# WINDOW FRIENDS

BY
CAROL DARLEY DOW

*a novel*

ISBN: 979-8-9856551-0-0

*One real friend*
*changes everything.*

cdd

# *Chapter One*
# SARAH:
## *Three Things I Like About Scotland*

The early morning fog seemed to dance around to unheard music, first ebbing away slowly in a twirling motion then suddenly flowing back toward the second floor window in a dramatic rush of passion. For a moment, the world stood still, not a breath taken, not a particle of air moving. Then as abruptly as it stopped, it began again. The gambol of the gray mist mesmerized Sarah, as she watched from her lofty antique four-poster bed. A heavy down comforter and four down pillows did their job keeping her warm while she stayed put looking out the window. If only she could linger here, safe and protected in the security of her large Victorian bedroom. Her only complaint would be how cold and drafty the room was, even with a few embers glowing in the fireplace. Moving to Scotland and living in a house that was well over a hundred years old, was quite a new experience. Seriously, who had a fireplace in their bedroom? With all the old world charm, she wasn't sure she would ever get used to crawling out of bed and dressing in a damp chill? Weighing the pros and cons, there was only one logical answer that made sense to the fifteen year old girl…pull the heavy down comforter over her head and begin her morning ritual: think of three things she liked about living in Scotland.

"Good morning, Sarah Sunshine. Time to rise and shine."

Her father began every day with a knock on her door and the cheery greeting. Too bad she wasn't feeling his optimism. Today was her first day at a new school where once again she would get lost, wouldn't know anyone, and truthfully, wasn't interested in making friends. What was the point when she would probably move again in a year or two? This was the fourth school in the third foreign country of her nine years of education. If it were up to her, she would stay in bed under the comforter, warm and toasty, and read. Books were a fine substitute for friends in her opinion. They never talked behind your back or made fun of you and were always there when you needed them. Whatever happened to home tutors anyway? Seemed like a fine idea!

"I know you're in there," her father continued lightheartedly outside her door. "Mrs. MacAughtrie has your tattle scones and sausage ready, and I haven't seen your new school uniform yet. I'll be waiting to hear the three things you love about Scotland over breakfast."

Sarah buried deeper in her comforter in an effort to escape the world. Knowing her father, who was early for everything, she figured she had a few extra minutes to enjoy the last pleasure of the day.

In the two weeks they had spent in Edinburgh, Scotland, Sarah was already enchanted with winding cobblestone streets and towering stone buildings with spires and peaks that reached to the sky. Everywhere you looked was something wonderfully old and endlessly interesting with history that went back forever. Her father's new job would keep him very busy, so he made sure they arrived early enough to explore their new town together. Sarah cherished their days of adventuring, it was rare that it was just the two of them.

Their first experience was a long walk up Castle Hill toward the iconic Edinburgh Castle, built on top of a huge volcanic rock. It was constructed in the year 1103 with sturdy stone walls that survived many attacks throughout the centuries. It loomed impressively over the city, keeping watch over the inhabitants. As the most popular tourist attraction in Scotland, there were hundreds of people waiting to join tours. Before long they were grouped together with about ten other visitors and a guide named Hercules. He was humorous and shared all kinds of information, some facts more useful than others.

"The castle is 443 feet above sea level, consists of 35,737 square meters of buildings, and is overflowing with history," Hercules shared with pride.

Sarah found herself far more interested in the stories behind the statistics. Who knew an elephant once lived in the castle mews for several years? It was brought by a Highlander Regiment returning from Sri Lanka in 1838 and kept as a mascot. She and her father laughed that this brought new meaning to the term 'mucking out the stable.' Later on, they saw one of the biggest cannons in the world, Meg Mons, a gift to King James II in 1457 and weighing in at six tons. It found its way to the Castle in 1829, sitting outside of St. Margaret's Chapel and looking ready to fire.

"Throughout history, the Scottish castle was often besieged by the British, so better to have your big gun ready at all times," their guide explained.

Later, as they strolled through the castle grounds, Sarah and her father were visibly startled by an ear-piercing gun shot.

"Oh my gosh! Are the British attacking again?" Sarah asked with some sincerity.

Her father got out his guide book and scanned it quickly

"No, it appears to be a tradition," he answered, continuing to read, "Nearly everyday a shot is fired at exactly one o'clock and it is known as..."

"The One O'Clock Gun," they said in unison, laughing.

Toward the end of the day, they saw The Honours of Scotland, Britain's oldest existing crown jewels. Consisting of three heavily encrusted pieces, the crown, the sword and the scepter, who's history was bizarre at best. The priceless jewels had been misplaced for over a hundred years, then found by Scottish author Sir Walter Scott. Another time, they had been smuggled away from the castle in a creel basket full of seaweed and hidden in a minister's bed for safe keeping. The jewels had been buried in more than one graveyard, but by far the strangest tale of all was when they were hidden in David's Tower...in the toilet.

"Eeeewwwww," was all Sarah could say, making an awful face.

"I'm sure they have been carefully washed," her father responded cooly, with a straight face.

Down the hill they walked toward Holyrood Palace, located at the opposite end of the Royal Mile from the Castle.

"It's where the Queen stays when she is in Scotland," her father read from the guide book.

"Much of the Palace is open to the public when she is not here. You'll love this, there is scandalous history!"

They caught up with a tour just as the female guide was explaining.

"David Rizzo, was a musician and private secretary to Mary, Queen of Scots in 1566. Mary was in the late stages of her pregnancy when her husband, Lord Darnley and his crew of nasty assassins burst into her bed chamber and stabbed David Rizzo as he hid behind Mary. He was stabbed fifty-six times and drug away. If you look carefully, you might still see Rizzo's blood on the wooden floor. It is said Lord Darnly was a dreadful man who drank too much and had many affairs…possibly even including David Rizzo. Records show that Lord Darnley was murdered a year later by the Earl of Bothwell, who then kidnapped Mary and forced her into marriage."

"My goodness, the Scottish people are far from dull," Sarah commented as they walked toward the ruins of the 13th century Augustinian Holyrood Abbey next door to the Palace.

"Do you feel how peaceful it is here?" her father asked as they carefully walked through the crumbling church, with birds singing in the branches of the tall trees adjacent to the ruin.

"Maybe it just seems peaceful after all the drama at the Palace," Sarah laughed.

"Actually, even Felix Mendelssohn found inspiration here. He wrote his famous Scottish Symphony after a visit."

"That's one of your favorites, isn't it?" she asked as they strolled back through the Palace garden.

"It is, very much so."

By far their best adventure took place one rainy afternoon to the Royal Botanic Garden. With no idea what to expect, Sarah thought it sounded a little boring, but at least she would be with her father.

However, once the taxi drove into the garden and she saw the grand Victorian structure, nearly seventy-two feet tall, with its huge, arched paned windows, ironwork roof and massive glass dome, there was nothing boring about it. And that was only one part of it! They ran from the car, holding umbrellas which were of little use in the downpour, toward the Tropical Palm House. They were unexpectedly hit with warm, humid air when they entered, creating the perfect antidote to the chilly day outside. The cavernous interior had a feeling of being in a lush, tropical paradise, even with cold raindrops pelting the window roof. They wandered through a series of enormous glass houses with hundreds of varieties of ferns and plants and came upon an extraordinarily tall palm tree. Craning her neck up she saw it reached the top of the towering ceiling! Sarah read the description out loud.

"It is a Bermuda Fan Palm, *Sabel Bermudana*, and it's the oldest known plant in the Royal Botanic Garden. It was transported nearly four thousand miles from Bermuda to Germany, before being shipped to the Port of Leith in the late 1700's. In 1834 it was moved to its current location as a potted tree, and was planted in the ground in 1910."

"And, it says here," her father continued, reading from the pamphlet he'd been given, "the tree is native only to Bermuda and its sap is used to make an alcoholic drink, called 'Bibby.' That's really a coincidence, I went to primary school with a boy names Bobby Bibby. He had a twin sister named Libby."

"Libby Bibby?" Sarah asked incredulously.

It didn't take much for the father and daughter to find this wildly funny, hardly able to breathe.

"You made that up," Sarah jokingly accused her father, as she wiped the tears away.

"I swear it's true," he answered, "but it was never funny until I told you."

This brought on another fit of unbridled hilarity. Sarah remembered thinking that laughter had to be good for the soul. Far from being bored, this was one of her favorite days ever.

Wriggling her toes under the comforter, reality came into focus.

"Well, that was then," she thought wistfully, throwing off the warm comforter, "and this is now. Today is still the first day of school. Time to get up and face the music."

"Waverley Station, Belted Galloways and...Khushi's," Sarah said with conviction.

"Interesting choices. You like the Edinburgh train station, black cows with white belts or is it white cows with black belts and Scotland's first curry restaurant. Excellent assortment! You are a very well-rounded young lady indeed."

Her father seemed to enjoy this game they played every morning, and she loved to make him laugh. Most people thought her handsome father was formal and reserved, but with her he was funny, attentive and even silly. After years of working in the American Foreign Service he had an air of sophistication, but when they were together life was simple and good.

Seaneen McAughtrie bustled in with their breakfast on a large tray. "Here's your favorite, pet. I'll pour your tea, unless you'd rather have hot chocolate."

"Thank you, tea is fine," Sarah answered.

"Here you are," she said filling the china tea cup, "Now, the first day of school is always a wee bit of a fright, but a lovely girl like you will do fine."

Sarah wasn't at all sure she would do fine, but it was a comfort to hear anyway. The consulate had hired Mrs. McAughtrie and she was the perfect housekeeper, in addition to being a wonderful cook. In her mid-sixties, the bright-eyed, grey haired woman combined warmth, wisdom, and good humor, splashed with the scent of lavender. Not exactly a mother figure, more like a grandmother whose only mission was to care for you. Sarah was naturally shy, but she liked Mrs. McAughtrie and was glad she lived in the house with them.

Richard finished his breakfast in short order.

"The consulate car will be here in about fifteen minutes to pick us up and drop you at school on the way to work. Do you have everything you need?"

"Oh please! No! I'm already the new kid at school. If you drop me off in that big black car, no one will ever speak to me." Sarah often had to remind her father that this wasn't her first rodeo at being the new student at a foreign school. "Please let me walk. It's only a few blocks."

Using her best wide-eyed, pleading look, her father finally smiled and shook his head.

"How is it I can negotiate with world leaders, and yet continually cave in to my fifteen year old daughter? There's something not right with that. Here's my offer–you can walk, but we will drive at a respectable distance behind you. Take it or leave it."

"Is that's your best deal?"

"It is."

"Then I'll take it. But no car on the way home."

Her father leaned in close, with his most intense stare.

"Then Mrs. McAughtrie will be watching from down the street when you walk home."

Sarah stared back with equal intensity.

"At a respectable distance?"

Richard Duncan, new Principal Officer of the U.S. Consulate General in Edinburgh, Scotland, laughed in complete delight at his only child, who was growing up too fast.

"Yes, Sarah Anne Duncan, at a respectable distance."

*Chapter Two*

# SARAH:

## *The Young Man in the Window*

Edinburgh was divided between Old Town, the medieval part of the city that began around the 1100's, and New Town, the Georgian section, established in 1770's. Sarah guessed the word 'new 'was a matter of perspective. She once asked Mrs. McAughtrie how far it was from Old Town to New Town.

"Why, pet, they are 2,641 feet apart. Hard to get lost."

The house where they lived was constructed in the 1820's and located in the Blacket area of Newington, one of the first suburbs built in Old Town. The odd, historical facts of their location fascinated Sarah. She had seen the remnants of the large, iron gates at the four entrances to the neighborhood, then learned that in the old days residents had to hurry home in the evening before the night porter locked them out until morning. It was interesting to live surrounded by so much history. She recently overheard Mrs. McAughtrie mention that Newington was an unusual location for a diplomat to choose to live, as most preferred the grand Georgian houses and fancy restaurants in New Town. Without hesitation, her father said that he specifically chose this area far from the lavish trappings of New Town, so their life could be as normal as possible. Plus, it was only a short distance to Sarah's school.

Sarah closed the front door and looked up through the thinning fog, or 'haar' as Mrs. McAughtrie called it. There just might be a bit of sunshine later, but for now it was damp and cold. The walking route to Campbell Manor School for Girls consisted of three turns and two long blocks down narrow cobbled streets lined with elegant three and four-story sandstone Victorian townhouses. Low, stone walls and heavy iron gates separated each property, giving a tiny garden area in the front for each owner to bring their personality to the residential neighborhood.

Tightening the soft scarf around her neck, Sarah casually flipped her long dark hair, with the intent of sneaking a peek to see if her father's black car was still trailing her. Indeed it was. While she could appreciate the need for security, living in a protected bubble was very frustrating. Looking heavenward for divine patience, she glanced at the house across the street. It looked much like the others, except this one had two large dormer windows, connected by two smaller windows on its third floor. Her gaze was caught by a young man with brown curly hair in the window who looked to be around her age. He stared down at her, smiled, and raised his hand in a brief wave. She had been taught not to communicate with strangers, but was so caught up in the moment, she tentatively lifted her hand, shielding it from her father, and waved back. Then off she went towards school, her spirit a little brighter.

"Here we go again," Sarah breathed softly to herself as she walked through the large black iron gates to her new school. There were girls of all ages, dressed identically in blazers, checkered skirts, black tights and flat shoes, gathering in small groups. The main school building was an enormous old mansion, perched on several acres of land, with a tall stone wall around the perimeter. The huge wooden front door led into the vestibule, a left turn to the administration office, a right turn to the large reception room, and straight ahead up the curved stairway to most of the classrooms. She needn't have worried about getting lost as nearly all the indoor classes were in the main house and all the outdoor activities took place in either one of the outbuildings or somewhere on the property. Sarah was forced to admit this school was a bit different, fewer students and much more progressive than the others she had attended.

The school booklet said the classes were small and extremely diverse, from ancient history and foreign languages (some she never heard of) to knitting and horse riding. She was quite sure she would be better at riding than knitting.

"Now, girls, I want to introduce our newest student, Sarah Duncan. Sarah is Level S4 and originally from America, but most recently attended schools in…now, where was it you were schooled, Miss Duncan?" Miss Jardeen asked.

"Washington D.C. for primary school, a home tutor in Malta, and middle grades in London." This was a litany Sarah had repeated a jillion times. Next would come the inevitable questions of why so many locations, what did her father do, did she have any siblings, and the one she dreaded most, 'tell us about your mum.'

Miss Jardeen continued, "And Sarah's father is the new head of the American Consulate here. Isn't that grand, girls?" A small smattering of clapping, equalled by a similar number of young girls looking bored and impatient. At least that's one question answered. They knew what her father did.

It wasn't likely that Sarah would find a best friend in this group. Maybe it was her fault. It was hard to get attached to people she would leave behind when her father got his next post. Maybe it was a trait she inherited from her mother, who had absolutely no trouble abandoning her daughter and husband. Thinking of her mother was never a very positive experience, so she rarely did it. Was she too old for imaginary friends? She thought of the boy in the third story window. Even if she never saw him again, she would pretend he was her best friend and that they would have lots of imaginary conversations about very important and interesting things.

# *Chapter Three*

# RICHARD:

## *The Consulate ~ Home Away from Home*

The black car followed Sarah at a respectable distance as promised. Richard Duncan wished he could tell his daughter that he completely understood her reluctance to facing her first day of school. He wasn't a big fan of first day adventures either. He mused that he had chosen an unusual profession for one who disliked repeatedly starting over. As a young man, he was drawn to the Foreign Service because he was intrigued by representing the United States around the world and he truly believed in public service. He had worked his way through the levels, from Washington D.C. to several foreign posts, and now found himself as Principal Officer of the U.S. Consulate General in Edinburgh, Scotland. This made him the highest ranking U.S official in the city, showing the face of America in a positive and sympathetic way. Richard knew he was good at his job, and other than the first few days when the staff in the office would be vying for position, he thoroughly enjoyed it. This post, however, would be a special challenge. The American Consulate's reputation had suffered greatly in the months since the last Principal Officer left. The interim director had made quite a mess of things with shocking reports of unprofessional conduct, and inappropriate, rude behavior. Richard was quite sure they hadn't told him everything, but what he did know was bad enough. The scandal had reached all the way to London and it was made clear that it fell on his shoulders to correct this unacceptable situation.

His driver guided the car past Waverley Station, turned east on Princes Street, and continued uphill along Waterloo Place to Regent Road. There a series of thirty-four classical attached three-story townhouses perched on the north side of the street. At the top of the hill was Number 3 Regent Terrace, with it's imposing Greek columns and black lacquered door. It would become Richard Duncan's home away from home. This area was considered very exclusive with many of the townhouses being privately owned by wealthy and often famous inhabitants. While the prestige wasn't important to him, he did appreciate that his stately office windows faced Holyrood Palace, Arthur's Seat and Old Town. He looked up at the three-story sandstone building with the American flag waving in the breeze, and felt a surge of pride. Richard said a quick prayer that he would lead his staff well and accomplish the mission assigned to him.

# *Chapter Four*

# SARAH:

## *The Daily Routine*

"Fenteman's Ginger Beer, Mayfield Church and Highland Cows!" Sarah was pleased with her well-thought out choices, even though she was kind of on a roll with the cow thing.

"Soft drink with a recipe from the 1900's, our neighborhood church dating to the 1800's, and shaggy fringed cattle from the second millennium BC. I notice all have 'old' in common and what is it with you and cows?" Her dad laughed, something he hadn't done much lately.

"Probably too many Country Life magazines with cow articles." She leaned forward and asked intently. "Have you ever seen a Highland Cow?"

"Have you?" he challenged right back.

"Actually, I have. Well, not actually, but I've read all about them in the magazine. They live way up north, are considered very charming, and have lovely Gaelic names. Maybe we could take a train trip up north and see them."

"There is nothing I'd rather do, Sarah Sunshine, but I'm afraid that will have to wait until I sort some things out at work."

Sarah knew that was an understatement. She was aware the situation was far more complicated than he had been led to believe and it was going to take a great deal of his time to make it right.

"I understand, Dad. No worries, we will look forward to going another time."

And so it went. Every morning she would walk to school, and her curly haired young man would be in the window. They would wave and smile. It was the highlight of her day. Her father would follow in the black car, thankfully occupied with work, then go his own way once she was safely behind the iron gates of the school. As she suspected, the girls at school had all known each other since birth and were not terribly interested in befriending her. If she were to be honest, she was not terribly interested in them either. No matter. She had her books and her dad and Mrs. McAughtrie, and her friend in the window.

Walking home was always a welcome relief with another day of school behind her. For twenty minutes her life was her own, other than Mrs. McAughtrie keeping an eye on her. The housekeeper kept her promise, and her distance, for the half-mile back to their house. As with her morning walk, the best part was always when she turned onto the now-familiar block, and smiled and waved to her friend in the window. He was always waiting at just the right moment when she was passing by. She wondered if he stood there all day just for her, then laughed out loud at the absurdity of that thought. Seriously, though, why wasn't he in school? Was he being punished and kept at home? She laughed again. Actually attending school felt like punishment to her. She would love to be able to read all day and just walk about without the confines of Campbell Manor School for Girls. Perhaps he was ill, or being held prisoner in the third floor of his house. Except he didn't really look sick or like he was an unhappy captive. He looked like a really nice person. He looked like someone who would be a good friend.

# *Chapter Five*
# RICHARD:
## *The Confrontation*

The elegant wood paneled room was deadly quiet. Ornate crown moulding and priceless oil paintings looked down on the proceedings below. Staring directly into the watery, bloodshot eyes of the older man across the desk, Richard's voice remained calm and controlled, masking the fury he was feeling. He spoke slowly and chose his words carefully.

"With all due respect, Mr. Ratchford, your time as interim director has not had the desired effect the Ambassador in London had hoped for. The complaints from visiting Americans and the staff have been overwhelming. Even now, your efforts to subvert my position here has backfired and you have unfortunately lost the last shred of credibility you had."

"Duncan, you have a mighty high opinion of yourself. Most of the staff here…"

"Mr. Ratchford, most of the staff here are intimidated by your raging temper and threats of retaliation." Richard watched as the large man's face turned several shades of red and his eyes bulged out.

"Why, you sniveling, jack-ass."

"Mr. Ratchford, don't say anything you will regret. This doesn't have to be the end of your career with the Foreign Service."

"How dare you! I'll see you burn in…"

"I caution you, Mr. Ratchford, your conduct is completely out of line and most unbecoming of a Foreign Service officer. Your insults to me are useless. The Ambassador has ordered your return to London immediately."

Mr. Ratchford opened his mouth to speak, but Richard held up his hand.

"This conversation has come to an end. It was my hope that we could work amiably in this transition to restore the damage done to the reputation of the Edinburgh office. Instead, I have seen that you are single-handedly the catalyst for most of the problems. Treating Americans who are entitled to our services with your rude, superior attitude has caused no end of trouble. May I remind you, Mr. Ratchford, that we are in a service business."

"So, they bring in the golden boy to make nice with these ignorant fools who are stupid enough to lose their passports, or want to waste our time with a tour of the consulate, or worse yet, you and your kind want to pander to the people who want to undermine our government with liberal propaganda. You have no clue, Mr. Duncan, what goes on here."

It was clear to Richard that this conversation was at a dead end and he was weary of it.

"I am not here to defend my position to you, Mr. Ratchford. In life you are either part of the solution or part of the problem. In this case, it appears you are the entire problem. The Ambassador will be expecting you tomorrow." Richard stood up to signal the end of the meeting. "Good day, Mr. Ratchford."

By now Richard could almost feel the hiss in Ratchford's voice.

"I will collect my things then. There are several large containers of personal belongings I have stored that I will move out by this afternoon."

"Actually, you won't. We have already sent your so called 'personal belongings' to the ambassador in London. He seemed most interested in why you would be receiving gifts from the Far East."

Conrad Ratchford's face lost all color and he couldn't speak for a moment. Seething with an anger Richard had never seen, Ratchford finally uttered an ominous threat.

"You can bet you haven't heard the end of this, Richard Duncan. I will get you!"

With his suit coat button straining against his ample frame, Conrad Ratchford stood up and stared at Richard for a few moments, walked to the door, opened it, and slammed it with all his might on his way out. The oil paintings on the walls swayed a bit and even the large, paned windows of the old building shook slightly. Richard wondered about the tales these walls could tell. He disliked conflict, but felt a genuine relief that Conrad Ratchford was gone and not his problem any longer. Being accepted into the Foreign Service was not an easy process, and Richard was at a loss as to how someone could go so wrong. It had taken years for Conrad Ratchford to achieve the level of director. No doubt he had worked hard and made sacrifices, and must have at some point been dedicated to the principles of the job. Everyone knew the risk of burn-out in this intense career, but Richard had never been face to face with it. The damage done by Mr. Ratchford would take a long while for Richard to undo. Feeling suddenly tired and a little drained, he straightened his tie, put on his wool overcoat, and walked toward the main reception room. To his absolute astonishment, the room was filled with the staff who broke into applause, and a rousing version of 'He's a Jolly Good Fellow.' Grinning sheepishly at the spontaneous accolade, the weariness faded and Principal Officer Richard Duncan felt renewed. Now, it was time to head home and spend time with his daughter.

## *Chapter Six*

# SARAH:

## *The Note*

November in Edinburgh was even more daunting than Sarah had expected. The chill in the air and frequent rain were one thing, but the persistent wind was absurdly annoying. Some days were so bad she actually considered giving in to the idea of her father's car to and from school. The walks would've been absolute drudgery, if it weren't for her friend in the window. How she wished he was a real friend.

The Campbell Manor curriculum was fairly interesting, though the social side continued to be dismal. It wasn't as though the other girls were openly mean to her, they were just indifferent. Lunches were spent alone with a book, which suited her fine, but hardly being acknowledged by her class mates was discouraging. She tried a few times to say hello or join in a conversation, but was ignored. The worst was when it came time to be chosen for sports teams–or not chosen, as it was most times. Rejection by people she didn't much care for shouldn't make her feel so demoralized. Several of her teachers must have noticed and tried to be friendly, but there was always the division of student/teacher that didn't lend itself to a personal relationship. While she hated to admit it, Sarah missed talking with someone her own age.

Today had been one of those days her father referred to as a 'blue devil.' Everything in her path went south instead of north, topped off by overhearing several of the girls making fun of her. Trying hard to contain her tears as she walked home, she nearly forgot to look up. There he was, like a bright light, waving to her with his usual smile.

She stopped and waved back, and smiled as tears streaked down her cheeks. No matter, nobody could tell with the rain hitting her face. Her window friend began to gesture, as though playing Charades. She felt silly not knowing what he meant, and was also aware Mrs. McAughtrie was lurking somewhere behind. He kept pointing down to something outside. She stood stock still and focused on trying to read his lips, which wasn't easy when he was three flights up.

"Wall. In the wall!" she whispered to herself.

That was it! She laughed out loud at the pleasure of figuring it out, and began to search the mossy stone wall in front of his house.

She looked up at him several times, trying to get a clue of what she was looking for,

"In the wall. In the wall," she repeated.

Ah ha! There tucked in a recess between two adjacent stones was a small plastic bag with a folded paper inside. A thrill ran through Sarah as she realized he had actually communicated with her! Looking up delighted to show him that she had found it, the window was dark and he was gone.

The fireplace in the living room warmed Sarah with logs that flamed with great enthusiasm. Dinner had been pleasant with her father, and she was pleased to hear that he resolved a big problem at work. He never shared details, but his relief was obvious. Thankfully, there had been no questions from Mrs. McAughtrie about Sarah suddenly stopping to look carefully at a rock wall on her way home. Putting her hand in her pocket, she felt for the folded note, as yet unread. At this moment it was the most precious thing in her life and she wanted to savor the secret and all the possibilities of what it might say. Her plan was to wait until she was alone in her room to read it.

"It's getting late, and I think I'll go upstairs now," she said, trying to sound casual.

Richard Duncan looked up at the grandfather clock ticking away in the corner of the room.

"It's only half-past eight. Am I such boring company?" he asked as he put down the newspaper.

"Of course not," she laughed, kissing her father on the cheek. "It has been a long day and I'm looking forward to a hot bath and early bed," she said, secretly thinking about her folded note. "Good night."

"Sleep well, Sunshine," he answered.

*Dear Friend,*
*Thank you for stopping to wave to me everyday.*
*Did you know that there is a black car*
*following you? Perhaps it should be a*
*concern to you.*

At the bottom was a perfect, small pencil sketch of a house that looked to be in the neighborhood. She was absolutely thrilled. She really, truly had a secret friend who seemed as happy as she was to make a connection. He was even concerned about her safety, which gave her a giggle, and he must be artistic from what she could tell. Wow! It kind of took her breath away. What would she write back? How would she ever sleep tonight? How could she tell her father that one of her favorite things in Scotland was a curly haired boy in a third story window?

The rain began pelting her windows, coming in waves of varying intensity as the branches from a nearby tree banged the roof. Snuggled under her down comforter, Sarah watched the dying flames in her little fireplace cast shadows on her tall ceilings. Having a fireplace in her bedroom was magical. It created a wondrous world in which to think and dream. After reading his note over and over, and looking at the pencil drawing from every angle, she tried to write back. It was harder than she thought–be friendly but not too friendly, grateful but not needy, casual but proper. Another benefit of a fireplace in your room was the ability to burn up all of the discarded replies. After several hours she was finally satisfied with what she had written. Reading it one last time, Sarah carefully folded the note and slid it in the plastic bag. If it was still raining in the morning, she would carry an umbrella which would be perfect cover to put the note in the wall without anyone in the black car noticing. How on earth would she focus at school wondering if he would leave another note?

## *Chapter Seven*

# PETER:

*The Reply*

Peter wiped his stained hands with a rough cloth just in time to see the girl carrying a large umbrella stop in front of his house. She tilted the umbrella up and waved to him. He watched her put something in the wall, hopefully back far enough so the rain wouldn't get it. She waved again and walked away. Odd how he was looking forward to what she had written. It was on a whim that he waved to her when he saw her passing by several weeks ago. There was just something about her demeanor that he recognized–a sense of loneliness and not fitting in. His mother always said he had a sixth sense about people, but making an overture to someone he didn't know was unusual and quite out of his comfort zone. He laughed to himself thinking how arrogant it was to make such an assumption about her. In the meantime, he would hurry down to see what she had written with more anticipation than he expected.

*Dear Window Friend,*
*(as I have come to think of you in my mind)*
*I look forward to your wave as well.*
*It is a highlight of my day.*
*Yes, I am aware of the black car that*
*follows me, and you have no idea the*
*negotiation it took for me to not be riding*
*in that car! My name is Sarah.*
*P.S. Your drawing is amazing.*

Ha! He knew it! If seeing him was a highlight, her days must be difficult. What could be so troubling to a lovely, young girl who walked to school with a black car following her? He enjoyed putting pieces of a puzzle together to make a complete picture, and this had all the makings of an interesting picture.

## *Chapter Eight*

# SARAH:

## *Arthur's Seat*

The end of the school day could not come soon enough. Thankfully, the rain had stopped and the walk home was far more pleasant than her morning walk. Sarah knew there was a time coming when she would have to give in to being taken to school in the big, black car. Everyone knew winter in Edinburgh could be very cold and windy. At this point, she was long past caring what the girls at school thought of her, black car or not. After all, now she had her own friend!

*Dear Sarah,*
*How nice to have a name to put to*
*your face. From what I can see you*
*look like a Sarah, though I'm not sure*
*what that means.*
*You were very brave venturing*
*out in the rain to walk to school*
*and it causes me to wonder why you*
*choose to walk rather than ride*
*in that nice car that follows you?*
*Of course, it's none of my business*
*if you'd rather not say.*
*My name is Peter.*

Sarah read his words with delight. This time the little pencil sketch at the bottom of the note was of Edinburgh Castle. She had so many questions, but didn't want to appear overeager to know everything immediately...even though she really did want to know everything immediately! When she realized it was Friday and she couldn't converse with him until Monday, her spirits sank. It was the one and only time she wished school was seven days a week. Trying to look on the bright side, it would give her two days to craft her reply.

"Arthur's Seat, the fireplace in my bedroom, and...Shetland cows!" Sarah said triumphantly.

Richard watched his daughter for a moment. She seemed a bit happier the last few days, but he hesitated to ask directly what had changed. He hoped her school experience was improving.

"You know I can see Arthur's Seat from my office. I've been reading about it in a guide book. If the wind holds off this morning would you like to hike up? We don't have to go the entire way. I've heard it's quite a trek to the top."

"That would be fabulous! Yes! Just the two of us? I'll go change."

Sarah was out the door and running up the stairs before Richard knew what happened. He yelled after her, "And would you like to take the bus?"

"Yes! Yes! Yes!" She answered without missing a beat.

They walked up Minto Street to the bus stop at a leisurely pace, though it was everything Sarah could do to not run ahead and secure their place in line. Their coins were put in the little slot near the driver, and Sarah gave him a big smile and "Good morning!" The driver couldn't help but respond to the enthusiastic young girl.

"Don't you make the day a bit brighter, Lass?" he said in return.

Up the curvy steps to the top of the double decker bus, they found the very front seats available. Sarah knew Liam, her father's driver and body guard was somewhere nearby, but chose to ignore the thought. She loved Minto Street, though it was a bit confusing because the same street changed names over the course of many blocks–Minto, Newington, Clerk, South Clerk, and South Bridge.

There were still some things in Scotland that were a mystery. A right turn on High Street, then curve down toward Holyrood Garden and there it was, Arthur's Seat!

"Ready to learn?" Her father asked as they walked across the massive Royal Park adjacent to Holyrood Palace, toward the volcanic rock. "Arthur's Seat is 823 feet in elevation, and is the main peak within a group of hills. It should take about two hours round trip, or we can choose a shorter route."

"Let's go to the top!" Sarah answered with excitement.

"Sounds good. It says in the book that the view from the highest point is fantastic. You can see for miles and miles, all the way to the North Sea sometimes."

It was one of Edinburgh's finest November days, just enough sun and a gentle breeze, though still quite nippy. Over the past few weeks it had become obvious the weather in Scotland was fickle. A bit like a whiplash, clear and sunny one minute, then gray and rainy the next. For now, it felt like half of Edinburgh had come out to walk up the volcanic trail. There were groups of people, families, couples, school kids, and of course, those over achievers who felt it was their calling to run up the massive hill as though mocking those who were walking. They would then turn around and run right back down again. How could they possibly enjoy the journey? Many hikers spoke in foreign languages, Italian here, Chinese there, Spanish behind them and any number of other languages she didn't recognize. The narrow pathways up the hill were steeper than she had read about. The stone and mud made it a little slippery, as well as the large rock steps that occurred from time to time. It was referred to as an easy hike, but easy was obviously a subjective word. In her exhilaration, Sarah forged ahead and quickly found she was out of breath and had hardly gone any distance at all. Her father caught up and they continued on at a little slower pace. To their left was a beautiful, glassy loch nestled between the hills. Suddenly two enormous swans took flight. The large shadow they cast over the hikers caused most people to stop and look up in wonder until the large white birds flew out of sight.

"That is St. Margaret's Loch, and in the distance is Saint Anthony's Chapel Ruins," her father said.

Up and up the dirt path they hiked, until they reached the cliff at the very top.

"We made it!" Sarah said breathlessly.

The views were in every direction, from the castle to the Firth of Forth and everything in between. With uncharacteristic abandon, Sarah spun around in a circle, with her arms outstretched, and began singing, 'The hills are alive…' Her father laughed heartily, and several of the other hikers applauded. With an exaggerated bow, she ran over and hugged her father.

"I love you, Sarah Sunshine."

"I love you, too, Dad."

Out of the corner of her eye, Sarah saw Liam catch her father's eye, and slightly incline his head in an abbreviated nod, and she knew it was time to go home. That was okay, the sky was clouding up and rain would surely follow. This was a day to remember.

*Dear Peter,*
*I agree that it is very nice to put a name to a face, and*
*I quite think you probably look like a Peter as well. Though*
*it is a little hard to see details through the high window.*
*Today is Saturday, and I won't put this*
*in the wall until Monday, but I couldn't wait*
*to share what happened today!*
*Have you ever hiked Arthur's Seat? I'm sure you probably*
*have because everyone who lives here probably has, and*
*you will think me somewhat silly, but I went with my father*
*and it is glorious! Really, truly spectacular!*
*Well, that's all for now. I look forward to hearing*
*from you and want to thank you for being my friend.*
*Sarah*

## Chapter Nine

# SEANEEN McAUGHTRIE:

*More Than a Housekeeper*

Seaneen McAughtrie finished the breakfast dishes and put the pot roast in the oven to cook for the rest of the day. It was Mr. Duncan's favorite and the whole house would smell delicious by dinner time. He had patiently given her explicit details of his mother's special recipe and was always so appreciative when it was served. Now, it was time for a cup of tea and a sit down. How had she done without an electric kettle for so many years? What a fine invention it was!

This assignment couldn't be better suited to her. She enjoyed all the cooking, and the old house was a joy to take care of and live in. Most of all, it was good to be needed. Her wonderful husband, Seamus, had been her best friend and companion for over forty years, and when he died five years ago, she had been completely lost. Everything changed so abruptly, even to the point of wondering who she was. Often she didn't recognize the wrinkled, gray-haired woman looking back at her in the mirror. The reflection was of a woman who had no purpose, who felt useless. Life with Seamus had been full and exciting with a dash of danger. While they were never blessed with children, they had each other and that had been enough. But with Seamus gone, one day slid into the next, and the next, and the next. Sundays found her sitting in the church pew with a vacant look, wondering not only where Seamus was, but where God was. More than once she yearned for the peace of the next life.

Early one spring morning, she felt slightly less lost than she had the day before. It was the slimmest kind of breakthrough, but she was grateful for it. In hindsight, it was her turning point. She began to actually hear the sermons by the vicar, and his words were aimed directly at her. Before long she began to look forward to each day instead of dreading it. *"Commit thy works unto the Lord and thy thoughts shall be established."* (Proverbs 16:3). Before she realized it, her thoughts were reaching toward what lay ahead, rather than buried on what she had lost. She still missed Seamus with all her heart, and often consulted with him about things on her mind, but now the smiling, plump, gray-haired woman in the mirror was happy to see her.

Glancing at the clock, Mrs. McAughtrie was surprised to see it was almost time to walk toward Sarah's school. It had been a long time since she had reminisced about days gone by.

"Yesterday is the past, tomorrow is the future, but today is our present," she reminded herself.

Yes, it was good that she had taken this assignment. She had become quite fond of Mr. Duncan and his sweet daughter. Young Sarah was an extraordinarily bright child, constantly reading and able to carry on quite adult conversations, yet, there seemed to be a deep loneliness about her. The one topic that was never discussed concerned Mr. Duncan's wife, Sarah's mother. It was almost as if she didn't exist. Undoubtedly, that must have had a devastating impact on the poor, shy girl. A few times Seaneen had speculated whether it had been an accident or an illness or some other tragic turn of events, but of course, it was none of her business. It had taken several weeks for Sarah to warm up enough to have tea with her in the kitchen after school, rather than retreat to her bedroom. And that might've been prompted by warm shortbread cookies coming out of the oven. Slowly, their conversations had become comfortable, though perhaps still a bit guarded.

As she put on her boots and raincoat, there was the slightest twinge of guilt that neither Mr. Duncan nor Sarah knew the entire reason she was chosen to be their housekeeper.

## Chapter Ten

# SARAH:

## *The Nightmare*

*Dear Sarah,*
*Yes, I have hiked Arthur's Seat and I completely agree with you–it is amazing. When it is the least bit foggy, one can almost imagine that it was indeed King Arthur's Camelot as some theories maintain.*
*May I ask, are you not from around here? It occurred to me that if that was your first time on Arthur's Seat perhaps you are new here? If I'm mistaken, please forgive my curiosity.*
*Peter*

Sarah's laugh echoed off the walls of her quiet bedroom. For some reason she assumed Peter knew she was American, but why would he? She looked like every other school girl in her Campbell Manor uniform, and he had never heard her speak. It delighted her to know that he was interested in where she was from. Once again, there was a beautiful pencil sketch at the bottom of the note–this time it was a view of Arthur's Seat. She smiled as she pulled up the down comforter and watched the last of the red coals burn in her fireplace. Shadows danced and all was right with the world. It was really nice to have a friend. Sleep came quickly. But not for long.

It was very dark when Sarah woke up with her heart pounding, terror gripping her. Hot sweat ran down her face and her breathing was ragged and irregular. For the briefest moment she didn't know where she was. Slowly, reality seeped in and the shadows around the large, yellow room began to be familiar. It had been months since the terrible nightmare had haunted her. Hugging her knees close to her chest and pulling the comforter around her chilled body, thoughts of Victoria Duncan's abandonment overwhelmed her. For so many years she simply accepted the situation as it was. Her mother left shortly after she was born–that was that. Hard to miss something you never had. The dreams began a few years ago, and was always the same. Sarah was a little girl running after her mother in a dark forest, catching glimpses of the woman's long brown hair just out of reach. No matter how fast she ran, Sarah couldn't catch up to her. "Mama, wait for me," she cried out over and over, but the elusive shadow would disappear. Little Sarah would drop to her knees on the prickly pine needles of the forest floor and sob, and blackness would overtake her. Then she would wake up. It was always the same, shaking, sweating and deeply disturbed.

She reached over to the nightstand and turned on the lamp. The small, white leather Bible given to her by her grandmother was right there waiting in the drawer. The thin pages fell open to Psalm 23, and the photo was exactly where it was supposed to be. Touching it gently with her fingertips, she traced the faces of her father, holding baby Sarah in his arms, and her mother looking at the camera with a wistful smile. She stared at it a long time as tears ran down her cheeks. "Mama, why couldn't you love me?" Hardly realizing she had spoken out loud, she placed the photo back in the Bible, put it on the nightstand and turned off the light. Pulling up the comforter, Sarah mentally returned all thoughts of her mother to an imaginary box and carefully placed the lid on it. Until next time.

# Chapter Eleven
# RICHARD:
## *Remembering*

A weak shaft of sunlight landed on the antique Persian rug, which accepted what little warmth it offered. Of the three long windows in his beautifully appointed office, the December morning sun chose only to shine through the middle one. Richard studied the particles of dust dancing in the light. What was the purpose of dust? There were so many mysteries he didn't understand. Life for everyone in Foreign Service was complex and fast paced, and for the most part, Richard thrived on the intensity. He liked the challenge of responding to a crisis and finding a solution. Part of his personality was anticipating every turn of events and having options for anything that might come up. These days it was rare for him to have a quiet moment to gather his thoughts. The situation in Edinburgh continued taxing his energy to the limit. Even with Ratchford gone, it was like a stone thrown in a still pond, with ripples of trouble going on and on. Add the additional normal consulate activities, and his days were over-flowing. It was the crack of dawn and here he was at in his office waiting for an important telephone call. How did it all get so complex? For the first time in years, he wondered what life would have been like if he'd chosen a different path. Thoughts of his sweet mother, Rosemary, always brought a sense of perspective.

"Trust in the Lord, but row away from the rocks," was always her answer, no matter how dire the situation.

In reflection, there had been any number of significant situations to deal with these past twenty years. By far the most impactful had been his relationship with Victoria, the lovely, charismatic, artistic woman he married. Despite never wavering in her position of not wanting to be a mother, she agreed to carry the child in the unexpected pregnancy. Richard was certain once Victoria saw the beautiful child she had carried for nine months, she would feel a bond and stay. When Sarah was a newborn, hardly a month old, his wife walked away just as she told him she would. He prayed for years they would one day be together as a family. To say he was young and naive was obvious, but to this day he couldn't understand not wanting to love and parent their child. It had been a very confusing and difficult time in his life. He was just starting his career and completely at a loss of how to go forward with an infant in tow. Without hesitation, his mother gladly stepped in and helped him care for little Sarah for over eleven years. Rosemary was a woman of quiet dignity and great faith, and was the most important influence in Richard's life. He never knew his biological father, though he had been told he resembled him a great deal. Much like Victoria, his father left the family when Richard was very young to seek business opportunities in Great Britain and was killed in an accident. Rosemary's second husband, Henry, had stepped in to love and support his step-son as his own. Henry passed away shortly before Sarah was born, leaving mother and son well off financially, but with a lasting heartache as they mourned his loss. Rosemary died twelve years later leaving a huge void in Richard and Sarah's lives.

The telephone ringing roused him from his thoughts.

"Good morning, Mr. Ambassador. Yes, tomorrow is fine. I'll see you then."

The call from the Ambassador was not unusual, though the request to come to the Embassy in London tomorrow was a little odd. Overall the atmosphere of the Edinburgh Consulate had improved enormously in the last weeks and he couldn't imagine the Ambassador finding fault. The trip to London would be only for the day, with he and Liam, his driver and bodyguard, flying out of Edinburgh airport in the morning and returning home by evening. Leaving Sarah always tugged at his heart, but she would be in school most of the day and Mrs. McAughtrie would be here. He had hoped by now Sarah would have made a friend or two, but his daughter had always been a little timid with people her age. She had no idea how beautiful and smart she was. Maybe he would ask in the morning if she knew the purpose of dust.

## Chapter Twelve

# SARAH:

*No Cows on My List*

*Dear Peter,*
*With a little fear, I will tell you that I am American.*
*I've lived in several foreign countries and found*
*not everyone is a fan of Americans. I profoundly*
*hope you are not one of those people.*
*From our correspondence, I don't think you are.*
*My father is the head of the American Consulate,*
*though I'm not supposed to tell people other than*
*school staff and students, but I think it's safe*
*to tell you. That's why the black car follows me*
*to school every morning and our housekeeper,*
*Mrs. McAughtrie, watches me walk home in*
*the afternoons. It has something to do with*
*security, though I've never had any scares.*
*Now you know my secret! Can you tell me*
*something I've been curious about? Are you*
*schooled at home? For the life of me, I can't figure*
*out why you're always home when I pass by*
*in the mornings and the afternoons! However,*
*like you said in your note, if this is private,*
*please forgive my curiosity.*
*But, after all, I am American.*
*Sarah*

She folded the note, put it back in the plastic bag and went down the stairs to breakfast.

"Walker's Shortbread, double-decker buses, and Dundee Orange Marmalade!" Sarah was quite pleased with her morning list, and looked at her father with a Cheshire Cat grin. She was rewarded with Richard's laugh and his admiration of her choices.

"What? No cows on your list?"

"I just wanted to see if you're paying attention. They'll be back!"

"I can hardly wait!" The smile faded from his face, "Are you happy, Sarah Sunshine? Sometimes I worry your childhood has been anything but traditional. I've never heard you complain, but I'm sure there are times when it isn't easy."

"You've never asked me that before. I guess it's the only life I know, and I love being with you. But hasn't worrying about me made your life more complicated?"

"You are my favorite complication!"

"Thank you for not sending your favorite complication to boarding school. I know some Foreign Service kids are sent away. I would really hate that."

"That was never an option in my mind. I couldn't imagine not seeing you for months on end. We've been a team for a long time and you've grown into an amazing young lady and I'm very proud of you."

"And Dad, for the record, I'm happy!"

"That, my little dumpling, makes my day! By the way, I have to travel to London this morning after we see you off to school. The Ambassador has requested a face to face meeting, but I will be back tonight, hopefully for dinner."

This was the first time her father had left her since they had arrived in Edinburgh.

"Is everything all right?'

"I'm quite sure it is. Sometimes meetings simply require one person to look into the eyes of the other person. Nothing to worry about. I'm sure you and Mrs. McAughtrie will have a lovely time."

As if on cue, Mrs. McAughtrie came bustling in the dining room with two bowls of steaming hot oatmeal, or porridge as they called it in Scotland, and a tray of small dishes containing brown sugar, and different fresh fruits.

"You are quite a wonder, Mrs. McAughtrie!" Richard said, "Fresh fruit in December!"

"All depends on who you know, Mr Duncan," she replied with a wink.

## Chapter Thirteen

# PETER:

## *Robert the Bruce and the Spider*

The plastic bag was looking a little tatty, but still did its job keeping their notes dry when they were in the wall. Peter slid Sarah's carefully folded paper out of the bag and sat down in the old, worn wing back chair. Talk about tatty, he thought. This chair had been in the family for generations, but when it landed in his mother's possession, she suggested giving it to the thrift store. He protested so dramatically she relented with the clause that he had to keep it in his room. At times, Peter could still smell the familiar pipe tobacco his grandfather used to smoke when the chair lived in the country with his grandparents. The memory of sitting in his grandfather's lap, as the white-haired, bearded gentleman would weave stories of Scotland, was one of his favorites. Smoke would rise from the bowl of his pipe and little Peter would sit very still, looking into the blue eyes of his grandfather, and whisper, "Grandfather, tell me the story about Robert the Bruce and the spider!" His grandfather would immediately begin speaking in a strong, Scottish brogue.

*"Aye, lad, robert the bruce, the greatest ruler scotland iver haed. Well, many years ago, robert the bruce went tae battle with edward the first, king o england. He was known as edward longshanks because o his long, spindly legs. Edward an his english soldiers badly defeatit robert an his men, an edward hunted robert unmercifully throuch the land. The weather was dreadful, with the drenchin rain an howlin wind. Robert the bruce finally found refuge in a deep cave.*

*Aye, he was sorely defeated, an e'en questionit if the scots shoud surrender tae edward. Was it aw worth it? aw the lives lost, aw the orphanit children. Robert was lower than low. Suddenly, he caucht sicht o a spider in the mouth o the cave tryin tae spin a web across the openin. Robert wis fascinatit watchin the spider work creatin the web, only tae have it torn apart by the wind. Again an again the spider would repair the damage until finally the web was complete. Robert the bruce was inspirit by the little spider tae carry on the ficht for scotlands freedom an peace. "if at first ye don't succeed, try try again," became his motto. He went on tae ficht for eight more years an finally defeatit the english at the battle o Bannockburn!"*

"But, Grandfather, didn't Robert the Bruce ruin the spiders web when he left the cave?"

"Aye, lad, that he did. But Robert stayit long enouch tae watch the spider rebuild the web. Try try again till ye succeit."

The memory made Peter smile. He loved everything about his grandfather–his way of speaking, his love of Scotland, and his pride in the 214 acre family estate in the Scottish border country. He was especially glad his grandfather had shared his love of fly fishing. Peter knew he'd been blessed with a wonderful role model.

The plastic bag recaptured his attention and he carefully unfolded the note and read it.

"Well, what do you know! She's American!"

## *Chapter Fourteen*

# SARAH:

*The School Meeting*

No one at Campbell Manor school was happier to hear about Fiona Farnsworth then Sarah Duncan. Finally there was a new girl in her grade level who would claim all the attention and be the target of the nasty remarks from the other girls. It was now mid-December and this term would end several days before Christmas. One week to go. Sarah worked hard and studied quite a bit, which was not difficult considering she had no distractions from social activities. Her teachers told her they were very impressed, especially since she was American. She had no idea what that meant and was quite surprised when the head of the Upper School requested a meeting in her office.

Mrs. Andrews was a tall woman with short, brown hair and wire-rimmed glasses. Her face lit up with a wide smile as Sarah walked into her office.

"Please sit down, Sarah. I'm glad to see you."

"Thank you, Mrs. Andrews," Sarah replied quietly. After two months at the school this was the first time she had been called to the administration office and was astonished anyone knew her name.

"I've noticed you have progressed quite well during your time here," Mrs. Andrews said, looking at a folder on her large desk with Sarah's name on it. "Would you please tell me your impression of Campbell Manor?"

Sarah paused slightly before answering, gathering her thoughts. Mrs. Andrews must have felt her discomfort.

"You can be candid with me Sarah."

"Well, I quite like the school. The courses are different from the other schools I've attended, and all my instructors are very good."

"And what about the students? How have you got on with the other girls in your level?"

Sarah wasn't sure how to answer. What she said about the courses and the teachers was absolutely the truth, but the girls…that was another matter entirely. She wasn't sure where this conversation was going, but knew that lying was rarely a good idea. If she said the girls were friendly or even tolerably decent, that would be a complete fabrication. What came to mind was they were rude, unmannered twits.

"By your hesitation, may I guess that you have not had an easy time of it?"

"That would be a good way of looking at it," Sarah answered, very glad to have words put in her mouth.

"I was afraid of that. I'm sorry your social experience hasn't been as positive as we had hoped. Many people think education is strictly about studies, but we know there is so much more. The girls in your level are of particular concern to me this year. They are an especially close group and I've observed they are not very welcoming to new students. Between us, may I suggest they border on mean-spirited. I've known many of them for years and I am working with their parents to address these issues. In watching you, it seems you have dealt with it in a very mature way. You've done exceedingly well in your studies while remaining open with your teachers. I'm very proud of you."

There were so many parts of this conversation that Sarah wanted to respond to but at the moment she was trying not to blush any more than she could help.

"Thank you. I appreciate that." Sarah wasn't sure if she was supposed to comment on the behavior of the other girls, or what more she should say.

"By now you must be wondering what this is all about."

"Yes, I am a bit curious," Sarah said, trying to hide the fact that she was a lot curious.

"I would appreciate if you would treat this conversation

confidentially."

"Of course. It's not as though they speak to me anyway," Sarah said with a laugh, relaxing a little.

"Yes, there is that fact," Mrs. Andrews answered with a smile. "A young American girl from another school will be transferring here. She is currently in Level 2 and is going to be moved up to Level 4 with you. She is exceedingly bright and needs the challenge of more intense studies. My concern is that she is new to Campbell Manor and is extremely shy. Any ill treatment from the other girls may have a very detrimental effect on her being successful in this transition. We want to keep her at Campbell Manor, as do her parents. It is a very large leap for her socially, much more than academically, and being younger than the Level 4 students, this concerns me." Mrs. Andrews paused and cleared her throat. "I've been thinking, and I may be asking too much, but would you be interested in being her friend, and help guide her this next term? Of course, I will speak to your father as well as her parents to make sure they are keen for this idea."

"Sort of a mentor?" Sarah asked, knowing if she accepted this situation, that would end any possible chance of being accepted by the other girls in her class. On the other hand, she wasn't making any progress in that department anyway. She certainly wished there had been a friend around when she started at Campbell Manor. Her thoughts brightened when she thought of Peter. His friendship had made all the difference. "Yes, Mrs. Andrews, I would be delighted to help."

## Chapter Fifteen
# RICHARD:
*The Ambassador Calls*

Heathrow Airport was crowded as usual, and getting to the British Airways gate was a hassle. Richard and Liam made it just in time to board the flight home and find their seats. The meeting with the Ambassador was not at all what Richard expected. Truthfully, he was stunned, but being well-versed in disguising his emotions, no one would've guessed. He expected inquiries concerning how he liked Edinburgh, how Sarah was adjusting, how competent did he find the staff at the consulate and so on. It was when the conversation shifted to personal threats and the need for additional security that Richard became inwardly uneasy. The Ambassador assured him repeatedly that the threats were being taken seriously and people were now in place to protect them. For the first time, Richard knew what it must feel like to get a punch to the gut. He felt both selfish and foolish exposing his daughter to anything remotely dangerous.

As the plane lifted off the tarmack, Richard turned to his body-guard, Liam, and spoke in a quiet voice, barely audible over the engine noise in the airplane.

"When did you become aware of the problem we discussed today?"

"Just recently, sir. I was taken into the ante room today and given the update and the solutions they thought were proper."

"And do you agree with the plan they are implementing? Please think before you answer. This is my daughter's safety we are talking about."

"And your safety as well, sir." Liam paused as if to replay the information in his mind. "If Sarah were my child I would not alter her schedule any more than was necessary. I believe we should assess the times during her day when she might be vulnerable and reduce the exposure. We can cover you fairly easily, though it will mean reducing your public visibility until this is resolved."

"The Ambassador said you've had a great deal of experience with this, so I am trusting your instincts. How many more men will be assigned to us?"

"Four at the moment, plus, of course, Mrs. McAughtrie."

"Mrs. McAughtrie?? What the blazes does she have to do with this?" Richard whispered loudly, suddenly realizing there was more to this than he had been told.

Liam stammered and his face blushed all the way to his red hair. The tall, well built man looked at Richard with his mouth open. No words came out.

"I can see that the cat has been let out of the bag, Liam. This is probably not the place to continue this discussion. We will resume it on the drive home."

"Yes, sir." answered the guilty bodyguard.

The rest of the flight was silent, the landing fairly smooth and the walk to the car was in the rain. Once they were on the road, Richard broke the silence.

"Where would you like to begin?"

During the forty-five minute drive to Newington, Liam told Richard everything he knew, including some information he probably shouldn't have shared. The Ambassador had informed Richard with the utmost secrecy, that not only was Conrad Ratchford a most unlikable person, it seems he was also running a money laundering operation out of the consulate. Apparently Ratchford had become associated with a cartel who needed an outlet to move large sums of stolen money. The plan was to send personal gifts to Mr. Ratchford at the consulate, filled with illicit cash. The cash would be stored until it could be safely sent to a secure Swiss bank account. Ratchford's previous experience in international banking meant he knew his way around global transactions. It would start small then increase as the plan became integrated throughout Scotland and

England. The scheme was moving forward as planned, with the expectation that Ratchford would become the permanent Consulate General. Once that happened, the door would be wide open for him to make a substantial amount of money illegally. Then without any warning to Ratchford, Richard Duncan was sent to replace him. The abrupt change rocked the entire arrangement for Ratchford and his cohorts, resulting in chaos and extreme frustration. The home office had done everything covertly with the utmost secrecy to be sure no one else at the consulate was involved. Once that was established, the decision was made to move quickly. According to what the Ambassador had told Richard today both Ratchford and the cartel blamed Richard Duncan for ending their well-laid, lucrative plan. Neither was pleased.

"But the order to replace him came from you, with all due respect, Mr. Ambassador."

"Richard, you are dealing with people who are exceedingly focused on what they wanted, which was money. It is rarely a good idea to get caught in the cross fire. These people are not interested in logic or morals, only greed."

A chill ran down Richards spine, which was interrupted by Liam's voice.

"Did the Ambassador tell you security detected the cartel already sent people to Edinburgh to check on the situation?" asked Liam.

"Not in so many words. He alluded to the fact that Sarah and I would have added protection until this mess is cleaned up."

The two men drove on in silence for a few minutes.

"Did the Ambassador happen to mention that they have misplaced Ratchford?"

"You've got to be kidding!" Richard answered, very alarmed.

"The Ambassador was trying to keep the entire affair quiet, letting Ratchford think he was dismissed because of poor performance. He didn't want to bring attention to the situation by arresting him. Somehow on his return to London, he outwitted the security cars following him and has disappeared. My guess is he is hiding from both the Ambassador and the cartel."

Richard knew Liam was telling more than was appropriate, but knew instinctively that Liam felt a loyalty to him and Sarah.

"Is there concern that the cartel will come after me? After all, I am the one who sent the shipping containers to London," he asked.

There was hesitation in the bodyguard's next words.

"There is concern, yes, but my experience tells me you are in more danger from Ratchford. We don't know exactly how far this scheme went. One looming question is if there is any cash hidden in the consulate itself. We've searched the offices, and Ratchford's home is being gone through meticulously. So far nothing has turned up."

"Perhaps Sarah and I should go away for a bit."

"That was discussed, but it was decided that things need to appear as normal as possible on the surface, and we now have expanded security to protect you. This brings me to Mrs. McAughtrie."

By now the car was parked in the driveway of the house. All was dark from the front, except for the light from Sarah's bedroom on the second floor. A wisp of smoke from one of the chimneys rose in the air and was lost in the rain. The enormity of this information was settling in on Richard.

"Please tell me Mrs. McAughtrie is one of the good guys."

Liam laughed out loud, breaking the tension in the car.

"Yes, she is one of the best. Her husband, S.A. McAughtrie was considered one of the finest, most honorable men in the international security world. Seaneen was right by his side, and is well-trained. Behind her congenial manner and motherly behavior, is a very savvy woman, who would not hesitate to take out anyone who would threaten you or your daughter. Originally, when she was assigned to you it was to be helpful with Sarah. You know, having another female in the house. As things became more complicated, her role has been amped up to bodyguard as well as housekeeper. You weren't told straight away because, again, they wanted things to appear normal."

It was obvious to Richard that he was out of his element with all the security details and behind the scenes organization. There had been a small amount of safety instruction during his early days with the Foreign Service, but nothing on this level.

"So how do we proceed from here?" he asked, his voice betraying weariness from the very long day.

"I will be moving into your downstairs bedroom for a while, and the others will be at their posts outside the house."

"Liam, I do appreciate everything you are doing and I trust you. It is just a little overwhelming at the moment. Let's go inside and see if Mrs. McAughtrie saved some dinner for us."

They entered the mostly dark house and Liam began turning lights on, cautiously looking around. Richard went upstairs to Sarah's room and apologized for missing dinner. She was ready for bed and full of enthusiasm, but agreed to wait until tomorrow's breakfast to tell him all her news. Seeing her happy was the perfect antidote to the day's turn of events. And Mrs. McAughtrie had indeed left a delicious dinner waiting for them in the Aga stove.

## *Chapter Sixteen*
# SARAH:
*Savor the Moment*

Sarah shoved the note under her pillow, and pretended to be reading Jane Austen's 'Pride and Prejudice' as her father walked up the creaking wooden stairs. You would think the lovely carpet runner would muffle the sound a bit more.

"Hi, Sunshine. I'm so sorry I missed dinner with you."

"Don't worry, we were fine. Mrs. McAughtrie made an amazing folded pie thing that was really good. I think she left you and Liam dinner in the kitchen."

"Then I'll go find it. I'm starving!"

"Dad…was your trip okay? You look tired."

"It was fine," he answered as he kissed the top of his daughter's head, "but I'm glad to be home. Goodnight, sleep well."

"Love you, Dad."

"Love you too, Sunshine."

Sarah waited until she was sure she was alone to open the folded paper.

*Dear Sarah,*
*This is your lucky day! I think Americans are brilliant,*
*talented, and very funny people! Actually, my older*
*sister, Ainslie, is a dancer with the Pacific Northwest Ballet*
*in Seattle Washington. She quite likes it there,*
*something about feeling right at home with the*
*rainy weather.*

*I have finished school, so no homeschooling.*
*For the moment I am working on a number*
*of projects that take up most of my time.*
*My parents are both university professors here*
*in Edinburgh and I would say they can be a bit formal*
*but also loads of fun. My extended family has a small*
*estate in the Scottish Borders near Walkerburn, and*
*growing up I spent most of my free time there.*
*The River Tweed is a famous salmon river, and it runs right*
*through the middle of the land. The fly fishing there*
*is exceptional. When I was a wee lad, my grandfather*
*taught me how to tie flies and how to be a*
*Compleat Angler (that's a joke, it's the title of a famous*
*book on fly-fishing by Isaac Walton from the 1600's).*
*Can you tell it's a bit of an obsession? If you haven't been to*
*that part of Scotland, try to make a visit sometime. It's a lovely*
*drive, about an hour and a half south of the city. By the way, have*
*you ever been fly fishing?*
*I'm afraid I don't know much about the American*
*Consulate here in Edinburgh, other than it's in a quite nice*
*building up on Regent Terrace with an excellent view of*
*Arthur's Seat. Your father must be a very smart, accomplished*
*gentleman to have such a prestigious position. I'm sure you're*
*very proud of him. Still, it must be a little disconcerting to have*
*the need for security. But I guess that's normal for you.*
*Are you looking forward to Christmas? Will you stay in*
*Scotland? Did you know that Christmas was actually*
*banned in Scotland for a time. It had to do with the*
*Puritan led English Parliament in 1647,*
*who thought there was no Biblical justification.*
*Have you heard of Hogmanay? That's our New Years Eve*
*traditional holiday. It's quite amazing.*
*I'd better close, my projects are calling me.*
*I really do enjoy our communication.*
*Peter*

At the bottom of the note was a sketch of an American flag waving. He really was talented. Reading the note again, she was fascinated by Peter and his life. There was so much she didn't know. Turning the light off, she noticed the rain had turned to snow outside her window. This was a lovely place to live when you had a friend.

The snow piled up overnight much to everyone's surprise, and the wind was howling. The old house was a bit drafty, so Mrs. McAughtrie asked Liam to light the fireplaces in several of the downstairs rooms. The smell of the slow burning wood was comforting, as was the warmth that poured out. The dining room was on the exposed side of the house, so breakfast was served in the large kitchen, which happened to be Sarah's favorite.

It became obvious that this crazy winter weather had moved in for a long stay. Edinburgh was not prepared nor equipped for this much snow, and schools, shops and businesses, including the consulate, were closed. Breakfast took on an unusually leisurely air with no rush to be anywhere.

"Unicorns, John Duncan Fergusson, and Guernsey cows." Sarah announced proudly.

"All right, Miss Smarty, explain your choices."

"The unicorn is amazing. It's the National Animal of Scotland."

"You know they don't exist, right?" Richard interrupted.

He was met with the look that only a teenage girl can give her parent when the obvious has been stated.

"As I was saying, the unicorn was first used by James I, King of the Scots in the 15th century. I read that it was thought to be majestic, proud and fearless, and considered to be the opposite of the lion, the English icon, which is considered the natural enemy of the unicorn."

"I can see your expensive education is paying off," Richard answered, taking a bite of toast and orange marmalade. "And is John Duncan Fergusson a distant relative of ours you've uncovered?"

"Actually, I'm not sure of that, but he was an impressionist painter in the early 1920's. He was going to study medicine and be a surgeon, but didn't like it after all, so he entered an art academy in Edinburgh to train as an artist, but didn't like how that was going either and left. He became a famous self-taught artist and has a large gallery in Perth. Of course, he's dead, but there is a lot of his work there, and I'd really like to see it sometime. I love that he was self-taught."

Mrs. McAughtrie was listening as she stirred the porridge pot and looked at Richard with a wink. Richard could only shake his head in amazement.

"Did you learn this from school or your own independent reading?"

"Self-taught," Sarah quipped, "much like John Duncan Fergusson."

"Touché! Now, about the Guernsey cow and what's so special about this lovely four-legged beast?"

"Oh, this is really interesting! Did you know that it's thought that this particular cow was brought to the Island of Guernsey in the 10th century by monks who were banished from Mont Saint Michel? They are very gentle and have nice, extra rich milk. The cows, not the monks…"

Sarah was pleased she was making her father and Mrs. McAughtrie laugh.

"You're in fine fettle this morning. Can I guess it's because there is no school today?" Richard asked.

"My gosh, I forgot to tell you the most exciting thing!" And with that Sarah recounted her conversation with Mrs. Andrews and the young student she was to mentor.

"So, Mrs. Andrews said she would call you and make sure it's all right, and also call the girl's parents and see what they thought." Sarah was beaming.

By now Liam had come into the kitchen and was making a cup of tea. Sarah saw Richard and Liam exchanged glances. Her father's voice was oddly sharp.

"I'm not sure this would be a good idea. Would it take place strictly at school during the normal hours?"

"As far as I know. I think Mrs. Andrews is still working out the details, and of course, she needs the okay from the girl and her parents. I don't think it would begin until after the Christmas holiday in any case."

Sarah was disappointed by her father's reaction and a little curious about his direct question as to the location. Why would that matter?

"I thought you would be pleased," she said wistfully.

"It's just that we have a good routine and I'd hate to make any big changes," Richard said, his voice a little softer.

That excuse didn't do much to erase the feeling something was off, she just didn't know what. Mrs. McAughtrie spoke up and cheerfully suggested it was a perfect day to make cookies and think about Christmas. Never having met a cookie she didn't like, Sarah readily agreed. Her father's odd behavior was quickly forgotten when he began talking about Christmas.

"Sarah, I have an idea. What would you think of having Christmas here instead of going away? We could show Mrs. McAughtrie and Liam our American traditions."

"Do you mean it? Can we get a big tree and lots of lights?" she asked with great enthusiasm. "And do we have our old ornaments, or should we make new ones?"

The spirit of the holiday took over, and it never occurred to Sarah that Mrs. McAughtrie and Liam might have somewhere else to be for Christmas.

"I can help with the tree," Liam offered. "I've a friend who has a Christmas tree farm not far from here. He grows Nordmann Firs and some are older than you!"

"Me? Older than me?" Mrs. McAughtrie said astounded at the thought.

"Well, I meant Sarah," Liam answered sheepishly.

"How about if I go with you?" Richard said.

"And Sarah, why don't we plan a menu with all your favorite things for Christmas dinner?" Mrs. McAughtrie, brought out a tablet and pen. "I want to learn all about your family recipes."

The day went on delightfully with growing anticipation of the upcoming holiday. Richard and Liam settled in the living room in front of the fire to discuss the various merits of different species of fir trees and the ladies stayed in the kitchen near the warm Aga and made long lists of things to be done for their Christmas holiday.

Later that night in her dark bedroom, Sarah listened to the rhythmic ticking of her grandmother's antique clock. It was very measured, much like the beating of her heart. Looking out the window, snowflakes seemed to float slowly down to the street below, gradually covering everything in a sparkling white blanket. In the soft light from the streetlamp, the world looked perfect. If only she could capture this moment and keep it safe in a secret place. Then, when life became sad or difficult, she could open it up it and be filled with this same joy and contentment. The warmth she felt wasn't only from the burning logs in her fireplace, but from a deep, inner peace within her heart. Sarah began a note to Peter. Who better to share her thoughts with?

# *Chapter Seventeen*

# SARAH:

## *The Anticipation of Christmas*

By that night, the air turned frigid, and the snow continued. Word went out that Campbell Manor School for Girls would close for the remainder of the week as the weather showed no sign of improving. With Christmas holiday on the horizon, there was little sense in forcing students and teachers to make their way to school. The U.S. Consulate also closed until after Christmas, except for emergencies, which made life easier for Richard, Liam and the other security people.

The sky was barely light when Sarah woke up and remembered school was cancelled. In a near panic she realized this meant she wouldn't be walking past Peter's house and couldn't drop off her note. Without hesitation, on went a warm sweater over her pajamas, and down the stairs on tip-toe. She threw on her heavy coat and boots and out she went in the deep snow to leave the note in the wall. She'd never seen so much snow, but the trip was successful and the note was deposited in the wall. Sneaking back to her house she had a feeling she was being followed, but decided it was simply paranoia. Everyone still seemed to be asleep, and she hastily cleaned up the snow her boots brought inside. Up the stairs and back into her warm bed she went. It was after ten when she finally came down to breakfast. Even with the fireplaces burning, the house was chilly, save for the kitchen which was cosy as always.

"Well, there you are, pet," Mrs. McAughtrie greeted her with a big smile. "Ready for a wee bit of breakfast? We have much to do today to get ready…make our lists and plans, and see how we want to set the table. I've found some hidden treasures in this old house we can make use of."

Sarah's eyes widened with excitement.

"Really? What have you've found!"

"I'll show you. Follow me."

Mrs. McAughtrie led her into the dining room where the big table was loaded with all manner of silver serving pieces, all in need of a good polish, and beautiful antique china plates and bowls.

"This is perfect!" Sarah whispered as she touched each treasure on the table.

"I think we will set a lovely table, don't you?"

Sarah impulsively gave Mrs. McAughtrie a heartfelt hug.

"Thank you so much for everything you do. I can't imagine life without you."

Mrs. McAughtrie hid the tears as she held onto the young girl.

"Your father and Liam ventured out a bit earlier into the country to the Christmas tree farm, and promised to return with a large tree, garlands and anything else they can find. Let's hope they don't get stymied in the snow and have to be rescued. In the meantime, we'd best get on with our shopping list and silver polishing. I hope the grocery shops won't be closed."

The morning was happily spent in the warm kitchen thumbing through Rosemary Duncan's old family recipes looking for her Southern Cornbread Dressing and Special Turkey Gravy. They laughed at the names of some recipes in the collection, and were fascinated by how tattered and old others were.

"Tell me, pet, where does one find red eyes for Red Eye Gravy?"

"I suppose at the Red Eye store?" Sarah giggled. "And imagine someone's shock when they are served Sauerkraut Surprise Cake!"

Mrs. McAughtrie groaned and made a gruesome face. "You Americans certainly like some peculiar food."

"At least we don't make haggis," Sarah said making an equally gruesome face.

"On a much better note, here's your grandmother's recipe for

Great, Great Grandma's Great, Great Snapping Ginger Cookies. My, isn't that a mouthful?! This paper is almost transparent it was written so long ago," Mrs. McAughtrie marveled, holding up the thin paper.

"That was one of her favorites," Sarah said, a wave of sadness passing over as she thought of her beloved grandmother.

With recipes chosen, silver polished and the heirloom dishes carefully washed, they settled down for a cup of tea. As Mrs. McAughtrie poured out, she brought up the subject of a shopping trip.

"There is a very old, charming antique shop on Cockburn Street owned by some dear friends of mine. It's a treasure trove of bits and bobs. Would you like to go?"

"Absolutely! I would love that." Sarah began mentally making a list of gifts she could look for. What could she find for Peter?

"We'll ask your father when he and Liam return, and possibly go tomorrow if the weather isn't too dreary."

It was nearly dusk when the big black car drove up filled with evergreens, and two Christmas trees securely tied onto the top. They made dozens of trips from the packed auto, into the house, dragging snow with them. There was a very tall, bushy tree, a smaller thin tree, several large wreaths, and an abundance of garlands. The smell of evergreens was intoxicating and filled every corner of the house. If ever a home smelled like Christmas, this was it.

After dinner, Sarah and Mrs. McAughtrie hung the green garlands all over the house, tying them with bright red ribbon. By the time a perfect place for each Christmas tree had been debated and decided, they all agreed it was too late to decorate, and it would have to wait until tomorrow. Going up the stairs, Sarah overheard her father and Mrs. McAughtrie discussing the shopping trip and was a little surprised to hear her father's concerns.

"Do you really think this is a good idea? We must not put her at risk."

"I've given it a fair amount of thought. I will be right with her, and Liam will follow. The shop is very small and my friends will agree to close it for a bit to other shoppers. The poor lass needs to get out, don't you think?"

If she weren't so tired and happy, she might have given it more thought. By the time she crawled into bed, her mind was filled with what gifts she could find for her father, Mrs. McAughtrie and Liam. They were her family for this Christmas. And, of course, the wondrous pondering of what she would get Peter.

*Chapter Eighteen*

# PETER:

*The SnowNote*

Without a doubt this was the most snow Peter ever remembered seeing in Edinburgh. The wind caused tall snow drifts to gather in corners, then white powdery dust would gust up in the air. He happened to glance out his window about the same time a suspicious looking figure, dressed in a large, heavy coat over what looked like pajamas with a knit hat pulled down low tucked a note in the wall, then disappeared. What a funny girl Sarah was! He ran down the stairs and threw on his old Wellies, and slogged his way through the deep snow to the wall.

Back upstairs in his old wingback chair, he set his steaming cup of tea on the wooden side table and anxiously unfolded the paper.

*Dear Peter,*
*There is so much to tell you! Isn't it amazing how little things*
*can bring new perspective? First off, I am delighted*
*that your sister is enjoying America, and how fabulous that*
*she is a professional ballet dancer–she must be very*
*talented. Have you been to visit her in Seattle? I was there*
*once several years ago and it's a lovely place,*
*especially down by the waterfront.*
*Your parents sound wonderful and interesting. It is*
*good to know not everyone thinks Americans*
*are obnoxious, aggressive and loud mouthed.*
*I will ask my father if we can make a visit to Walkerburn so*
*I can see first hand this land that is your favorite. I think*

*my father has been fly fishing, and I'll use that as bait (good pun, huh?) to whet his curiosity to go. There are so many things I don't know about you, but somehow we seem to get on well. Does that sound crazy?*

*Now to the big news: The Head Mistress of the Upper School asked me to mentor a young American girl who was advancing from level 2 to level 4. They are concerned that a girl that young will be treated badly by my classmates.*

*I haven't really shared with anyone how hard the last few months have been, but somehow the Head Mistress must have known. Being new and not making any acquaintances in Edinburgh, I'm sure you understand how grateful I am for your friendship. I'm hoping I can help her as you have helped me.*

*The second big news is that we will stay here for Christmas! Normally we travel to somewhere else and stay in a hotel and have our Christmas dinner in a nice restaurant. This will be the first time in a long while that we will get to decorate our house and celebrate with a real, home-cooked Christmas dinner! Mrs. McAughtrie, our housekeeper and Liam, my father's security man will be here, too. The thought of decorating our house with garlands, candles, mistletoe and Christmas trees is so exciting! We will make ornaments and bake cookies! This probably seems silly to you, but it is really a big deal for me! Would it be okay if I brought you a little Christmas gift? If that is not appropriate, please let me know. I promise it won't hurt my feelings. Well, it might a little, but it's okay. You mentioned Hogmanay and I am burning with curiosity about the custom and how it is celebrated here. In case you hadn't noticed, I love to read and learn about everything. Books have been my best friends forever.*

*Please forgive the length of this note which has somehow become nearly a novel. I'm sure I could write into the night but you would most likely be bored and forever sorry you befriended this silly American girl.*

*Good night, my friend.*

*Sarah*

*Chapter Nineteen*

# SARAH:

*Cavanagh's Antiques*

The next morning, Liam dropped Sarah and Mrs. McAughtrie off at the bottom of the steep set of stairs called Fleshmarket Close. Up, up and up they walked, pausing from time to time to catch their breath. Mrs. McAughtrie explained that a 'close' was similar to what Americans would call an alley. But Sarah had never seen anything like this in her life. It was a narrow, stone, vertical stairway between towering, ancient buildings with pubs tucked in here and there along the way. What intriguing people these Scottish were.

At the top of the steps, they finally reached Cockburn Street, (pronounced "Co-burn Street" Mrs. McAughtrie pointed out). It was a serpentine, cobblestone road, with four and five-story medieval buildings, each with unique peaks and spires, and chimneys reaching high into the sky. Sarah tried looking up to the rooftops, but it only made her neck hurt.

"What is that very tall building over there?" Sarah asked, looking at one structure that dominated the others.

"That's the City Chambers and it is twelve stories high, leaps and bounds taller than the rest. Now, if you look over there on the northside, you will see sculptures of an owl and a pussycat on top of that building," Mrs. McAughtrie said, obviously enjoying her role as tour guide.

"You mean like the Edward Lear poem?" Sarah asked incredulously.

"Depends on who you ask," she answered with a twinkle in her eye.

Small shops and restaurants lined each side on the sidewalk level, with apartments 'to let' in the stories above. Cars parked on both sides of the road made driving on the one way street a bit tricky. Sarah could now understand why Liam had dropped them off at the bottom of Fleshmarket Close. He said that this was a short cut between Waverley Train Station and High Street. Somehow walking up hundreds of steps didn't qualify as much of a short cut in Sarah's mind.

Cavanagh's was a tiny, age-old shop that could accommodate about three customers at a time, and then only if they were on the small side. To the left of the glass door entrance were antique wooden display cases filled with timeworn silver serving pieces of all sorts. Clusters of mismatched silver spoons and forks were tied with string and small white price tags. Rising above to the tall ceiling were vintage military posters urging boys to 'enlist today,' or proudly announcing the Women's Royal Air Force. There were framed sepia photos of long gone families, dressed in centuries old styles, standing rigidly looking at the camera. Casually overlapping was a relic theatre poster advertising "The Pickpocket" play at the Royal Lyceum Theatre. Old maps, well-worn military helmets, bowler hats, and an actual suit of armor, shared space with flags of various countries, classic clocks, multi-armed silver candelabras and ancient suitcases. On the crowded counters were ribboned military medals, jeweled brooches, many strands of pearls and a multitude of rings. Toward the back of the store high up, a large banner proclaimed God Save the King. Every available surface was covered with things old and curious. Sarah was in heaven!

They were greeted warmly by Maeve and Robbie, the older couple who owned the shop. The small sign in the window was turned to read "closed" to any potential customers who might wander by.

"Oh! Seaneen! It's been far too long. We mustn't let such time fly between visits," exclaimed Maeve. "And, Sarah, I am delighted to meet you. Please have a look around and if anything catches your fancy, do let us know. Robbie will be at the register taking care of some things." With that, the two old friends chattered like magpies, and walked through a black and red tartan fabric curtain to a private area in the back of the store. Their talk was of memories and recipes, and soon became background noise as Sarah explored every nook and cranny of this extraordinarily wonderful place.

"Were you looking for anything in particular, lass?" asked Robbie, a charming man with dimples and twinkling eyes behind his wire rimmed glasses

"A few Christmas gifts for friends and family. This is the most amazing shop I've ever been in. I'm quite sure I could spend all day here."

"And you'd be most welcome. I'll be happy to show you anything you care to see."

"Thank you," Sarah answered with unbridled sincerity.

Robbie beamed and went back to his tasks at hand.

Sarah was aware that they had closed the shop for her visit, but hadn't really given it any more thought. Before she knew it half an hour had passed and she had chosen perfect items for each person on her list. Glancing through the paned windows, she saw several people waiting for the popular shop to open. She turned toward the back where the two ladies were still chatting. They had lowered their voices to whispers but Sarah could still hear their conversation.

"She is a darling girl. I can see why you are quite attached to her," said Maeve.

"Like a granddaughter I never had," answered Mrs. McAughtrie.

Sarah smiled at the affection Mrs. McAughtrie obviously felt. What she heard next stunned her.

"Does she know you have a gun?"

"Of course not. Her father has chosen not tell her anything for now."

"Seaneen, Is that really fair? I know you can protect her, but this is a real threat."

"I am well aware of that. Both Liam and I are on high alert, and we have additional invisible guards stationed everywhere."

At that moment, Robbie spoke up in a loud voice.

"Ladies, the young lass has her purchases made and I think it's time we opened our doors for business."

The two friends gave a hug and one for Sarah, and they made their way back to the sidewalks of Cockburn Street.

# Chapter Twenty

# LIAM:

*Thinking of Home*

Light snowflakes drifted down onto Liam as he stood by the car parked near Cavanagh's Antique shop. He glanced right, then left to make sure his additional guards were in place. Thankfully, there were not many people on the streets this morning, as it was one of the coldest winter days in many years. He suspected most shoppers were not venturing out, opting to stay home and 'kennel' up as his father used to say. He thought of the windy, cloudy winters in Shetland growing up, and how as kids he and the sisters would play outside for hours oblivious to the weather. He must be getting old, because even just standing here the chill was reaching his bones. White twinkling lights in the storefront window caught his eye and he thought of Christmas at home. This would be the first time he missed the family celebration, but he was at peace with it, having no doubt where his duty lay. His mum and dad and three sisters would carry on just fine without him. He must remember to get with it and send a few packages to them straight away. With air mail delivery now, they should arrive on the island before Christmas. Sarah reminded him very much of his youngest sister, Ava, and he decided he would enlist her help with gift ideas for his sisters. He knew just what to get his dad and mum, which left only one gift undecided. What should he send Mairi, his girlfriend?

Liam's thoughts were interrupted as Mrs. McAughtrie and Sarah arrived with arms loaded with treasures. Once the ladies were inside the car, the nod was given to the waiting security men, and the entourage slowly made their way down Cockburn Street back to

Newington. Looking in the rear view mirror, he could see Sarah staring back at him. His lifelong experience with the sisters told him that this was a girl with something on her mind.

He spent the rest of the afternoon avoiding Sarah for fear she would corner him and ask questions he was not at liberty to answer. There was much relief when she asked Mrs. McAughtrie if she wanted to take a walk around the block to get some fresh air. Far be it for Liam to mention to the ladies that the fresh air outside was icy cold, with more snow predicted. He would take this opportunity to talk to Mr. Duncan, who was working in his home office. The tall, red-haired man knocked lightly on the partially opened door.

"Sir, may I have a word?"

"Of course, Liam. Has something happened?" Richard asked, trying to mask his concern. "Is everything all right?"

"Everything is security tight, not a hint of anything amiss. However…"

"However?"

"However, I have a strong feeling Sarah suspects something. Perhaps she overheard a conversation or made the deduction herself. So far, I've been able to keep a distance, but I didn't want you blindsided if she asked you directly."

"She's a very smart young lady so I'm not totally surprised, but I had hoped to keep this amongst ourselves until after Christmas. There doesn't seem to be any point in alarming her just yet." Richard stared out the window to the bleak winter day. "And you're comfortable we are safe?'

"I am for the moment. I've been doing this long enough to know you never know completely, but we've taken serious precautions to secure the house and watch the neighborhood."

"Then let's hold off as long as we can. We will make every effort to keep her distracted through Christmas Eve dinner tomorrow night. I am hoping that the excitement of the holiday will override her curiosity."

"That sounds like an excellent plan. Oh–and are you still planning to attend the midnight service at the Salisbury church tomorrow night?"

"Yes I would like that, unless you feel there is a real danger in doing it."

"No problem. My men will do a sweep of the church prior to your arrival."

Liam knew that the thought of all that extra work and disruption for the church went against Richard's ingrained good manners, but security was a priority. Being in church on Christmas Eve was a tradition that was obviously important to Richard and he would do everything in his power to make sure they were safe.

"Thank you, Liam. We will count on the Lord to protect us. I am in your debt for all you and the other guards are doing for us."

"My pleasure, sir."

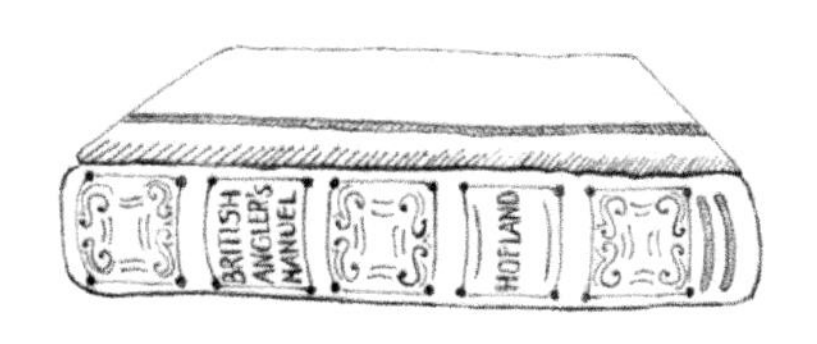


# *Chapter Twenty-one*

# SARAH:

## *Tomorrow is Another Day*

"It's freezing out here!" Sarah's breath came out as a frosty cloud. She pulled her knit hat lower on her forehead and held tight to Peter's Christmas gift with gloved hands.

"Let's make quick work of this wee trip, and hurry back to our warm kitchen," Mrs. McAughtrie replied with her teeth chattering.

"How can I thank you enough for coming out with me? I think Liam thought we were crazy. You've never questioned me about my friend in the window."

"I trust you, Sarah Duncan. You're a lass with good sense."

They walked along, their boots crunching in the snow on the sidewalk. Sarah's mind was racing on how to approach Mrs. McAughtrie about the odd conversation she had overheard when she suddenly caught sight of Peter in the third story window. All thoughts fled as she looked up at the young man who had come to mean so much to her. He smiled and waved. She waved back and showed him the gift before laying it down on top of the wall so he would be sure to see it. She carefully retrieved the note he had left for her in the crevice and when she looked up again, he was gone. Tucking the note in her coat pocket, Sarah looped her arm through Mrs. McAughtrie's and they headed home hastily to get out of the cold winter afternoon.

The tea kettle was on and well heated by the time they arrived back in the warm kitchen.

"Did you ladies have a brisk walk about?" Liam asked with a hint of amusement.

"Aye, we did, young man," Mrs. McAughtrie answered, "And now it's time I saw to dinner, so be off with you."

Sarah quickly caught that this was the housekeeper's way of ending any further conversation about their excursion.

"What can I do to help?" Sarah asked. After dragging Mrs. McAughtrie out in this weather, it was the least she could do. Peeling potatoes and scrubbing vegetables was a low price to pay for a co-conspirator. The note from Peter was calling to her, but she would save it for later as a treat to look forward to.

The comfort of one's warm bed should never be taken for granted. With two sweaters and an extra blanket, Sarah was finally warm and content, and the best part was reading her note.

*Dear Sarah,*
*Never would I be sorry we became friends. Your notes are delightful*
*and often the nicest part of my day. What a vote of confidence that your school headmistress has*
*recognized your brilliant ability to mentor a younger student.*
*You will, no doubt, make a positive difference for the*
*young lady. I'm sorry your school year has been so difficult.*
*The first time I saw you I had a rather odd feeling that*
*you were struggling with something, and now*
*I understand a bit more. Looks like happier days ahead though.*
*Christmas is a lovely time in Edinburgh, even though*
*we are a bit new at it compared to America.*
*Your plans sound very festive and full of spirit, and*
*I'm sure you will have a memorable holiday.*
*My sister is dancing a principal role in the Nutcracker*
*ballet this year and won't be here.*
*It's the first time she will miss our family gathering*
*and we are all rather sad. Our tradition is to have*
*a big Christmas Eve dinner with neighbors, then*
*Christmas Day will be here. Shortly after we will go to*
*Elibank House in the Scottish Borders*

*and spend time with grandparents.*
*If it isn't too cold we will go fly fishing on*
*the River Tweed for salmon, which I enjoy tremendously.*
*Someday you must try it. Our plan is to return the day*
*after Hogmanay (or New Years.)*
*I will be leaving a little gift for you*
*tomorrow in the regular place. I do hope you like it.*
*Merry Christmas my friend Sarah Duncan.*
*May God bless you.*
*Peter*

With the warm glow of the fireplace filling her room, Sarah read the note again and again. There was much to think about in all that he wrote. She was struck with the thought that she couldn't have found a more wonderful person to be her friend. Tomorrow was Christmas Eve and he would be leaving her a gift at the wall. The anticipation was thrilling. What could it be? She cautioned herself to not get too excited, but she just couldn't help it. It looked as though another walk around the block would be in order tomorrow. Bless Mrs. McAughtrie for being a willing participant. That reminded her of the conversation she overhead in the antique shop. She really needed to find out what was going on, but for tonight she recalled what Scarlett O'Hara said in Gone with the Wind, 'Tomorrow is another day.'

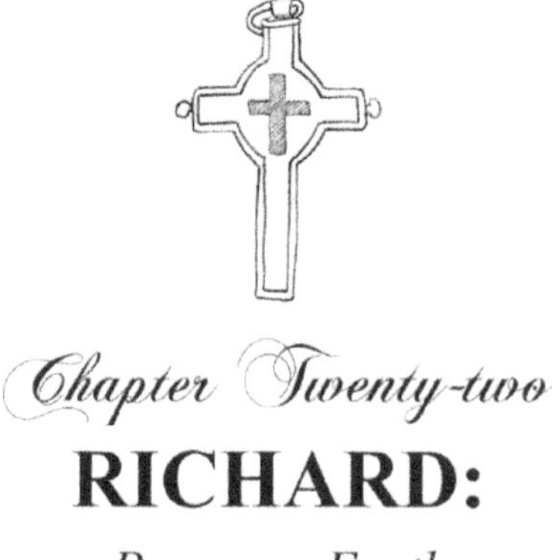

## *Chapter Twenty-two*

# RICHARD:

### *Peace on Earth*

Christmas Eve morning began early with Mrs. McAughtrie getting breakfast out of the way so she could proceed with making their big evening meal. With just the four of them, it was decided to still do it in grand style with all the silver and china they had found, and prepare a mélange of everyone's favorite Christmas dishes. Christmas morning would be their time for opening gifts.

"Hogmanay, Scottish salmon…and Christmas secrets," Sarah volunteered as she finished her porridge.

"Wait a minute! You're supposed to share three things you like about Scotland. How did Christmas secrets sneak in?"

The familiar look of teenage exasperation crossed his daughter's lovely face.

"Well then, *Scottish* Christmas secrets. Will that do?"she asked.

"That certainly clarifies it," Richard answered with amusement, raising his eyebrows up and down, making Sarah laugh. "So, what are your plans for today?"

"I've a few presents to wrap, and I promised Mrs. McAughtrie I would help with dinner. The table is already set and is gorgeous! I'm so excited we decided to stay here for Christmas. Thank you, Dad."

Richard looked across the table at his daughter and felt the familiar pang of guilt. Most of her childhood had been spent abroad with only her grandmother as her companion. What kind of upbringing and stability does that give a child? After his wife abandoned them, he vowed to do his best to make sure Sarah knew how much he loved her. The fine line between a successful career and parental responsibility was constantly in the back of his mind, like a balancing act. Sarah seemed bright and content, if a little shy, but he worried about the long term effects of her less than traditional childhood. Today, however, was Christmas Eve and they would enjoy every minute of this holiday from start to finish.

"Remember church service is at eleven-thirty tonight. I'm trusting you will stay awake."

"Bet I'm more awake that you'll be! Will the others go with us? I hope so. It will be like our little family!"

"They will, yes. As cold as it is, we had better dress warm."

Once again, Richard was given the amused teenage roll of her eyes, silently saying, 'Duh!' then off she went to help in the kitchen. Richard retreated to his office to wrap his few gifts and put them under the tree. There had been no reports from Liam of any unusual activity the last day or two. He sent up a silent prayer asking for peace on Earth, if only for today. It was probably wishful thinking, but he hoped the worst of the threat was over and life could return to normal. Starting fresh in the new year seemed the natural order of things. The consulate was closed until December twenty-sixth, but he had been warned that when it reopened, it would be very busy. With these extra days off due to the snow, he was actually looking forward to getting back to work. For now, there were three security people spending their Christmas holiday in surveillance around his house, meaning they weren't with their families, and that bothered him. Unfortunately, at this point there seemed no recourse. He must make sure to ask Mrs. McAughtrie to provide them with food and hot drinks, and anything else they might need. It was the least he could do.

Even with the shadow of an unknown threat hanging over them, Richard knew blessings overflowed. He was extremely grateful for Seaneen McAughtrie and Liam Morrison, who had embraced the idea of spending Christmas together with complete, unabashed excitement. He hadn't cleared it with either of them when he first mentioned it to Sarah, though he assumed they had families they would rather be with. Yet, both knew the security limitations that Richard and Sarah faced and completely stepped up without hesitation. The blessing of friendship. There would come a time when Sarah would have to know the reality of their situation, but Richard hoped they could make it through Christmas without burdening his daughter with the perils of the life he had chosen.

# Chapter Twenty-three
# SARAH:
## *Liver Koogs for Christmas*

The delicious aroma of Christmas dinner filled the kitchen. After hours spent preparing an enormous variety of dishes, Sarah and Mrs. McAughtrie finally hung up their aprons and sat down for a cup of tea.

"I don't remember cooking Christmas dinner being so involved," Sarah sighed.

"I doubt you ever cooked each persons favorite fare in addition to normal Christmas recipes."

"Well, on that note, I think you win the prize, preparing those fish liver things for Liam. Eewwww!" Sarah grimaced, wrinkling up her nose.

"Aye, Liam's a fine lad and I'm happy to bring a wee bit of home for him."

"I agree," Sarah answered, "but I can tell you there is no way I will ever be sold on Liver Koogs."

"It would never occur to me to bake fish livers in a hollowed out potato, but I'm with you lass, they wouldn't be first on my list of favorites. Good Liam could give me some idea how to prepare them. He said they used to be cooked among the hot peat on the fireplace hearth."

"I know he is from Shetland Islands, but isn't there some…less exotic food he might've preferred?" Sarah asked, scrunching up her face. "My guess is he will have all of them to himself."

"He'll not be fighting me for them," Mrs. McAughtrie laughed and changed the subject. "I must say I am quite taken with your method of making the cornbread dressing. It smells mouthwatering. I believe cooking comes quite naturally to you."

Secretly delighted, Sarah tried to act like it was nothing out of the ordinary.

"I guess I did watch my grandmother make it a few times. When I was little she would cook our holiday meals, but later when we began to move around a lot and she got older, we got into the habit of going to restaurants. I mean it was nice, but not the same as Christmas at home, wherever home happened to be. I miss her quite a lot. You would've liked her. She was always full of fun and she loved Christmas. You remind me a little of her."

"I can't think of a lovelier compliment, lass. Knowing you and your father, I'm sure I would've thought the world of her. She must have had quite an adventurous spirit if her recipes say anything about her."

Each sipped their tea, lost in their own thoughts.

"Do you think Liam misses being with his family this time of year?" Sarah asked.

"I suspect he does, but he's become quite attached to you and your father. It appears he's rather enjoying it."

"What about you? You must miss being with your family."

"There's only my sister, Marjorie, her two grown children and myself these days. Since my husband passed on, the holidays aren't quite the same. But I suppose that's the way of life, isn't it? Things change and we adjust." A hint of sadness was quickly replaced with her usual cheery demeanor. "And I am thoroughly enjoying being part of your Christmas."

"Our Christmas!" Sarah answered, as she put her hand on top of the older woman's. "I do hope you know how much it means having you here."

"Lass, there is no where else I'd rather be."

Once the tea things were washed up, Sarah summoned the courage to ask if they could take another walk around the block before it got too late. Looking out the window at the impending weather, they agreed the sooner the better. With coats, hats and scarves securely in place they were out the door in record time. Sarah had her note to Peter tucked in her coat pocket, and was excited to discover what he could possibly have left for her. As they walked toward the sidewalk, she noticed Liam and Mrs. McAughtrie making eye contact, and an ever so slight nod of his head. She really needed to find out what all this mystery was about.

## *Chapter Twenty-four*

# PETER:

### *Christmas Eve Dinner at the Holt's*

The ribbon on the small package had been tied and re-tied so many times, Peter was afraid he had worn the fabric thin. He wanted it to look perfect before he put it in the plastic bag with his note, and poked it in the recess of the wall. Several times he had questioned his judgement on choosing this for Sarah, but here it was, all wrapped. He dearly hoped she liked it.

To say that he had been overwhelmed by Sarah's gift to him would be an understatement. Where could she have possibly found a second edition of one of the most famous fly fishing books in all the world? Originally published around 1840, with the unwieldy title of 'The British Angler's Manual, or The Art of Fishing in England, Scotland, Wales, and Ireland with Some Account of The Principal Rivers, Lakes, and Trout Streams, in the United Kingdom; with Instruction in Fly-Fishing, Trolling, and Angling at the Bottom, and More Particularly for the Trout.' It was written by T.C. Hofland, an artist who would fish while painting his famous landscapes near the streams and lakes in Britain. The book is filled with Hofland's sketches and drawings, as well as fly fishing instruction and information. For years he and his grandfather had haunted second hand book shops looking for a copy, but to no avail. What a brilliant gift! The more he interacted with her, the more amazing she seemed. In fact, he found himself thinking about the lovely Sarah Duncan more often than not.

"Peter! We must arrive at the Holt's on time. Please get a move on, son."

"I'll be right down."

His father was quite adamant about being prompt for engagements, even if they were only going next door for Christmas Eve dinner. It had been a tradition for more years than Peter could remember, and always great fun being with their old friends and their four dogs. While their house layouts were nearly identical, the interiors were as different as night and day. Peter's home was beautiful and formal, quite a showplace for his parents art collections, and frequent dinners with important people. On the other hand, Albert and Allison Holt next door chose a much more casual approach to entertaining in their warm, charming home where large fireplaces roared with huge flames and comfortable overstuffed furniture filled the high-ceilinged rooms. Their children were grown and scattered all over the world, so it was not uncommon for Peter to be the only young person in attendance during the holidays. Their four King Charles Spaniels were the centerpiece of every gathering. Each dog's name started with an 'A' in keeping with their owners names, Anton, Abigail, Angus and Annabelle. Playful and engaging, the dogs pretty much had the run of the house, scamping about until they dropped from exhaustion. It often surprised Peter that his parents were able to relax in this slightly chaotic atmosphere. Even visiting his grandparents country estate on the River Tweed, his parents tried to keep an air of formality, though not with much success. The family joke was that his mother never got her shoes dusty. Even her Wellies looked brand new. It occurred to Peter that he loved being at the family estate probably because of the lack of formality, and of course, because of the fly fishing. He startled when he realized Allison Holt had directed a question to him, as he was casting a fly over the River Tweed in his mind.

"I'm terribly sorry, Mrs. Holt. My mind was a hundred miles away. You were saying?"

"I was wondering if there was a young lady in your life these days. We hoped you might bring someone special."

"No, not yet," he answered. She asked the same question every year since he began high school. It was awkward for him to explain that in addition to being very shy, he was completely passionate about his work. "I have been quite busy with my latest projects. It doesn't leave much time to socialize."

"Your mum says your work is brilliant."

"As any loving mum would say about her son."

"Well, that would be true of most mums, but not yours. She knows what she is talking about and she's not one to embellish. In any case, Albert and I invited some new neighbors to join us tonight and they are bringing their daughter. I'm not sure of her age, but you might find her interesting. I hear she is extremely bright and accomplished."

Peter used every muscle in his face not to react in a negative way and show the complete indifference he felt. There was a part of him wanting to cross his eyes and stick out his tongue like a five year old, but that would certainly not be appropriate.

"How long have they lived in Newington," Peter asked with feigned interest.

"Not long, perhaps a month or so. They are from America, the East coast I believe. Their daughter is an only child and is a new student at Campbell Manor. Didn't your sister attend Campbell Manor?"

Hearing the name Campbell Manor after everything Sarah had shared about her troubles there, brought new interest to this conversation. He already felt sorry for any new girl who was expected to thrive in that environment.

"No, actually Ainslie attended Salisbury School. Interesting though, I've recently heard some rather disturbing things about Campbell Manor," Peter spoke without thinking

"And just where would you hear gossip about a local girls school?" Allison asked with an amused twinkle in her eye.

As if on cue, Albert interrupted to announce their new guests had arrived, and Allison was thankfully sidetracked.

"May I introduce to you all Jelena and Cabot Worthington and this is their daughter, Jonquil."

The middle aged couple smiled pleasantly and shook hands around the room as they met each guest individually. Peter estimated Jonquil was a very young thirteen or fourteen year old, complete with all the awkwardness that age produces. Nothing about her quite fit. Her hair was an odd color, neither blonde nor red, and it hung down limp and straight. Her nose was a bit too large for her face, but adequately held her thick glasses in place, and her mouth was not much more than a thin line. Peter was reminded of the terrible phrase he once heard at school to describe a classmate, 'potato chip lips.' Jonquil was quite small and thin, and obviously terribly uncomfortable. Pity overwhelmed him, and Peter walked toward the girl. The look she gave him was reminiscent of a deer facing the headlights of an oncoming car. He thought if it had been possible, she would have dissolved on the spot rather than speak to him. No matter, he was his parents child and they had instilled good manners in their only son.

"Hello, Jonquil. My name is Peter and I live close by." He held out his hand and received a limp fish handshake in return. Then she simply looked at him, not saying a word. If he hadn't just heard how bright and accomplished she was, he might have thought, at the very least, she had a hearing problem.

"I understand you are attending Campbell Manor school."

She silently nodded her head up and down.

"And you are from America?"

Another up and down nod.

"Are you enjoying Scotland?"

A third silent nod.

Not sure which one of them was the greater fool–him for asking only questions requiring yes or no answers, or the mute treatment she was using to respond. Well, he wasn't born yesterday. He would trick her by asking a question that needed more than a one word answer.

"How do you find school?" It was a sincere question as he was curious to know if she was as unhappy as Sarah was at Campbell Manor.

After a slight hesitation, she spoke in a soft voice.

"I walk down the block, turn right, go three more blocks and it's on the corner. That's how I find it."

Peter couldn't hide his amusement and laughed out loud. Behind her awkwardness hid a girl with a sense of humor.

She finally looked him in the eye and nearly smiled.

"Well, Jonquil, I have a friend who goes to Campbell Manor and perhaps you could meet her."

He watched as Jonquil's eyes brightened immensely.

The Holt's Christmas table was quite large and overfilled with an incredible variety of food, keeping with the tradition of making sure no one went home hungry. Dinner began with Cock-a-Likee soup, moved on to roast turkey, sausage meat stuffing, bacon rolls, glazed brussel sprouts, mashed carrots and turnips, red wine gravy and finally homemade cranberry sauce. Conversation was lively and diverse, running from one topic to another. Peter's father, Stuart, chatted with Cabot Worthington and Albert Holt comparing views on football and politics, while the women seemed more focused on the new art gallery that was opening, Hogmanay plans and the weather. This left Peter and Jonquil to either dine in silence or find common ground. He'd give it another try.

"What has been your experience so far at Campbell Manor? I've heard girls schools can be a bit brutal."

A moment of silence lasted long enough to make Peter slightly annoyed. Then the dam broke and she launched into a low-voiced diatribe about the dreadful students, girls schools in general and Campbell Manor in specific. She took no prisoners! He was both stunned and amused at the same time with her passionate sentiments. In an equally low voice, he leaned close to her and responded.

"Well, tell me how you *really* feel, Jonquil. Please don't hold back!"

Shy Jonquil burst out laughing loud enough to cause the others at the table to momentarily look over at what they had missed before returning to their previous conversations. In the same quiet conspiratorial voice, Jonquil continued on.

"The school's latest idea is to pair me up with another girl at school. Can you imagine? Why would I want to do that? Those girls are wretched?"

A bell rang in Peter's brain as the pieces instantly fell together. Jonquil was Sarah's student. He wasn't sure where to go with this conversation. He felt he had been told of the situation privately from Sarah and in confidence.

"Maybe the girl they pair you with will be…nice. It might be helpful."

That was met with an incredulous stare as though he was dumb as a rock.

Dessert was brought in to a chorus of "ooohs" and "ahhhhs." Flaming Christmas pudding, Cloutie Dumpling, and Scotch Trifle were placed on the side board, along with coffee, tea and brandy, next to the dessert plates, cups and saucers. The old custom of the men retreating with brandy and cigars was not honored at the Holt's home, so everyone remained at the table in the relaxed atmosphere. The conversation comfortably settled in to who was going to Watchnight service at church and who was going home. One last drink in the drawing room and everyone began to get ready to depart. Peter had kept the situation with Jonquil and Sarah in his mind. This poor girl was dreading her time with Sarah, not knowing it would be the best thing that would happen to her. As they said their goodnights at the door, he leaned close to Jonquil and quickly whispered, "I know the girl they have paired you up with at school and she is quite remarkable. She is also American and her name is Sarah Duncan."

"Why should I trust you?" she whispered back.

"Why shouldn't you?" he answered sincerely.

# *Chapter Twenty-five*
# SARAH:
## *Happy Christmas*

The dining room table sparkled with the silver, crystal and the exquisite china Mrs. McAughtrie had found hidden in the back of the pantry. Sarah gently touched several of the pieces, and wondered who else had set such a fine table with these treasures. Mrs. McAughtrie was quite certain most pieces were at least a hundred years old. Were they wedding gifts to a young couple ages ago or were they family heirlooms handed down from one generation to the next? The dining room itself was a work of art, with its raspberry red walls, high ceilings with white crown molding and Carrara marble fireplace. It had been her father's idea to put a second Christmas tree in the dining room near the tall window, and the fragrance of the Nordmann pine completed this perfect picture.

Everyone helped bring dinner to the table, with Richard leading the way carrying the browned turkey on a silver platter. They held hands as Richard prayed over the meal.

"Lord, we thank you for this day to celebrate the birth of your son, and for the friends and family to share it with. We pray for your grace and mercy on our loved ones, and for the world. Thank you for keeping us safe and out of harms way. Amen."

Sarah opened her eyes when her father finished the prayer and could not remember when such happiness filled her heart.

"Thank you so much for spending your holiday with us. This is the best Christmas I've ever had and I'll remember it forever!"

Her bubbling over-excitement might also have something to do with the small gift upstairs in her room waiting to be unwrapped. Receiving a present from a young man was a new experience for her and she wanted to bask in the wondering of what it could be for a little while longer. She decided to open it after dinner, just before they left for the Watchnight service at church. It was a little hard to focus on the dinner conversation with her mind upstairs. She tuned in just in time to catch Liam talking about his family on Shetland Island.

"Aye, it can appear a bit windswept and barren, but there is really no place like it. Mum and Dad and my sisters live on a 300 acre farm with about 150 ewes and 70 calving cows, both native Shetland breeds. We also have a few of the famous Shetland ponies and Highland cows."

"Is Shetland part of Great Britain?" Sarah broke in, a little embarrassed she didn't know more about it.

'It is, but just barely. In fact, the Shetland Islands, are a wee bit over 100 miles from mainland Scotland and are considered the most northern extremity of Great Britain. Norway is only about 140 miles east of the islands."

"Oh my, it sounds so isolated," Sarah said, "and so far away."

"Well, in a way it is, but I think that isolation brings the locals together in a fellowship not seen elsewhere. There's a great pride in the people who call it home. Most think of themselves as being Shetlanders first, Scottish second and then finally British... somewhere down the line."

"Do you think you'll ever return to live there permanently?" asked Richard, taking a second helping of his mother's southern cornbread dressing.

"That is my plan, sir. I want to make enough money to help my family buy more land and secure a larger property, enough for my parents, and my sisters and for myself to be self-sufficient. Make no mistake, it's a rugged country, but our place is right on the ocean and that makes it a wee bit better than most other properties."

"And might there be a lass you've got in mind to share this bonny property with?" Mrs. McAughtry asked mischievously.

Sarah cringed, thinking she would never have the nerve to ask

Liam such a personal question, and was surprised when he answered quite happily and forthright.

"Aye, there certainly is! Mairi Edwards, the loveliest girl on the island. She and her family have been native to Shetland for generations as well, and are quite popular in the pony world. We've known each other since we were wee ones and plan to be married soon I hope. Our family's friendship goes back eons."

"You must miss your family and Mairi very much," Richard said.

"That I do, and I miss life there in general, but I'm happy to be here for now."

"I have to know, do people on Shetland eat other things besides Liver Koogs?' Sarah asked, making a funny face.

"Actually, no, that's all we eat, every day, every meal," Liam answered trying his best to look serious. "It's mandatory eating."

"Oh my, that is distressing news. I must remember to pack some snacks if I ever visit," Sarah answered seriously.

"Really, we have wonderful food, lamb, beef and lots of seafood. Our Shetland black potatoes, which are really blue not black, are perfect for making…Liver Koogs."

"Perhaps we should plan a visit to Shetland, what do you think?" Richard addressed the question to Sarah.

"Absolutely yes," she answered with her usual enthusiasm, "but no Liver Koogs please!"

"You'd all be most welcome on the farm anytime. Mind you, there's a bit of a long ferry journey between Aberdeen and Lerwick, which is the largest town on the main island. But once you arrive, and stand atop of a wee hill and look around at the rolling green hills then look out to vast sea, it will make your soul ache to try to take in so much beauty."

Conversation shifted to other subjects, but Sarah could feel warmth and genuine friendship between each person at the table, as if they knew this was a night that would be remembered for a long time.

## *Chapter Twenty-six*

# SARAH:

*The Gift from Peter*

With the dishes cleared off the table, Sarah ran up the stairs two at a time under the guise of locating something in her room. It was pretty much the truth. Making sure her door was closed, she retrieved the package from it's hiding place under her pillow. In a flash, the ribbon was untied (with no notice of how thin the material had become), and a small, black velvet drawstring pouch fell out along with a folded note. Gently pulling the strings to open the bag, Sarah took out an exquisite antique gold locket that looked exactly like a miniature book, about an inch long. The cover had very ornate engraved initials which were hardly decipherable, and a tiny clasp to hold it closed. Carefully releasing the clasp, she opened the book locket. Under the tiny glass windows, written in very small handwriting, one side said, "To Sarah from Peter." Written on the other side was "Friends Forever." Sarah would recognized Peter's writing, no matter how minuscule it was. She held the locket and could feel the metal warm in her hand. His thoughtfulness and insight in finding exactly the right gift left her mind in confusion. How could he know she had very little personal jewelry of her own? And to connect that with her love of reading. Sarah felt her heart might burst right then and there. She picked up the note that accompanied the locket and unfolded it.

*Dear Sarah,*

*There is absolutely no way you could have known*

*my grandfather and I have been searching for an early edition of this book for many, many years. To receive it as a gift from you makes it even more special. Simply saying thank you seems rather inadequate, but please know I mean it with all my heart. I am wishing you a very happy Christmas and brilliant new year. I will look forward to my return from my grandparents in a few days, to hear all about your holiday. I am enclosing a gift I found in a small antique shop on Cockburn Street. It reminded me of you.*

*Yours,*

*Peter*

It took going over the note over several times for Sarah to fully grasp all he had written, warning herself not to read too much into every word. She reduced it down to two main points: he really liked the gift she gave him, and it would seem, he really liked her! She must write him back right now, even though she wasn't sure how she would get it to him. Maybe she and Mrs. McAughtrie could walk home after the church service tonight and put it in the wall. Without time to truly sort her feelings and articulate them fully, she wrote quickly, sealed the note in an enveloped tucked it in her pocket. She could not conceive of a better, more splendid Christmas. Her thoughts soared to how extraordinary the new year would be, full of hope and new beginnings. And Peter! All thoughts were disrupted by her father telling her it was time to leave for the Watchnight service. Running back down the stairs, Sarah didn't notice the note slip out of her pocket. Ever vigilant, Mrs. Mc Aughtrie, quietly stooped down, picked it up and put it in her purse.

## *Chapter Twenty-seven*

# PETER:

## *A Watchnight Like No Other*

It was half an hour before midnight, and the magnificent interior of the old stone church was lit by scores of flickering candles located around the sanctuary. This gave the holy space a heavenly glow and feeling of intimacy. The smell of pine and melting wax was in the air mingled with a slight mustiness. Every wooden pew was filled, yet the only sound was a rustling of clothes as people settled in. No conversation, simply a quiet reverence in an atmosphere of awe and anticipation. Out of nowhere, the high, clear voice of a child singing a cappella captured everyone's attention.

"Away in a manger, no crib for a bed,
The little Lord Jesus laid down his sweet head;
The stars in the sky looked down where he lay
The little Lord Jesus asleep in the hay."

As the last word hung in the air, a light from above slowly became a bright shaft revealing the nativity scene on the top step of the sanctuary. The choir joined in the second verse:

"The cattle are lowing, the poor baby wakes,
But little Lord Jesus, no crying he makes;
I love Thee Lord Jesus! Look down from the sky,
And stay by my cradle to watch lullaby."

A moment of silence followed, then Reverend Christopher Chambers spoke, his deep voice echoing slightly off the high arched ceiling and tall stained glass windows.

"And it came to pass in those days, that there went out a decree from Caeser Augustus that all the world should be taxed. And all went to be taxed, everyone to his own city. And Joseph also went up from Galilee, out of the city of Nazareth, into Judaea, unto the city of David, which is called Bethlehem, because he was of the house and lineage of David, to be taxed with Mary his espoused wife, being great with child. And so it was, that while they were there, the days were accomplished that she should be delivered. And she brought forth her first born son, and wrapped him in swaddling clothes, and laid him in a manger; because there was no room for them in the inn."

Peter looked down at the printed order of service sheet he had been given when he entered. He knew exactly what came next. After all, the service hadn't changed in all the years he had attended. Some people found this to be a problem, but he appreciated and looked forward to the tradition of the Watchnight service. Somehow, it meant that all was right with the world, even for just this little moment. Surrounding him were people of all ages, incomes, and races, all gathered to share the moment. Some he knew and others were strangers. Christmas did that to people, he thought, brought a unity of spirit, if only for a short time.

The choir walked up the center aisle quietly singing 'Silent Night,' each carrying a candle. Peter knew this was when the congregation joined in the singing.

"Silent Night, holy night, all is calm, all is bright

Round yon virgin mother and child. Holy infant so tender and mild,

Sleep in heavenly peace, sleep in heavenly peace."

They went on to sing the next three verses of the familiar hymn, as the choir took their place. Hardly anyone had to look to the hymnal for the correct words. Another perk of tradition–familiarity. A moment of reflective silence followed, then Reverend Chambers continued:

"And there were in the same country shepherds abiding in the field, keeping watch over their flock by night. And lo, the angel of the Lord came upon them, and the glory of the Lord shone round about them, and they were sore afraid. And the angel said unto them, fear not, for behold, I bring you good tidings of great joy, which shall be to all people. For unto you is born this day in the city of David a saviour, which is Christ the Lord. And this shall be a sign unto you; ye shall find the babe wrapped in swaddling clothes, lying in a manger. And suddenly there was with the angel a multitude of the heavenly host praising God, and saying, Glory to God in the highest, and on earth peace, good will toward men."

After a moments silence, reverberating organ music filled the space with 'Hark the Herald Angels Sing.' The enthusiasm of the hymn was contagious and the congregation joined in with the choir. 'Joy to the World' followed, and finally the benediction.

"May the grace of The Lord Jesus Christ, and the love of God, and the communion of the Holy Ghost, be with you now and forevermore. Amen."

Right on cue, the church bells began ringing out the midnight hour. There was much hugging, hand-shaking and shouts of "Happy Christmas" as the crowd made their way toward the large double doors leading to the entry hall at the front of the church. Peter smelled the spiced cider and mincemeat pies he knew were waiting on the long tables. After all, it had been hours–okay, maybe only two hours since dinner! He waited patiently while his mother and father chatted with Reverend Chambers. Looking around the large group, his gaze landed on Sarah Duncan standing next to her father on the other side of the church. He had no idea she had attended the midnight service. She looked beautiful with the candlelight shining on her face. At that moment, she turned and saw him, and her face lit up with a huge smile. She lifted the gold locket that hung around her neck, and mouthed the words, 'Thank you.' Peter smiled broadly back at her, and stepped forward to interrupt his parents conversation.

"Sorry to interrupt..."

"Don't be sorry, lad, it's time I found my way to the entry for a wee bit of mincemeat pie before it's all gone," replied Reverend Chambers in his cheerful way. "You have a very blessed Christmas time."

"What's this about, son? Not like you to interrupt the Reverend," his father asked.

"There's someone I would like you to meet."

"Well, lead the way," his father answered, ushering his wife ahead of him.

Peter looked over where he had last seen Sarah and she was gone. Scanning the room, he caught a glimpse of her walking out the huge wooden doors to the outside with her father and the tall red-haired man he recognized as the driver of the black car. An older lady followed behind them, probably the housekeeper Sarah had mentioned.

"Follow me," he commanded his parents uncharacteristically.

He knew they must be a little baffled by his behavior as he was usually quiet and respectful, and certainly not in the habit of coaxing them through the throng of worshipers toward the exit. They followed, nearly running into him when he stopped abruptly at the top of the outside steps.

Looking this way and that, Peter couldn't see her anywhere in the mass of people. Where could she have gone?

"Who is this mystery person?" his mother inquired.

"She's….a friend."

His parents exchanged glances, silently noting the odd behavior their son was exhibiting.

They never knew him to be particularly interested in any specific young lady.

"Oh, there she is, over by the black car."

They watched as the black car drove up to the curb and the tall red-haired man got out, walked rounded the front of the car and was about to open the rear passenger door for Sarah and Richard Duncan. Peter yelled above the crowd.

"Sarah!"

She looked up toward Peter's voice. At that moment there was a deafening noise, a crack and a bang, and flashes of light. Richard Duncan crumbled to the sidewalk. Everything became chaotic slow motion. A large man ran away, rounding the end of the block followed by two men giving chase, several people rushed to Richard's body, the older lady kneeling to administer first aid. Sarah was pushed into the passenger seat of the black car by the tall red-haired man. All Peter could see was her profile as the car rushed away into the night. Suddenly, lights and sirens of the ambulance and police cars swirled and echoed in the snowy neighborhood, creating a surreal atmosphere. Sarah's father was quickly loaded onto a gurney and slid into the back of the ambulance. Police were urging bystanders to go home, telling them there was nothing more to see.

"Oh, dear God! Peter! Who was that?" asked Peter's mother.

Peter was completely speechless.

## *Chapter Twenty-eight*
# CONRAD RATCHFORD:
## *The Great Getaway*

He hadn't intended on shooting Richard Duncan when he woke up that morning, but his overwhelming frustration created an uncontrollable desire to lash out. The only person in his sights was his replacement at the consulate. After all, Duncan had it coming after ruining his brilliant scheme.

For well over a year he had maneuvered and conned the people around him to make his strategy work. Hours and hours were spent carefully arranging details to make the most of an unexpected opportunity. The fact that it was highly illegal and completely immoral were never factors in agreeing to be involved. He'd be lying if he said the fantastic sums of money to be made was his sole motivation. Almost as intriguing was the mental challenge of actually manipulating things to make it all work. If he were to be honest, a certain amount of boredom had crept into his work with the Foreign Service. This sideline sparked his creative juices and he found he very much enjoyed the art of the game, even if it was unscrupulous.

The groundwork had been laid, the first shipments had been successful and it looked as though it would run like clockwork. Then it all blew up in his face. Like the incoming tide washing away the sandcastle, all was lost. Worse yet, he was now considered a criminal and would have to out run the CIA and his underworld connections. Once he decided to fall off the radar instead of meeting the Ambassador in London, it made sense to create a diversion that would give him just enough time to grab what was rightfully his and disappear.

As soon as the shot was fired, he faded into the immense crowd and ran around the corner. Once out of view he went as fast as an overweight, out of shape, middle aged man could manage. Rounding the second corner, he saw two men on his tail, and knew he would have to outwit them rather than lose them in a foot race. By chance, a side door to a garage had been left ajar and Ratchford slipped in. In the dim light, he found a cubby closet under some stairs and squeezed in. Other than spider cobwebs and the faint rustle of mice running about, this would do for the moment.

It didn't take long for him to reconsider his lack of planning, but what was done was done. But there was more yet to do. After a few hours passed, Conrad Ratchford stealthily crept from his hiding place, and pulled his hat down to just above his eyes. There was no one about at this early hour, and given it was Christmas morning, it was doubtful he would run into anyone. Edinburgh was a maze of narrow streets and closes, and if you knew your way, it was possible to stay hidden in the shadows. He carefully made his way toward the back of the American Consulate, and climbed up the slippery hill on the backside. The thought of being caught began to gnaw at him. He must be swift about this, but watchful for anyone lying in wait. There was an old, abandoned door to a basement room at the Consulate that had been long forgotten. Enough bushes and underbrush had grown up in front of it to make it nearly impossible to see. Feeling his way along the wet, unstable slope his hand reached the rusty door handle. A few good shakes and it gave way. He had always been a bit curious as to why this entrance hadn't been permanently sealed up, but for the moment it served his purpose perfectly. Stepping inside the dark, dank room he lit a match, which gave just enough light to locate the battered briefcase he had hidden there. The match burned his finger and he uttered an oath before he lit another one. He didn't have time to waste, if he was going to make his way to Glasgow before sunrise. The lock on the briefcase opened on the first try and the sight of all that money gave Ratchford a thrill.

"Well, Happy Christmas to me!"

He closed it back up, making sure the clasps on the case were tight, grabbed it by the worn handle and left the damp room pulling the old door shut behind him. He was off with an almost giddy sense of victory, ready to steal someone's vehicle and make his great escape. Curiously, he was beginning to enjoy being undercover. The thought that he had shot another human being didn't enter his mind.

# *Chapter Twenty-nine*
# SEANEEN McAUGHTRIE:
## *Cleaning House*

The house in Newington was dark and cold, and echoed the sadness Mrs. McAughtrie was feeling. She was nearly finished packing up the Duncan's belongings, but found herself looking at the only remnant of their lovely Christmas–the wrapped gifts on the sideboard where they had been put when the large tree had been taken down. The presents had seemed so important at the time, each carefully chosen for the recipient. Now they were destined to collect dust and never be opened. All the garlands and greenery had been removed as though Christmas never happened. She had carefully wrapped each ornament from both trees and put them together with the lights in several large containers. They were labeled and set aside. The hardest part had been organizing and boxing all the personal items. Mr. Duncan's things would be put in storage for now, and she would send Sarah several boxes of items she thought would be meaningful. With one last look around, it was time to go.

"Michael, would you please carry these boxes to the car?" she asked the guard at the front door.

"Yes, ma'am."

The house would be secured with only Foreign Service personnel having access for at least several weeks. There were still many unanswered questions in this tragedy. In all her years, this was the most difficult situation Seaneen McAughtrie had been involved in. Her job required her to be professional and take care of the business at hand, but inside she was heartbroken. This felt too much like family. With a deep sigh of resignation, she put her coat on and reached in the pocket for her gloves. There was a curious rustle of paper. Along with her gloves, out came the note that Sarah had dropped on their way to church Christmas Eve. It had the name "Peter" on the outside. With an air of spontaneity, Mrs. McAughtrie knew exactly what she had to do. Scribbling something on the back of the paper, she called out to Michael.

"Please finish with these boxes and wait for me. There is something I must do around the corner. I shan't be long."

"Yes, ma'am," he answered.

## *Chapter Thirty*

# PETER:

### *A Miracle at His Door*

The sharp ring of the telephone startled the core of Peter's brain. He must have dozed off sitting at the desk. Not entirely surprising, as sleep had been scarce since the shooting three days ago. Looking around the room, it was already dark outside. Edinburgh winters were famous for short days and long, black nights. How long had he been asleep? The persistent phone rang several more times before he answered it.

"Hello?" he answered a little disoriented.

"Hello, Peter. It's Mum. Are you all right? Do you have any news?"

Hearing his mother's voice was unexpectedly comforting, which wasn't always the case. She could be formal and demanding, and sometimes distant, but this voice was of a mother who sounded deeply concerned, and Peter responded openly.

"No news! Absolutely nothing. I've walked around outside and nothing seems amiss in the neighborhood. The church is closed and I've called the American Consulate but there is no answer. There is very little in the news other than a reporting of a brief skirmish at the church. It's as though life is just going on. How can a tragedy just fade into thin air?"

There was a pause and Peter realized he probably sounded like a mad man who had not had contact with the outside world in several days, which was exactly the case.

"Have you thought to call the police? You might get some information from them."

"I decided that might not be wise. From what small amount Sarah shared, I gather their lives have been under security lately, and I wouldn't want to cause any trouble by inquiring when I shouldn't. I had hoped to hear from Sarah by now, but that doesn't seem likely."

Peter wasn't sure any of that made sense to his mother, but she had the grace to not argue the point.

"Your grandparents miss seeing you. Do you think you might come down later in the week?"

"I honestly don't know. I just want to be sure that Sarah is safe. She is pretty much alone without any family I'm aware of. I can't imagine what she must be going through or where she is."

"It is all so awful, poor dear, but I'm not sure how you can help," he mother said softly.

Peter knew she was right, but he couldn't bring himself to leave the house just in case Sarah should need him. That's what friends do for each other.

"Grandfather said to tell you the spey rods are ready to go whenever you feel like it."

"I'd like nothing more than to be on the river with him. Tell him I promise it will be soon."

"I will pass that along, but Peter, please take care of yourself. You've had a dreadful shock. I'm not sure we did the right thing leaving you alone the past few days."

"I am nearly twenty-one, and it was important you spend time with family. No worries, I'm fine."

"The kitchen is full of food, in fact there's some lovely cheese and fruit and some biscuits…"

Peter had to stop her before she gave him a complete run-down of everything in the kitchen.

"I will go find the lovely cheese right now," he promised.

"You will ring us up if you hear anything?"

"Of course…"

"And, Peter, your father and I love you."

That was such an unusual proclamation, that it took him a few beats to respond.

"I love you, too."

He hung up the phone and stared at it for a bit. What an interesting conversation, yet on a certain level he understood. None of them had ever witnessed such a violent, senseless act and it inevitably must bring to mind how fragile life is. Looking around, he realized the room had become rather dark and had grown cold. He stirred up the wood in the fireplace, and placed fresh logs on top of the embers. The talk of food was a reminder that he was quite hungry. On the way to the kitchen a loud knock at the front door halted him in his tracks. Who could that be? He felt his heart stop as a wild thought filled his head.

"Oh please, God, let it be Sarah."

Swinging open the door with urgency, he looked into the face of a sixty year old, gray haired woman. With no jacket, the cold wind hit him hard, as did stinging disappointment. He could hardly focus on what she was saying to him.

"Might you be Peter?" she asked expectantly.

"Yes. Yes, I am. And who are…"

As soon as the words left his lips he realized who she was. Without thinking, he pulled her into the house, closing the door with a slam.

"You're Mrs. McAughtrie! I've heard so much about you. Is Sarah is all right? We were there, we saw it all! I can think of nothing else."

She put her hand over his which was still clinging to her arm.

"Aye, poor lad. I'd a feeling you'd been a might worried."

"Where are my manners? Please come in and sit by the fire. A cup of tea?"

"I'll warm my bones by the fire for a wee moment, but no tea, thank you. I couldn't leave without speaking to you."

Peter motioned her to sit in the wing-backed chair next to the fireplace, and he took the matching chair opposite her. He leaned forward so he wouldn't miss a word of what she was about to say.

"Peter, I am aware that Sarah thought highly of you. She never shared much about the details of your relationship, but I know she trusted you. Much of what I am going to tell you should not leave this room. As it is, I'm bending the rules a wee bit just by being here.

Lad, I'm not exaggerating when I say lives might depend on your discretion. For Sarah's sake, please keep this between us."

"I care very much for Sarah, and I promise you, Mrs. McAughtrie, I would never do anything to hurt her. Please tell me she is safe."

She looked directly into Peter's eyes as if assessing one more time if sharing with him was a good idea. The expression on her face carried the seriousness of the situation.

"First of all, Sarah was not physically injured. She has been taken to stay with the family of one of the security detail in a remote area."

He let out a breath that he must have been holding without realizing it.

"That is very good news, but she must be devastated about her father. They were so close. What a terrible tragedy this is! I've heard little in the news about the entire incident. It would seem when an American diplomat is murdered, it should've been noteworthy to say the least."

Another long pause, as she appeared to choose her words carefully.

"You will hear nothing more about the incident. Not for a time anyway."

Peter looked at her curiously. What was she not telling him? He opened his mouth to ask when she interrupted him.

'I can say no more about it, so please don't ask."

Mrs. McAughtrie reached in her coat pocket and took out a familiar tattered plastic envelope with a note in it.

"Before Watchnight church service, Sarah had written a note and was planning on leaving it for you. It fell from her pocket and I found it, meaning to give it back to her after the service. Obviously, that never happened."

She placed the crumpled envelope tenderly in his outstretched hand.

"And I've done something I hope I won't regret…I've scribbled her address on the back of the envelope. It's fond I am of that little lass, and if hearing from you would bring her a moment's happiness, then so be it."

Peter looked at the envelope he held in his hand. It was as though it was a miracle from God. He was actually holding a new note Sarah had written! Mrs. McAughtrie rose from the chair.

"I must go now."

They walked to the door, and as Peter opened it, Mrs. McAughtrie leaned toward him as if to kiss his cheek. Instead, she whispered in his ear.

"Richard Duncan is alive." And with that she was gone.

# Chapter Thirty-one

# LIAM:

## *A Night to Remember*

Liam glanced at Sarah quietly looking out the window of the car as it sped through the cold, wet, night. How in God's name had this happened? Over and over he wracked his brain trying to figure out where the gunman had come from. He and his team had scouted the area earlier that evening, and were constantly scanning the crowd for anything suspicious. Granted, there had been quite a crowd, but they were well trained and knew what to look for. And it was Christmas Eve…who does something like this on a Holy night? The worst part was he had assured Richard Duncan several times that he and Sarah were safe.

The day had gone so well with the special dinner and the candlelit church service, then BAM! Out of nowhere all hell broke loose! Suddenly, Richard was on the ground, with a pool of blood forming on the sidewalk, and Mrs. McAughtrie was shouting at him.

"Go! Go! I've got this. Take Sarah and go."

He grabbed Sarah and literally shoved her into the backseat of the black car, jumped into the driver's seat and sped off through the deserted streets of Edinburgh. His sole focus was on getting her out of town to safety. Ironically, several days ago he and Richard had discussed options if anything should happen. It was decided Liam would take her to Shetland temporarily to be absolutely sure she was far away from any danger. That was where the conversation ended, with no further planning or details.

Sarah silently wiped tears away, but didn't say a word. Liam's training had not included what to say to comfort a young girl who had just seen her father shot. He took a handkerchief from his coat pocket and handed it to her.

The drive from Edinburgh to Inverness in the north of Scotland would take close to 4 hours. Straight away he realized it was Christmas and neither the ferry nor the airline would be in service. Driving in silence gave him time to think of a plan. The pain in his gut had to be ignored while he formulated their next steps. There were three telephone calls he needed to make as soon as possible. It niggled his conscience that calling people in the wee hours of Christmas morning was bloody rude, but it couldn't be helped. They finally arrived in Stonehaven, a small fishing village about fifteen miles from Aberdeen, and he found a call box near the crescent shaped bay. The streets were empty and it was still dark so he felt confident leaving Sarah in the car alone while he made his calls.

The first call was to his cousin Gordon, who lived in Aberdeen and happened to run a small airplane charter service on the side. With a minimum of details, Liam explained the urgency of the situation to a very sleepy cousin, who readily agreed to meet them in an hour. The second call was to his parents, asking them to drive forty-five minutes from the farm to the airport in Sumburgh and pick them up. Again, the details given were sketchy, but there wasn't a moments hesitation. Before making the third call, the tall, strong bodyguard took a deep breath to calm his nerves. Liam's superior answered on the third ring.

"I've been waiting to hear from you. Is the girl safe?" The voice on the other end of the line sounded weary, but wide awake.

"Yes. We are nearing Aberdeen. My cousin will fly us to Shetland and we will house with my family on the farm."

"Excellent. Call me when you arrive and we will discuss future arrangements."

"Sir, about Mr. Duncan……"

"He is out of surgery and should fully recover. You must have shielded him enough that the shooter didn't get a direct shot. Good work, Morrison"

"He's really alive?" he asked incredulously.

There was a brief silence.

"My boy, doctors rarely operate on deceased people. Yes, he is very much alive."

Liam couldn't breath. The relief was overwhelming.

"Thank you, sir. Thank you."

"Stay in touch," and the line went dead.

Standing alone in the call box, tears ran down his face.

"Thank you, God, for saving this good man."

Since he gave Sarah his handkerchief, he had to wipe his eyes with his coat sleeve. The smile that took over his face couldn't be dimmed. The term, 'feet never touched ground' to express feeling complete joy, was never more meaningful. He walked out of the familiar red phone box and opened the passenger side door and looked into the face of a child who's father was alive. Reaching his hand out to her, she stepped out of the car looking completely bewildered. Without thinking it through Liam circled Sarah with his strong arms and gave her an all encompassing hug, twirling her around, then said the words he knew she never expected to hear.

"Your father is alive! He's had surgery and he's going to survive! Sarah, your father is alive!"

Sarah fell out of his arms and collapsed on the damp ground, shaking and crying.

"Are you sure you know what you're saying? I can't believe it. He's really going to be all right?"

The lanky red-haired man reached out his hands and pulled her up.

"Yes, I heard it from the highest source. He is going to recover. Now, we must get going and get you to safety. We are flying to Shetland and you will meet my family."

"Are you sure they won't mind?"

"Lass, they will be delighted to meet you. We need to hurry to meet my cousin at the airport."

"Oh, Liam, I'm confused and a little dazed but I trust whatever you tell me to do. I am so grateful. My father is alive and that's the most important thing," she managed to say before a fresh round of tears began. "Happy Christmas, Liam."

"If I'm not mistaken, this will be one Christmas none of us will ever forget."

The rest of the trip went as planned. Gordon met them at a small airport and they boarded a compact private airplane for the flight. Once in the air, it felt as though they were flying in a universe of bright stars. Even though the ride was a little bumpy, Sarah and Liam were so fascinated by it all, they lost all track of time.

"Just for your information, Sarah, Sumburg airport is surrounded by two different seas," Liam shouted over the engine noise. "Over there is the North Sea, look this way and it's the Atlantic."

Before they realized it, Gordon landed the plane and taxied toward a building off to the side of the main runway. Liam thanked Gordon repeatedly as they got off the airplane, and the cousins discussed a visit to the pub next time. Waiting for them, as scheduled, were Liam's parents who warmly welcomed Sarah, and ushered the two travelers into the car for the drive back to the farm.

Liam watched as the sun rose up over the water. He thought to himself that this was the most bizarre Christmas he had ever experienced.

Since their arrival in Shetland a few days ago, Sarah had remained quiet and reserved. She kept to herself–as much as that was possible in a house full of people, and just as Liam thought, Ava had been the one of his sisters to relate best to Sarah. They were close in age, personality, and size. Ava had given her warm clothes to wear and a stack of books to read and Liam's mum had rearranged Ava's bedroom to accommodate the two girls. For her part, Sarah offered to help out, whether in the house or on the farm.

"One more set of hands is always welcome, lass," Liam's father said. "Thank you for the asking."

Liam knew Sarah must be full of questions. He wished he could ease her mind, but there had been no news and there were no answers. While it was obvious she was relieved knowing her father was recovering, the shadow of what the future held was always on her face.

One afternoon, after all the chores were done, Liam was in the kitchen making a cup of tea, when Sarah came in.

"Would it be all right if I took a walk to the cliffs?" She asked softly.

"Of course. Would you like me to go with you?" he asked.

It was the first time she had wanted to venture beyond the house or the nearby stables, and he felt this was a good sign. It was important for her to feel as though she had a little freedom.

Their farm was very secluded and he was absolutely certain she was safe. The cliffs were the most beautiful vantage point on the farm and he wouldn't mind accompanying her.

"Thank you, but I'd like to go by myself, if that's all right with you. I don't want to be any trouble."

"You are no trouble. Off you go, but don't stay away too long."

After a few minutes, Liam put on his heavy coat and quietly followed her. He would not let anything happen to Richard Duncan's daughter, no matter how safe she was.

## Chapter Thirty-two

# SARAH:

*Sitting by the Sea*

Standing on top of the jagged cliff, Sarah looked down at the North Atlantic and watched the waves crash on the rocks below. The sea air was clean and cold as she filled her lungs with several deep breaths. She could feel the salty mist on her face, which was the only part of her body exposed to the elements. Liam wasn't kidding about how chilly Shetland could be in the winter. Clothes and warm boots had been graciously loaned to her by Liam's youngest sister, Ava. The entire family had been very kind and sensitive, treating her like family rather than a surprise guest who had been thrust upon them on Christmas. Even so, she felt guilty for intruding on their holiday, forcing them to adjust their lives to accommodate her. Worse, there was nothing she could do about it. Offering to help with the chores seemed a small repayment for their generosity.

A few yards away Sarah saw a rough hewn bench. Apparently she wasn't the only one mesmerized by this view of the wild, raging ocean. She sat down on the damp wood and drew her knees up to her chest, wrapping the long woolen coat tightly around her body.

Closing her eyes, her mind began to replay the horrible scene at the church–the shots, the screams, the flashing lights.

"No! I'm not going there!" she shouted out loud, her words lost in the noise of the angry sea.

There was some relief in releasing the pent up emotion she had been holding in. The terrifying memory could easily overpower her with thoughts of what could have happened. What if her father had died? What would have become of her? What if Liam hadn't protected her and she had been shot? Grandma Rosemary kept coming to mind, with her confident faith that everything worked out in God's plan. She was trying with all her might to not be discouraged or overwhelmed and to find God's purpose. The huge blessings were obvious, her father would recover, she was safe, and no one else had been harmed. Yet, at times she could hardly find the courage to take the next breath. Here she was in a far away land, with people she barely knew, facing the reality that her secure life had been destroyed. She opened her eyes and looked across the vast sea, the world seemed very big and she felt very small and alone. Was her chin trembling because of the cold or was it more to do with the tears welling up in her eyes? She looked up at the swirling mist and began to speak to heaven.

"God, I don't know what to do. How to get through this? I want my Dad. I want my life back. Please help me. I'm so lost. I really need to know you are there."

For the first time since she had been in Shetland, she let the sobs take over and cried until there was nothing left. She mourned for the past, the present and an unknown future. Where did she belong? Another crashing wave hit the rocks and spewed droplets of water into the air, as though it shared her intense pain. She watched the ocean rise and fall in its divine rhythm. Ever so slowly, her breathing became more regular, though hiccups interspersed now and then. There was no telling how long she had been sitting on the bench, but it was beginning to be uncomfortable and there was rain looming in the distance. Out of nowhere her thoughts turned to Peter for the first time since everything had happened. She remembered seeing him in church, and trying to tell him across the crowded room how much she liked the locket he had given her. Had he called out to her before the shots? Her mind was fuzzy about details, and she didn't want to think about the incident. She couldn't help wonder if she would ever hear from him. But how could she? No one knew where she was and there was no way for her to communicate with him. A new wave of sadness came over her as she realized yet another loss.

The first raindrops came fast and furious, and Sarah was sure her mind was playing tricks when she heard someone call her name.

"Sarah! Sarah!" The faint voice could barely be heard over the ocean roar. "Sarah!"

She heard it again. Turning around she saw Ava running towards her, waving her arms.

"Sarah! Come quickly! You must hurry!"

## Chapter Thirty-Three

# RICHARD:

*Call From Henley Manor*

Holding the phone to his ear, the wait seemed forever until he finally heard his daughter's breathless voice on the other end of the line.

"Hello?"

Richard was nearly overcome with emotion, but tried to not show it. There had been so many times during the past weeks he had wanted to hear her voice, and just know she was safe.

"Sarah?"

There was a moment of silence.

"Oh, Daddy! Is that you? Where are you?"

Just hearing the relief and excitement in her voice was like a healing balm. She hadn't called him 'Daddy' since she was a little girl. It crossed his mind again how blessed he was to be the parent of such an extraordinary child. His first impression was that she sounded strong as though she was coping. Now he needed to sound equally strong for her. He lightened his tone to reflect her mood.

"Actually, I am staying in a lovely estate that has been turned into a medical rehabilitation center southwest of London. The care is very good, and I was fortunate to be allowed to stay here. It is usually reserved mostly for Royal Air Force pilots."

"Oh Daddy, by where are you, I really meant how are you? When can I see you?"

"You are not to worry about me. I've had two surgeries, one on my right arm and one on my right leg, and the doctors tell me both were quite successful. They expect me to make a complete recovery after I spend time here doing physiotherapy. Now, tell me about you. How are you getting on with Liam's family?"

"They have been kind to me, really making me feel part of the family. But I've been worried about you so I'm afraid I haven't been a very cheerful guest. But Shetland is beautiful and I can't wait for you to see it."

"What three things do you like best about it?"

Without hesitation, Sarah joined in their old game.

"I haven't been here very long, but so far the little horses are quite adorable and the sheep are interesting, too. They are kind of small and are used mostly for their wool. They've been on Shetland for over a thousand years!"

Oh, how he loved his daughter's interest and curiosity in everything.

"And the third thing?"

"Let me think…oh, the third thing would be…the cliffs. When I'm standing there looking at the sea below, I feel like Rebecca in Daphne Du Maurier's book. It's scary and powerful and kind of moody all at the same time. Will you be coming to Shetland soon?" she answered full of animation.

There was a pause before he continued. This would be the hard part of their conversation.

"Well, that's the thing. The doctors are insistent that I stay here at least three to six months in order to heal completely."

"Really? Are you sure?" The disappointment in her voice was almost worse than the pain from his wounds. "I could take care of you. Really I could."

"Oh, Sunshine. I'm so sorry about all of this. You never asked to be raised all over the world, with no permanent home, and now here we are involved in this horrific mess. I would do anything to change the situation, but I'm afraid it is what it is for the moment. The gentleman who shot me has not been found, and it cannot be confirmed whether he was working alone or had accomplices. For the time being, I've been advised that we must remain cautious. I am fairly well protected here, and I believe you are safe in Shetland. Liam has been given orders to stay there with you for as long as necessary."

"So, I'll stay on Shetland for maybe six months?" Richard could hear the strain in her voice. "And I'll go to school here?"

"It was decided that it was the safest place for you. There was talk of a boarding school, but there was not enough security available to protect you."

"No. No, I wouldn't like that. If I can't be with you, then staying here is probably best, though I feel as though I'm imposing on Liam's family."

He knew she was trying to be brave, but could hear she was close to tears.

"Liam has already spoken to the school and explained the situation. You will be in his youngest sisters class. I suspect you will be ahead of them academically. Before I forget, there will be some boxes arriving for you from Mrs. McAughtrie. She packed up clothes and books and other belongings she thought you might want."

"That's so thoughtful of her. Ava has been very generous sharing clothes, but it will be good to have some things of my own."

"Yes, it will be nice for you to have some familiar belongings. I'm going to have to ring off now. There is a line of fellows waiting to use the telephone. I'll try to call you every Sunday if I can. Never forget how much I love you, Sunshine Girl."

"I love you too, Daddy. Please be careful…you're all I have."

No words could've stabbed him deeper.

"Goodbye."

Staring at the telephone as if in a trance, the full impact of everything that had happened hit him. This close call could have left his daughter, the light of his life, an orphan. She truly would've been all alone in the world. Dear God, what was I thinking with this career?

"If you're done, old chap, I'd like to call my wife."

"Of course, of course. I'm sorry."

"No need to be sorry. We are all in the same situation, more or less, Just trying to heal so we can return to our families."

Richard looked at the smiling young man with the bottom part of his left leg missing. It didn't take long to see that each man in this rehabilitation unit was fighting his own personal battle to recover both physically and mentally from their injuries. He remembered his mother telling him to always be kind to everyone, because you never knew what they were going through.

The main house of Henley Manor had been outfitted to meet the needs of RAF pilots recovering from impairments, but much of the majesty of the house remained. It was obvious that the original architecture and interiors were designed to impress and entertain guests long ago. The entrance lobby with its painted panelling, and the impressive stairway and first floor landing particularly impressed Richard. The attention to detail in the wood work was astounding. He had always been intrigued by the sheer magnitude and opulence of some British country homes. Limping over to the great bay window in the stair hall, he looked out over the garden. There was a peace about this place he sorely needed. It was several hours until his next rehabilitation session, perhaps he would just sit by the window and let his mind rest. Maybe just close his eyes for a moment. He was suddenly so very tired.

# *Chapter Thirty-four*
# RICHARD:
## *Lady Elizabeth Rose*

Opening his eyes, Richard was struck by two things. First, he was disorientated and could not place where he was. Blinking a few times, as if that would clear his mind, he secondly became aware that he was looking into the face of a very old, very wrinkled, very elegant woman. She sat on a chair close to him, leaning over her carved wooden cane, staring at him with piercing eyes.

"You ARE the American, are you not?" She inquired with a forthright manner.

Still trying to fully wake up, Richard hesitated before answering.

"Now, either you are or you're not. This is not a trick question, young man," she continued with veiled amusement.

Catching her mood, he responded.

"Well, if you're quite sure it's not a trick question, then yes. I am the American."

"Good that we've established that. Tell me, is your physiotherapy going well?"

"I believe it is," Richard answered, very curious where this conversation was going.

"Well, that's fine, isn't it?"

There was an awkward silence, but her piercing eyes never left his face.

"May I ask a personal question, young man?"

"May I first know with whom I have the pleasure of speaking?"

A slow smile crept across her ancient face, as she leaned closer to him.

"I am Lady Elizabeth Rose and Henley Manor used to be my home. Every once in a while I am allowed to come visit and see what they are up to here, though between us, they don't much encourage me."

"Then it is truly my pleasure to meet you, Lady Rose. What personal question could you possibly have for me?"

She continued to look closely at him.

"Your name is unusual."

"Richard?"

"You're playing with me, Mr. Duncan."

"That I am, Lady Rose," he answered amused.

"Your complete name on the registry is Richard Wayde Galloway Duncan. By any chance was your father William Wayde Galloway Duncan from St Andrews, Scotland?"

Racking his brain, Richard tried to conjure up anything he might have heard about this woman in connection to his father. William Duncan left their family early on, and Richard was too young to have formed many memories. According to his mother, Mr. Duncan died shortly after leaving, and from then on he was not often spoken of. Several years later his mother remarried a wonderful man, and life proceeded in a normal fashion. Richard was always curious about his father, but out of respect for his mother he never asked any questions. As time went on and he grew into adulthood, she would share a memory here and there, but all very small glimpses of what his father was like. He was left with the impression that his father was very smart, ambitious, loved playing golf and was a bit of a ladies man. And not particularly attached to his only son.

"I don't have many memories of my father, but yes, that was his name and he was born in St. Andrews."

Lady Rose didn't answer immediately, but rather seemed to be lost in thoughts of long ago. Richard watched her face as a variety of emotions seemed to pass through her mind.

"Your father and I knew each other in our youth."

"You actually knew my father?" Richard was struggling to get his mind around this strange revelation. "You knew him well?"

"We were practically engaged. I certainly thought I knew him well." she answered.

"You're joking?!"

"Women rarely joke about the men in their lives," Lady Rose snapped back at him.

"Please tell me anything about him. You see, I really know very little."

Richard realized he sounded like a young, vulnerable child, anxious for any breadcrumb of information about his father. He thought he had put to rest any longing to know about his paternal side of the family. Suddenly, his enigmatic father, so closely related yet so completely foreign to him, was practically coming to life in the words of this old woman.

"He was very handsome and very charming, and I cared a great deal for him."

"Yet you didn't marry him."

"No I didn't," she paused again as though weighing what she was going to say next. "Your father enjoyed the company of wealthy people, who in turn found him a great asset to any gathering. He was witty and athletic, everything that segment of society values.

Hunting, riding, and fishing came naturally to him, but it was on the golf course that he excelled. He was very popular on The Old Course at St. Andrews. If my memory is correct, he once played there with the great Bobby Jones…but my memory doesn't remember who won," she said with a slight smile.

"So, you were in the same crowd as he was? Is that how you knew him?"

"Indeed not! He was a high flyer, I was a down to earth girl more interested in my studies than a charming young man. He was an acquaintance of my older brother's and was invited to our home from time to time. A group of young people spent time together on our small estate, riding and enjoying picnics by the stream. Your father nearly drove me crazy trying to get me alone. In hindsight, I'm quite sure he was more interested in the chase than the capture."

"But you did enjoy the chase as well?" Richard asked mischievously.

Again, Lady Rose looked at him for a moment or two before

answering.

"The summer before your father left for his last year at university we spent quite a lot of time together. Most of it with friends and siblings, but it seemed we enjoyed each others company the best. It was all innocent and great fun. He was easily the most interesting, good looking young man I had every been around, and I looked forward to every day in his company."

"You fell in love with him, didn't you?"

"It was hard not to. In fact, everyone fell in love with William."

"What happened, if it's not too forward of me to ask?"

"The afternoon before William was to leave, we went to the ruins of St. Andrews cathedral. We often went there to walk and talk about all sorts of things. Your father was interested in everything and liked nothing more than exploring a topic until he knew everything about it, then became the resident expert. Our conversation that day centered around the architecture of a new building being constructed in St. Andrews. We talked on and on about historical versus modern, William always insisting he was correct. As we passed through the Pends at the ruins, I reminded him of a local superstition that claims that if a true genius walks through them, the ancient archway will collapse. I asked if he wasn't afraid to walk through for fear it would fall down around him. He looked amused then became serious, and out of nowhere asked if he were to ask me to marry him, would I say yes. You can imagine how stunned I was. I was quite sure I was in love with him, but I was barely seventeen. Nonetheless, I told him that, yes, I would marry him. He picked me up and twirled me around and said, "Then we are practically engaged, Lizzie girl." He went on to tell me he how he would go off to university, and get his finances in order, then speak to my father. We agreed until that time, we would tell no one. I was in a strange fog, excited and scared at the same time."

At that moment, they were interrupted by an aide asking if they would like a cup of tea. Both agreed that would be nice.

"Please go on," Richard urged.

"I was in the clouds knowing a handsome, brilliant man wanted to marry me of all people! It was very difficult to not tell the world, but on the other hand, there was something almost sacred about keeping the secret. Time passed slowly, and we exchanged a few brief letters, never mentioning anything personal. He told me about university life, and I filled him in on things going on in St. Andrews. Never knowing when he might appear to speak to my father added to the anticipation of the whole situation. As the holidays drew near, I was certain he would show up and make the engagement official. I recall thinking how clever of him to wait until everyone was gathered for celebrations. When my brother arrived home, it was all I could do to not ask about William, and if and when he would make an appearance. That night at dinner we were all around the table, having lively conversation when my older brother announced, "Oh, I have news of William Duncan. You remember him from last summer when he stayed with us a bit? Well, it seems he is to be married this week to that wealthy Ashley Clark-Patterson. Her father is a powerful MP from somewhere. Can't believe the chap is tying down to one girl so young and in such a hurry…" I'm sure he went on and on, but my brain stopped hearing anything except the screaming pain in my heart. Trying to breath, I sat for a few moments then whispered to my mother that I wasn't feeling well and asked to be excused. Once safely in my room I remember being quietly hysterical, knowing any outward sound would bring my family curious to know what was wrong. I was able to convince them that I had caught something and was not at all well. Thankfully, I was left alone for several days, only having food brought up periodically. It was a very dark time for me."

"What a dreadful thing to do. How did you ever get over it?"

"What makes you think I'm over it?" Lady Rose responded softly. "I'm afraid the story continues. Months passed by, then we heard that Ashley Clark-Patterson Duncan was with child, due to be born in the summer. It didn't take much finger counting to figure out the reason for the sudden marriage. This latest bit of information only added to my heartache, and I began to dislike William Duncan, dare I say, hate him. They say it is a fine line between love and hate."

The young aide arrived with their tea tray, and poured out a cup for each of them. When they required nothing more, she disappeared back to the kitchen.

"Did you ever see him again?"

"Yes. Poor Ashley had a difficult delivery and died a few days after her daughter was born. It was a tragic situation really, as Lord Clark-Patterson insisted the child be sent to relatives in western Scotland to be raised. He was adamant that William would not have care of the little girl. As William was still a student and intent on completing his education, I'm not sure he put up much of a fight. But in fairness, what do I know? As month after month passed my sadness rarely left, but I knew I had to get on with my life. Somewhere during that time I was introduced to Lord Alistair Rose, who was a widower and much older than I, and most anxious to get married and father an heir to his fortune. In what I now remember as a blur of time, we had a lovely wedding and settled into life at Henley Manor. Alistair was a politician and often in London, so I was left alone to attend to the local social obligations and really whatever I chose to do."

The name Lord Alistair Rose rang a bell in Richard's mind. As he recalled the man was something of a pompous, abrasive, self-important tyrant who got mixed up in high level government, and came out looking very sinister. He couldn't imagine Lady Rose with this notorious man.

"Truthfully, life was much easier alone than with Alistair home. He had been a bachelor too long and was quite set in his ways. He was demanding and generally disagreeable. Somehow, we managed to have two lovely children, James and Lily."

"So, there was a happy ending?"

"Not particularly. Shortly after Lily was born, Alistair was in London when I was informed I had a visitor. You cannot imagine the shock of seeing William Duncan in my drawing room, as handsome and charming as ever. Oh, dear me, I am sounding like a Jane Austen novel, aren't I?"

"Please continue, I'm fascinated. I need to know this story."

"You would think my good sense would warn me to not be drawn in, but my heart was pounding and I was very glad to see him. It didn't hurt that he began apologizing from the depth of his soul for all the pain he had caused. I forgave him immediately and we sat and talked as old friends all afternoon. It was as though nothing had come between us. I had a selfish sense of relief sharing how difficult life with Alistair had become. He held my hand and listened without judgement. He told me how well his engineering career was going and his plan was to leave for New York in ten days to pursue a partnership with an American inventor named Thomas Edison. It all sounded very exciting. His daughter was never mentioned and I chose not to ask. When it came time for him to leave he begged me to come with him to America, and bring the children. Being caught up in the moment, the offer was very tempting. I knew in my heart I didn't have the courage to do it, but I was so enjoying the fantasy of pretending. Finally, I told him I couldn't do it, no matter how much I wanted to. Life had moved on and we each had responsibilities to tend. His last words to me were, "I will always love you, Lizzy girl." With tears, he embraced me and we held together for a bit too long. You see, unbeknownst to me, Alistair had come home and walked in at that moment. I'll spare you the details, but it was dreadful to say the least. Alistair had always been extremely jealous, and in his mind now he had proof. For several years after that, I was forbidden to leave the estate and kept loosely as a prisoner with my children. He threatened to take them away if I protested in any way."

"My God! How could you live with that?" Richard was truly appalled.

"In this life you do what you must do. As it turned out, Alistair only lived a few years after that."

"Did you try to find my father?"

"My brother told me that William found much success in the States and had married a lovely American girl…"

"My mother!"

"Yes, I'm guessing it was your mother. Then, I lost track of him until I heard of his fatal equestrian accident."

A single tear slid down her wrinkled face.

"Once again I mourned the loss of William Duncan."

Richard was at a complete loss of what to say. Processing everything he had just heard was like trying to drink from a firehose– the velocity was overwhelming. He reached across and took Lady

Rose's hands in his and just held them. Neither spoke for some minutes. It occurred to him that these were the very same hands his father held so many years before.

"You are my only living connection to my father. I didn't think I cared, but now…this changes everything," he said, noticing his heart was beating double time.

"Remember, you should have a half sister somewhere. I never knew the Clark-Pattersons, but perhaps you could make inquiries and find her," Lady Rose reminded him.

"Yes, maybe I will. It's quite incredible I might have a sibling. May I ask what my father looked like? Was he tall? Was he fair or dark haired? I'm sorry be so inquisitive, but you see, I've never seen a photo of him."

Lady Rose unclasped the catch on her handbag and slowly withdrew a well-used small envelope. With a hint of reluctance, she handed it to Richard.

"This is very precious to me."

He opened the envelope flap and carefully pulled out the old black and white photo. For the first time in his life, he was looking at the face of his father. It was oddly like looking in an old, cracked mirror. Looking up at Lady Rose, she smiled back.

"Yes, you bear a very strong resemblance to him."

"It is almost uncanny. I always thought I took after my mother, but there is no denying this is my father. It is so strange to be seeing him for the first time."

From across the room a man a bit older than Richard approached them and leaned down to Lady Rose.

"Mother, the car is here. Are you ready to go?"

"Oh, thank you, Jamie, in a few moments. We are just now finishing our visit. Allow me to introduce you to Richard Duncan, he's an American who is staying here to recover."

Richard stood up, unsteady on his injured leg, and the two men shook hands.

"Very nice to meet you, Mr. Duncan. My best wishes for a speedy recovery."

"Thank you. I can't imagine a better place to heal."

"It is marvelous, isn't it? Exactly what mother always envisioned." Turning to Lady Rose, Jamie continued. "Take your time. I'll be in the entry when you're ready."

Lady Rose watched her son walk away.

"I've been very blessed with my children. Both were young when Alistiar died and remember very little about him. It makes it much easier to pretend it wasn't as bad as it was.

Now, Richard Duncan, as we have just a short time before I must go, tell me about you. I want to know William Duncan's only son."

As best he could, Richard shared the highlights of his life, spending the most time telling Lady Rose about Sarah. He showed her a photo he carried in his wallet of the two of them when they climbed Arthur's Seat.

"What a beautiful child, and she sounds wonderfully bright. You must miss her a great deal. A perfect incentive to heal and reclaim your life. I would enjoy meeting this Sarah of yours someday. "

"Honestly, Lady Rose, I don't know where my life will be when I leave here. It will be with Sarah, of course, but I've much to sort out in terms of our future."

"You will find your way. Life has a strange way to leading us down pathways we never could have imagined."

"I can't thank you enough for telling me your story. There's quite a bit there for me to think about."

"Thank you for letting an old lady relive her youth again. It's a story I've never told anyone, and likely never will again. William Duncan was the love of my life and for me to sit with you and hold your hand is nothing short of a miracle. You have given me a peace I never expected or knew I needed."

Richard took a long look at the photo and returned it to the envelope. He handed it back to her.

"Would you please keep that photo for me until I see you again?" she asked. "I know it means as much to you as it does to me." She reached in her handbag and took out an old fashioned calling card with her name and address engraved on it. "I expect to hear from you. May God bless you and Sarah."

"And you as well, Lady Rose."

With that, Lady Rose indicated to her son that she was ready to go. Jamie helped the beautiful, elegant woman to her feet and they walked out together.

Richard overheard Jamie speaking to his mother.

"You seemed to get on quite well with the American chap."

"Yes. Yes I did…"

# *Chapter Thirty-five*

# PETER:

## *The Letter Finally Arrives*

Peter licked the envelope flap and pressed it down to make sure the seal was closed tight. He made a face at the taste of the adhesive, thinking what a diabolical plot it would be to wipe out mankind if someone were to poison the glue on the flaps of envelopes. One lick and 'poof' you're gone! Perhaps, he had read too many Sherlock Holmes books.

The slot of the bright red pillar post-box opened easily and he slid the letter to Sarah through, waiting to hear it drop on top of all the other letters. He wondered about all those envelopes inside the cast iron cylinder. Was it full of love letters or overdue billings? Since Mrs. McAughtrie's visit yesterday, he found himself feeling a heightened sensitivity to everything around him. There was a lightness, something like a sun break after a dark, rainy morning. He figured hearing really excellent news would do that to a person.

His letter to Sarah had been written several times and discarded several times before he decided shorter was better. He had reviewed it so many times that he committed his words to memory. Walking home from the post-box he recited it in his mind.

*Dear Sarah,*

*Your friend, Mrs. McAughtrie, came to visit me and brought the best news imaginable. Knowing you were safe and that your father was alive brought me such great relief. I have been thanking God for saving you both.*

*Hoping this letter finds you well, and I will look forward to hearing all about everything when you have a chance to write. Do you have any idea how long you will be in Shetland?*

*Your friend,*
*Peter*

For hours he had struggled with what to write, wanting her to know how concerned he had been, but not overly suffocating or too familiar. He had no idea how traumatized she might be from such a shocking event, and certainly didn't want to burden her with unimportant details of his life. Thinking back, Peter realized he never had many close friendships, especially one with a smart, funny, pretty girl. This was all new territory for him and he would have to tread carefully. For some reason, Sarah being far away was bringing their relationship to a new level in his mind. He often wondered what she was thinking.

The wind and the rain began early in the morning and hadn't let up all day. There were times when the drops hit the windows so hard, it felt as though they wanted to come inside. It was well known mail to Shetland Island was notoriously slow, but he had written Sarah over two weeks ago and hadn't heard back. It was a constant battle to keep his mind focused and not on endless speculation about Sarah's situation. The dark, gray day was not helping his mood. Looking up, he saw his mother standing in the doorway of his room watching him. He wondered how long she had been standing there, and hoped she couldn't read his mind. Since the shooting incident, she had changed and become a bit softer and more…motherly. It had been a long time since he had felt like a son rather than one of her clients. It wouldn't do for her to know how depressed he had been, so he tried to act more cheerful than he was feeling.

"Come in, though I doubt the weather is any better up here than it is downstairs," he said trying to be animated.

"Perhaps I can bring some sunshine to your day. There is a letter here for you, and it looks as though it might be from Shetland!"

There was no point in trying to hide his elation as he jumped from his chair. The happiness on his face negated all the soggy weather outside.

"Oh, Mum! Thank you!"

She handed it to him and spoke softly.

"Well, I'll go downstairs and prepare our tea and leave you to it."

Holding the long-awaited letter in his hand, he stared at the handwriting on the envelope.

"I'll be down shortly," he said, absentmindedly, then remembering his manners, "Thanks awfully for bringing it up."

"You're quite welcome, son," she said, smiling.

With that, she closed the door and left him to himself.

*Dear Peter,*

*You would never believe how surprised I was to receive your letter. I had wanted to write to you so many times the last five weeks, but realized I never took the time to notice your address. Far more embarrassing than that, I realized that I didn't even know your full name. The vision of writing on the envelope 'To Peter who lives in the lovely house on Salisbury Street with the third floor gable window' just didn't give me confidence that it would arrive in your hands. Now I know that you are Peter Michael-McGregor. Such a grand name! I'll be forever grateful to Mrs. McAughtrie for her thoughtfulness in finding you and actually coming to your house. I'm sure she broke all kinds of rules by sharing my new address, but she knew it would be important to me. I miss her very much and the thought of possibly not seeing her again makes me sad. Her kindness was so like my grandmother's, who I also miss.*

*To answer your question, we don't know how long I'll be in Shetland. The authorities are quite sure of the identity of the man who shot my father, but can't find him. The big question is whether there was anyone else involved. From what Liam says, they are thinking more and more that he acted alone. However, until he is caught there is concern that he might try to harm my father or me. The good news is that my father is recovering from his wounds and taking physiotherapy to heal completely. We are able to talk on the telephone once a week which I look forward to. Nothing has been mentioned about the future. I have no idea if we will go back to America or remain here. It's a bit unsettling and I have to work at not thinking about it, and sometimes at night I go crazy trying to sort it. Everyone here has gone out of their way to make me feel at home, but between us, sometimes I am lonely and afraid. I try to be brave and get through everyday living in a foreign place with people I don't know very well. This must be what it's like to be adopted into a new family. If my father had been killed, I have no idea what would have become of me. Oh, there I go slipping into the pity pot. Sorry!*

*In some respects, the days go by quickly. I am enrolled in school, though because of my private education I'm quite a bit ahead of the local school here. I'll tell you all about that in another letter. Quite an adventure and too long for now. Liam has started letting me help out on the farm, mostly with small tasks like feeding the animals or cleaning the barns. I can see these jobs would be much more pleasant in the warmer months, but I love being busy. It's still very cold here and they tell me it will be a while before things warm up. Most of my life I've lived in cities, so being in the country on a farm on a remote island, four hundred miles from Edinburgh is about the last place I would ever expect to end up. The odd thing is that I like it. There is such beauty in the starkness of the land and being bound by the sea is extraordinary. Have you ever been to Shetland? If you have, please tell me what you think of it. I am intrigued by many things here like the Shetlandic dialect and the its history with Norway. Burning peat in the fireplace is another first for me.*

*It is getting late and I'm sure I am rambling, but it is very comforting to know that you will be reading this soon. Please fill me in with your news. Did you spend Christmas with your grandparents, and were you able to fly-fish? It seems like years since life took such a big detour. I'll wait impatiently to hear from you. Take care of yourself.*

*Your friend,*
*Sarah*

## *Chapter Thirty-six*

# LIAM:

### *Riding Horses Always Helps*

It's a funny thing about the weather in Shetland. You could experience nearly every element nature could throw at you in the span of one day. A windy, rainy morning might very well find snow drifting down by noon, and end with the sun sparkling off of the sea. Even in the dead of winter, a fine day could appear out of nowhere. Liam recognized such a day and lost no time in heading to the barn to saddle a horse for a quick ride. There was much on his mind that needed his undivided attention and a gallop around the land sounded ideal. He was surprised to see Sarah gently brushing Golden Girl, one of the farm's Welsh ponies. Not sure if she heard him come in, he spoke quietly.

"Well, hello. How are you today?"

"Liam! Good morning. I hope you don't mind that I came out here without asking. It was so nice to see the sun shining."

"Of course not. I want you to feel as comfortable as you can…given the circumstances."

Sarah paused brushing for a moment and looked straight at him.

"Do you think I'm safe here?"

His first thought was amusement at her directness, but on second thought realized this must be on her mind constantly. She was not looking for an evasive answer, just the truth.

"Before I answer that, would you like to take a ride around the farm with me?"

This had the reaction he hoped for. Her face lit up.

"Really? Do you mean it? Yes, of course I would!"

The horses were saddled and within minutes they were cantering gently across the open expanse of permanent pasture land dotted with ancient cottage ruins. Sarah was a good rider and he could tell she was thoroughly enjoying the abandon of galloping with the wind. The horses hooves kicked up the light frosting of snow which sparkled in the morning sunlight. Liam slowed to a walk, and Sarah followed beside him. He spoke thoughtfully to her.

"Look around you. Shetland is a very remote island, with a limited population. Most of these people have lived here for generations and we all know each other and watch out for one another. Getting to the island is not an easy journey, and strangers are noticed readily. What I'm trying to say to you is, you are protected here more than almost anywhere else I can think of. It is still my job to keep you safe, and I will do that with every ounce of my being for as long as you need me."

"Oh Liam," her voice catching in her throat, "I'm so sorry you are stuck with me but I want you to know I really, really appreciate everything. I don't know what I would've done without you and your family."

Fearing she was about to cry, Liam changed the subject. With so many sisters, crying was the one thing he never knew how to handle.

"Well, tell me what you think of my daft family?"

This had the desired result of making her laugh.

"They are not daft! I never had siblings, so it's interesting to watch your sisters get on with each other. One minute they are terribly upset over something, and the next they are friendly and dovey. It's really funny, but please don't tell them I said that."

It was Liam's turn to laugh.

"Dovey? That's a new one. The thing is, they really do love each other and would defend each other to the death, but woe be to the sister that borrows another's scarf or gloves!"

"Your mother and father are extraordinary. I've never been around people who work so hard, but always seem to have time to visit or have a cup of tea. Would you think I was dreadfully shallow if I said how good looking they are? Your mother is gorgeous and your father is positively handsome. Good thing for you!"

Liam was enjoying the lighter conversation. It was good to see her relax and her mind diverted.

"Very good for me, indeed, and my sisters. I agree."

The horses seem to know their way, and ambled along without much guidance from the riders.

"Has your family lived on Shetland for generations like other families?"

"My father's side definitely. The farm has been in our family for five generations. I would be the sixth. I love the farm and everything about it, but it is a big responsibility. Farming gets more complicated every year, but I can't imagine settling down anywhere else."

"And your mother? Her name is beautiful and so unusual. Is she a native Shetlander?"

"No, she was raised on the Isle of Skye."

"I've read a bit about Skye. Fishing villages and medieval castles, part of the Hebrides, right?"

"Aye, aren't you the smart girl? That it is. The story I've heard is she was raised by her aunt and uncle. Her mother died when she was quite young and her father is a bit of a mystery. She's always said she had a lovely childhood and was very happy, but true love came to Skye and it moved her to Shetland."

"How did they meet? That's such a far distance."

"It seems my father's father, Grandfather Donal, heard about a chap on Skye who had a well-known fold of Highland cattle or Coos…"

"You lost me already. I love Highland cattle with their long bangs covering their eyes, but don't know what a 'Coo' or a 'fold' is."

"Highland cattle are nicknamed 'Coos' and herds of them have always been known as 'folds.' It has something to do with them sheltering in stone places in the winter that are called 'folds.' So, Grandfather Donal sends his only son, Mark, to Skye to learn all he can and bring back a head full of knowledge to help their fold. Well, in addition to bringing back all his new cattle wisdom, he brought back a wife, the niece of the gentleman who owned the fine fold of Highlands."

"Seriously? That's a wonderful story!"

"Mum is brilliant. The way she runs the house, works the farm with my father and still manages to raise her children is impressive. She has set the bar very high for my future wife."

"And speaking of your future wife, when will I meet her?"

"You will soon. It's just I've had my hands a wee bit full with one thing or another the past weeks."

Sarah looked at her body guard and realized how lucky she was.

"And I'm guessing one thing or another would be me?"

"You are top of my list," he said.

In an instant the wind changed direction and the dark clouds that had seemed far away a moment ago were headed their way. Sarah pulled the woolen scarf tighter around her neck.

"We had best get back," Liam said. "When you live on an island, you get used to the weather changing quickly. Let's see if we can beat the rain."

The horses needed no coaxing to head toward the barn. Neither did their riders.

*Chapter Thirty-seven*

# CONRAD RATCHFORD:

## *The Great Getaway*

Life on the lam wasn't as exciting as he thought it would be. Even with a graying beard, and his long hair covered with a knit hat pulled down to his eyebrows, Conrad Ratchford was constantly looking over his shoulder. Reykjavik, Iceland was full of people during the day, but when the cold night fell, the streets were deserted and it was hard to not be visible. The cheap room he rented was helping conserve his money, but was drafty and he was sure he was sharing it with a family of rats. What good was all this money if he couldn't indulge himself? Maybe it was time to come out of hiding. There were plenty of women in a certain part of town who would be happy to spend the evening with him. He wouldn't even have to clean up much, they were not a choosy lot. Stuffing his pockets with money from the battered case, he walked the dark streets until he found what he was looking for…love in all the wrong places.

It's curious how life can turn and twist and lead you down a path you never expected. Ten years ago Conrad Ratchford was a well thought of foreign diplomat, even sacrificing family relationships for a promising career. Growing up in privilege on Long Island, New York, he and his sister wanted for nothing, except parental attention. Boarding schools and summer camps were a way of life and for all appearances both children thrived. Being top of his class, Conrad was a natural for Foreign Service. With his father's influence, he was fast tracked and found himself working in consulates all over the world.

It was glamorous at first and he enjoyed becoming more powerful as he rose in the ranks. When the opportunity arrived to be the interim head of the Edinburgh office, it seemed somewhat interesting. He had never lived in Scotland and hoped by being in full control, it wouldn't be as boring as his previous stations. He had no idea he would be approached to be part of such a profitable, illegal side business. A few introductions to some key players and he was sure he could take advantage of his new position. Things were just getting started and had all the appearances of going well until Richard Duncan suddenly showed up and spoiled the set up. Conrad did everything possible to maneuver around Duncan, but to no avail. The deal was sunk.

Anna was not the kind of woman Conrad would've given a second glance to in his former life, but enough liquor and the dim, smoky light in the dockside bar made her seem almost pretty. That and the fact that she returned his attention with gusto. The last thing he remembered was stumbling out into the nighttime air with his arm around Anna. He woke up on the sidewalk with a large lump on his head and all of his cash taken. Rising to his feet, he unsteadily retreated to his rented room. He didn't want any involvement with the police and the best way to avoid that was to go back into hiding.

It was nearly noon when Conrad finally roused himself out of his rumpled bed. The thin walls were not doing much to keep the cold out, and he listened as the wind whistled through the cracks in the window casing. Weak, mid-day light was trying to filter through the dirt crusted on the small window, doing little to illuminate or warm the room. He turned on the one lamp and looked around at his disheveled surroundings. The magnitude of how far he had fallen hit him almost as hard as the bat that caused his head to swell. Dropping to his knees, he retrieved the old suitcase from under his bed and opened it. At least a large amount of his cash was still there, but how long before Anna's thugs would come looking for him figuring there was more money to be had? It was time to make a move. Maybe Iceland wasn't his brightest idea. Whoever said money can't buy happiness, might have had a point. Still, there was enough cash to get him out of Iceland, but where would he go?

An idea came slowly, but once it took root Conrad couldn't let go of it. Examining it from every angle he could think of, the idea only grew stronger. If only his brother-in-law would cooperate, Conrad could end this downward spiral he had fallen into for something more suiting of his upbringing. Working out the broad details of this plan, he decided it would be best to appeal to his sister first and win her over. Jelena had married an extremely wealthy man who's family owned extensive land holdings along the northern east coast of the United States. Her husband, Marcus, had retired from his legal career to oversee the development of the raw land portion of his family's large portfolio. Obviously, Marcus could run the operation from anywhere, as they had been traveling the world for the last few years with their daughter. Ironically, they had come to Scotland just prior to his departure. Jelena had tried to connect, but Conrad's world was collapsing around him at that moment and he couldn't take the time to get involved with his little sister. But now, she looked to be his only way out of this dreadful mess he had created. Yes, that would be the answer.

*Chapter Thirty-eight*

# SARAH:

*Fondly, Peter*

*Dear Sarah,*

*Your letter was the perfect antidote for a long, winter day. The snow is all gone and has been replaced by windy, rainy weather. As you are aware, the daylight hours become less and less and one is not particularly motivated to get much done. Perhaps bears have the right idea by hibernating for much of winter.*

*Once I knew you were safe and your father was on the mend, I was much more in a mood to celebrate the holidays with my family. They had gone earlier to my grandparents house in the Borders, and I joined them later. Sadly, it was too cold and the river was too high to go fly fishing. It is traditionally a much anticipated adventure with my grandfather, but not to be this year. I brought the new book you gave me to show my grandfather and he was astounded at what a clever girl you must be. My grandmother and mother prepared loads of food and it was good to be together. Having gone through your terrible ordeal on the periphery, I found I was much more introspective than usual, and enjoyed just walking through the meadows near the river, watching the sheep. Makes me sound a bit of a dolt, doesn't it? I just kept thinking what a fine thread we exist on. And like you, I am remembering to NOT think about the 'what if's' of the situation. May I ask you a question? Feel free to not answer if you don't want to, but do you believe in God?*

*It must be interesting to attend school in such a remote part of the world. I'll look forward to hearing your thoughts on it. Do you have enough books to read? It wouldn't be any trouble to send you some. In fact, it would make me feel like I was helping you. Let me know.*

*Of course, the big question–has there has been any progress on finding who did this? Seems everything in your life depends on that, one way or the other. Is there any news?*

*And how is your father mending? I can understand why the future must look scary, but I really feel it will all work out.*

*It delights me to know you are finding so many redeeming things about Shetland. You are quite a remarkable girl, you know.*

*I'll be anxious to hear from you.*

*Fondly,*
*Peter*

Sarah read the letter twice, smiling more the second time than the first. Then she read it again, stopping at the part where he asked if she believed in God. That was going to take some pondering, and honestly, it was something she knew it was time for her to confront.

Ava popped her head around the corner, "Dinner time, Sarah. Your favorite, Liver Koogs!"

Both girls shared hearty dislike of the Shetland dish, but they knew Liam would be thrilled. So far, it was really the only thing about Shetland she didn't care for.

*Chapter Thirty-nine*

# JONQUIL:

*The Phone Call*

How could it be that she had never read *Swiss Family Robinson* before? Jonquil started it that morning and couldn't put it down. Curled up comfortably in front of the fire in a large overstuffed chair, every page was an adventure. Taking a sip of tepid tea, she looked over at her mother who was completely engrossed in knitting yet another scarf. This one in shades of blue and lavender. She wondered idly who would be the lucky recipient of this latest creation. Glancing at her father, she noticed his glasses had slid partially down his nose, as he concentrated on the stack of papers from the latest mail delivery.

The telephone rang loudly. Then rang again and again and again. Finally Jelena Worthington looked up in some exasperation at her husband and daughter, and put down her knitting.

"Isn't anyone going to answer that?" she asked.

The black phone rang again as she picked up the handset.

"Good afternoon," her mother answered pleasantly. She repeatedly told Jonquil that it was much nicer to say 'Good morning or afternoon' or whatever time of day it was rather than say 'Hello.'

"Jelena? Is that you?"

"Connie? Is that you? Where are you, dear? The connection is crackling."

Jonquil lost interest in the conversation almost immediately. Her Uncle Connie was not one of her favorite people. He smelled like cigars and thought he was dreadfully important. More than once he had made it clear that he had no time for his only niece. It was hard to imagine that he and her lovely mother were siblings. How could two such different humans come from the same gene pool?

"We've been here for two months and haven't been able to find you? The consulate acted very oddly when we called there looking for you. In fact, they said if we heard from you to let them know. Wasn't that a strange thing for them to say?"

"Jelena....you must listen to me very carefully. Don't say anything until I finish. I'm not sure how long I can stay on this telephone line or when I will be able to ring you back."

"Well, I'm listening, but you're acting very dramatic and there is so much static on the line..."

"Jelena! Listen to me! I have done something very stupid and I need your help."

"Oh, Connie, what have you done that's so terrible? Surely, it can't be that bad. You never needed my help before."

At this last pronouncement, both Jonquil and her father looked up with curiosity. This conversation was obviously more interesting than either originally thought.

"I shot someone and I am in hiding, and now I am in a lot of danger," Conrad spoke urgently as though by telling someone it would ease his fear.

"You shot someone???" Jelena answered, her voice very loud and several octaves higher than normal. "What are you saying, Connie? Are you drunk?"

"It's a long story, but I need Marcus to help me get somewhere safe. I'm thinking somewhere out in the wilderness, on the land his family owns. I must disappear for a while."

"Marcus is not going to do that. Who did you shoot? When did this happen?" She was almost screaming by now.

By now, Marcus was on his feet, standing over Jelena, ready to pounce on the telephone. Jelena wasn't giving the phone up until she had some answers.

"I shot Richard Duncan on Christmas Eve at the church in Edinburgh. It's a long story. Please, Jelena, you must convince Marcus to help me. I'm begging you. I have a false passport and can arrange passage. I am desperate."

"You shot Richard Duncan? His daughter went to school with Jonquil! How could you shoot him? What were you thinking?"

At this latest information, Jonquil sat up and took in every word. Sarah Duncan! The girl who was supposed to be her mentor at school. The one Peter, the young man at Christmas dinner, had told her about. Her uncle shot Sarah's father! The fact that her uncle shot anyone was bad enough, but shooting Sarah's father was incredulous! When school started after the holiday break, she wondered why they never met. She had overhead rumors that Sarah left school with no explanation.

"Jelena, I'm going to have to hang up. I hear someone coming. I will call you later if I can. Please, please convince Marcus to help me."

With that the line went dead and Jelena continued to hold the phone aloft, looking very confused.

"I think I am going to throw up. How could Connie shoot someone? I had no idea he knew how to shoot a gun. I'm speechless."

"I think we need to talk. Jonquil, will you give your mother and me a few minutes alone?"

"Of course," Jonquil answered, knowing full well she would hide behind the door and listen to what was going to be said.

Her mother and father talked back and forth quietly, as the details were revealed to Marcus. Then when her mother asked if he would help Conrad, her father blew up and it was one long argument. Jonquil was incensed that her mother would actually think of helping to hide her smelly, criminal uncle. Her head was beginning to ache, and she was growing weary of sitting on the floor by the door eavesdropping when the phone rang again. This time she heard her father answer it.

"Hello!"

They recently had a speaker added to their telephone and the sound was loud enough for Jonquil to hear every word. At first there was only silence, with sporadic static.

"Conrad, is that you?" her father demanded.

"Yes it is. Marcus, I wouldn't ask if I weren't desperate."

"Where are you?"

"Can I trust you?"

"If you're asking for my help to hide a fugitive, then I need to know where you are," her father answered firmly.

Jonquil was now equally appalled that her father, her straight-arrow father, was going to get involved in this as well. How could this be happening to her family?

"Fair enough. I am in Iceland."

"Where are you in Iceland? I'm guessing Reykjavic?"

"Yes."

"How quickly can you arrange transportation to the States?"

"I'm not sure. Probably within a week."

"It will take me at least that long to make arrangements on my end. I will need you to call me in the next few days. We have much to talk about."

"Thank you, Marcus."

"Goodbye."

All was quiet in the room, and Jonquil carefully stood up to see if the coast was clear to go back into the study, when her mother began to cry.

"I'm so sorry about this. It is all so shocking that he would shoot someone. I know in my heart that he should come forward and turn himself in, but he is my brother and he would die in prison. Oh, what a mess."

"Jelena, you need to realize that by hiding your brother we become accomplices to his crime. I am going to really need to think about this. I have spent my career as an attorney and all of this goes very much against everything I have stood for my entire life."

"But you said…you told him…"

"I said what needed to be said for now."

With that her mother began to sob uncontrollably, and Jonquil escaped to her room to sort this all out in her mind.

Several hours passed as she ran all this information around and around in her brain, trying to put it chronological order. Peter had mentioned Sarah to her at Christmas Eve dinner. Now she knew that was the night her uncle shot Richard Duncan. Next, when she went back to Campbell Manor after Christmas holiday, expecting to meet Sarah, she heard that she was gone. Where did she go? Did her uncle try to kill her too? Today, her stinky uncle calls and wants her parents to hide him. Like a lightening bolt, it hit her that the police or whoever looked for criminals like her uncle, probably had no idea where he was! And to further complicate this situation, her father was considering helping Uncle Conrad, which would make her parents part of the crime. She would not let her mother and father become part of this.

"Okay, Miss Smart Girl. So what are you going to do about it?" she said out loud, hoping an answer would appear out of thin air.

And it did. She would talk to Peter. It was obvious, even to a fourteen year old, that Sarah was special to Peter.

## Chapter Forty

# PETER:

*A Surprise Guest Knocks*

"Peter, I'm putting on the kettle for tea," Jessica Michael-McGregor said at the foot of the stairs in a voice loud enough for him to hear.

It had been a long day for his mother. She had been up since dawn making all the arrangements for the Royal Botanic Gardens event to be held at their home in two days. Peter knew she enjoyed fund raising for worthy causes, but like everything she undertook, it had to be done to a certain standard. Flowers would be delivered tomorrow afternoon, catering would arrive the day after, musicians will show up two hours before the guests. Peter knew the drill well, and so far, all appeared to be in order.

"I'll be right down," he answered.

Halfway down the stairs there was an urgent knock at the door.

"Who would that be?" he asked loudly.

"No idea. I'm not expecting anyone," she said from the kitchen.

"I'll get it," he said, opening the heavy carved door. "Jonquil! Hello, come in. This is a surprise. Mother, you remember Jonquil from the Holt's Christmas Eve dinner. Her family moved into the neighborhood several months ago."

"Why, of course. Lovely to see you, dear. Come in, we were just about to have tea. Join us, won't you?"

Peter loved how gracious his mother was in all circumstances, but he was very curious to know why Jonquil was standing in his entry way looking rather uncomfortable.

"Thank you very much, Mrs. Michael-McGregor, but I would

just like a word with Peter…if that's all right?"

"Oh yes, of course. Please give my regards to your parents," his mother said, heading back to the kitchen

"I will, thank you."

Peter guided Jonquil to the small library where they could have the privacy she obviously wanted. Sitting across from one another in the dark green velvet chairs, he looked at the young girl expectantly.

"I'm not completely sure where to start," she said in a shaky voice.

He let her organize her thoughts and waited for her to continue.

"Peter, Sarah Duncan is someone special to you, right?"

Wow! He didn't see that one coming.

"Yes she is."

"And her father was shot and she went away, right?"

"Yes. That's the short version of what happened."

"Is she all right then? I mean she wasn't hurt, was she?"

"Yes, she is all right. No, she wasn't hurt," he answered cautiously.

"And the authorities haven't found the man who killed her father, right?"

This caught Peter off-guard even more. He knew he shouldn't tell Jonquil that Richard Duncan was still alive, but she was struggling with this conversation and he wished he could ease her mind. But he chose not to.

"You are correct, to the best of my knowledge, the man who shot Mr. Duncan has not been caught."

Jonquil gave him the most pained expression he had ever seen on another human being.

"Are you quite all right, Jonquil?" he asked.

"I don't know who else to talk to. Remember you told me to trust you on Christmas Eve?"

By now she was wringing her hands to the point of tangling up her fingers. He hoped she wasn't going to faint or cry.

"I meant it. You can trust me," he said trying to sound more reassuring than he felt.

The diminutive young girl squeezed her eyes shut, as though

trying to block out something terrible. Peter's heart began to pound. He knew he was about to hear something earth shattering.

"Oh, Peter…my uncle is the one who shot Sarah's father!"

With those words out of her mouth, she broke down crying and began to run words together so fast he couldn't make sense of any of it. Something about her parents, and land in Maine, and a false passport, and her uncle smelling of bad cigars. He took hold of her hands.

"Okay. Let's start at the beginning."

She hiccuped then seemed to settle down. Peter handed her a tissue and she blew her nose. It might take more than one tissue.

"My uncle called my mother today wanting my father to hide him. He admitted to the shooting and was desperate to find a place to hide. He wasn't safe where he was. I'm afraid my parents are going to get involved and get into trouble."

With a deep breath, Peter hesitatingly asked the big question. The answer could change Sarah's life.

"Where is your uncle, Jonquil."

Silence filled the room, as tears streamed down her face.

"He's in Rejekyvic, Iceland."

## *Chapter Forty-one*

# SARAH:

*Up Helly Aa*

*Dear Peter,*

*Holding a piece of paper that you have actually written on means so much to me. I'm not sure I can explain why that is, other than it makes me feel closer to you and gives me the feeling that someday my life might not be so uncertain.*

*Several large boxes arrived recently filled with things from our house in Edinburgh. Mrs. McAughtrie took the time to send some 'bits and bobs' as she would say, to help me feel less alone here. Other than my clothes, the best things were a few of my favorite books. I've read most of them two or three times, but no matter, they are like old friends. If you happen to find a book you think I would like, it would be most welcome, but please don't go to any trouble.*

*I still have moments when I feel sad, but it has gotten better. Everyday I discover marvelous new things about Shetland. The other night Ava dragged me out in the cold and made me walk a long distance in the dark. Suddenly the sky exploded in what she called the 'mirrie dancers.' Later I learned everyone else calls it the Northern Lights or aurora borealis. The colors that danced across the sky in waves were absolutely thrilling. Ava said it's a natural phenomena that happens off and on all winter long. I've never seen anything like it!*

*Since Shetland is such a remote island where there are more sheep than people, I'm amazed how many events there are here. I've just experienced my first Up-Helly-Aa festival which is pretty crazy. Liam took us to Lerwick, the big city, to see the celebration. He said that during the year a full size replica of a Viking ship is built. During Up-Helly-Aa, men carry torches and dress in costume, then march through the streets dragging the Viking longship. When they finally get it where they want it, they surround the ship and sing songs before setting it on fire. Once it has burned completely, the men sing, "The Norsemen's Home," and go off for a night of drinking and partying. Isn't that the oddest thing? No one in Liam's family could quite explain it, other than it was a nice way to break up the long winter nights. I would have to agree.*

*My father is healing well and his rehabilitation is going faster than the doctors expected. While this is very good news, we are all held captive where we are until that man who fired the shots is found. According to Liam, there is just too much uncertainty as to what he might do. People from the U.S. and Great Britain are madly searching for him, but nothing so far, as he seems to have vanished into thin air. I'm not sure what happens if he is never caught.*

*School is going along fine, and everyone is nice. Working on the farm with Liam and his family is great fun. It's wonderful to be part of a large family and help getting the chores done. Who knew I would like to get dirty? The girls at Campbell Manor would be shocked. So would my father.*

*You asked if I believed in God. For the past few months I have been avoiding those thoughts, but by asking you opened the door for me to begin think about it. Before you anticipate an answer, don't be disappointed because I am still gathering my thoughts. A short answer is, yes, I do believe in God. The confusing part is why terrible things happen to good people. My father is the best person I know and I don't understand why God allowed him to be hurt. I'll keep pondering and have more on the subject when next I write.*

*Please tell me what you have been up to. Sometimes, I realize I really don't know very much about you. What books do you like? That tells a lot about a person.*

*Thank you again for your letter.*

*Your friend,*
*Sarah*

*Chapter Forty-two*

# PETER:

## *Consulate General Parker Pays a Visit*

After a long discussion lasting into the wee hours of the morning, Stuart and Jessica Michael-McGregor finally agreed their son should contact the American Consulate. It was important to Peter that Jonquil and her family be protected as the source of the information concerning the whereabouts of Conrad Ratchford. He was a dangerous man who had already tried to kill Richard Duncan. There was no telling how he might react if he found out the authorities were closing in on him.

Sleep had been elusive, but a strong cup of tea helped Peter clear his brain. Most of the night had been spent rehearsing what he would say. He even made notes to insure he didn't divulge anything he didn't have to, yet still communicated the urgency of his information. A promise had been made to Jonquil to not mention her family if at all possible, and he intended to keep that promise.

Sitting in his father's office alone, Peter dialed the telephone. There was one ring before it was answered by a pleasant sounding woman.

"Good morning, American Consulate."

"Good morning. May I speak to the Consulate General? It is an urgent matter."

"I'm sorry, but the Consulate General is not available at the moment. May I take your name and leave a message?"

"Yes, of course, but please understand this is of vital importance and is quite urgent."

"Your name, please?"

Peter gave his name, address and telephone number, but felt she was not grasping the gravity of his call. Out of frustration, he tried one last time to impress his compelling need to speak to the Consulate General.

"In your message, would you please inform the Consulate General that I have information regarding the whereabouts of Richard Duncan's assailant."

There was a dead silence that went on long enough for Peter to ask if she was still there.

"Would you stay on the line, please," she responded curtly and put him on hold.

An eternity passed until a gentleman with a deep voice came on and addressed Peter in a commanding, clipped manner.

"Mr. Michael-McGregor, this is Interim Director Parker. I have received your message and am not at liberty to discuss this matter on the telephone. Are you certain of what you know?"

"Yes, sir. I am."

"I will meet with you personally within the hour. I assume you are available."

"Yes, sir."

"My secretary has your address. We will be there shortly."

There was barely time for Peter to alert his parents about their visitors before two black cars were parked in front of their house. He answered the front door and was met by two large men who explained briefly that they would need to do a quick search of the house. Inwardly groaning, Peter could only imagine how unamused his mother would be by strangers peeking behind the drapes and looking in closets. The men did their job efficiently and within a matter of minutes gave the driver of the second car the signal that the house was cleared. Director Parker exited the car quickly and entered the house, shaking hands with Peter and his parents. Jessica, ever the correct hostess, offered tea to the three gentlemen.

"Thank you, no, Mrs. Michael-McGregor. We need to get right

to the point."

"Of course," Jessica answered, "We will leave you to it."

It had been agreed that Peter would meet with the Consulate people alone. While a bit intimidated, he kept reminding himself that he held the key to Sarah's future.

Two other men had joined Director Parker, though they stayed in the background. Peter was asked a number of personal questions, things like his age, schooling, occupation, and finally what his involvement was in regards to this situation.

"Sarah Duncan, Richard Duncan's daughter, is a friend of mine."

At that statement, Director Parker raised an eyebrow.

"And do you know where Sarah is?"

Richard's brain went into overdrive. Should he lie to protect her or tell the truth to protect her? His split second decision was to be carefully honest.

"Yes, sir, I do."

There was a brief silence, as the older man seemed to process this information.

"And are you aware of Richard Duncan's location?"

"No, sir, I'm not."

A mild look of relief crossed Parker's face.

"How were you made aware of Conrad Ratchford's whereabouts?"

"That I can't tell you. I promised my source not to involve him or her. The source is aware that I was going to contact you, and sincerely hopes that you are able to find Ratchford before he moves on to another location, which could be imminent."

"Do you believe this source to be reliable?'

"Absolutely, I do."

"And where, Mr. Michael-McGregor, do you believe Mr. Ratchford is?

"He is in Rejekyvic, Iceland."

Director Parker gave a slight nod to one of the gentleman standing in the background, who then left quietly through the door.

Silence once again filled the room. Several minutes passed before the gentleman who left returned and gave a brief, affirmative nod to the Director.

"Well, young man, if your information is correct, the government of the United States will owe you a tremendous debt of gratitude."

Peter looked down, a little embarrassed. Director Parker continued, "However if it proves to be a wild goose chase, we will be holding you personally responsible and charge you for any cost we incur."

Peter looked up, startled and shocked, to see the Director with a hint of a smile.

"That's a joke, son. My associate has made a preliminary telephone call and we believe your information might be on target. I'm sure I don't need to tell you how sensitive this is and we would appreciate your discretion in mentioning it to anyone. You may tell your source, however, that we will be taking immediate action to apprehend Mr. Ratchford."

Director Parker stood up, shook hands with Peter and thanked him again.

"Sir, would it be possible for you to let me know when you apprehend him? It would put my mind at ease to know Sarah was safe."

"Yes, I think we could manage that. Good day to you."

Peter opened the front door and the three men exited quickly. He watched them get in the black cars, then slowly drive down the road. All the adrenaline pumping through his body rapidly vanished, and he was suddenly very tired. More than anything he wished he could talk to Sarah and tell her that she was about to get her life back. A tiny part of his soul wanted her to think of him as her hero, but of course, that would entail betraying Jonquil and he vowed not to do that. He would just have to let it all play out in God's time.

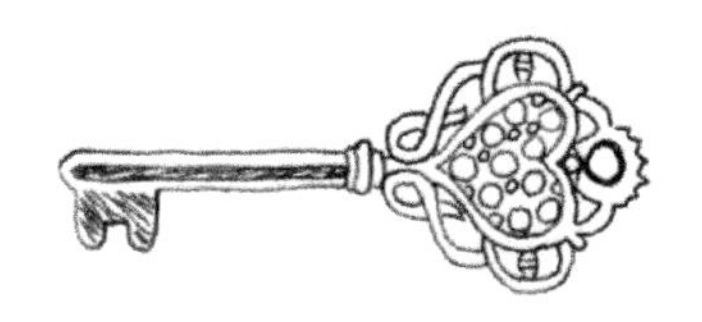

## *Chapter Forty-three*

# SARAH:

### *The Trauma Ends*

*Dear Peter,*

*This will be a short, but I couldn't wait to tell you. Sit down and take a deep breath–they found and arrested the man who shot my father! Liam says it's a complete miracle because they had no idea where he was, then suddenly they got a lead and found him and it's over! It's really over! My father just called and he will arrive in Shetland in a few days. His rehabilitation has gone so well, he will be released a little early. Can you believe this all happened so quickly? I have no idea where our lives go from here, but the important thing is I will be with my father again. Maybe God was watching over us after all.*

*I need to get this in the post right now because I can't wait for you to know. I'm so excited! I'll write again when I know more. Thank you, as always, for being my friend.*

*Sarah*

With the envelope sealed and stamped, Sarah handed it to Liam. He was going to Lerwick to pick up some supplies for the farm and offered to put it in the post.

"Do you want to ride with me?" Liam asked, "The threat is gone and you are free to come and go as you please. I know I am relieved, you must be as well."

"No, but thank you for asking. I know I'm safe, but it's almost become part of me to be wary. Every time the telephone rings, I'm terrified that something has happened to my father. I guess it will take time to adjust to being out of danger."

"Your feelings are not unheard of. A lot of soldiers come home from war to their lovely families who have no concept the trauma they've been through. The soldiers can't forget nor can they explain, it just takes time. You have had a miserable experience and it will take a while for you to learn to feel safe and confident again."

"How do you know all this?" she asked.

"You'd be surprised what I have been through, young lady," Liam said with a bit of humor that closed the door on any further discussion of his past. "Right now, let's focus on reuniting you with your father."

Spontaneously Sarah wrapped her arms around the waist of her tall, red-haired body guard.

"I honestly don't know what would've happened to me if your family hadn't taken me in. I hope someday I can repay you all for your kindness."

"Not necessary. You have pitched right in and been surprisingly helpful on the farm.

Everyone has enjoyed your being here, especially mum. I'm afraid we will miss you when you've gone."

"Thank you for saying that. You all feel like family and I'm going to be sad to leave. You know, I really never knew my mother, but I wish she had been just like your mum."

"I know she feels the same. Now, your father arrives day after tomorrow, and I've asked Mairi to join us for dinner so you can meet my fiancé before you leave," Liam smiled as he leaned close to Sarah. "And if you can keep a secret, we are going to announce a date for the wedding."

Sarah squealed with excitement, then lowered her voice.

"This is so exciting–all of it! You and Mairi, seeing my father, the end of our nightmare…" Sarah bubbled over, then a devastated look took over her face. "Oh, Liam! I just realized that you've been postponing your wedding plans in order to look after me. I am so sorry."

"Never you fret, my lass. Everything happens as it's supposed to.

I must be off to Lerwick and remember, keep a lid on our secret."

Sarah put her fingers up to her lips as though locking them with an imaginary key. She watched him drive away, realizing she liked being part of a big family. One day, God willing, she would be married with a houseful of kids. The very thought made her laugh out loud.

"Where did that come from?" She asked the empty room, and to her surprise, Liam's mother answered.

"Did you say something, Sarah dear?" She asked, walking in with a basketful of clean laundry.

"I was thinking out loud how grateful I am to know you."

Liam's mother opened her arms, and the two embraced for the first time. Sarah's barriers were crumbling and this sweet woman recognized it. Before she knew it, Sarah was weeping for no apparent reason, but for the first time in a long while she felt safe as Liam's mum comforted her. A runny nose ended the moment, quickly remedied by a lace hankie.

## Chapter Forty-four

# RICHARD:

*The Road Less Traveled*

Sunlight filtered through the bare winter trees, and the musty smell of last night's rain filled the air. It is said that one wanders through the woods to find tranquility. Nature often provides a soft clarity for finding answers to the confusions of life. Walking through the forest sanctuary, Richard was aware of a lone bird singing high above him. It sounded like a robin, declaring the first days of spring. Sensing motion to his left, Richard turned his attention to a small, red fox peering at him from behind the ferns and undergrowth. Neither he nor the fox moved a muscle, each sizing up the other. Finally, the fox, sensing no danger, turned away and disappeared with a flourish of his furry tail, as if to say, 'you're welcome here so long as you don't cause any trouble.'

There was much on Richard's mind that needed sorting. He knew decisions must be made sooner rather than later. News that Conrad Ratchford was in custody brought relief that was indescribable. The American Ambassador to Great Britain had paid a visit to Henley Manor to personally share this information and offer options for his future. He had assured Richard that Ratchford acted alone, and that his cohorts had vanished. The Ambassador also made it clear that he personally hoped Richard would stay with the Foreign Service, as his record was outstanding and his future was quite bright. They both agreed some time away would be beneficial to evaluate what lay ahead.

Naturally, he would include Sarah in the decision making. It was a bit of a shock to realize she would be going off to university before long, following her own life's journey. How had his little girl grown up so quickly? The thought of being alone put a new wrinkle in planning the next chapter of his life. His work in Foreign Service was fulfilling and he was good at it, but it was a very demanding career. Did he have the energy and desire to tackle another assignment? It wasn't fair to take on a job with anything less than a full commitment. Maybe he was still tired and weary from his recovery, and would bounce back. Or perhaps not. On the other hand, if he left after all these years, what would he do? Financially, he didn't have to work, thanks to his inheritance, but he was never one to be idle. His thoughts were bouncing around his brain like a pinball machine.

Making his way across the wide lawn toward Henley Manor, he noticed the small purple and yellow crocus flowers blooming. A new season was beginning and things were about to change–what an accurate metaphor for his life. While being shot was not for the faint of heart, his time at Henley Manor had certainly changed his perspective of things. He had made friends with several of the fellow patients and hoped to keep in touch when they went their separate ways. It was an interesting bond that seemed to occur when men were vulnerable, each fighting to heal and win their health battles. It must be somewhat like the camaraderie that took place during war. They cheered one another's little victories, and were supportive when times were difficult. They were a team. This was new to him.

Of course, meeting Lady Rose was in a category all its own in terms of changing his life. The events that led up to his being sent to Henley Manor were uncanny. You couldn't write that in a Hollywood script. What were the odds of meeting his father's former girlfriend while in rehab from gunshot wounds? His mother would say it was God's divine hand. How he wished he could share all of this with her.

As he walked through the tall french doors into the drawing room, Richard was met by Brian, one of the young aides who served the patients.

"Did you enjoy your walk, sir?" Brian asked.

"Very much, indeed, thank you." Richard replied, hanging his outdoor coat on a nearby hook. "Spring never ceases to be a wonder after the cold, gray days of winter. I hope you find time to warm your face in the sun today."

"I do as well, sir. By the way, there is someone in the front room to see you. Would you like me to bring in tea?"

"That would be very nice, thank you. Brian."

A familiar face looked up as he entered the room, and graced him with a warm smile. Richard took her outstretched, gloved hands in his and sat across from his friend.

"Lady Rose. I'm glad you received my note. I was afraid it wouldn't reach you in time."

"The postman is very good about bringing my mail promptly. It arrives so quickly, I sometimes wonder if he follows all the postal rules. But never mind about that. Tell me what has happened. I'm guessing it must be good news."

For the next few minutes, Richard relayed the story as he knew it. There were still gaps to be filled in, but no matter, nothing could dim the feeling that both he and Sarah were safe and could return to their lives. Lady Rose shared his high spirits, with a slight hint of sadness.

"I make no secret that I shall miss our visits, but I am quite pleased for you. Where do you go from here?"

"I leave tomorrow to meet my daughter, Sarah, and then…truthfully, I don't know what I'm going to do with the rest of my life," he answered, surprised that those words fell out of his mouth.

"Well. Is this a private conflict, or can anyone join in?" she asked with a wry smile.

"Your guidance is most welcome, in fact, much needed."

He reached in his pocket and produced a small, leather bound volume of poetry.

"Have you ever heard of the American poet Robert Frost?"

"No, I'm not familiar with your Mr. Frost."

"He wrote a poem about a road less traveled. May I read it to you?"

"Of course."

Opening it to a bookmarked page, he began.

*Two roads diverged in a yellow wood,*
*And sorry I could not travel both*
*And be one traveler, long I stood*
*And looked down one as far as I could*
*To where it bent in the undergrowth;*

*Then took the other, as just as fair,*
*And having perhaps the better claim,*
*Because it was grassy and wanted wear;*
*Though as for that the passing there*
*Had worn them really about the same,*

*And both that morning equally lay*
*In leaves no step had trodden black.*
*Oh, I kept the first for another day!*
*Yet knowing how way leads on to way,*
*I doubted if I should ever come back.*

*I shall be telling this with a sigh*
*Somewhere ages and ages hence:*
*Two roads diverged in a wood, and I—*
*I took the one less traveled by,*
*And that has made all the difference.*

Lady Rose was silent. Richard closed the book and lay it on the table.

"This poem was published in 1916 when Europe was immersed in World War I, and within a year the United States would join them. Here we are decades later and the message is still as relevant. I don't know which road would be best." He searched the face of the older woman seated across from him, yearning for her to direct him. "I trust your judgement, Lady Rose, and I need help with this decision. Which road should I take?"

Lady Rose was contemplative before answering.

"Well, young Duncan, what road, in your world, would be the one less traveled?"

It was Richard's turn to be quiet and give thought. She leaned in closer, with her hand on top on her cane to steady her frail body. Her words were spoken softly and she looked directly into his eyes.

"What is your passion, Richard? What is it that sings to your soul? Is there more to accomplish with the Foreign Service or have you come to the end of that journey? Do you have financial needs you must fulfill?"

"No, we are financially secure and I've really no need to work, but I'm not very good at doing nothing."

"Then is there something burning in your heart that you want to pursue? I have found life without passion is merely surviving. My only advice would be to surrender to your dream, honor that spirit and let it lead you. Do not be influenced by what others might think or boulders that block your path. I won't presume to ask where your passions lay, but I do urge you to let your mind open up to all possibilities. From my perspective, I can tell you life is very fleeting."

With that simple answer, delivered by someone who had experienced so much in life, the fog lifted from his mind. Yes, it was time to consider how he really wanted to spend his remaining time on this earth.

"Lady Rose, you just gave me permission to dream. It's been a long time since I've traveled that road. Thank you."

"You silly boy, you just gave yourself permission to dream. Now, go pursue it, but do promise you will stay in touch. I will wait anxiously to hear what you and your beautiful Sarah decide. Promise you will pay me a visit before too long. Oh, before I forget…"

She reached in her small purse and produced an envelope with his name on it.

"This is the name of your half-sister. I was able to come up with it from old friends. The last they heard she had married and was living on the Shetland Island mainland. It is an island quite far off the northern coast of Scotland, if you're not familiar with the name."

"Shetland? Did you really say Shetland? Shetland Island?"

"As I'm not aware of losing my mind, I'm quite sure that's what I said."

"Sarah is staying on Shetland right now. That's where I am going tomorrow! That is absolutely....unbelievable!"

"Life is full of surprises, my boy. Why does that always astonish us?" she asked, struggling a little to rise from her chair.

"You, Lady Elizabeth Margaret Rose are one of my favorite people in the world!"

Grinning broadly, Richard offered his arm to the elegant, elderly lady and they slowly walked toward the front door.

"And you, Richard Duncan, are the same. What a blessing you are to an old woman with young memories."

He bent down and kissed her wrinkled cheek. A moment later Jamie Rose was at her side and led her to the waiting car. Richard waved until they were out of sight at the end of the long

driveway. He felt for the envelope in his jacket pocket.

"Well, I'll be. Life is indeed full of surprises."

## Chapter Forty-five

# LIAM:

## *That Dreadful Ferry*

Standing at the dock waiting for the ferry to arrive, the wind swirled around and brought a chill to Liam Morrison. He felt a strong sense of anticipation as the big boat bounced up and down on the waves coming into the harbor. In a few minutes he would greet his client, a man who had become a close friend, and who, by the way, had almost been killed on Liam's watch. Security personnel were taught to keep a professional distance from clients, but given what they had been through, Liam couldn't help but feel close to him.

The first glimpse of Richard Duncan confirmed his thought that the ferry boat might have had a turbulent crossing. It was interesting how a person's face could literally turn a slight shade of green after a rough 12-hour overnight ride. The ferry must have had encountered the infamous "roost" between Fair Isle and Sumburgh, where two tidal streams meet in the gap between the islands with undesirable effects for the passengers on the ferry. As anxious as he was for Richard to like Shetland, it would probably be best to let the man get his feet on solid ground before touring him around the sights. Besides, Sarah was waiting impatiently for them to get back to the farm, and he was sure Richard would be eager to see his daughter. The friends clasped hands like long lost mates, and Liam got both Richard and his luggage in the old car.

"If the only way off this island is to take that ferry again, I may *never* leave!" Richard exclaimed with great emphasis on the word 'never.'

The car lurched ahead as Liam struggled to get it into the proper gear.

"That bad, eh?"

"Beyond bad. I cannot think of a word in the English language to articulate how…bad. Seriously, it makes getting shot feel like a walk in the park. There was not a moment in twelve hours that was calm. You people are hardy sorts."

"I've taken that ferry my entire life, and I cannot imagine what you're talking about," Liam replied, trying to disguise his amusement.

"That is possibly the first untruth you have ever told me."

"Aye, you're right about that. To be honest, the ferry ride can be a horrid ordeal, but not always. I've been on it when the sea is glassy and the stars feel so close you could touch them. I'm sorry you had the worst of it. It's not quite the introduction to Shetland I had hoped for. I think you'll find Sarah quite likes it here."

"Did you bring her here on that wretched ferry?" Richard asked, a little alarmed.

"No, we flew with my cousin who has a charter airplane."

"And you are just now telling me about your cousin with an airplane? After twelve hours of unimaginable horror on the open seas?"

Liam laughed and suggested Richard and Sarah might want to arrange to fly back to Inverness, if and when they leave Shetland.

"I think you will be surprised, sir, at how much Sarah has fit right in with our family and with the work on the farm. Since she is so advanced in her school work, there wasn't much she could be taught at her current level. The administrators were reluctant to move her ahead, not knowing how long she would be here. I'm sure you are aware what an extraordinary daughter you have, but seeing her courage throughout this ordeal has been quite incredible."

"I'll not disagree with you. She really is something special." Richard looked out the window of the old Land Rover. "Liam, I'm not sure I will ever be able to thank you and your family for taking such good care of her. The situation happened so fast and I was completely helpless. For years it has just been the two of us and it never dawned on me that I needed a back up plan. I always thought I would be able to protect her. Laying in the hospital, my biggest consolation was knowing my Sarah was safe."

"Sir…about the shooting…"

"Please call me Richard. Our relationship is certainly more personal than professional at this point."

Liam took a deep breath and kept his eyes on the road as they traveled through the rolling hills. His words came slowly.

"Richard…about the…incident…" There was a long pause before he continued. "I feel completely responsible for what transpired. In recreating the entire sequence of events again and again in my head, for the life of me I cannot sort how it came about. We had searched the area, watched the crowd, and there was no sign of anything out of the ordinary. How could this have happened? I'm so sorry."

These were thoughts and emotions that haunted Liam and he had to share them with Richard, maybe in the hopes of easing his own pain. They drove on in silence before Richard spoke.

"One of the things I've learned in getting older is sometimes you get a bit wiser. The last few months I've had time to ponder what happened, both before, during and after. There are a few things I want, actually I need, to tell you. First of all, in no way are you to blame for what happened and I mean that. You willingly gave up your holiday to stay and protect us, and we had one of the most wonderful Christmas times I can remember thanks to you and Mrs. McAughtrie. Liam, if there is larceny in someone's heart, there is nothing you can do to stop it. Conrad Ratchford was not going to be denied his revenge. It's as simple as that. From what I heard, if you hadn't stepped toward me seconds before he fired, the shots could have been fatal. But you did and they weren't. You graciously brought my daughter to safety with your family and stayed by her side safeguarding her from harm. Other than booking me on that dreadful ferry, you are pretty much a hero in my book."

"I don't know what to say. I hardly feel like a hero."

"My mother taught me that God always brings good out of bad in every situation, and I definitely have seen that in this case. There are things that happened, and people I met while I was at Henley

Manor that are life changing. I can't imagine any other way these connections would have come about. Oh, before I forget, there is someone on Shetland I want to look up. I'm hoping you know everyone on Shetland and can help me find a certain woman."

"Oh, a woman? A certain woman. This is getting interesting." Liam couldn't help teasing his friend, and he was glad to change the subject. Richard's words did go a long way toward healing his self-esteem and confirming his opinion that Sarah's father was about as a fine man as he'd ever known.

The aging green Land Rover Defender hardly came to a stop when Sarah came running out of the house and into her father's arms. After tears and several bone crunching hugs, Liam led the way inside. It was still fairly early in the day and the rest of the family were off doing chores, or in the case of the younger girls, attending school. It had been agreed that they would all gather for dinner at the table that had already been set. Richard was given Liam's bedroom, and in turn Liam would sleep in the front room on the couch. Richard protested, but was met with Shetland stubbornness and a gracious sense of hospitality. It was obvious his friend was exhausted and Liam suggested he take a little rest. Then if there was time before dinner they would get back in the old Land Rover and tour around the farm so Richard could see first hand the beauty of Shetland Island.

# *Chapter Forty-six*

# SARAH:

## *Treasured New Books*

Momentarily forgotten in the absolute elation of seeing her father was the box wrapped in brown paper and tied with string that Liam brought her from the Lerwick Post Office. Sarah saw that it was from Peter, and must be books by the weight of it. With her father upstairs taking a rest, and Liam busy with farm work, it was a perfect time to unwrap the parcel in private.

As she hoped, four books each individually wrapped in brown paper filled the box along with an envelope with her name on it. Seeing Peter's handwriting still gave her a thrill. What an thoughtful friend she had found. Did things happen by chance or was their meeting a divine appointment, as her dear grandmother would say? It was so easy to believe in God when things were going well.

*Dear Sarah,*

*What wonderful news your letter brings! This horrific nightmare is finally over for you and your father. I imagine you must be filled with so many emotions. One day I will share an interesting story pertaining to all of this. I'm sure I am premature in asking, but do you have any idea of your plans? Do you know if you will be returning to Edinburgh anytime in the next few weeks? I'm asking not only for the hope of seeing you in person, but I have a bit of news myself. I will be leaving for Italy in a week or two, and might be gone for up to a year. An opportunity to study abroad arose suddenly and the honor of being chosen was too great to pass up. I'll try to write more as the details become clear.*

*I have enclosed several books that I found at my favorite booksellers in Edinburgh last week. It is a marvelous little shoppe in Old Town with a treasure trove of old and rather well-priced books. The first is two stories by Jane Austen in one volume, 'Northanger Abbey' and 'Persuasion' by titles. My sister has always enjoyed Jane Austen, though I know not everyone is a fan. This particular book was once part of a full set, but lost its way and became separated. It's a reprint from 1933 and in good condition. What especially caught my attention is that the illustrations in this version were done by Hugh Thomson, who is a fascinating character and one of the most famous illustrators during the late nineteenth century. You would enjoy researching him. The second book is 'The Fair Maiden of Perth' by Edinburgh's own Sir Walter Scott. Everyone who lives in our city should own at least one Scott novel. This is the story about the Battle of the North Inch in the 1400's, following the adventures of Henry Gow and the Fair Maiden. One of my favorite things about Sir Walter Scott was his love for the Scottish Border country. He used to live in a fabulous house called Ashlestiel on the banks of the River Tweed, where he wrote a number of his famous books. It isn't very far from Elibank, my grandparents land and the lovely river where we fish. Thirdly, I came across a little book that relates to nothing except that the author's name reminded me of your father's name. I also loved the blue cover with the sporting green vintage Rolls Royce motor car gliding past an exotic tall tree with fly fisherman in a body of water next to the road. Not sure there's much interesting reading inside. Lastly, I've enclosed a journal book with blank pages for you to fill with your brilliant writings.*

*As I close, I realize that shortly it will be more difficult for us to communicate. Until we know where each of us might end up, I suggest you send your next letter here in the hopes of it being sent on. If you find out your next location, please drop me a note. I can't help but feel that this is a change in our friendship, which is a little distressing, but let's do try to stay in touch.*

*Fondly,*
*Peter*

She folded the letter and carefully placed it back in the envelope, then gently unwrapped each book one at a time. It was almost spiritual feeling the old leather bindings, and thumbing through the yellowing, aged pages. A scrap of paper fell out of the Jane Austen book, and landed near her foot. It was Peter's hastily written note with the location of the bookseller in Edinburgh. He had made a special trip there to find books just for her. The lump in her throat became almost impassible and the tear in her right eye slid down her face, landing on the cover of Sir Walter Scott's Fair Maiden.

What was she to do? She could not demand her father take them back to Edinburgh immediately like a spoiled child so she could see a friend who was about to walk out of her life. She knew in her heart if she asked he would try to accommodate her wish. Though Richard Duncan looked the picture of health, he was still in recovery and had been cautioned to take it easy. The ferry trip to Scotland alone must have taken a lot out of him. The alternative was not seeing Peter for a long time, or maybe never again. Thoughts of her window friend were one of the secret pastimes that kept her going when days were difficult. With a deep breath, Sarah Duncan took a big step toward adulthood, and decided to not mention anything to anyone about Peter and follow whatever her father had decided. Her blessings were abundant, her father was alive and well, and that was more than enough for now.

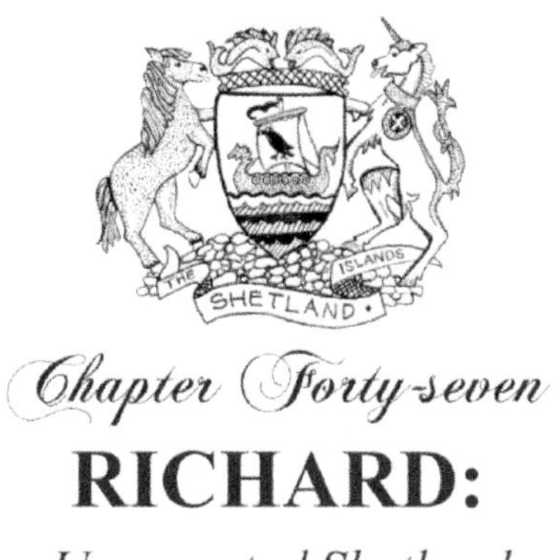


*Chapter Forty-seven*

# RICHARD:

*Unexpected Shetland*

When Liam used to talk about his family home, Richard had absolutely no recollection of him referring to a stately, two story stone house situated in a green meadow with a view of the sea in the distance. It wasn't an overly large house, but obviously quite old and well taken care of. Thinking again how kind the Morrison family had been to Sarah, and even now Liam giving up his bedroom, it was almost overwhelming. How could he ever repay them? Shaking the cobwebs out of his brain from his nap, he took note of his surroundings in the small, but comfortable bedroom. The walls were whitewashed which helped keep it bright, and a nice sized window gave a view of the countryside. It was nearly dark outside now, but Richard could tell the scenery was unusual. An antique armoire with a mirror on the door, a worn wooden desk and the bed situated under the sloping ceiling gave the room an intimate, warm feel. He smiled thinking of the tall, lanky Liam growing up in this room.

He closed the door and walked the narrow hallway to the stairs. With his leg injury not completely healed, maneuvering steps was still a bit of a challenge. Holding the handrail, he made it down the steep stairway without incident. Liam was sitting by the fireplace in the main sitting room reading a newspaper. Even though spring was evident, there remained a chill in the air and the burning fire in the fireplace lent much needed warmth.

"Are you feeling a bit better, sir?" Liam asked, putting the newspaper aside.

"Yes, thank you. I slept longer than I expected and it's Richard. I'm quite sure we settled that."

"Well, I wasn't positive after your ferry ride if you were still speaking to me," Liam teased.

"Oh, please do not remind me!" Richard said with mock horror. "Where is everyone?"

"My parents and sisters are finishing up the chores, and Sarah is in the kitchen seeing to dinner."

"Sarah? Cooking? I think I had better see this firsthand."

The kitchen was toward the rear of the house, and larger than Richard expected. A well-used, Aga cooker had several covered pots simmering, and the door of the top oven was opened revealing a perfectly browned, enormous pie. The delicious smells reminded him of how hungry he was. Sarah was stirring something in a large bowl, and hadn't heard them come in.

"Sarah Sunshine! Look at you, queen of the kitchen! "

The wooden spoon dropped and his beautiful daughter hugged him fiercely. He didn't think he would ever tire of seeing her face. She in turn was slow to release him from her grip, then words fell out of her mouth with hardly a breath.

"You're finally awake! How are you feeling? Everyone is out and I am in charge of the final preparations for our dinner. Oh! I'm so happy you're here! Can you believe it? Me? Getting dinner ready?"

"I can see a lot has changed in these few months. You look the very much at home in the kitchen. Mrs. McAughtrie would be quite pleased."

"Mrs. Morrison actually did most of the cooking, and showed me the last minute things to do. They should be here anytime…"

The words had hardly left her lips when the back door into the mudroom burst open and three lively young ladies came in, hanging up well-worn jackets, and kicking off mud-caked Wellies. Richard watched the good-natured teasing and laughing, getting a glimpse of what Sarah found so appealing in this close knit family. Not for the first time did he feel a twinge of guilt over the nomad life he had given Sarah. The oldest young lady looked up and saw Richard for the first time.

"Hello. You must be Sarah's father. I would shake your hand, but I'm afraid I've not washed up yet. My name is Davina, this is the middle sister Emily, and the youngest, Ava."

Each girl inclined her head towards him as her name was spoken. He could feel their friendly, unabashed curiosity looking him over from head to toe.

"I'm Richard Duncan and I'm very glad to meet all of you. Sarah has told me how kind you've been during her stay."

That caused some blushing and smiling, and a little embarrassment. As if prompted, Liam came through the door arms laden with peat for the fire.

"Out of the way, girls. You're holding up my progress. It's looking to be a might chilly tonight and we don't want the fire to dawdle."

The group of girls parted so Liam could continue on to the fireplace. As the two youngest walked upstairs, Emily spoke in a loud whisper.

"Isn't he handsome?"

That was met by giggles and more whispering. The last one up the stairs, Davina spoke to anyone who was listening.

"I'm suppose to tell you to sit for dinner when it's ready. Mum and Dad will be home shortly but didn't want us to wait. And Liam, don't forget to pick up Mairi."

"Dinner in ten minutes," Sarah answered in a loud voice with great authority.

Liam groaned as he set the peat in the fireplace.

"I'll be back shortly. I don't know where my head is today."

With everyone gone in their separate directions, Richard sat down near the fireplace in a well worn stuffed chair. After being on Shetland, and in the Morrison's house, for less than twelve hours he was surprised at how comfortable he felt. Thinking back on the complicated turn of events that led Liam into their lives, thus leading he and Sarah to Shetland, it could only be a heavenly plan. It didn't take much to realize that taking Sarah away from this pleasant environment was going to be yet another disruption. His thoughts were interrupted when Ava, the youngest sister approached him.

"Might I share a word with you, Mr Duncan?" She spoke very quietly so he had to strain to hear her. This was a far cry from the laughing girl that had come through just a few minutes ago.

"Of course, Ava. Please sit down."

Richard could see the girl was a little troubled and unsure of herself. She looked around surreptitiously, then sat on a low footstool very near him so she could continue to whisper.

"I'm not sure I should be telling you this, but I'm so very fond of Sarah. She has become as close as a sister and I would never want her to think I was going behind her back."

Richard waited for her continue.

"You see, we've been sharing a room, and....it's just that sometimes, in the middle of the night she wakes up very frightened. It's happened more than once and I don't want her to be scared and sad."

Richard was deeply touched by the young girl's obvious concern for Sarah.

"You must care very much about her to worry so. I don't know what Liam has told you, Ava, but I was shot by an angry man with a gun and Sarah was standing by my side. Then she was whisked away not knowing if I was dead or alive to a place she had never been before. I can't imagine how terrible that was for her. We are the only family left. I am all she has, and she is all I have. I don't wonder that she might be sad and emotional."

"Actually, Liam told us briefly what had happened, and I could never have be as brave as she has been." The young girl leaned in closer, "But I think it's about her mum. She kept calling out for her."

Richard was silent, heartsick that Sarah's nightmares had come back. With all that had happened the past year, she had not mentioned them, nor had he heard her call out like she used to. In all honesty, he had forgotten. To think his sweet daughter had been dealing with this all by herself was unconscionable. He wasn't sure how to explain the story of Sarah's mother to this sweet lass looking up at him.

"Thank you very much for telling me..."

The conversation was interrupted by Liam's parents arriving and the remaining sisters coming back downstairs. A moment later Liam and a petite red-haired young lady came through the door holding hands and all smiles. Brief introductions were begun by Liam's father.

"It is a glé pleasure to meet you, Mr. Duncan. Liam has spoken well of you."

Mark Morrison was tall and strong, and rather imposing. His ruddy complexion was in contrast to his very soft blue eyes, and Richard suspected that this large Scotsman had a heart of gold.

"Well, thank you, but I believe I owe my life and that of my daughter to your son, and will certainly always hold him in the highest regard. I am honored to call him my friend."

"I can see where your lass gets her charm, Mr. Duncan," Mark answered with a smile. "May I introduce my wife?"

The beautiful woman before him hardly looked old enough to have grown daughters.

"Mrs. Morrison, it is a pleasure to meet you and to thank you in person for taking care of Sarah."

"Please, Mr. Duncan, my friends call me Anje, and I've become very fond of your Sarah. It has been a delight to have her. She fits right in with the sisters, always so helpful. It is my hope she will always feel welcome here."

"Thank you. As a parent I'm sure you must know how deep my gratitude is."

"May I call you Richard? I do feel as though I know you after all we've heard from Liam and Sarah."

It was easy to see why his daughter would be captivated by the love and warmth of the Morrison family. Of course, they must get on with their lives, but for today they would enjoy the gift of togetherness.

"I would much prefer that," he answered.

Sarah announced dinner was ready and nine people gathered at the long table.

"Richard, please sit next to Sarah, and Mairi, I see you're planted next to Liam," Anje Morrison instructed.

"Mark? The blessing?" Anje asked.

Liam's father looked lovingly at his wife, "Yes, my lovely lass."

*'Bless this house and those within*
*Bless our giving and receiving*
*Bless our words and conversation*
*Bless our hands and recreation*
*Bless our sowing and our growing*
*Bless our coming and our going*
*Bless all who enter and depart*
*Bless this house your peace impart.'*

The simple blessing was a balm to Richard's heart, as though it had been written especially for this occasion. There was no time for contemplation as lively conversations broke out immediately covering a range of topics from weather, farm life to an upcoming church festival. It was still hard for him to believe that Sarah had been involved in preparing such a feast. Tattie soup, Saat Beef and Shetland Bannocks, with roasted black potatoes (which he was told again 'were really blue not black, with yellow inside'). As dinner wound down, Liam cleared his throat, to which no one payed any attention. Repeating the action a little louder, there was still no response. By the third time, Anje inquired if he was coming down with something.

"Liam, have you caught a chill?" she asked.

Judging by the blush that quickly hit his hairline, this was not the problem. He gently tapped his glass with his knife.

"If I may have everyone's attention…"

Conversations ceased and all looked curiously at Liam as he stood up. Mairi took hold of his hand as if to give him courage. Richard was amused watching his seemingly unflappable bodyguard suddenly looked like a naughty schoolboy.

"Well…the thing is…Mairi and I have spoken to the vicar and both he and the church are available next weekend…for our wedding." Before anyone could reply, he rushed on. "I know it seems very sudden, but most of the preparations are complete, and Mairi's mum and dad have agreed, and it would be a shame for Sarah and

Richard to miss our wedding, wouldn't it? So, what do you say? Mum? Dad?"

Richard watched Mark and Anje exchange a glance that could only be described as loving amusement at their only son. Mark stood up straight and looked around the silent table.

"I don't think we want Richard to have to take that ferry ride again quite so soon…so yes, we agree with your plan, lad."

An uproar began with all the women gathering at one end of the table to talk about the details of the wedding, Sarah included. This left the three men to reposition themselves at the other end of the table for a celebratory dram of whiskey.

"You will stay, won't you?" Liam asked. "It would mean a great deal to all of us. You're practically family."

"We wouldn't miss it, and I'm honored you would move the date up to accommodate us."

Liam's face returned to the deep pink blush.

"Well, that might not be the only reason…"

Richard laughed and gave his former bodyguard a wink and a firm handshake. Mark returned with a bottle of 1937 Glenfiddich whiskey and Richard gave a low whistle in appreciation.

"Mark, there were only 60 bottles of 1937 Glenfiddich made."

"And how might you know about Scotch Whiskey, coming from America?" Mark countered curiously.

"When I was at the Embassy in London, Charlie Gordon came by for a visit to talk about his plans to market the family whiskey in the States. He's quite an interesting gentleman with an intriguing history. It turns out he was stationed in Malta with the Royal Navy during the war, and I had a short stay in Malta with the Foreign Service. We hit it off immediately and he gave the Embassy a bottle of 1937 Glenfiddich, which my superior promptly took control of."

"The rascal," Mark said as he opened the bottle and poured out a dram for each man.

Mark raised his glass for a quiet toast, "To my only son, may your marriage be as happy as your parent's has been."

Even though Richard was a light drinker, one sip of this dark amber whisky was unlike anything he had ever tasted.

"Aye, I see you can taste the difference in this fine whisky," Mark said. "It's smooth with a trace of dark roasted coffee, bitter chocolate and heather. Can you sense the edge of tobacco smokiness?"

"Aye, I can," Richard answered, adopting the Scottish way of speaking.

The liquor warmed his body, but the easy friendship of the Morrison family warmed his soul.

Liam took a sip of the fine Glenfiddich and turned to his father.

"There is something we need to discuss, Dad. By moving up the wedding, and adjusting all the plans, we cannot invite the entire island of Shetland. We are limited to only 75 people total from both families."

"That's not so easy, lad. I've lived here my whole life and know about everyone."

"That I know!" answered Liam, "That I know!"

Suddenly, Richard remembered the envelope in his jacket pocket and withdrew what Lady Rose had given him. The abrupt move caught the attention of the two men, who stopped their conversation and looked at him.

"I'm sorry to change topics, but may I inquire if you know a woman who I've heard lives on Shetland?"

Mark took another sip of his whisky, and responded with a good-hearted laugh.

"You've been here nigh on twelve hours and you're looking for a woman?"

Richard was immediately embarrassed and looked to see if Sarah had heard, which of course, she had. All conversation stopped and he was the center of attention. Setting down the small glass of whisky, he began to mentally prepare to tell this story as simply as possible. It was not a simple story.

By now everyone in the room had abandoned wedding talk, anticipating what they were about to hear. He looked to Sarah first.

"I had intended on sharing this with you privately before making it public, but as I see the friendship around this table, I hope you will forgive me telling the story to everyone."

Watching his daughter closely, he could see the wheels of her mind spinning as she tried to sort what on earth he could be talking about. Looking back at him, Sarah took a deep breath.

"I trust you. I think..." she answered trying to lighten the moment.

"I'll try to keep this as straightforward as possible, it's a bit complicated. You see, I never knew my father as he left when I was quite young. My mother told me very little about him and I never asked. After a few years she married a wonderful gentleman who was everything I could have ever wanted or needed as a father. My real father rarely crossed my mind. When I had my recent...accident, for want of a better word, I was sent to a special rehabilitation facility outside of London. It had formerly been a lovely country estate, owned by an aristocratic family. While I was there, an older woman, Lady Elizabeth Rose, sought me out. The estate had belonged to her in years past, and she enjoyed coming by now and then to chat with the patients–mostly RAF pilots. I could not imagine why she singled me out or why I intrigued her, until she told me that my name was similar to that of an old flame from her youth. Well, it turned out that her old flame, who became her fiancé...was my father."

There was a gasp all around the table.

"Of course, this was all years before he married my mother. To continue on, her fiancé went off to finish his last year of university, when shockingly she got word that he had married someone else."

"The scoundrel!" exclaimed Mark, totally caught up in the story.

"Sadly, a while later his young wife died in childbirth. The daughter survived, but was given to relatives to be raised as their daughter."

"That poor lass," Anje whispered with compassion. "Not knowing her mother or her father."

Liam, being one step ahead of everyone, interrupted his mother.

"That means you have a half-sister you never knew about!"

"Is that true? We have family?" Sarah gasped.

"I am hoping so. It's been many years, and she may not welcome us, given the situation. Lady Rose gave me her name and indicated the last information she had was the woman lived somewhere on

Shetland Island."

Mark was intrigued. "And what might this woman's name be? I know nearly everyone."

The sisters laughed, well aware of their father's bent on exaggeration.

"It's written on this paper. I can't figure how to pronounce it. I know there's little chance you would know her, but the coincidence of her living on Shetland is a small ray of hope."

Richard handed the card to Mark, and attention shifted to Liam's father as he read it. Sarah reached for her father's hand and squeezed it. A look of total shock came across Mark's face as he silently read and reread the name. He looked up and opened his mouth to speak, but closed it without uttering a word. Finally, he addressed Richard.

"Are you sure this is the name?"

"Yes. Lady Rose seemed certain of it. Is it someone dreadful?"

He'd been so overwhelmed at the thought of connecting with a long lost relative, it hadn't crossed his mind that perhaps his half-sister was someone notorious or even a criminal.

Mark burst out laughing.

"No. No, indeed. It is someone quite wonderful."

"Someone you know, Father?" Davina asked excitedly.

"Mark, you must tell us who it is," Anje urged her husband. "Don't keep us in suspense."

"Well, the name written here is… Azjanae Clark-Petterson."

Without hesitation Anje answered.

"But that's MY name."

## *Chapter Forty-eight*

# SARAH:

### *You Won't Believe This!*

*Dear Peter,*

*My mind feels like it is about to explode! I have so much to tell you and don't know where to begin. There is a very good chance this letter may make no sense whatsoever. It is well past two in the morning and I'm sitting in a large chair by the fireplace with only a candle for light. The last bits of a peat fire are sending out smoke curls, making the room seem very surreal. Given all that has happened tonight, it's quite appropriate. Everyone has finally gone to bed, though I doubt there will be much sleep, but I'll get back to that.*

*It has been a monumental day. The box of books you sent arrived today, along with my father. He looks wonderfully normal with only a slight limp as a reminder of all he's been through. I must remember that he tires easily and shouldn't do too much. The books are a very welcome surprise as I have read nearly everything here at least twice. I'm not familiar with the two Jane Austen books, and look forward to starting them. I've been anxious to read something by Sir Walter Scott and this sounds like a good one. The blank journal is absolutely perfect as I've so many thoughts to write down. I agree with you that the author of the motor car book shares a name very close to my father's. I'll show him the book tomorrow and I'm sure he will find it interesting. Thank you for your overwhelming thoughtfulness and generosity.*

*Now, what I am about to tell you is about as astonishing and amazing and fantastic as you could ever imagine. Right now, in my mind, I'm trying to simplify this story, which is exactly what my father said as it all unfolded earlier tonight. You might need to get a cup of tea and settle in while I try to explain. It seems my father's father (my grandfather) had been married before he married my grandmother, which no one knew about. His first wife died soon after having a child, and the baby girl was given to relatives to raise. As she grew up she knew very little about her real parents and simply accepted that she had been adopted. Through a recent chance meeting, my father found out about his half sister, and then discovered, to his surprise, that she might live on Shetland Island. At dinner tonight he asked Liam's family if they knew the woman, thinking maybe Shetland was small enough for them to recognize her name. Much to everyone's shock, my father's half-sister is Liam's mother, Anje! Can you believe it? She is the most caring, loving woman you can imagine. This means we have a real family! I have an aunt and an uncle, and four cousins! This must sound a bit odd to you as you've always had relatives around you. But I still can't believe it, nor can anyone else. I can't explain this miracle except to thank God. I guess He hasn't forgotten me. Our family (I'll never tire of saying that) talked until they were too tired to utter another word, and finally all went to bed. I was too excited to sleep and couldn't wait to share this with you.*

*Forgive me for writing all about me. The news that you are going to Italy for a year is intriguing. It made me realize that much of your life is a mystery to me. Have you told me or given hints that I didn't understand? Or maybe I'm just not as bright as I think I am. You mentioned that you will 'study abroad,' but I'm not sure I know all that entails. I feel a little embarrassed by my ignorance. The important thing is it seems to be something you are very much looking forward to and I am delighted that you are delighted. I must admit I feel I will be losing a big part of my life when you go. The lateness of the hour must be making me terribly bold. I truly am excited for you.*

*As always, thank you for being my friend, and for the lovely books. I'll send this letter to your home and look forward to hearing about your adventure.*

*Best,*
*Sarah*

*P.S. My candle just went out–good night, my friend.*

# Chapter Forty-nine
# PETER:
## *Who's Idea Was This?*

Why was life so much scarier in the middle of the night? Peter tossed and turned unable to sleep. He listened intently to the clock ticking as though the rhythmic marking of time would calm the tumultuous thoughts in his brain. What was he thinking when he said yes to spending at least a year as a student in Italy with this strange man he hardly knew? Adventure was one thing, but rumors churned about this man's reputation for being cynical, pessimistic, hard to please and outright mean. On the other hand he was charming, charismatic, and world famous.

Everything inside Peter wanted to beg off and keep on with his work. If his parents hadn't made such a big deal about it, he might have done just that. Instead, an Edinburgh newspaper asked to interview him for a front page article, and his ego was inflated to capacity. Somehow, he had gotten lost in all the prestige of the opportunity, but now he merely felt insecure and unhappy, like a little boy who was being sent away against his will to a dreadful, boarding school. The pounding of his headache kept time with the clock.

In his heart, Peter knew that leaving was only part of his turmoil. The letter from Sarah had arrived yesterday, and while he was dumbfounded by the coincidence of Liam's mother being her father's half-sister, there was a small, selfish bit of him that felt like Sarah didn't need him any longer. Now she had a family to share her life with and his importance would be diminished. The immaturity of this thought stunned him, but he really enjoyed his exchanges with the smart, funny, inquisitive young lady and found he rather liked having someone to think about, even to worry about. Their connection revealed a side of Peter he thought had been lost. It was completely intentional that he hadn't revealed much about himself to Sarah. She responded to him so innocently and honestly and he relished that. He hadn't had that luxury in several years. Past experiences had wounded him and he was wary of getting too close to anyone. Somehow Sarah was different. He trusted her and that made this all the more difficult. He found himself angry with her and wasn't sure why. In fact, he felt mad at the whole world, which made no sense whatsoever. The clock, like a metronome, continued to punctuate passing moments in a rush that couldn't be stopped.

Morning arrived with an overcast, dark gray sky and the usual spring drizzle. He pasted-on good cheer, and said good bye to his parents at the front door. He reasoned it would be easier to take a cab and not prolong his parting. The driver took his leather satchel and small suitcase, and put them in the trunk of the car. Peter waved a final goodbye to life as he had known it.

"Going far, lad?" the cab driver asked.

"Maybe too far," Peter answered cryptically.

Florence, Italy felt like it was on another planet.

## Chapter Fifty

# SARAH:

*Palm Court Tea Room*

The North British Railway Hotel was located in the heart of Edinburgh, and was the perfect place for Sarah and her father to spend a few days. Originally built in 1902 to entice wealthy railway passengers north to Scotland, no expense had been spared on the elegant Victorian building. The attention to detail was legendary, even the hotel's landmark clock tower that loomed over the city ran three minutes early so guests wouldn't miss departing trains. The first time they walked through the hotel's revolving glass door, both she and her father were awed by the lobby's sparkling chandeliers and grand staircase that led up to the mezzanine level. It felt as though you had entered a marvelous world where nothing could go wrong. During their short stay at the NB Hotel (a nickname it acquired early on), The Palm Court Tea Room with it's massive atrium ceiling and plethora of potted palms had become Sarah's favorite spot. A harpist played softly in a balcony above creating an intoxicating atmosphere.

"May I bring you more tea, Miss?" the young waitress asked Sarah.

"Thank you, no. I won't be here much longer," she replied.

Putting her pen down, Sarah looked at her watch, surprised two hours had passed since she sat down. Her father was finalizing some business at the American Consulate before they boarded the train for London. She chose to spend her last hours in Edinburgh having tea in this lovely room and writing in her journal.

Being in Edinburgh the last few days had been a mixed blessing. While the city itself was as captivating as ever, memories of her father's shooting, and knowing Peter was in Italy left her feeling a little flat. Still, there were so many positive things for her to focus on. After all, she and her father were about to begin a new life. The journal Peter sent while she was in Shetland awakened a love of writing. The daily habit of capturing her thoughts and chronicling events happening around her was now an activity she relished. Most recently, she had written about Liam and Mairi's wedding.

Never having been to a marriage ceremony, she found it all fascinating, and terribly exciting. The wedding was held in the northern part of Scalloway Bay in mainland Shetland. Weisdale Kirk was an old church associated with Liam's family for generations. It stood alone at the top of a grassy meadow, where wildflowers gently swayed with the breeze and a slight fragrance of lavender wafted through the air. The afternoon of the wedding saw a break in the clouds allowing a beam of sunshine to highlight the lone bagpiper leading the way to the church along the gravel pathway. He was playing a tune called 'Mairi's Wedding' which Sarah learned ironically happened to be a traditional song for processionals. Liam, his sisters and Sarah walked behind the bagpiper, followed by Mairi and her parents, then Marcus, Anje and Richard. To be included in the wedding family still felt slightly unreal to Sarah. The rest of the guests trailed behind, up the hill to the wide open door of the church. The wedding service began with the vicar reciting a customary prayer. Ava sat next to Sarah and whispered explanations of the Scottish traditions as the ceremony went along. At one point, Liam and Mairi each took a lit taper to light a central candle.

"This is the Unity candle that shows our families joining together, and honors the new family of Liam and Mairi," Ava whispered.

Toward the end of the ceremony, the vicar did an odd thing–at least it seemed odd to Sarah. He took the bride and groom's hands, placed them one over the other, and tied their wrists together with a piece of white fabric, then with some impressive moves, Liam and Mairi pulled their hands apart, leaving the fabric knot in tact.

"They are literally 'tying the knot," Ava whispered. "Mairi and Liam will keep it to remind them of today and their vows. Now watch, they will drink from the Quaich to seal the deal."

The vicar handed a shallow two-handled silver drinking cup to Mairi and Liam, who each held one of the handles and both took a drink out of it. It was Liam who finished the liquid, with a lip smack and big smile.

"What are they drinking?" Sarah whispered.

"A wee bit of fancy whisky, I'd be guessing by the look on Liam's face."

The two girls let a giggle escape and looked around to see if anyone noticed. The vicar announced Mairi and Liam man and wife, and the bagpiper began the tune that would take them through the meadow to the reception hall. Once there, the piper was given a few coins to follow the tradition of 'paying the piper.' There were lots of people dancing about to Scottish music and enjoying the festivities, including she and her father. The food was traditional, without a Liver Koog in sight. The beautiful two-layer brandy-laced wedding cake would never be forgotten. It had been a completely happy, joyous day.

The next few pages in her journal recounted the emotional parting when she and her father said goodbye to their new Shetland family. There were lots of tears, and promises of keeping in close touch and lofty plans for future visits. Liam and Mairi even drove to the airport with them for one final farewell. The British European Airways flight from Sumburgh airport to Aberdeen meant that her father didn't have to brave another ferry ride across the North Sea. Liam couldn't help teasing Richard, who took it with good humor and genuine gratitude that he had been spared the ferry ride. Sarah noticed a special moment between the two men when they were shaking hands, where a look of understanding and genuine caring was evident. How wonderfully odd to realize that Liam was her cousin.

With a deep sigh, she turned to a fresh page in her journal, and thought of Peter. She mentally reminded herself that this journal was a record of thoughts and events, not a diary of sappy, sentimental feelings. Admittedly, being in Edinburgh, she longed to connect with him. He had been so interested in everything she shared, just like a real friend would be. In a few hours she would be on a train headed to London with no idea if she would ever be back. An overwhelming sadness crept over her and she closed the journal book. Touching the leather cover, she was reminded that Peter had chosen this book especially for her. He had carried it in his hands, wrapped it up, mailed it...and thought about her. Sarah closed her eyes and held the book close to her chest as though uniting with him in a spiritual way. But who was Peter Michael-McGregor really? Why would a young man make an effort to befriend a lonely, young girl? Her thoughts were interrupted by a group of rather loud talking young ladies who had entered the quiet, dignified Palm Court Tea Room. Looking closer she recognized the school uniforms, and several of the girls who had tormented her at Campbell Manor. They walked past her as though she was invisible and not worthy of a glance. One girl said something to another one and they both half turned to look at Sarah, then sniggered and continued on. Thank goodness for Peter! Whatever his motive was in taking her under his wing, she would be eternally grateful.

"Sarah?"

She had been so lost in thought that she hadn't noticed her father standing beside her.

"Oh! I'm so sorry, I didn't see you!" she said, thinking she would never tire of seeing her father.

"I brought a friend," he said, obviously delighted in surprising her.

For one quick, crazy moment, she thought it was Peter and her heart skipped. Of course, her father knew nothing about Peter. What was she thinking?

"Ah, Lass! Aren't you looking the picture of loveliness?" Standing in front of her was Mrs. McAughtrie! If it couldn't be Peter, Mrs. McAughtrie was the next best thing. They hugged, then hugged again.

## Chapter Fifty-one

# RICHARD:

*The Plan*

Waverley Station was a marvel with its expansive clear glass roof. Richard was fascinated by Scottish architecture and the tendency for skylights in so many of it's buildings. He mused that with all the gray skies and rain, finding a source for natural light must be important. Even the famous glass dome in the booking hall lit up the area on this cloudy day.

As they got closer to the tracks, travelers were madly going this way and that, looking for departure platforms, or trying to hike up the wide stairway that led out from the train station to Princes Street. Sarah and Mrs. McAughtrie led the way toward Platform 15, walking arm in arm. Richard and the NB Hotel porter followed closely behind.

"I'm guessing you're not from around here," the porter shouted to Richard.

With all the noise and the luggage cart between them, Richard had to lean in to hear what the older gentleman had said.

"No, but we lived here for a few months. We're very sorry to leave."

"Well, I've heard you always take a piece of where you've been with you when you go."

The porter, dapper in his three-piece black wool uniform with gold buttons, carried an air of dignity and wisdom. Richard smiled and responded warmly.

"I quite like that! Scotland is a fascinating place and we will miss it."

"Might you be coming back again then, sir?"

Richard looked straight ahead, scanning the crowd, then answered with conviction.

"Yes, I believe we will be back."

"That's good to hear," the porter responded.

They reached Platform 15 and the porter unloaded their luggage efficiently in the individual sleeping compartments. In that brief conversation, Richard had, for the first time, admitted out loud that he wanted to return to Scotland. He realized in that moment he had turned a corner in his thinking and now was anxious to talk with Sarah about their future. No doubt there would be obstacles, but once a goal was identified, all the details would simply be worked out, one at a time.

The restaurant car was about half full of travelers who appeared ready for a nice meal before settling in for the overnight journey to London. Dining tables were covered in white tablecloths, and the settings were silver with linen napkins. A small vase of fresh flowers had been carefully set next to the window where it wouldn't jiggle all over the table with the movement of the train. The wine steward had come and gone as they declined his services, and a young man nattily dressed in his jacket and bow tie uniform handed them menus. He looked like a young Cary Grant and was obviously interested in making a good impression on Sarah.

"May I tell you about our specialty for your evening meal?" he asked very formally, his gaze lingering a little too long on Sarah.

Richard looked across the table at his lovely daughter, who was blushing at all the attention and looked flustered. He realized this was just a glimpse of what his future held–fending off 'would be' suitors. Where had the years gone?

"Yes, young man, we would ALL like to hear about your specialty," Richard answered in a commanding tone intended to slightly intimidate.

Before the Cary Grant look-alike could begin his recitation of the evening's speciality, Mrs. McAughtrie came to his rescue and made her order off of the menu.

"I would like Filet of Cod Mornay with roast potatoes and garden peas, please."

"I'll have the same," Sarah followed suit, never making eye contact with the waiter.

Richard, however, asked him to recite the entire specialty offering and then ordered it, mostly out of guilt for wanting to punch the kid in the nose for looking at his daughter. He smiled to himself for his papa bear reaction. It was going to be a long few years, indeed!

Dinner far exceeded their expectations, and once dessert of chocolate trifle was finished, they were all feeling comfortable and mellow. The Scottish countryside passed by their large window in the dark with only an occasional light from a faraway farmhouse visible. The rhythm of the cars on the rails was slightly hypnotic and quite conducive to conversation. Only two other people remained in the restaurant car, and they were at the far end engrossed in a deep discussion. Richard decided now would be a good time to talk about their future.

"We have had quite a time of it lately, haven't we?" He went on not giving Sarah a chance to respond. "And it has caused me to consider what comes next in our lives. There is much to consider."

"Do you mean in the next few weeks or forever?" Sarah asked lightly.

Mrs. McAughtrie gently interrupted and offered to leave so they might talk privately.

"Please stay, Seaneen, as my thoughts include you."

Turning to Sarah, he continued on.

"To answer your question, my Sunshine Girl, both. For the short term, we will stay in London for a while. I must take care of things with the Ambassador, and we need to straighten out just where you are in school. Education in England and Scotland differ and it's important to determine what level you have completed and should you prepare for university, if that's what you think you want to do, or if you will need another year to qualify and graduate."

Richard could see Sarah was beginning to grasp the importance of what he was saying. She leaned in closer to hear every word. He knew she must be eager to know where they were going and what was to come, but he wanted her to know that nothing was definite and it was important for her to share her thoughts. It was time he included his daughter in their plans. He continued on.

"Once that is sorted, and depending on the outcome, I have several options I want to present to you for long term. It is essential that you tell me how you honestly feel about them and don't hold back. First off, I will be resigning from the Foreign Service."

This was met with a slight gasp from both Sarah and Mrs. McAughtrie.

"Really?" was the only word Sarah could manage. It was one more word than Mrs. McAughtrie could say.

"I didn't mean to be quite so dramatic, but I have given the decision a lot of thought. For many years I have thoroughly enjoyed my time with the Foreign Service. I have taken my job representing the United States all over the world seriously and am grateful for all of the opportunities I have been given. But the negative side has been relocating every few years and moving you from place to place with no real home."

"You know I was happy as long as we were together, and you never made me go to boarding school, of which I was deathly afraid. I'm sure it wasn't always easy to drag me along."

"You are the light of my life and have never, ever been a burden. Whenever I had a difficult day, coming home to you put everything in perspective. After all that has happened the past months, I feel confident it is time for changes…big changes."

Sarah and Mrs. McAughtrie exchanged glances and turned back to Richard, neither saying a word.

"So here goes…and remember there are options." He took a deep breath, and proceeded.

"Because of the new family we have discovered on Shetland, and the wonderful friendship of Mrs. McAughtrie, and others, I think we should plan on living in Great Britain semi-permanently. We will have to return to the U.S. periodically as we have citizenship there, but our home would be here."

"I can't think of anything I'd like better!" Sarah responded instantly. "That would be amazing!"

"If you have not completed enough courses to qualify for graduation, we would stay in London until that's done. When you sit for the exam and if you do well, the first decision is if you want to go on to university or take time off."

Richard paused to give his daughter a chance to respond. She didn't hesitate.

"One of the things I think I'm passionate about is…writing. I was given a journal a few months ago and am finding writing has become my favorite thing. You know I've always loved to read, and writing seems the perfect way for me to express myself. Since you asked, I think I would like to go to university and learn more about writing and literature. Do you think that's silly?"

"I think that's brilliant!" Richard answered, flashing back to his last conversation with Lady Rose. "A very wise woman recently told me to 'find the passion that sings to your soul.' It seems you might have found yours. I couldn't be happier. With the tentative plan that you want to go on with your education, let me share what I'm thinking. In doing my own, personal soul searching, I believe, I too, have found the direction I want to take. However, I will pursue it only if it corresponds with your ideas."

Both Sarah and Mrs. McAughtrie were looking at him, with rapt attention, waiting to hear his grand scheme. A sudden hesitancy washed over him, and he began to doubt the validity of his plan. He had gone over it a thousand times in his mind, taken preliminary steps and made modest contacts, but who knows if he could actually pull it off? Sarah interrupted his thoughts.

"Dad….you were saying?"

Richard laughed a little and regained his confidence. It was interesting how exposed a person can feel when they so want the approval of others, in this case his daughter. Yes, his idea was rock solid, and he knew in his heart that it was exactly what he wanted to do.

"Well, you remember all of those lovely Country Life magazines you have found so interesting? While I was in rehabilitation, they had a subscription and every week I spent hours examining available properties, mostly to fill my vacant hours. As my time to leave was approaching, I knew decisions had to be made. Did I want to continue in Foreign Service? Did I want to move again, and make you start over? Had I accomplished all I wanted with that job? Was I leaving out of fear of being hurt, or God-forbid, you being hurt? If I left, then what? I'm a bit too young to retire, and have never had the time to really develop any hobbies. You would be gone soon with your own life…"

"Well, I haven't left yet! Maybe I'll be one of those children who never leaves home."

"As lovely as that is to hear, you must live your own life."

At that moment their Cary Grant look-alike waiter approached the table to see if there was any further service he could offer, and to take another look at the beautiful young lady. They assured him they were fine, and inquired whether he minded if they sat a while longer at the table. Gazing at Sarah, he told them to stay as long as they liked, then walked back to the galley kitchen.

"Let me take back what I said earlier," Richard spoke in a low voice, "maybe you should plan on living with me forever so I can protect you from young men like our dining Lothario."

After being silent the last half hour, Mrs. McAughtrie gave out a laugh.

"Who's Lothario?" Sarah asked inquisitively.

That produced more laughter between Richard and his former housekeeper, and the mood lightened considerably.

"I digress. Here's what I am thinking for the future. I have seen men who are world-weary. Whether it's war, work related, family tragedy, or just worn out from life, the thing in common is a need to take a break from their situation, a chance to lay their burdens down and see things with a fresh perspective. Sarah, you and I have been blessed with a secure financial position. I never need to work if I choose not to. That puts us in a unique place to help."

"I'm a little confused," his daughter confessed.

"I'm about to tie it all up and I sincerely hope you share my vision. As I read about all the magnificent properties for sale in the

Country Life real estate sections, it came to me that I wanted to buy a large manor house with some land, and establish it as a short term haven for men who need time and rest. It must be a location with woods for walking, lots of wildlife, streams for fishing, equestrian facilities with horses, a few separate cottages, but mostly a space to reconnect with God and nature. A place of kindness, a place to lose the fear of life and maybe find a dream to follow. Your grandmother was a very spiritual woman, who taught me much, and I think it's time I used the resources she left us. I wouldn't be counseling anyone, but would be there to offer whatever wisdom and knowledge I could share. My plan is to be a listener."

"I think Grandmother would really like that," Sarah answered thoughtfully.

"Now, here is the tricky part, with a lot of 'if's' attached. Sarah, IF you like this idea, we would live in the main house, and you could attend the University of Edinburgh by commuting or you could go away to school. Maybe London or wherever you would like."

"I don't think I'm ready to fly too far from the nest yet, thank you. After months of being apart, I'm not tired of you yet," she laughed, "plus, I might run into another…Lothario! I'll have to think about it."

Richard took that as a positive and continued, turning his attention to Mrs. McAughterie.

"This is where you come in. IF you like the idea, I can't think of anyone I would rather have run the house and all it would entail. Of course, you would have a small staff and there would be workers to tend the outdoors. You mentioned you've been living with your sister, and perhaps you don't want to change your situation?"

"I am intrigued and quite interested. While I love my sister and her family, I've been a wee bit anxious to have a busier life, and being with the both of you would be lovely."

"IF we decide to move ahead with this, I've been thinking about what a wonderful place for Liam and all the Shetland family to visit and stay as long as they wanted."

"That's a great idea! We would have family," and turning to Mrs. McAughtrie, "and very close friends."

Feeling elated with their full enthusiasm, he moved to the last portion of his plan.

"The area I have been focused on is the Border country between England and Scotland."

There are several properties that are close to meeting what I'm looking for, and as I mentioned, the University of Edinburgh is not far away. I've yet to contact a real estate agent, wanting to know your thoughts, but it sounds as if you approve. I know I've given you a lot to digest and if you want to think about it, that's fine. We have a somewhat limited timeline however, with summer approaching properties will be selling more quickly."

"I've heard from a friend that the Border country is really beautiful," Sarah remarked. "I don't think I need time to think about it. Having a real home where we won't have to ever move is....well, I guess it's something I never knew I wanted. It sounds like a dream."

"I think you can count me in as well," Mrs. McAughtrie added. "There will be plenty of details to sort, but it sounds like just the ticket for me."

"Then I will begin setting the wheels in motion for this new adventure as soon as we arrive in London!"

Spontaneously, all three raised their water glasses to toast their future together.

## Chapter Fifty-two
# SARAH:
*Reading on the Train*

Sarah's sleeping compartment was sandwiched between her father's on the left and Mrs. McAughtries on the right. She had never been in a train sleeping cabin and was fascinated by how so much was packed in such a small space. It was like her own personal bedroom on wheels. The bed was next to the wall, a lamp above it and a place for your pocket watch. There was a window, and a large mirror over a small wash basin with hot and cold water. An added bonus was a chamber pot underneath the basin. Instructions on the pot read 'contents could be emptied directly onto the train track below when necessary.' Right then and there, she decided she would not go to the bathroom until they reached the hotel in London! Aside from the chamber pot, it was pretty cosy, if just a little chilly. The attendant had offered an extra blanket and a hot water bottle, which now seemed like a good idea. As she pushed the button to summon him, there was a knock at her door.

"Sarah, it's Mrs. McAughtrie."

She opened the door, Mrs. McAughtrie handed her the most recent Country Life magazine.

"I thought you might be a wee bit interested in reading this..." she said hesitantly.

At the same time the attendant arrived and assured Sarah he would be right back with a blanket and hot water bottle. Mrs. McAughtrie took her leave and wished Sarah a good night's sleep. The blanket and hot water bottle arrived moments later.

Finally settled in with the bedside lamp on, she took out her journal and began writing of all the incredible things that had happened at dinner. Her father mentioning the Border country brought a deep longing to share the news with Peter. How she had missed him and their friendship. It was the only time in her transitory life that she had really confided in someone, and in turn, he seemed to greatly enjoy having her as a friend. At least she hoped he did. Maybe he was just being kind, like when you're nice to someone who looks needy. No, she would not let her mind go there. At least, she would try not to.

The sure cure for feeling sorry for oneself was to thumb through the magazine Mrs. McAughtrie had brought her. Country Life had pages and pages of amazing properties for sale, most of them historic estates and ancient castles. With any luck, she might find something her father would like, plus it was fun to read about the details and imagine what it would be like to live in a castle. It was always amusing to find a property that had twelve bedrooms and only one bathroom. There is no way that could work under any circumstance, even with chamber pots. Sarah reached toward the foot of the bed to pull up the extra blanket just as the train came to an abrupt stop. Being off balance, she tumbled onto the floor with a thud, and both the magazine and the hot water bottle hit her in the head. Grateful no one witnessed her less than graceful thump to the floor, the absurdity of the situation struck her. She found herself laughing so hard she could hardly breathe. The bedside light flickered off and on several times before the train started up again slowly moving down the tracks. Instantly there was a knock at her door and her father's familiar voice.

"Sunshine, are you quite all right? I heard a bump and wanted to make sure you weren't hurt."

Trying to stifle her giggle, she stood up and opened the door.

"I did fall out of bed and was accosted by my hot water bottle, but I think I'll survive."

This brought on another fit of laughter, as her father merely smiled, shook his head, and closed the door to return to his cabin.

Snuggled back in bed with her hot water bottle and magazine, Sarah opened the glossy pages, turning them one at a time so she didn't miss anything. Tucked between the ad for the Georgian country house near Glasgow and the three hundred acres for sale in the Highlands, there was a neatly folded Edinburgh newspaper. Turning the newspaper from front to back, she wondered if Mrs. McAughtrie had forgotten she left it in the magazine. Then she saw the headline and the photo of Peter…her Peter! With a pounding heart, Sarah fought to process what she was seeing. Her Peter was a famous artist, a very famous artist. The photo was a candid shot of him smiling, and looking quite appealing. She touched the photo lightly with her finger, as if he might somehow turn his head and cast his gaze her way. Slowly, deliberately, she opened the newspaper and began to read. Gone was the humor of the last few minutes, replaced with a foreboding anticipation.

**MYSTERY ARTIST REVEALED BEFORE GOING TO ITALY**

**By**

**Graeme McPherson**

*Rarely has the art world been so taken by an artist that their work is praised and lauded by both critics and the masses alike, yet their identity is a puzzlement. By that we don't mean that they are new and unknown, we mean rather that this person's identity is truly a mystery. Several years ago, The Pure Arts Guild in Edinburgh, promoter of exceptional Scottish artists in their gallery, chose to exhibit two paintings by this artist. The response was immediate and within the year the gallery hosted a rare one-person show. Each piece was signed with only the initials PMM. The Guild has maintained that they dealt with the artist's agent and sincerely did not know the artists name. I am happy to report that the mystery has been solved, and the reluctant artist has been made known. Saying it is a surprise would be an understatement.*

*Ladies and gentlemen, may I present to you Edinburgh's own Peter Michael-McGregor.*

*Born and raised in Newington, his parents are both university professors–father in engineering and mother in design. From my recent interview, I learned that he has not had much in the way of formal art training, and that a majority of his time is spent at Elibank, the family estate near Walkerburn, where he does a great deal of his painting. His latest news is an upcoming opportunity to study with the famous Italian artist, Paulo Antoneli, in Florence, Italy.*

*Barely into his twenties, young Mr. Michael-McGregor has presented paintings that far exceed his chronological age. Skilled in both oils and watercolors, his work is evocative of masters that came before him, but with a refreshing newness.*

*In my recent interview with Peter Michael-McGregor, I found him to be an intelligent and engaging young man, who is a wee bit disconcerted by his fame.*

Sarah re-read the opening paragraphs several times. Her mind was trying to wrap around all that her eyes were reading. He had kept the major part of his life a secret from her. A few of the details she knew–the part about his family, and the estate in the Borders, but why wouldn't he tell her everything? Obviously, he didn't trust her, and why should he? After all, he didn't owe her any explanation. She was just a lonely, young girl who…who what? Who developed a crush on someone she hardly knew. She read on.

**GM:** *It is a pleasure to finally meet you. What a stir you've caused in the art world. Was your anonymity devised or happenstance?*
**PMM:** *Thank you, Mr. McPherson. No, in no way did I set out to be anonymous. I have found that I work best without distractions and for that reason I choose to simply concentrate on painting, and have an agent deal with the business side.*
**GM:** *As I understand it your agent is your mother.*
**PMM:** *It worked out to be a perfect arrangement. She had connections in the art world and who could be more trustworthy than your mother? We also decided to keep my name and identity quiet for*

*the time being.*

**GM:** *That makes a great deal of sense. May I inquire when you began painting?*

**PMM:** *I've been told that as soon as I could hold a pencil, I began to draw. I would sketch on any flat surface, driving my parents mad. Somewhere around age ten I was given paints and canvas.*

**GM:** *And the rest, as they say, is history. I am fascinated that you have had very little formal training, and in fact, could be considered self-taught. This is incredible in light of your abilities. Where do you believe this talent originated?*

**PMM:** *My great uncle on my mother's side was very artistic, and as a child I was captivated by watching him sketch scenes, then bring them to life using paint and brushes. He was mentored for a time by Joseph Farquharson.*

**GM:** *To refresh those who might have forgotten, Joseph Farquharson was a Scottish artist, famous for painting landscapes in the early twentieth century. He was quite skilled at capturing the warmth and light of sunrises and twilights, though snow scenes were his trademark. In fact, he painted so many scenes of cattle and sheep in the snow he was given the nickname of "Frozen Mutton Farquharson."*

**PMM:** *He and my uncle were great friends and would travel together to Finzean, Farquharson's family estate in the Highlands, and paint 'en plein air' together.*

**GM:** *They would paint outdoors in that harsh climate? That's madness.*

**PMM***: Yes, but Mr. Farquharson cleverly built a hut on wheels with a wood stove and large glass window where they painted their landscapes in relative comfort, surrounded by whatever countryside they chose for that day. My uncle was certainly not the artist that Mr. Farquharson was, but his work was quite good, and his love for painting was contagious. Some of my happiest memories were of painting alongside him at Elibank.*

**GM:** *So you credit your great uncle for inspiring you?*

**PMM***: I believe by watching him, I learned to not be afraid to try. Painting is a process of putting scenes on canvas that grab your* *creative brain and won't let go until you've satisfied yourself that you've done all you can. I guess that is true of all creative avenues, you follow your passion until you have exhausted it. My parents are great devotees of all the arts. Growing up we spent hours as a family visiting the Scottish National Gallery, the Queen's Gallery at Holyroodhouse, and most of Edinburgh's private galleries. We went to plays, symphonies, dance performances and the like. My mother is an incredibly creative person and she made sure both of her children where exposed to as much of the arts as possible. My father is a professor of engineering at the University of Edinburgh and his job is to keep us grounded financially and practically in our artistic adventures.*

**GM:** *You have a sibling? Is he or she in the arts as well?*

**PMM:** *Yes, my sister, Ainslee, is a ballet dancer with the Northwest Ballet in Seattle, Washington in the States. She is two years older and extremely talented.*

**GM:** *Tell me about your style of painting. You favour landscapes in what I would call a somewhat traditional, romantic style, a wee bit reminiscent of John Constable, and Alexander Nasmyth, but with a brilliant fresh look. Would you agree?*

**PMM:** *Yes. I find that I most like painting what I enjoy seeing. For me, that has always been our countryside. Where is there anywhere more beautiful than the Scottish outdoors? Nature fascinates me, the colors, the textures, the light and the shadows, that sense of something about to happen. As a young man visiting museums, I was always drawn to the landscape artists. I would study individual paintings for hours, taking notes on style and composition and techniques. Then I would go home and try to duplicate it. I've been able to collect dozens of books about painters and their techniques, and spent countless hours studying them.*

**GM:** *Most landscape artists have specific ways they like to paint. Are your paintings done from scratch or en plein air or do you paint from photos?*

**PMM:** *Really, I use every avenue that is available to me. There is nothing like being outdoors as though you are part of the natural order of things. Have you ever waded into a stream to fly fish and felt* *one with creation? Capturing that fresh feeling; the scent of the air, the feel of the mist, the sound of the wildlife, the warmth of the sun. Those are the things I am most passionate about conveying in my paintings. However, there are times when plein air painting is not possible. Usually I carry a journal to take notes and do quick sketches of things that catch my attention. From time to time, I will use photos for reference. I have been blessed to have family property in the Borders and it is one of my favorite locations to paint.*

**GM:** *Your family home, Elibank, is perhaps one of the most beautiful properties in the Borders. What a breathtaking spot to set up an easel and create. As we mentioned, you are self-taught, and to this point quite successful with your painting. I'm curious why you, a landscape painter, have chosen to spend time in Italy with Paulo Antoneli, very famous portrait painter?*

**PMM:** *It's quite a nice story actually. I met Mr. Antoneli about seven years ago. He was a guest at a reception in my family home, and I'm quite sure I was a precocious teenager engaging him in conversation about my art. He seemed mildly amused by me, though not terribly interested until he realized we shared a bond in having very little use for modern art. That cemented our relationship. I showed him some of my paintings and he was very encouraging. Nearly every year I would receive a letter from him inquiring how my painting was progressing and professing the earnest hope that I still hated modern art as much as he did. In one letter he mentioned that perhaps one day I should come to Florence and apprentice with him. It wasn't until years later that I found out he was an internationally famous portrait artist. To me, he was just a funny, eccentric fellow who told stories of fencing duels and drinking too much wine. I was intrigued at the thought of being his student and being in Italy. When he wrote to me last year and mentioned the apprenticeship, I thought it might be a good time to take him up on the offer.*

**GM:** *And obviously he said yes.*

**PMM:** *More than said yes, he told me to hurry up and get to Florence so we could paint side by side in his studio. He further told me he felt it was his job to teach me how to draw properly, and how to fight a duel, just in case the situation ever arose. How could*

*anyone turn down such an offer?*
**GM:** *What do you hope to learn from the great Master of portraits?*
**PMM:** *Honestly, I'm not sure. My plan is to surrender to Mr. Antoneli's teaching and soak up everything I can. As you say he is one of the greatest artists in the world and the importance of this is not lost on me.*
**GM:** *Are you concerned that his influence might alter your style, one that has become quite successful?*
**PMM:** *My painting is very personal and I paint what is in my heart, not what I think will sell well. I'm sure my father would shake his head at that statement. As a painter I am always evolving, always learning, always trying new techniques and new ideas. I think it will be exciting to see what new skills I will learn from Mr. Antoneli.*
**GM**: *Well, along with the rest of the art world, I look forward to watching your progress as an artist. One last, perhaps more personal question. You are about to travel quite a distance, into a foreign land and dare I say, a rather exotic lifestyle. Do you have any qualms about leaving family and friends behind?*
**PMM:** *I'm quite certain my parents have already booked passage to visit Florence under the thin guise of visiting their friend Paulo Antoneli. As for friends? I learned a long time ago that acquaintances are easy to come by, but friendships are rare and must be maintained to be meaningful. Painting, for me, is all consuming and by nature a solitary sport. There is no one, other than my cocker spaniel, that I will miss.*
**GM:** *Thank you, Peter Michael-McGregor for meeting with me. You are a talented, articulate, interesting young man and it has been a pleasure to spend time with you.*

She swallowed hard as the hot tears ran down her cheeks. A myriad of emotions raced through her mind–embarrassment, betrayal, confusion, anger, but mostly she was completely heartbroken. If she made any noise her father would hear her and inquire as to the problem. This was something she was going to have to bear alone. Of all the difficult events the past year, this one crushed her soul.

Turning off her bedside light, the train continued its rhythmic journey into the night, with the wheels offering a clickety-clackity cadence. Sarah held the newspaper against her heart and quietly sobbed.

Blessed are they that mourn, for they shall be comforted.

END OF PART ONE

# Five Years Later

## Chapter Fifty-three
# RICHARD:
## *Leigheas is Home*

It was a magnificent morning after a roaring thunderstorm the night before. Tree limbs had been ripped from their trunks and were strewn about, but the air was crystal clear and fragrant with the smell of wet soil. Early morning sun filtered through the few leaves that were left, reflecting sparkles on the shallow rain puddles. Richard guided the big, chestnut gelding through the forest, and gave thanks, once again, for this beautiful property that he called home. In the pasture clearing, he gently pulled on the reins, slowing his horse to a walk. He needed to give the other riders a chance to catch up. Before a minute passed he heard the pounding of hooves behind him, and saw the two riders headed his way. Looking at their flushed, happy faces, there was no need to ask if they were enjoying the morning.

"It's been years since I've galloped around the countryside. I didn't realize how much I'd missed the joy of an equestrian outing," said James Bradbury, a retired vicar of the Church of England.

"Nothing like time spent in nature to calm the soul, vicar." Richard was pleased with the positive reaction of his guest.

"Please call me James, young man," answered the vicar with a twinkle in his eye, "After all, you are the Laird of Leigheas."

The humor found its mark, and Richard continued their banter as their horses walked side by side.

"Indeed, I am and you best not forget it or I'll have you thrown in the dungeon!"

"Do you really have a dungeon?" asked the vicar incredulously.

"Actually…I don't think so, but I bet there are some frightening places Mrs. McAughtrie has found. Speaking of which, we had better turn toward the stables, and make haste to the house for breakfast. Mrs. McAughtrie is not amused when we're late.

"I've learned you never want to raise the ire of the cook. Tell me a bit about Mrs. McAughtrie. Does her husband work for you as well?" James asked.

"No, she has been a widow for quite some time. We met in Edinburgh where I employed her to take charge of my home there."

"Well, she's a lovely lady indeed."

The smile on the vicar's lips didn't go unnoticed. The question was, should Richard tell his old friend that she might have an admirer? Richard stifled his own smile.

"Yes, she is. Indeed."

"On another note, tell me about the name, Leigheas? Is it Gaelic?" the Vicar asked.

"You have a good ear, James. Yes it is, Scottish Gaelic and literally means 'healing.' My dream has always been for Leigheas to be a restorative, peaceful place for…healing."

"Is the proper pronunciation 'lee-az' or 'lay-eez?' Words fascinate me, and I enjoy learning about their origins.

"We pronounce it 'lay-eez' and if you're interested, I have several books in the library on Scottish Gaelic."

"I would very much like to explore the subject, thank you."

The other rider, Ian Patterson, didn't join in the conversation, but couldn't mask his pleasure at the morning outing. It was obvious to Richard this young man had a lot on his mind, and if an hour ride in the countryside helped ease his burden, then the morning had been a success. All applicants wishing to spend time at Leigheas are asked to send a personal letter outlining their reasons for requesting a short stay, and Ian's letter had touched Richard's heart. In essence, he was a man in his early thirties from a wealthy, successful family who owned a newspaper conglomerate. He had been made CEO of the large corporation about a year ago at the untimely death of his older brother. The letter indicated that he was overwhelmed and fearful of letting his family down, and didn't feel qualified for the position. He felt he just needed some breathing room and space to plan and face his future. This was precisely what Richard had in mind five years ago when he bought this property. Ian had only been at Leigheas for about a week, and while he kept primarily to himself, Richard noticed that he was spending much of his time at the stables with Stephen, the retired vet who took care of the livestock on the estate, and Stephen's son Henry, a delightful, down syndrome youngster.

As promised, breakfast had been set out on the long side table in the dining room, kept warm in several large chafing dishes. Hot coffee and hot water for tea were at one end, and glass bowls of cut up fresh fruit were at the other end, with sausage, eggs, bacon, kippers, oatmeal and toast in the middle. By the time Richard, James and Ian had cleaned up and made their way to the dining room, the two other guests were halfway through their meal.

"Gentlemen, good morning," said Richard, as he dished up the delicious smelling food. "I hope you all slept well, which might have been a challenge with that thunderous storm raging."

Edward, the engineer, was the first to comment. "I had no idea the Border country was subject to storms of that magnitude. Does that happen often?"

"Thankfully no, though we do get our share of unpredictable weather. September and October tend to be the rainiest, but last night's storm was a bit over the top."

"You should have a weather station on the premises to gauge exact amounts of rain and other important information. It's imperative to know exactly what you can expect year to year. You would then have statistics to refer to. You need to get on doing that. You cannot expect your guests to enjoy their stay with so much…unpredictability."

In the two weeks Edward Davies had been a guest, it had become exceeding clear that the forty-six year old man was a bit tightly-wound. In his introductory letter he mentioned that his compulsive need to control everything was having a negative impact on his business, as well as his wife and teenage twin boys. A close friend of his had heard about Leigheas and suggested a few weeks away might be helpful. Richard noticed Edward gravitated toward spending time with the head gardener, Marcus.

"That's an excellent idea, Edward," Richard answered pleasantly, "I'll speak to Marcus for his thoughts on the matter. I must admit that I've found part of the charm of nature is its unpredictability."

"Well, there's nothing like factual information to aid in planning things. Spontaneity is rarely the best course," Edward answered in typical clipped engineering fashion.

"I've a thought. Why don't you speak to Marcus about a weather station?" Richard said, continuing to enjoy his breakfast. "I'm quite sure he would value your opinion and ideas."

The reed-thin man with the wire-rimmed eye glasses looked gratified, "Why, I think I'll do that. Marcus has a keen sense of the way things should be."

The door between the kitchen and the dining room swung open and Mrs. McAughtrie came through carrying a piping hot apple strudel.

"Aye, gentlemen, I thought you might like a little sweet before you go on about your day."

There were happy groans all around as the fragrance settled over the table. Everyone except Becket McTavish, the out of work actor who had been unpleasant since his arrival several weeks before. The portly man seemed to have trouble controlling his biting tongue.

"Why must you insist on serving useless foods that are entirely unsuited for men our age? What is wrong with you?"

Other than a slight flicker of one eye, Mrs. McAughtrie replied with her usual graciousness.

"You know, meeting you in person, Mr. McTavish, I was surprised at how much younger you appear than you do on stage. Is that due to a strict diet regime you maintain? If you have any special requests I would be most happy to accommodate you."

The aging actor scowled, as he took his first bite of the apple strudel. Richard was reminded once again why he admired Seaneen McAughtrie so much. Her gentle forbearance was genuine, always peppered with a dash of humor. The actor was one of the few guests that hadn't responded to the calm, serene atmosphere of Leigheas. His inner turmoil appeared very deep, which was somewhat understandable. Recent newspaper articles reported the death of Becket's wife in a dreadful car accident in Glasgow. In his letter to Richard, he mentioned great sadness and a paralyzing fear that his acting career was coming to an end. He wrote that he must find other interests in life. Optimistically, Richard hoped that time in the country would help heal Becket's troubled soul and give him guidance. Unfortunately, his demeanor had not improved, and now, instead of being rude to everyone, he seemed to be targeted on Mrs. McAughtrie. For the first time in five years, Richard was considering telling someone they would have to leave Liegheas. He would not allow Becket McTavish or anyone else to verbally abuse Seaneen or the staff. If there was no improvement by the weekend, he would have no choice.

Becket, responded under his breath in an almost guttural growl, "No, no. Everything is fine…thank you."

"Well, then," Mrs. McAughtrie continued on as though nothing had happened, " I will be going to the village this morning. Is there anything I can bring anyone back from the shops?"

"Perhaps I could accompany you?" asked Vicar James with the enthusiasm of a new puppy. "I'm quite good at carrying a load."

"Why, that would be lovely, James. We will plan on leaving within the hour."

Richard held his amusement in check and proceeded on with the morning announcements.

"There are a few things I'd like to mention. If you had any problems in your cottage such as leakage, or wind damage from the storm, please let Marcus or Joseph know. Sometimes the windows aren't quite as snug as they should be. I haven't heard of any power outages."

There were eight self-contained cottages on the property, five for guests and three slightly larger ones for live-in staff, all fairly close to the main house. Each cottage had a sitting room, bedroom, bathroom, small kitchen and a fireplace that helped when the weather turned chilly. Sarah and Mrs. McAughtrie had spent months redecorating each cottage, making sure they were comfortable and attractive.

"The river is too high, too fast and too muddy for fly fishing after the storm last night. We will have to wait until it settles down. However, Colin, our fishing guide, will be here this morning checking gear and would be available if anyone would like to fish on the loch. It's an excellent way to practice fly-casting. As to the horses, there should be four available…"

Ian spoke up, "Actually, there will only be two, as the other two will be getting new shoes today."

"Good to know, thank you Ian," Richard replied, impressed that the young man spoke up given his reluctance to join in conversations thus far. "As always, the library here in the main house is available. Feel free to make yourself at home with a cup of tea and light the fire if you wish. I checked on the chapel this morning and it only sustained minor damage which I imagine Joseph has repaired by now. Today looks to be as bright and sunny as yesterday was wet and windy. I'll be around if there is anything you need or just want to chat."

There were no takers to his invitation and they all casually disbanded, each going his separate way.

Mrs. McAughtrie spoke up, "Richard, might I have a wee word with you in the kitchen?"

"Of course," he answered.

The kitchen at Leigheas had been the first area remodeled, resulting in a large, open, bright room, with plenty of white cupboards with glass doors. Countertops were white marble and a four-oven white Aga stove was on one side, with the kitchen sink opposite under a large window that overlooked a grass meadow. In the middle of the room was a big table, ideal for more workspace or for pulling up a chair and having a cup of tea. To the left, an antique French door with etched glass panels was the entrance to the butler's pantry. It was filled with china, crystal, silver, and overflow supplies, making it look much like a small, charming shop. The kitchen was a perfect blend of modern conveniences blended into a traditional early nineteenth century house. By far, it was the most favored room for all who lived or visited Leigheas, not only for its aesthetics, but because of Seaneen McAughtrie's caring personality. Long ago

Richard recognized she was the ideal person to share his dream of offering a place for healing. He particularly enjoyed how informal their relationship had become since beginning this adventure five years ago.

"What could possibly be on your mind, Seaneen," Richard queried with amusement. "Might it be the attentions of a certain vicar?"

"Do stop that!" she answered, with a slight blush and a rap on his arm with her tea towel.

"Well, you know…I quite like the chap, if that has any bearing on anything," he replied.

"Richard! I hardly know the man. He's barely been here a month."

"But he is quite interesting, and well-read and, by the way, quite besotted by you."

"Besotted? Wherever did you discover that word? Have you been reading Jane Austen again? I will only admit that I do enjoy his company and that's the end of this discussion, lad."

"For now…" Richard raised his eyebrows in a mock sinister way. He just couldn't let it go, he was enjoying it too much.

Mrs. McAughtrie rolled her eyes, much like Sarah when she was exasperated with her father. "Two important reminders you mustn't forget. First, we are expecting a new guest in three days and the JM Barrie Cottage Is fully prepared for him."

Early on they came up with the idea that each cottage would be decorated to honor a specific Scottish author. The theme would be throughout the interior, and include the author's books, photos, framed news articles, really anything they could find that was appropriate. For example, the Sir Walter Scott Cottage had a complete collection of all twenty-seven fiction novels, a framed quote from his book, 'Marmion' which read 'Oh what a tangled web we weave, when first we practice to deceive,' an oil portrait of Sir Scott, and an etched print of Abbotsford Estate, Scott's home in nearby Melrose. Every cottage was a labor of love by Sarah and Mrs. McAughtrie. Richard was often in awe of the two women in his life.

"And, you've no clue who our mystery guest is?" she asked.

"No idea. He used the name Leonardo da Vinci in his letter, so if the person who arrives is not four hundred years old with a long, gray beard, we can be pretty darn sure the name is an alias," Richard said with his usual humor. "I suspect he is a fairly young man. His letter merely indicated he was in dire need of rest and reflection from some unfortunate choices he made. He seemed familiar with the Border country, but didn't expand on that. Let's hope he isn't expecting royal treatment."

"I'm sure you will be up to the task, Laird Richard," she responded teasingly. "Secondly, I'm sure you haven't forgotten Sarah is coming in on Friday evening. Do I get the feeling the wee lass will be here for an extended stay? I do hope so, I've missed her now that she's living in London and busy with her career."

"We had a long visit on the phone last night and her job at the book publishers has taken a bad turn. The fellow who originally hired her right out of university left for another company. It seems his replacement and Sarah don't get on. Her agreement to come in as an Assistant Acquisitions Editor was based on a hand shake agreement that she be given priority on submitting books she has written. Her previous boss saw great promise in her writing, but now the new man is unwilling to uphold the bargain. She's disappointed and a bit angry, and thought a leave of absence for a few weeks to sort out her feelings might be a good idea."

"Oh, poor lass! She had such high hopes when she started there. Jobs are so hard to come by in London, she must be very torn what to do." Mrs. McAughtrie's momentary concern was replaced with her inherent good cheer. "Well, it will do her good to come home for a wee bit. She does love being here, though that may have more to do with the horses and fishing than with either of us."

"You have an excellent point there. Colin has made a true fisherman out of her. Who knew that girl would take to fly-fishing?"

Their conversation ended there when James came bustling in, looking excited about his outing with Mrs. McAughtrie.

"I hope I'm not interrupting."

With veiled amusement Richard assured him he was not. Glancing at his watch he remembered he was to meet with Stephen at the stables in a few minutes.

"You two have a lovely time in the village. If you happen to run across any Fenteman's Ginger drink, please pick some up for Sarah. I think it's still her favorite."

"Aye, we will," said Mrs. McAughtrie, as James tucked her hand through his arm, with a wink to Richard.

*Chapter Fifty-four*

# SARAH:

## *The Flying Scotsman*

For over a hundred years, the Flying Scotsman train had been rumbling on the tracks from London's Kings Cross Station north to Edinburgh's Waverley Station. The 392 mile train journey took the eastern route through the village of Peterborough with its cathedral towers, onto York with it's charming nineteenth century train station, then to Newcastle, where the train crosses the River Tyne before going into Scotland. The scenery was breathtaking with open fields separated by dry-stone walls which kept the sheep and cattle from wandering afar. As the train went northward, it edged closer to the coast, with views of the North Sea, and small croft farms and little villages. Further on was the larger town of Berwick-Upon-Tweed, officially known as the most northern place in England, thus causing residents to never know whether they lived in England or Scotland. Sarah never tired of her trips on the Flying Scotsman, even though she had made the journey countless times over the last five years. For a little over six hours she could relax with the gentle rocking of the train car, and look out the large window at the world passing by. It turned out to be an ideal place to focus on writing without much interruption. Trial and error taught her if she booked a first class seat in the dining car, she could have the table alone for the entire trip. Most of the train staff knew her by sight, if not by name, and were respectful of allowing her space to work. An occasional nod and a smile, and they went on to their other duties.

There was much on Sarah's mind today and she was sure her face reflected the inner turmoil about her job situation. Trying to understand which feelings were valid and which were purely emotional seemed like a tangled mess. Was it even possible to make a rational decision as angry as she was? With her journal in front of her, she listed reasons for staying, and then pros and cons of leaving. Could she ever be happy working for Mr. Collier with his snide, superior attitude? His predecessor, Mr. Laurence Fraser, who originally hired her, was the exact opposite. She had known him to be a thoughtful, well-mannered gentleman who knew the book publishing business inside out and was well respected at every level. It didn't hurt that he thought Sarah was a brilliant, young writer who only wanted for a bit of guidance before she made her mark on the world as an author. Before he left, Mr. Fraser mentioned the possibility of taking Sarah with him to his new, elevated position with another firm, but it hadn't worked out. Oh! What to do? What to do? Her pondering was interrupted by one of her favorite, familiar waiters.

"Miss Sarah, would you prefer your usual tea and treats or a lunch menu?"

"Tea and treats would be lovely. Thank you, Mr. Hawkins."

The train took a wide curve and the dining car swayed this way and that. Sarah was fascinated that the waiters never bobbled or, heaven forbid, dropped their trays filled with food and drink. She once asked Mr. Hawkins how they were able to keep such a balance and he had regaled her with wonderful stories about a sealed off, special dining car, where waiters-in-training were taught to walk along a white line, carrying a full tray, blindfolded with the train moving at speed. He laughed as he shared funny incidents of food and drinks flying about that secret training car. She wondered idly if he had ever wanted to quit his job and become a writer.

Just as the tea and treats were set before her, Sarah noticed a conversation between a young waiter and a passenger a few yards away. She could see by the waiter's demeanor he was a bit flustered and looking around for help. The passenger was an attractive, blonde, well-dressed woman in her early forties who looked a bit embarrassed. Sarah watched Mr. Hawkins tactfully take over the situation and send the young waiter on to another task. The blonde and Mr. Hawkins were slowly walking in her direction when she overheard their conversation.

"My sincere apologies, Miss Turning. I've no idea how your restaurant car reservation was lost. Shall I bring tea service to your seat?"

"Please don't concern yourself with the confusion. Sometimes things happen," she answered pleasantly.

With a quick look around the restaurant car, Sarah could see it had filled up around her. Being so focused on her thoughts, she hadn't noticed how many passengers were seated, ready to order. Spontaneously, she spoke out.

"Mr. Hawkins, there is plenty of room at this table." Turning to the blonde passenger, Sarah smiled. "Please join me. There is more than enough for the two of us, and I would enjoy the company."

"Are you quite sure? I wouldn't want to disturb."

"Truthfully, it would be nice to escape my own thoughts for a bit. Do sit down."

"You are most kind. My name is Kaitlyn Turning."

She offered her hand across the table and Sarah shook it.

"I am Sarah Duncan."

Moments later Mr. Hawkins brought a second tea pot, dishes and silverware.

"Is there anything additional you require?"

Both ladies agreed they were well fortified, and Mr. Hawkins went off to another table.

"Is this your first trip to Edinburgh?" Kaitlyn inquired as she poured out her tea.

"No, our home is in Scotland, in the Borders actually. My father found a lovely property five years ago and has settled in. I did live in Edinburgh for a short time quite a while ago."

"Oh! Forgive me! You sound American and I made a silly assumption. Sometimes my wee brain is not fully engaged," replied Kaitlyn with a lilting Scottish laugh.

Surprisingly, for one who preferred being alone, Sarah found herself chatting more with Kaitlyn than with most people.

"I was born in Washington D.C. but my father and I have lived all over the world with his work. We both developed quite an affection for Scotland and when it came time to settle down we chose a spot near Peebles," Sarah shared.

"Isn't that a charming part of Britain? Peebles and Lauder are two of my favorite market villages. Have you taken the walk along the Lauder Town Trail? It's about a mile and a quarter. And have you seen Thirlestane Castle? It's one of the seven Great Houses of Scotland. Listen to me going on and on. You've probably explored the area to your hearts content."

"Truthfully, I have not spent as much time there as I would've liked. The first months we spent refurbishing and decorating the house with lots of decisions to make. It was very intense, but great fun. Then I started Girton College at Cambridge for the next three years and didn't get home often, mostly holidays, and now I am working."

"My goodness! You've left me winded! Haven't you had an exciting life? Did you enjoy Cambridge?"

"My time at Cambridge was…very focused on studying. Social aspects didn't appeal to me. Looking back, I think the education was worthwhile, and I'm quite sure having it on my resume gave me a leg-up in being hired, but I'm glad to be done with it."

'What is your job? Kaitlyn asked, gently dropping two lumps of sugar in her teacup.

"I work for Carlisle and Bryer Book Publishing in London, as Assistant Acquisitions Editor, which sounds far more important than it really is," Sarah paused, leaned closer and confided, "but at heart I am a writer."

Kaitlyn lowered her voice in acknowledgement that she had just been told a deep secret. "That is brilliant! But isn't it difficult to work full time and find occasion to write?"

Sarah answered in an equally low voice, "Yes it is, and I am facing a huge decision for my future, choosing which direction I should follow."

There was a quiet moment and for a split second Sarah wondered, 'what has gotten in to me to spill my story like a leaky bucket.' There was just something about Kaitlyn that felt easy and comfortable, like someone she could trust. The last time she had felt that way was with

Peter, but that was a lifetime ago and best left forgotten. She poured the last of the tea from the pot to her cup and looked across the table.

"Do you have any wisdom you'd care to share?"

"I'm sure you don't need the advice of forty-two year old stranger, but I guess I would tell you to follow your heart, if you can afford to. You're young, obviously very bright and a world of possibilities await you. Find what you love, then figure out how to get paid for it."

Sarah looked at Kaitlyn earnestly, "But do I give up a prestigious job and possible career in publishing to follow what could be a silly dream?"

"First of all, I believe there are no silly dreams. Secondly, do you absolutely love the publishing business? Are you completely fulfilled? Answer yes and you have your answer. But if not, think about this–if you had all the time and all the money in the universe, how would you spend your days? There's a wonderful saying by Confucius, 'Choose a job you love and you'll never work a day in your life.' If you look forward to a future in publishing, and are insecure about leaving, then perhaps you would be content to write as a hobby. However, if you yearn for a life of writing with stories to tell, and if your imagination leaps at the thought of spending each day creating, ask yourself if you would be satisfied not fulfilling that part of your soul?"

Handing the last biscuit across to Kaitlyn, Sarah took her time in replying.

"You've given me much to think about. I rarely share my concerns, and you have treated me with your wisdom and kindness. I am very grateful, thank you."

Mr. Hawkins and an assistant waiter came by to collect the dishes.

"Ladies, we shall arrive in Edinburgh shortly. As always, it has been a pleasure to see you Miss Sarah, and very nice to meet you, Miss Turning."

Both ladies smiled at the engaging waiter and thanked him.

"Kaitlyn, please tell me about you. I've taken up all our time together with my problems, and the stories of other people are always so much more interesting."

"Spoken like a writer! My story isn't much to tell really. I was born and raised in Edinburgh with lovely parents and three siblings, two boys and a girl. My father's family has owned a wee book shop on Victoria Street in Old Town for generations and much of my youth was spent there. My Da still runs it."

"I love book stores and I love Victoria Street. That sounds like a perfect childhood."

"It certainly was, and it is still one of my favorite places. Imagine second-hand books floor to ceiling, a huge fireplace and comfortable chairs where you can read or chat to your hearts content. There is even an old rolling library ladder that I was allowed to climb only when a customer absolutely required a volume from up top. The best part was the smell of old books." She looked across at Sarah in a conspiratorially way. "Did you know that when book glue, ink and paper all break down, they produce an aroma somewhat like vanilla, and that makes you want to read everything in the shop? And have you ever really thought of how old books carry their history by how they smell? Like a smoky scent if the owner used tobacco, or the fragrance of flowers pressed between pages or the reek of moldy water damage?"

The light in Kaitlyn's eyes, along with her enthusiasm, was contagious, and Sarah chimed right in.

"I know exactly what you mean. I have been a bit obsessed with books my whole life, especially old books. I've often wondered about their history, and who else held the very same volume I was reading. I can't believe you grew up in a book shop!"

"Well, you must make the trip to Edinburgh and come see me and the shop. Every few months I travel up from London to help my Da with the book-keeping. Mother used to take charge of that, but when she passed several years ago it was clear that he needed me. And it's a lovely excuse to visit him and the book shop. I'll be there for a few weeks and my Da would love to meet an aspiring writer. The wee shop is on Victoria Street, and it is called Turning Pages. We're open Tuesday through Saturday from ten in the morning until late afternoon or whenever Da decides to close."

Sarah was madly scribbling all the information in her journal.

"I can't think of anything I would enjoy more. My father is quite a reader as well, and I'm sure he would appreciate knowing a good place to find books. We will definitely see you in the next few days." Sarah ripped off a corner of a page in her journal, and wrote the telephone number of Leigheas as well as her London number and handed it to Kaitlyn. "I'm so glad we met. I hope we can stay in touch."

"I would like that. Besides, I will be curious to know what you decide about your future." Kaitlyn rose and gathered her handbag. "I'd better return to my seat, we're nearly there. Thank you again for sharing tea, and for the most interesting afternoon I've had in a long time."

After watching Kaitlyn disappear through the door at the far end of the dining car, Sarah found herself replaying their conversation over in her mind. What were the odds of meeting someone so engaging and interesting on a train? She thought of all the trips she had made alone the past few years and had openly, and possibly rudely, discouraged any conversation with anyone. Why would she want to share anything about her life with a stranger? It was much safer to keep to yourself, and 'mind your own counsel,' as her grandmother used to say. That was how she survived at Cambridge. Yet, the one time she opened herself up, it was with a delightful woman who seemed to understand and care. This was going to take some further thought, Sarah mused.

Ayton Castle came into view and that was the sign they were almost to Edinburgh. There was always anticipation when she arrived at Waverley. The first glimpse of her father waving to her, then the hour drive to Leigheas with just the two of them talking non-stop. Even after five years, the joy of having a real home to return to was exhilarating. Only one small downside she would never admit to anyone. The thought of Peter invariably crossed her mind as the train came to a stop in the station, and she was secretly afraid, yet secretly hopeful she might run into him. The old hurt rose in her mind and stabbed her heart. Looking anxiously through the window, she saw her father and that made everything okay.

## *Chapter Fifty-five*
# SEANEEN McAUGHTRIE:
## *A Walk to Remember*

"The River Tweed, our new dog Maggie and…having a real home," Sarah announced as she sat down to breakfast with her father and Mrs. McAughtrie.

Seaneen McAughtrie loved when Sarah came home for a visit. Everything was lighter and brighter, including Richard's already pleasant nature. It was rare when just the three of them could sit down in the kitchen and visit. Porridge was on the table, with raisins and brown sugar, and the tea pot was brewing their favorite blend.

"We are off to Edinburgh this morning, please do come with us, Seaneen," Sarah asked sincerely. "We're going to the book shop I told you about, and to Cavanagh's Antiques to see Maeve and Robbie. You know they would love to see you."

"Aye, it's a bit tempting but I think I had better stay here and get a few bits and bobs done. Our mystery guest might be arriving a wee bit earlier than we expected, and there are always last minute things to attend to. I like to keep a sharp eye on things."

Richard piped in, "Isn't that what Meara and Brennon are here for?"

"Those young lasses are busy tidying the house, and laying fires. Out of the blue they asked if they might prepare dinner tonight. I'm delighted, but will want to oversee their cooking to make sure it's edible. Once lunch is served I am looking forward to taking a long, leisurely walk about and enjoy a bit of this late October sunshine. I want to check the kitchen garden for any remains of vegetables we might find. The winter chill will be here before you know it. I promised little Henry I would bring him some fresh shortbread biscuits today. He's such a fine lad."

"Well, your day sounds fully planned. Maybe you would take Maggie with you on your walk? A nice run would do her a world of good," Richard said, then turning to Sarah, "As soon as you finish breakfast and are ready, Miss Sunshine, we will be off. I'll need to grab a few things in my office, then meet me by the front door."

Sarah helped clean up the dishes, and couldn't help herself from teasing Mrs. McAughtrie. "I hear you've an admirer hanging about."

"Oh, don't you start too, lass. Your father is enjoying this far too much. James is a lovely gentleman and nice to be around. Now, scoot, and get on your way. Give Maeve and Robbie my best regards."

A few minutes later they were gone and the big house was quiet. Other than mealtimes when their guests would congregate in the large dining room, the house was wonderfully peaceful. There were always tasks to be tended to and meals to plan and prepare, but overall life was quite good. Thinking back, she had enjoyed the year spent living with her sister. Marjorie's small house was over a hundred years old and located in Lacock, near the historic town of Bath. The home had been lovingly restored by Marjorie and her husband, Hugh, into the most delightful family home imaginable. Now, however, with Hugh gone and the children grown up, Marjorie's life had become far too quiet. At the same time Seaneen was very much at loose ends after the traumatic event in Edinburgh. In a telephone conversation, Marjorie suggested Seaneen come stay with her for as long as she wanted. It was an answer to prayer. Being with family proved to be the best remedy for both women. They took long walks through the countryside, and stayed up late reliving childhood memories and laughing unto tears. After a few months of staying close to the house, the sisters began venturing into the village more and more. They joined a book club, ate lunch at the pub, and attended church again. Marjorie even began keeping company with a pleasant older gentleman, Malcolm, who sang in the church choir. Seaneen was feeling stronger and more confident as the days went on, and truthfully, felt like a third wheel with Marjorie and Malcolm. As with most things that are meant to be, Richard Duncan's timing in contacting Seaneen to join him at Leigheas was perfect. It was hard to believe that it had been five, wonderful years ago. The position overseeing the large home fit her personality superbly, and the idea of being with Sarah and Richard pleased her enormously. Furthermore, when Richard explained the mission of the Leigheas, and how he intended it as a place for men to heal, she knew she had found her place. This was exactly where she belonged. But enough reminiscing, there were things to do if she was going to take a walk around the property today. The sun wouldn't be shining forever.

Lunch dishes had been put away, shortbread cookies were packed in a tin box for Henry, and she found a cloth bag to carry any vegetables she might find.

"Maggie, come on lass, let me get the leash on you."

She didn't need to call twice, as the golden cocker spaniel appeared instantly. Stepping out the side door into the fresh air, Seaneen caught sight of the rolling hills in the distance, and the sunlight glistening off of the River Tweed. This really was God's country on a day like today. That thought made her laugh out loud. She was equally sure this was God's country even when it was gray and pouring rain. It was simply a lovely day to be alive.

Her first stop was the chapel on the far northeast side of the property. To the casual observer it would appear that the small stone building had been there for centuries. Ivy crawled up the walls and encircled the leaded, stained glass windows and the arched wooden door had 'Rosemary's Chapel' carved in it. In reality, the chapel had been built only about four years ago as a loving homage to Richard's mother. It was important to him that the structure fit in the landscape as though it had always been there. Inside were wooden pews to seat around twenty people, and a small alter at the front. One of the first guests at Leigheas, Francis Finlay, was so enamored by the chapel, that he hand carved a tall cross out of elm wood, and had it shipped to Richard as a thank you for his time spent there. If you looked carefully, the initials FF were carved within the ornate design. Over the past years, Seaneen had noticed an interesting pattern by their guests. When they first arrived at Leigheas, they tended to avoid the chapel but the longer they were there, the more frequently they would stop by and spend time. Whether in times of trouble or simply in humble gratitude, the hushed, serenity of the chapel seemed to speak to everyone. There was hardly a week that went by that Seaneen didn't try to spend a bit of time there.

The walk from the chapel to the stable crossed a wide grass meadow, beyond was an area referred to as The Woods. The welcome smell of hay bales, and freshly polished leather saddles in the tack room reminded her of early days spent on her family farm. She inhaled deeply, and wandered through the long, L shaped stone building to the horse stalls. Maggie tugged at her leash, wanting to run free and explore the barn, but Seaneen held her tight.

"Not yet, Maggie, wait till we are outside."

Coming to the first stall, she peeked in. "Hello, you handsome four-legged creature," Seaneen spoke gently to the bay gelding who greeted her with a snort and nuzzled his nose into her open palm holding the carrot. "I've missed you."

"I see you're carrying on with my horses again," teased Stephen, walking up from behind. "They have missed you as well. Make sure you've enough carrots for all of them. Don't go playing favorites."

Opening her over-sized, fishnet bag Seaneen pulled out an entire bunch of carrots, complete with green tops.

"I'd never do such a thing," she laughed.

Visiting with retired veterinarian Stephen and his down syndrome son, Henry, was always a pleasure. Stephen was a widower in his early fifties who's wife had died in childbirth with Henry. In the early days as a single parent, he tried to work while others took care of Henry, but after three years he knew his place was with his son. It was about that time that Richard was looking for someone qualified to take care of the horses and other livestock at Leigheas, and heard about Stephen. Once Stephen knew the job paid well, came with a cottage, and Henry was welcome, he signed the contract and had never been sorry. Henry had taken to Seaneen early on, calling her Auntie-Neen. Never had she been around such an open, loving, engaging little person. His smile and captivating demeanor brought happiness to everyone he met.

Little Henry rounded the corner of the stable and saw his Auntie-Neen, and ran toward her with open arms. Shortbread cookies were his favorite and once he spied the tin box, he was overjoyed.

"For me, Auntie Neen?"

"Yes, indeed, sweet boy. Would you like to hold Maggie's leash while we find a bale of hay to sit on?

"Oh, yes," he answered with excitement.

The far side of the barn was a perfect spot, away from all the animal activity, but close enough for Stephen to know where they were. Little Henry snuggled onto Seaneen's lap and opened the top of the biscuit tin. Maggie's nose wiggled as she caught a whiff of the shortbread.

"Auntie-Neen, can we give a teeny, tiny, wee bit to Maggie?"

"Aye, just a wee bit," she answered, drawing the little boy closer as she took out a well-worn copy of Peter Rabbit from her mesh bag. "Look what I have!"

"Peter Wabbit!!" He sang out joyfully and listened carefully as she read, nibbling shortbread biscuits happy as could be. She began their ritual reading.

"Once upon a time there were four little rabbits, and their names were..."

"Flopsy, Mopsy, Cottontail and Peter!" He would answer triumphantly.

If she missed a word, or skipped a sentence, he was quick to correct her. As they got to the last page where Peter Rabbit was being put to bed with his camomile tea, little Henry had eaten three cookies and was ready to go back to playing. With one last hug, he was off.

"Love you, Auntie-Neen, love you Maggie."

"Love you, too, sweet boy."

The cocker spaniel wagged her tail in agreement.

With autumn headed toward winter, the sun was setting earlier and earlier. One more stop at the kitchen garden, then she would return to the house to check on Meara and Brennan and see how dinner was progressing. The unusual sight of a large, white-tailed eagle caught her attention as it soared overhead. The huge bird swooped down to chase a fleeing rodent, then flew up and away toward the loch. The absolute, pure beauty of nature always left her feeling humbled and grateful for the wondrous world God had created. She watched the graceful bird land on the far side of the water, and to her surprise she saw Becket McTavish seated on the wooden bench not far away. He appeared to be deep in thought, staring off toward the opposite shore. Knowing he had not seen her, it would be easy to quietly step away, avoiding another distasteful incident. Seaneen sighed deeply. On the other hand, hadn't she promised Richard she would do all she could to be a positive influence on their guests? Sometimes it was hard to summon up the energy to do the right thing. In her heart she knew she should at least speak to him, even if her brain was telling her to flee the cranky man. Right won out as she walked with the dog toward him.

"Good afternoon, Mr. McTavish," Seaneen spoke cheerfully, "lovely day, isn't it?"

"Yes," was his curt reply.

After standing beside the bench for a good minute and a half with no acknowledgement, she spoke again.

"Do you mind if I sit for a moment? I've walked quite a distance from the chapel, to the stables, to the loch."

Another one word reply.

"No."

"No, you don't mind, or no, you'd rather I move on?"

He looked up at her with tired eyes and finally answered, "You're welcome to sit down."

Another few minutes passed with nothing being said. A fish jumped in the loch, creating ripples that radiated out in concentric circles. A pair of Whooper Swans, visible at the far end of the water, spoke out with their familiar *kloo-kloo-kloo* honking call, breaking the silence of the late afternoon.

"I've a lot in common with those swans," the actor spoke out of nowhere.

"Really?"

"Yes. They mate for life."

Seaneen was not sure how to respond and didn't want to run the risk of irritating him. Another few minutes passed with only the vocal swans speaking to each other. Just when she was thinking of a reason to justify leaving, he spoke again.

"Mrs. McAughtrie, I have behaved very badly toward you and I am sorry. I have no excuse to offer and I ask your forgiveness with a promise that it will not happen again."

She opened her mouth to accept his apology, when he hushed her by lifting his hand in a silent command not to speak, but to let him continue.

"I have come to realize that for many years I have demanded to be the center of the universe, no matter the toll on those around me. I learned to use my temper to control people and situations. If something wasn't to my liking, I would brutally lash out, most often hurting and humiliating whoever was in my path. To my mind, I was owed adoration and respect."

A long silence passed before he continued.

"Being here, in the quiet and peaceful surroundings Mr. Duncan has provided, I have had the earth-shattering realization that I am an ass and an overall deplorable human being. For decades I treated my beautiful, loving wife shabbily, always making sure she knew I was the star and she merely had a supporting role. And now that she's gone..." he paused to wipe the tears rolling down his cheek, "whatever shall I do? It's too late to make amends to her, to tell her that I owe everything I've ever achieved to her. She was my mate for life. How will I live with the shame of all I've done?"

Becket McTavish, famous international stage actor, looked over at Seaneen McAughtrie, a woman he hardly knew, with desperation in his watery eyes. She's quietly lay her hand over his and held it firmly for a time before speaking. He made no effort to move it, and slowly turned back to watching the swans. They sat on the bench for some minutes, then she spoke in a soft voice.

"The first step toward healing will be to forgive yourself."

"I don't know how to do that."

And for the next hour they talked and shared about their lives, the choices they had made, mistakes that haunted them, and the fear of forgiveness.

"There comes a time when we must unlearn much of what we thought was acceptable and take responsibility. The past is gone, don't wallow in it, but learn from it. Be brave, Becket, and move forward toward the rest of your life. You've much to offer the world."

Realizing how much time had passed, Seaneen stood up, and added one final thought.

"I believe in you."

The weary actor looked up at his new friend and took her hand.

"Thank you, good lady."

"Now, I must be off to see if those lasses have prepared dinner. We might all be in for a wee surprise if they haven't."

Walking hastily toward the house, she neared the kitchen garden and decided gathering the vegetables would have to wait for another day. She turned quickly, when without warning her foot caught on a large exposed root from a tall pine tree. She felt herself falling. The ground was coming toward her very quickly, but she couldn't stop the momentum. Her head hit the hard earth with a thud and everything went black.

## Chapter Fifty-six

# RICHARD:

*An Eventful Day in Edinburgh*

Cavanagh's Antique Shoppe at 49 Cockburn Street was packed with customers, which meant there were three people plus Robbie and Maeve and no room to turn around. With quick hugs and promises to return soon, Richard and Sarah were off to lunch at Jenners, the elegant department store built in the late 1800's. Lunch was a quick affair in the cafe, and they hardly took time to appreciate the glamorous interior with it's ornate balconies and dark wood railings on their way out.

"Have you noticed how many buildings here have glass ceilings?" Richard asked.

"I have actually. Waverley station, the North British Railway Hotel, Jenners, the Botanical Garden, though I suppose that's more of a glass house," she answered.

"You know," Richard laughed, "you must be one of the few young ladies who is more interested in the building structure than all the beautiful clothes in this fine establishment."

"That must come from my splendid upbringing," Sarah chided, as she slid her arm through her handsome father's.

"It's a ten-minute walk to Victoria Street. Let's take Princes Street to Waverley Bridge. I think it's a short cut, though we might need to climb some stairs."

"Of course, we will," Sarah chimed in with a laugh, "It's Edinburgh. There are stairs everywhere! I'm so looking forward to seeing Kaitlyn and the bookstore."

They turned right at St. Giles Street, left onto Back Street, then continued on to the George IV Bridge and finally a right to historic Victoria Street. They walked up the curving, cobblestone street with five and six story Flemish style buildings towering on either side. All along the way, engaging shops with imposing fronts and large windows beckoned buyers to come in.

"Did you know this street was named after Queen Victoria?" Richard quizzed his daughter.

Sarah rolled her eyes, "Yes, Dad, I knew that."

"Well, did you know," he leaned down and said in a sinister voice, "there are still narrow medieval passageways lurking between these tall stone buildings?"

"Then it's a good thing we are standing in front of the book shop, so we won't get lost forever in a medieval passageway."

Richard looked up to see an aging wooden sign over the door with faded gold lettering, *Turning Pages Book Shoppe*. They peeked through the display window of the modest-sized store and saw Kaitlyn toward the back helping a customer. The tinkling bell over the glass entry door announced their arrival.

Sarah leaned close to her father and whispered.

"Now, remember her name is Kaitlyn and her father is Thomas Turning," Sarah instructed her father.

"You've mentioned that three times in the last two hours. Am I getting dotty and don't know it?" Richard laughed.

"No, it's just that I like her and I want her to like us."

"You want who to like us? Were their names Catherine and Todd?" he teased.

"Dad!"

"I'll behave and try to be my charming self."

"You mean your incorrigible self," Sarah responded. "Would you look around? I've never seen so many books in my life! The shelves go all the way up to the ceiling, and the ceiling must be twenty feet tall! This is the best store I've ever been in!

Richard was highly amused by his daughter's reaction. He followed her gaze around the long, fairly narrow shop and had to agree that there was a staggering number of books in such a compact space. Turning toward the back of the store he saw a lovely, slim woman with blonde hair and a beautiful smile walking toward them. He was a little disappointed when she made a beeline to Sarah, completely bypassing him.

"Sarah! I'm so glad you found us! There are so many shops on Victoria Street, it's a bit hard to tell one from the other."

"We had no trouble at all. It was a nice walk from Jenners, and we came right to it. This is an absolutely marvelous place, Kaitlyn. If I were you I would spend everyday just breathing in all these old books."

Kaitlyn looked up at Richard, who held out his hand toward her.

"Good afternoon, I am Richard Duncan, Sarah's father."

Placing her hand in his, they continued looking at each other for a few seconds, before a rather small, slightly bent, older gentleman with gray hair and a small mustache appeared.

"And I am Thomas Turning, Kaitlyn's father," the gentleman said with amusement.

Dropping Kaitlyn's hand, Richard reached to the outstretched hand of Thomas Turning.

"Very nice to meet you, sir. May I say, this is quite an impressive array of books."

"Thank you, Mr. Duncan. The shop has been in my family for three generations, and I feel as though I am just the caretaker until my Kaitlyn grows weary of London and comes home to take over."

Sarah brightened and turned to Kaitlyn, "Do you really think you might do that? That would be brilliant."

"We will see," Kaitlyn answered with a smile.

"And you must be Sarah," Thomas said, "I've looked forward to meeting you. I understand you are a writer."

"Well, I'm not sure about that, though I have written a few things," Sarah blushed.

"Then you are a writer, my dear. Never be afraid of calling yourself a writer. Now, becoming an author is quite another thing. Let's sit down so I can get to know you." Reaching for her hand he led her through the shop, past rows of bookshelves filled with leather bound books, toward the fireplace and the two overstuffed chairs opposite each other.

"We have much to talk about. Have you read *The Elements of Style* by William Strunk…." Almost immediately the two were engrossed in conversation about writing styles, authors and other such things.

Not totally sure what just happened, a bewildered Richard looked at Kaitlyn.

"I am not accustomed to Sarah opening up to people. She has always been a rather shy girl, but she certainly has taken to your father."

"His whole life has been about literature and writing and old books, and when he finds a kindred soul, there is almost always a connection. I think he was born an antiquarian."

"I suspect he will find Sarah shares those feelings and then some. Reading has been…I guess I would say, her refuge for most of her life. I used to worry about her spending so much time in books, often to the exclusion of everything else," Richard said looking at his daughter deep in conversation with Thomas Turning. "But it seems I needn't be concerned about her making friends."

"No, I think you can lay that to rest," Kaitlyn answered with her lilting laugh. "Sarah was absolutely engaging when we met on the train. I was taken with her immediately. I wonder if sometimes parents are not able to see their children objectively."

"I'm quite sure of that. After three years at Cambridge, and now London for nearly a year, she has quite outgrown the little girl I raised."

"From what I've seen, you've done quite well."

The door bell tinkled again as a young man came rushing in.

"I'm sorry, the bus was running a wee bit late."

"You're fine, Jacob. The afternoon has been quiet, and our new friends have just dropped in. Let me introduce you to Mr. Richard Duncan. Mr. Duncan, this is Jacob Silvers, our most helpful employee. He's actually our only employee."

The two men shook hands, as the younger one looked curiously at the older one.

"Are you THE Richard Duncan? The gentleman from the American Consulate?"

"Yes, I was at the consulate for a short time."

"And someone shot you!"

"Yes, I'm afraid they did," Richard answered wryly.

Kaitlyn jumped in before the inappropriate conversation went any further.

"Jacob, please put your things in the back while I show Mr. Duncan around the shop."

The young man lowered his head and walked toward the back of the store and turned right into the office area, but not before giving Sarah an appreciative look.

"My apologies. He's a very bright boy, but a bit prone to not filter his conversation."

"Youthful enthusiasm." Richard added in a lower voice, "Are you really going to give me a tour of your shop?"

"Indeed I am! I would not want you getting lost between Dante's Inferno and Elizabeth Barrett Browning."

"Interesting you choose those two authors, as one is Italian by birth, and the other, namely Barrett Browning, lived and wrote many of her poems in Florence, Italy."

The lilting laugh again, "Are you trying to impress me, Mr. Duncan?"

"Indeed, I am, Miss Turning," Richard answered.

They spent the next hour perusing the narrow aisles of the little bookshop, discussing literature, history, biographies and travel. Richard had developed a sudden interest in beautiful old books, or maybe it was the shopkeeper's daughter that had caught his attention. He looked at his watch and realized how much time had passed. They still had a long drive back to Leigheas and it was much later than he expected. About the same time Sarah and Thomas Turning were walking toward the front of the shop, where Jacob was helping a customer. Looking at the lovely Miss Turning, Richard held his hand out again.

"I can't thank you enough for this fascinating literary adventure."

She shook his hand, "It was my pleasure, Mr. Duncan."

"Richard, please," he said.

"Very well…Richard, please do come again."

"Rest assured on that, Miss Turning."

"Kaitlyn, please," she answered.

He was oddly reluctant to release her hand, and she seemed in no hurry to have her hand back. The moment was broken by Sarah walking up with her arms filled with books.

"Mr. Turning said these were essential."

In a flurry of confusion, with goodbye's and 'lovely to meet you' niceties said, they were out the door.

The drive between Edinburgh and Leigheas was familiar, but Richard never tired of it. The narrow roads and small market towns were all leading him home. Learning to drive on the left side of the street had been a challenge, with more than a few close calls, but now he drove like everyone else, a bit too fast, and a bit too close to the hedgerows bordering the roadsides. He was deep in thought when their comfortable silence was broken by Sarah.

"Wasn't that the most amazing afternoon?"

"Yes, it was. You seem to enjoy talking with Mr. Turning."

"He knows everything about writing and authors, and I think he's read every book ever written. He was so interested in me and what I want to do and had so many suggestions. Do you know he has a one of the original self-published versions of *The Elements of Style* by William Strunk from decades ago? It's that famous American book about rules that writers must know before they can break them."

"I know the book well, believe it or not, we used it when I was in school."

"Is it THAT old?" Sarah teased. "Wow, I had no idea."

"I admit it, I am very old!" He laughed, "But seriously, you seem very taken with Mr. Turning, and I can understand that. He appears to be very generous with his time and his knowledge, if he finds someone worthy of sharing."

"Speaking of being taken, you seem to be quite attentive to Miss

Turning."

"She is very interesting and certainly knows everything about…everything."

"And she's really pretty as well, don't you think?"

"Of course she is, but as you've reminded me, I'm very old…"

"Oh silly, you are not old, and besides she is about your same age."

Not sure where to go with this conversation, Richard said nothing. Talking about women to his daughter was unfamiliar territory and he suddenly felt uncomfortable. How did she grow up so fast? Nothing was said for several miles. Out of the corner of his eye he noticed Sarah looking at him as if she wanted to speak, but didn't. He tried to think of a different topic to bring up, but honestly, his mind was on Miss Turning. He really was quite taken with the Scottish lady, but certainly didn't want to discuss it with his daughter.

"May I ask you something?" Sarah queried. "It might be a little personal."

"Of course you may ask," her father answered as lightly as he could, "but we will see about the answering part."

"Were there any women in your life when I was growing up? I don't ever remember meeting anyone, or you talking about anyone. After all, now that I think about it, you were single and very handsome, and I do remember you went to lots of dinners and parties all dressed up."

"Well…there were a few, several of my choice, but mostly set up by well-meaning friends or colleagues. There was never any one lady that I had enough feelings for to introduce to you. Whether you know it or not, you have always been the top priority in my life, and I never thought it a good idea to risk the possibility of you becoming attached to a person only to find them gone the next week."

Sarah appeared to be pondering this new information.

"Would it be okay if I asked you about my mother?" she asked.

"Of course. What would you like to know?" Richard answered with a false bravado, not entirely thrilled with this conversation, but in his heart knowing it was overdue.

"How did you meet?"

"I had just started in the Foreign Service, and a gentleman I worked with wanted me to meet his sister. At the time, I was very involved in my new job and not looking for any outside distraction, but he was insistent. I finally gave in and arranged to meet Vincent, his wife Jenny and your mother, at a small Italian restaurant for dinner. The moment I walked in I saw your mother across the room. She was quite beautiful." For a brief moment Richard was back in that Italian restaurant gazing in awe at Victoria. She had been beguiling in every way, very bright and quietly charming. "She appeared interested in me, asking lots of questions, which by the way, is the best way to make any man feel important."

"I'll remember that. And then what happened?" Sarah asked.

"And then, we spent all of our free time together and got married, in hindsight, maybe a bit too quickly," Richard answered, hoping to end the discussion there. While he wanted to be truthful about the past, he wasn't comfortable sharing the trauma of his wife leaving so soon after Sarah's birth and cutting off all communication. Before he could change the subject, Sarah pressed on.

"Did…did you ever try to contact my mother?"

"In the beginning I gave photos of you to Vincent, my brother-in-law, and pleaded with him to send them along to Victoria. He always took the photos from me, but I never knew if he gave them to her or not. Before long divorce papers arrived and I reluctantly signed them. Within the next year, I was told she had moved out of the country and that is the last I've heard about her."

"What about her family? Vincent and his wife? None of them know anything?"

"Unfortunately, Vincent and Jenny were on assignment in Africa and got caught in a local, political uprising and have been missing for nearly twenty years. They are presumed dead, and there are no other relatives I know of. I'm sorry, I wish I could tell you more."

"We've just never talked about it and I wondered. Thank you for telling me."

For the next few minutes he let the past drift away, until reality came back into focus.

"Sunshine Girl, are you still having your nightmares?"

"Less and less," she answered looking out the window.

"So that means yes?"

"I guess, but they aren't as bad and not as often. It's okay, Dad."

Light rain landed on the windshield as they drove on.

"Well, little lady, let me ask *you* a question," Richard inquired determined to change the mood. "In all of your years at university, didn't some young man work his way into your heart?"

Her giggle lifted the mood.

"Like father, like daughter I think. There wasn't anyone important enough to tell you about. The closest anyone came was Jeff, a fellow in medical school. He was smart and funny, but after a few weeks I realized I wasn't much of a priority in his life. There were times he was really rude, then apologized and blamed the stress he was under. Well, guess what, mister-almost-doctor, we are ALL under a lot of stress. So, that didn't work out very well. It did make me realize I just wanted to study, graduate and go into the world."

"You have been blessed with so much wisdom for your age, almost like you were born an old soul. I'm sure you've no idea what an extraordinary person you are and I promise you, my beautiful daughter, that someday you will meet someone wonderful, who adores you and will compliment and enhance every part of your life."

# Chapter Fifty-seven

# SARAH:

## *The Afternoon of Change*

Listening to her father describe the perfect mate for her, it crossed Sarah's mind that one day she would tell her father about Peter, but not today. Even thinking his name still caused a pang of hurt. She reminded herself that he was in the long ago, and she lived in the here and now. And now she needed to think about her future.

The drizzle had become rain, and the windshield wipers were racing to keep the road visible. Thankfully, they were just turning into the gates of Leigheas and would be at the house before it was an all out downpour. Rounding the last curve, she could see a man carrying a body, running toward the house.

"Dad! Who is that? What's happening?"

"I don't know. Someone is in trouble."

As soon as the car stopped, they both jumped out and ran toward the house. It was Becket carrying Seaneen McAughtrie, who appeared to be unconscious. Most of the guests heard the commotion and were standing in the entry. A very wet Maggie the dog hung back from the crowd. Richard immediately began barking out orders as he led the way to the nearest room.

"Bring her into this reception room, Becket. Sarah, call Dr. McDonald, tell him it's an emergency. Ian, run to the stables and get Stephen. Meara, bring me blankets and brandy from the butler's pantry. Edward, could you take the dog to the kitchen? James, come with me."

By the time Sarah returned, Mrs. McAughtrie's limp body was reclining on a long sofa, covered in wool blankets. She opened her eyes and looked around in obvious confusion. James was kneeling next to her, holding her hand and whispering prayers. Richard was the first to speak to her as he held a snifter of brandy to her lips.

"Try to take a sip of this, not too much," he instructed.

She did as she was told, and began to cough. "Ohh. My head," she said before she closed her eyes again.

Stephen came rushing in, with Ian on his heels and Henry not far behind. Richard turned to Becket for an explanation of what had happened.

"We were chatting on the bench by the loch and as she walked away her foot caught on a tree root and she fell. My guess is she hit her head."

"Stephen, could you just look her over?" Richard looked at Sarah, "And Dr. McDonald is on his way?"

"He should be here shortly. I caught him at the surgery just as he was leaving."

James moved away as Stephen gently felt her limbs and asked questions in a low voice. The room was quiet as everyone strained to hear the conversation. Sarah could see the deep concern on her father's face as the vet examined their dearest friend. With an authority that hid her distress, Sarah spoke quietly to the others.

"I think it might be good to give them some privacy. Meara, Brennan, could you make tea and a few things? Let's serve in the orangery. Dinner will be a bit later than usual, so that should hold us over." Sarah caught sight of little Henry and her heart melted.

"Henry, do you think you could help Miss Meara while Auntie-Neen talks to your father?"

The boy shook his head up and down, and grudgingly took Meara's hand. The others had not completely gotten the hint.

"Gentlemen, tea will be in the orangery in a few minutes. I will meet you there with any news."

With that, Ian and Edward left, followed by Becket who kept saying how sorry he was. James was watching Seaneen, and hesitant to leave her. Stephen had finished his cursory exam and was reporting to Richard.

"I don't find any broken bones, but only an X-ray will tell for sure. I am not able to comment on her head injury, as that is completely out of my field. I don't see any open wounds, but there is what appears to be a sizable hematoma where I am surmising her head made contact with either a rock or hard soil."

"Thank you, Stephan. That is very helpful. I believe there is tea in the orangery and little Henry is helping in the kitchen."

It was finally Sarah's turn to comfort her long-time friend. She pulled up a chair next to the sofa and took the older lady's hand.

"How are you feeling? Is there anything I can get you?" Sarah asked, looking into the still somewhat dazed eyes that stared back at her. The response was delayed and brief, and somewhat slurred.

"All right. No, thank you."

The impact of the possibilities hit Sarah like bolt and the 'what ifs' of life assailed her once again. What if she doesn't recover? What if she is permanently impaired? What if…? Tears slid down her cheeks. Her father put his arm around his daughter and held her tightly. Seaneen closed her eyes, as if her lids were too heavy to keep open. James spoke up in an urgent voice. Sarah had forgotten he was even there.

"I don't think she should be allowed to sleep. I had a bit of medical training and I remember anyone with a head injury needs to stay awake for a few hours."

Richard gently stroked Seaneen's cheek, just enough to wake her up.

"The doctor will be here shortly, Seaneen, and it would be a good idea if you stayed awake until then. Can you do that?" His answer came with a slight nod of agreement.

"Would you mind terribly if I stayed, just until the doctor arrives?" James asked.

Richard was the one who answered, with kindness and compassion in his voice.

"I think that's a fine idea, James. Both Sarah and I should clean up a bit, at least wash our hands. Thank you. I know you'll take good care of her."

As father and daughter were leaving the room, Sarah looked back long enough to see the retired vicar gently rubbing Seaneen's forehead and speaking in a soft voice. He was rewarded with a slight smile from his injured friend.

Dr. McDonald arrived and spent about an hour with Seaneen. They moved her to one of the spacious upstairs bedrooms at the far end of the hallway where it was very quiet. For the most part his assessment agreed with Stephen's in terms of no broken bones. She had plenty of cuts and scrapes which would become colorful bruising in the days to come. His main concern was her cognitive ability and any more symptoms that might develop.

"We need to be alert to any visual changes such as the pupils of her eyes becoming larger than normal, any nausea or vomiting, a headache that becomes worse or any blood draining from her nose or ears. I would like for her to be watched twenty-four hours a day for the next two days. I will return then and we can see how she is progressing. If possible, keep her awake for the next four hours, then it should be fine for her to sleep. Do you have any questions?"

Neither Richard nor Sarah could think of anything, and the doctor took his leave. As the front door closed, they looked at each other, both feeling the adrenalin of the days events wearing off. Sarah saw that her father was exhausted, and offered to do the first shift. They spoke quietly while Seaneen was resting in the large four-poster bed across the room.

"Dinner is almost ready, so why don't I spend the next few hours with her and you can get some rest. Meara can bring me a tray and I will talk Seaneen's arm off and not let her sleep."

Sarah could see her father was too tired to protest.

"I think I will take you up on that offer," he said, then added, "The last I heard, our new guest will be arriving tonight. I had forgotten about it until just now. Obviously, he isn't here yet, so my best guess is he will arrive either sometime later tonight or tomorrow. He is coming in under an alias name, so I've no idea of who he is. I'll check with Meara to see if she has any more information. If I know Seaneen, she will have left all the paperwork in order in her office."

"No worries. We will sort it out when he arrives. Sounds like a celebrity of some sort. How exciting."

"I'm too tired to be excited. In fact, I think I'll ask Meara to bring me a tray as well when she's finished serving the guests. If I can sleep for three or four hours, I'll be ready to take my turn."

A knock at the door surprised them both. Carrying a tray with a few biscuits and a cup of tea, James walked in.

"May I offer to stay with Seaneen tonight? If you don't mind me saying, you both look a bit like you could use a rest, and honestly, I would like to be with her. I promise to keep her alert as the doctor mentioned. You have no idea how many racy clergy stories I can tell her, and if all fails I can give her one of my sermons, though on second thought that might put her to sleep. If I'm at all troubled by anything I can awaken you."

Huge relief washed over both Sarah and her father, and they could see James was looking forward to his time alone with Seaneen. They hurried out of the room before he changed his mind, though Richard had one last instruction.

"You know which room is mine, please don't hesitate to let me know if you're concerned about anything."

"We will be fine," he said turning to gaze on Seaneen, who was looking back quite contentedly.

Richard turned to Sarah as they stood in the hallway, "With another guest, I think we should try to get some additional help. While the girls can handle the kitchen, there are a hundred of other things that Seaneen takes care of," Richard said.

"You forget, I am here for a while…maybe a long while, and I can try to take care of some of the tasks. We need to be positive about Seaneen's recovery. I'm sure she will be able to help guide me once she is feeling better. Anyway, that's tomorrow's problem. I'll go down and see how everything is going while you relax and have dinner brought up to you."

"Sunshine Girl, how you have grown up! Thank you, I'll do just that."

"And dream about Kaitlyn," Sarah answered as she ran downstairs.

They needn't have worried about anything. Dinner went perfectly well, and Meara and Brennan had the dishes done and were planning the meals for the next day when Sarah found them in the kitchen.

"All the guests have retired to their cottages, and we've taken trays to both Mr. Duncan and Vicar Bradbury. Your tray is in the warming oven. We have been thinking and figured we can handle the kitchen, but someone will need to make grocery orders and see to the schedules."

"You girls are a wonder," Sarah said.

Looking shyly at each other, Meara, the older sister spoke out.

"Mrs. McAughtrie has been very good to us and taught us things we never would have learned."

Brennen interrupted, "And she's so patient with my mistakes. We really care for her and want to help."

Spontaneously, Sarah hugged both girls and thanked them repeatedly.

"We were thinking, ma'am, would it be a help if we stayed in the main house for a few days instead of going home? That way we would be here anytime if you needed us," Meara offered.

"Oh girls, I think that is a wonderful idea."

"If you could stay here for just a few minutes, we could run home and get a few things and tell our mum, if that's okay."

"By all means. Take your time, I'll have my dinner here and enjoy the quiet house. And, please tell your mum how much I appreciate your help."

Both girls nodded shyly and were out the back door in a hurry. Sarah retrieved her dinner from the warmer and sat at the big table in the middle of the kitchen. So much had happened in one day. From the exhilaration of their trip to Edinburgh to despair over her dearest friend. She could hear her grandmother Rosemary's voice in her mind, 'No matter how bad a situation seems, always look for the silver lining.' Indeed, there had been abundant blessings in this crazy day. Rinsing her dishes, a feeling of well-being settled over her and she knew that somehow they would get through this. Seaneen McAughtrie would get better and life would be back to normal, then she would decide the direction for her future. The loud, sharp doorbell startled her from pleasant thoughts.

"Oh darn! I was hoping the guest wouldn't arrive until tomorrow," she said out loud.

With no one else in the around, she knew she must deal with it.

"I'm coming, I'm coming," she grumbled, getting up from her comfortable chair in the kitchen.

The thought that she had never handled the details of a new person's arrival was hopefully the last hurdle of her day. The bell rang again. She must get it before it woke up the rest of the house.

She lifted the old fashioned latch and unlocked the old, heavy door. It had become stubborn lately, probably due to the humidity and all the rain. With a hearty tug it opened, almost knocking her over. There stood a tall, young man with an unkept beard, looking quite ragged in a large overcoat and a knit hat. His eyes were looking down when the door opened, but rose to meet hers. Taking off his hat, his brown, loosely curled hair surrounded a familiar face. Neither said a word for what seemed like an eternity.

"Peter, what are you doing here?" Sarah asked, her heart beating so fast she thought she might faint.

"Very much hoping I could come in out of the rain."

# Chapter Fifty-eight

# PETER:

## *Welcome to Leigheas?*

Her hesitation was obvious. He figured it might be because he looked like a drowned rat, and after all, it had been over five years since his last contact with her.

"I...I think I was expected," Peter answered, as the rain continued to pelt him.

"By whom?" she responded, strangely aloof.

"Your father? I am listed under the name Leonardo da Vinci?"

"YOU are the mystery guest?" she asked incredulously.

"Apparently. May I please come in? The taxi left me at the gate and I walked the distance to the house."

Sarah stepped back and Peter entered, leaving puddles wherever he stood.

"I'm sorry. You are the last person I expected to see tonight. Let me take your wet things," she said cooly. "My father has gone to bed, but I believe there are instructions in the kitchen. Follow me."

Of every conceivable reception he had anticipated at Leigheas, the indifference and distant behavior of the young lady he thought he knew so well came as a shock. Life had given him some difficult lessons the past years, but he had kept the memory of his friendship with Sarah as a beacon of light when he felt so lost. Maybe it was just the surprise of seeing him unexpectedly that was cause for her attitude. When his mother had suggested Leigheas, she mentioned that it was owned by Richard Duncan, 'your friend's father who was shot all those years ago.' There was part of him that was elated at the thought of being reunited with Sarah, but it was overshadowed by the embarrassment and shame of where he was now in his life. After all, he had reasoned when choosing to come here, he might not ever see Sarah. For all he knew she could be happily married with children and living God knows where. He would have carefully asked her father about her, and hoped she was doing well. Sarah opening that large wooden door was the last thing he expected.

The kitchen was warm with a small fire in the Aga. He watched a cocker spaniel sleeping soundly on a padded bed nearby. Sarah went into a small office off the kitchen to retrieve his paperwork. He would try again to make conversation.

"I am terribly sorry for arriving so late and throwing you into confusion."

"It's fine," was all she answered as she looked through the file with the name Leonardo da Vinci written on it.

Peter leaned over and stroked the sleepy dog, thinking of how much she reminded him of his own cocker spaniel.

The outside door to the kitchen flew open and two very wet girls in their early twenties came in laughing, carrying suitcases and leaving pools of water in their wake.

"We're back!" the taller of the two announced, before catching sight of Peter.

"Oh hello. Are you our new guest?" Meara asked.

"I am," Peter replied standing up.

The younger girl, put out her hand to him.

"Nice to meet you, Mr. da Vinci. My name is Brennan and this is Meara."

It was all Peter could do not laugh at the sincerity in her voice. Sarah walked in and heard Brennan's welcome and he could tell that for a brief moment she was as amused as he was.

"Shall we call you Mr. da Vinci? Or Leonardo? Or is there quite another name you might prefer?" Sarah challenged him.

He noted her momentary humor was gone.

"Peter would be fine, thank you."

"Well then…Peter. Meara and Brennan will show you to the JM Barrie cottage. As I understand it, there is food in the pantry and refrigerator and the fireplace is ready to be lit." Turning to the girls, she continued her instruction. "Please take…Peter…to his cottage and make sure all is in order. I suggest you take the umbrellas by the door and I will wait here to see if you need anything else."

"Thank you, Sarah. It really is good to see you," he said, knowing he was out on a limb.

"I doubt that," was her terse reply. "Girls?"

With a bit of confusion, all three were out the door. Peter noticed the downpour had slowed to a fine mist, and the air carried that fresh rain fragrance that made one want to breath deeply. His brain was overloaded and he was very, very tired, and bewildered by Sarah's behavior. His fall from grace haunted him, and perhaps this was further punishment.

Meara and Brennan led the way across the wet, grass meadow. It was dark now and lights were barely visible in the windows of the other cottages. The J.M. Barrie cottage was only about a two minute walk from the main house, but between carrying two suitcases, slogging in damp shoes, and a less than stellar welcome from Sarah, Peter was ready to call it a day. Maybe coming to Leigheas wasn't such a good idea.

The girls opened the door, and found the lights quickly.

"Brennan, see to the fireplace and get some warmth in here. Mr. da Vinci, would you like me to put your clothes away?"

"Oh no, thank you. I can see to that," he answered, ready to be alone. "And my name is Peter."

Meara called his attention to the packet of papers she set on the dining table.

"Everything you need to know is in here. Meals are served three times a day, but some guests prefer to keep their own company. Your kitchen is stocked with basic items but if there is something you would prefer, simply write it down and drop it off in the main house kitchen before ten in the morning. One of us makes a visit to the village nearly every day. There is a list and a map of all the areas at Leigheas, the stable, the river, the chapel. I'm sure Mr. Duncan will take you on a tour tomorrow."

"Meara, you sound like you've been doing this for years,"

Brennan marveled, still kneeling at the fireplace.

"Hush, Brennan and mind the fire."

"The fire is lit, if you'd take a look," then looking toward Peter, she continued, "We are all a wee bit befuddled since Mrs. McAughtrie had her accident this afternoon. She fell and hit her head and the doctor had to come. And now, we are in charge."

"Hush your gossiping! And we are not in charge. Miss Sarah will be in charge."

"Did you say Mrs. McAughtrie is here at Leigheas?" Peter asked.

"Yes, she is the manager of the house and Mr. Duncan runs everything else." Brennan piped up.

Meara took her sister by the arm and tugged her out the door with a final word.

"Is there anything else you need, Mr. da…Peter?"

"Thank you, no. You've done a marvelous job. Good night."

As he closed the door he could hear Brennan talking to her older sister.

"I mean it, you did a really good job. And isn't he a looker?"

"Oh, Brennan, do come along."

Finally he was alone in what turned out to be a beautiful, compact stone cottage with everything he needed. The firelight flickered on the walls, illuminating all things J.M. Barrie. There were photographs of the famous author with the bushy mustache and heavy bags under his eyes. There were even a few of him as a youth, one in particular that had written on it, *Nothing that happens to us after we are twelve matters very much,* signed James Barrie, aged twelve. Another wall was everything Peter Pan, from a large red poster announcing the Paramount Picture film complete with an evil looking Captain Hook and the sprightly Peter Pan. A simple black frame in the kitchen held a copy of J.M. Barrie's obituary from the London Times. An old bookcase was packed with Mr. Barrie's volumes, many Peter had never heard of. Knowing a bit about Mr. Barrie, since he was such a famous Scottish writer, Peter was curious as to who chose to name a cottage after him. The man was brilliant, and even knighted, but his personal life was a matter of rampant speculation and vicious conversation for decades. Truthfully, Mr. Barrie, Peter thought wearily, I have my own problems.

## *Chapter Fifty-nine*

# SARAH:

*No Rest for the Weary*

It was half-past eleven when Sarah finally got into bed. On the way she checked on Seaneen and found her awake, alert, and obviously enjoying her time with James. The possibilities of how bad her injuries could have been made Sarah's stomach turn. She sent up a prayer of gratitude for the wonderful woman who had become family. When she passed her fathers closed door, all was quiet, and Sarah hoped he was sleeping soundly. It had been a long day. Now, alone in her bedroom, the emotional shock of seeing Peter exploded in her brain. She was angry, confused, hurt, and scared all at once. How dare he turn up in her life and her home! Why had he left such a scar on her heart? Years had passed, yet standing face to face with him, the painful realization that she hadn't been important to him, hurt like it was yesterday. Her mind went back to the train five years ago reading the last line in that article, *'There is no one, other than my cocker spaniel, that I will miss.'* That pretty much summed up his thoughts. He had simply been an acquaintance, who took a passing interest in her at a time in her life when she was sad and lonely. She sat up and punched her pillow about five times, more out of frustration than an effort to make it comfortable. One question remained unanswered... why did her heart leap when she realized the man at the door was 'her' Peter?'

Sleep must've overridden the adrenalin at some point, as she was dead to the world when she became aware of banging on her door that wouldn't stop.

"Miss Sarah?" The voice outside the door said, "It's Brennan and I need to know about the kitchen order. Mrs. McAughtrie is sleeping and the grocer gentleman is on the telephone. Miss Sarah?"

Barely able to open her eyes, Sarah sat up, still not one hundred percent awake.

"Come in, Brennan," Sarah said groggily, aware of a dull headache. It was clear that the young girl was in a tizzy. "Now, what is this about?"

"I'm sorry, Miss Sarah, but Mr. Patterson, the grocer, is wanting the kitchen order early because of the bank holiday and Mrs. McAughtrie is asleep and Vicar Bradbury won't let me wake her up and Mr. Duncan is horse riding with Mr. da Vinci and Meara is out at the cottages and I don't know what to do."

"Please tell Mr. Patterson that we will return his call directly with the order. Thank you, Brennan."

The young girl escaped out the door, just as her father appeared.

"Good morning, Sunshine! What a difference a day makes! I'm surprised you are still in bed. Rise and shine, the day is waiting!"

"Aren't you a bit too cheerful this morning? Sarah asked with a slight sarcastic tone.

"Am I? I don't think so. Seaneen is doing well, and I might have had a telephone call with Kaitlyn earlier telling me she would be happy to accept my invitation to come visit Leigheas next week." Her father was not even trying to hide his pleasure. "And I had a lovely early morning ride with our new guest. He's a nice chap, and it turns out has family in the area."

Sarah's headache just got worse.

"Dad, I need to tell you something…"

A knock on the open door stopped her. Meara peeked in, and looked quite urgent.

"Sorry to bother, but a fish order just arrived and the invoice needs signing and I don't know…."

Just then the vicar poked his nose into the room, looking equally agitated.

"So sorry to interrupt, but Seaneen is trying to get up, and Dr. McDonald was insistent that she stay in bed another day. I thought maybe one of you could speak to her…"

It was her father who finally put up his hand to bring silence.

"Meara, please tell the delivery man I will be down shortly to sign. Perhaps offer him a cup of tea. James, please tell Seaneen I would consider it a personal favor if she would stay in bed one more day and behave herself. I will be in to see her shortly and offer her bribes if she will cooperate."

With that, Meara and James dispersed to take care of their missions. Richard returned his attention to his daughter who was still in bed, but now fully awake.

"My plan is to go put out these fires, then spend a few hours with our new guest fly fishing on the river. From my brief time with him this morning, I sense he is a good lad who took a wrong turn somewhere. I think you'd like him, come to think of it I don't know his real name yet. Now, what was it you want to tell me?"

Sarah, feeling totally overwhelmed by everything said in a loud voice, "His name is PETER!" Then, with a dramatic gesture, pulled the comforter over her head.

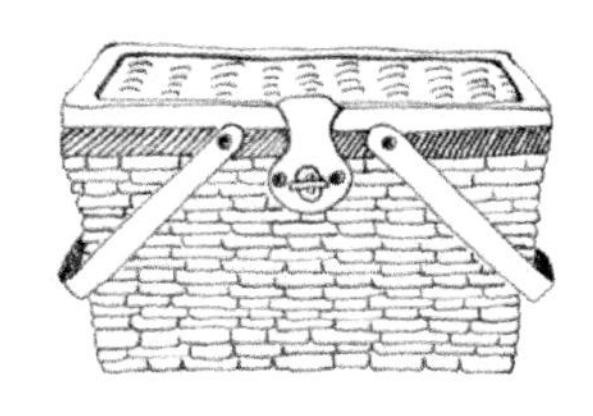

## Chapter Sixty
# SEANEEN McAUGHTRIE:
## *A Most Perfect Day*

By early November, autumn was long gone and winter was upon them. Clouds had become regular visitors, sometimes with rain, other times with wind, but always skies were gray. With the addition of dropping temperatures, the stage was set for contemplative thinking. It had been two weeks since her accident, and four days since she had been allowed to return to her cottage. The mark of real progress was Dr. McDonald approving a modest return to normal life for her.

"You can work a few hours a day for the next month, then we will see how you're feeling. If I find that you are overdoing, it will be back to bedrest for you," the good doctor had threatened this morning.

The girls were really taking hold and managing the day to day activities fairly well. They were comfortable asking for help or advice when needed, but that was less and less. Overall, things seemed to be going quite smoothly. There wasn't a day that passed that Richard didn't come by her cottage and fix them both a cup of tea. Yesterday, he had jokingly given Seaneen the new title of 'House Boss.'

"With your new rank, you will be required to take vacations, sleep in now and then and relegate tedious tasks to your proteges," he insisted. "Simply put, you will oversee the operation of the household, with Meara and Brennan, and for now, Sarah, doing the work."

Several weeks ago, the idea of slowing down wasn't anywhere

on her mind. She loved the challenges every day brought and found great satisfaction in being productive. How life had changed in the blink of an eye. It was a little strange at first, that feeling of being replaceable, but the more she became accustomed to the idea, the less she minded. She would always want to be involved, but maybe the bump on her head brought some perspective. Perhaps enjoying time with James was a lovely incentive toward a more relaxed way of life. After all, she wasn't getting any younger, as her upcoming seventieth birthday kept reminding her. Possibly this was the autumn season of her life.

"Oh my, what maudlin thoughts," she mused.

The jangling bell by her front door got her attention. The owner of the deep, theatrical voice had become a regular visitor recently, and she quite enjoyed his company.

"Do let me in, fair lady, for I know you dwell inside," Beckett spoke as though on stage.

Seaneen opened the door and a far different gentleman entered than she had known only a few weeks ago. Gone was the sarcasm and self-pity, replaced by an engaging, thoughtful man who appeared to have had a metamorphosis somewhat like Scrooge in 'A Christmas Carol.'

"Enlighten me, fair lady, how are you today?"

"I do quite well, kind sir," she responded. "Please sit down. May I offer you a cup of tea?"

"Thank you, no," he said, dropping the Shakespearean language. "I've only a few minutes before Mr. Duncan drives me to the train station. I'm shall be departing shortly."

"I had no idea you were leaving. Is this sudden or did I miss you telling me? I seem to lose a wee bit of memory now and then since the accident."

"You've missed nothing, my fair friend. On your advice I called my daughter and we had a cracking conversation. It had been far too long since we spoke due to my obtuse thinking that she was angry with me, and the 'old me' didn't want to deal with it."

"Was she angry with you?"

"She admitted she had been, but had long forgiven me and was too stubborn to tell me. Thanks to you, we have made amends and she will meet me at the station in London. But there's more to tell! My agent called…now, I'll let the suspense build…" he said with a mischievous look.

"Oh, this must be very good news by the looks of you."

"Well, fair lady, my agent said I am one of two people being considered to direct a play at the smallest theatre in London's West End! Do you know it?"

"I'm afraid I don't, but I haven't been to London in years," she said.

"A brief history: The Arts Theatre began in 1927 as a members-only club with illegal plays and experimental performances in order to avoid theatre censorship. But now, it is a sought after playhouse, with nearly every actor of any note wanting to appear there," he paused dramatically before continuing, "and they want me to direct. I'm absolutely thrilled! So, I leave today and meet with the owners tomorrow afternoon and they will make their decision."

"Becket, I could not be happier for you. This is indeed a new beginning."

The tall man rose and stood next to Seaneen's chair, taking her hand in his.

"I owe everything to you. Thank you for forgiving me and for helping me find my confidence and courage. I will always have my regrets but I swear to you, Seaneen McAughtrie, I will not go back to being an ass. I will make you proud."

"Becket McTavish, I will always be proud of you."

He opened the door to leave, then turned back with a parting comment, "And hold on to that Vicar. He's a good man."

Through the open door Seaneen could see James in the distance walking toward her cottage carrying a picnic basket. This had become one of the daily routines that she was most fond of. Meara and Brennan would send over dinner in the large wicker basket for she and James and they would dine in her cottage.

She watched with interest as Becket and James stood together in the meadow conversing. It seemed a bit odd as the two men had rarely acknowledged one another in earlier days. Becket lowered his head and it seemed James was praying with him. They parted by shaking hands and what appeared to be goodwill. Seaneen reflected that much had changed while she had been sidelined–to put it mildly.

"Your meal has arrived!" James announced as he came through the open door. "And I think you will be quite pleased." He unlatched the top to the basket and the fragrance of roast beef and Yorkshire pudding wafted through the small cottage. "Even a chocolate pudding for dessert."

"It smells wonderful. The table is set and I'll light the candles," Seaneen said as she scurried to find the matches.

This really was her favorite time of the day. They would hold hands while James said the blessing over the meal, then talk as old friends about everything imaginable while they enjoyed the delicious food. She looked across the table at his handsome face, with well earned lines and wrinkles, as he regaled her with stories of his youth. Being with James brought the enjoyment of sharing life with someone special. Finding friendship and companionship with this extraordinary gentleman was certainly an unexpected surprise.

With dinner finished and the chocolate pudding bowls scraped clean, they lingered at the table, never running out of conversation.

"I suppose Becket told you he is leaving this evening," Seaneen said.

"Yes. Hasn't he become a changed man? He says he owes it to you," James replied.

"I've no credit to take for that. I think he was simply ready to listen and I happened to be there."

"Ever humble, my friend. Your words spoke to his soul and awakened a part of him that had been dormant for most of his life. After your accident, he sought me out and we began to spend quite a bit of time together. He felt a trifle guilty about your fall, thinking if you hadn't stopped to sit with him it wouldn't have happened. I assured him that the blessing was that he was there to pick you up and get you to the house. Once that was sorted, he opened up about so many things in his life and we were able to develop a mutual trust."

"That is splendid news. I can't think of anyone better to help set his course than you."

James began to collect the dishes to wash, as was their custom every night. Seaneen would try to help and he would never let her, saying it was his pleasure to spoil her.

"I've something I'd like to run past you," he said as he sat back down at the table. "As I'm sure you're aware, you've come to mean quite a lot to me," he paused as though thinking his next words carefully. "When I first came here, I was at quite a loss as to what the rest of my life would be. My life as a vicar was gratifying in every way, but the last few years I was finding it hard to keep up with all that was expected of me. Retirement was the logical answer, however I quickly found out that I missed being busy. I was unable to identify how to occupy my time. I spent a year reading, painting, walking, doing all the things I thought I should be doing. By chance, I heard about Leigheas and uncharacteristically wrote to Mr. Duncan, who most cordially invited me for a stay. As a vicar, you are the one offering help and healing and it is the only role I know. For a change, I was the one in need of guidance."

He trailed off, as though taking a breath to gather his thoughts. Seaneen had often wondered had brought him here and how he was faring with whatever difficulty he was experiencing. It would have been a dreadful breach of confidence to ask, as each guest was treated with privacy. They, of course, were free to share their lives if they chose, but Richard never divulged any information.

"I'm quite sure meeting you was a divine appointment," he went on. "You are quite an accomplished woman! Which brings me to what I would like to ask you."

His last words caused Seaneen's heart to beat faster. She had been listening carefully, but only now guessing the direction he must be going. Thankfully, he had paused again, giving the hundreds of thoughts that suddenly were racing through her mind time to settle. How should she answer him, IF he should ask her…"

"You see, I think I have an idea for the future."

"You do?" she answered tentatively.

"Yes, I do!" he said with growing confidence. "What do you think, and please give me your honest opinion, about me asking Mr.

Duncan if I could stay on at Leigheas as a vicar? Most of the guests have come to me for some spiritual advice at one time or another, and he has a chapel, and he wouldn't have to pay me as my retirement is more than adequate and I think I would fit in rather well. Do you think that would be too forward of me?"

Seaneen wasn't sure if she was happy or disappointed by his question. It sure wasn't what she expected. What a silly old woman she had become. Romance at her age?

"I think that is a brilliant idea, James. It seems a perfect fit, and I'm surprised Richard hasn't thought of it first," she said with all sincerity, though secretly a little let down.

"Excellent! Now, the second part of my question. Should Mr. Duncan agree with what we both think is an extraordinary idea, I was thinking that perhaps in three days I would ask you to marry me."

"I'm sorry. What did you say?" she answered incredulously, as he knelt before her on one knee.

"Seaneen McAughtrie, I will be asking you…in three days time…if you would be interested in spending how ever many years we have left on this earth as my wife. Why you would want to tie yourself with a stodgy, old vicar is beyond me, but you have brought a light and a happiness to this tired old soul, and I adore you. It seems only right to give you three days to ponder the possibilities, but I do hope you say yes."

She wasn't sure if he stayed on his one knee waiting for her to answer or because he wasn't able to rise up again.

"What if I don't need three days?" She asked coyly.

"Oh. Well then. If your answer will be no, please don't tell me just yet. Kindly wait the three days in the off-chance you have a change of heart. But, on the other hand, if your answer is yes, feel free to make me the happiest old vicar in the world."

Pushing back her chair, she stood up and offered him her hands to help him up, then kept holding them.

"I'm afraid James Bradbury, extraordinary Vicar…that I adore you as well. And if you're really sure about this, I would very much like to marry you." Any further words were lost as the Church of England vicar kissed the Church of Scotland parishioner.

"By the way, Becket gave us his blessing…in case you said yes," James added.

"He told me you were a good man and I should hold on to you."

"Oh, please do!"

Another half hour of giddy conversation between the two ended when they decided it would be better for James to speak to Richard sooner rather than later. They agreed that they would marry, even if Richard wasn't interested in the vicar staying on. With the promise to stop by later with all the details of his meeting, he was out the door leaving Seaneen alone with a swarm of thoughts buzzing through her brain. She must call her sister with all the news. Since the accident, they spoke several times a week with Seaneen always assuring Marjorie that her head was almost as good as it ever was.

"Well, that is a bit of a low bar, don't you think?" Marjorie would laugh, and the sisters would have a good giggle.

No one answered at Marjorie's house, but then she remembered that it was Thursday evening. Her sister and Malcolm would be at early choir practice, then stop off by the pub for fish and chips. When Seaneen moved into her cottage, she told Richard having a telephone was not necessary as there were two in the main house, but it certainly had come in handy the past week. She would try Marjorie later and in the meantime she would bask in her happy thoughts of life with James.

By now it was quite dark outside, and the wind had picked up a bit. The knock at the door startled her, but she remembered James was to return with news. To her surprise it was Richard who stood there, looking like the Cheshire cat.

"Please come in out of the whether, Richard. I wasn't expecting you, but it's always a delight. Would you like a cup of tea? Sit here by the fire," Seaneen said, realizing she was rambling.

"Thank you for being pleased to see me, no thank you to a cup of tea and yes I will sit by the fire. I believe we have a lot to talk about."

"Yes, we do," Seaneen answered demurely. She couldn't gauge if Richard was perturbed or pleased. To hide her nervousness, she went to the kitchen for a plate of biscuits.

"First off, let me ease the suspense and tell you I am absolutely delighted about you and James. You are as close as family, and I never would have given my blessing to a lessor man. He is the genuine thing, caring, trustworthy and solid as the Rock of Gibraltar. I suspect you've not had time to sort the details of a wedding, but you know I am available to help in any way. To be honest, I am only out of sorts that I hadn't thought to ask him to be part of Leigheas before now. He's been here nearly four months and has spent a great deal of his time with the different guests, listening and offering counsel. They often mention how helpful he was during their visit. With him here full time, there are so many possibilities of how he can help our guests heal. It really is a superb idea, and the fact that you have found each other makes it all the more wonderful."

For the first time in a very long time, Seaneen felt tears slowly inching down her cheeks. This man had become like a son, and hearing him praise James was the final act in making this a most perfect day.

"Thank you, Richard. Your words mean more than I can say. I love you and Sarah, and your approval means the world. I don't know what I would've done if you had been unhappy."

"Having both you and James here is beyond anything I could've imagined!" Richard said with sincerity.

"Oh! I must tell Sarah! It wouldn't do to have her hear it from anyone else," Seaneen said.

"That was the other reason I wanted to talk with you. Have you seen Sarah lately?"

"Now that you mention it, I haven't seen the lass in several days. She would pop in to ask questions about this and that, but was always in a hurry. Is she under the weather?"

"I don't think so, but she has been acting very strangely for the past two weeks. The household has been humming smoothly, but she is rarely visible. It seems she is up before anyone, gets her work done and retreats to her room supposedly to write. We haven't seen her at meals and she hasn't been riding or fishing for quite some time."

"When did her behavior change? Is there a problem with her job in London?"

"I have no idea. Like I said, I rarely see her and I am reluctant to disturb her if she truly is writing. Thinking about it, I would have to say it began around the time our latest guest arrived."

"You mean Mr. da Vinci?" Seaneen laughed, and took a sip of the water glass in front of her. "Of all the aliases to choose."

"Well, he turned out to be an engaging young man in his mid-twenties. His real name is Peter Michael-McGregor…"

The glass slipped out of Seaneen's hand and landed on the floor, spilling what was left.

"No! No! You must be mistaken, Richard. It can't be Peter! Are you absolutely sure?"

"Yes, his name is Peter Michael-McGregor. From what he has told me, he is or was, an artist who spent time in Italy and it didn't go well."

"I must speak to Sarah right now," she said rising from the chair and moving faster than she had in weeks. "You can see yourself out, Richard. And please don't ask any questions!"

## Chapter Sixty-one

# RICHARD:

## *Who Knew Alexander Graham Bell was Scottish?*

Standing in the middle of Seaneen's cottage, watching a normally sane woman run across the meadow toward the main house at break-neck speed, he said out loud to no one, "What on earth just happened?" He looked around aimlessly as though the answer lay somewhere within the little house. For the life of him, he could not understand how the arrival of Peter Michael-McGregor had upset things, especially his daughter. Add that to Seaneen's adamant directive, 'Don't ask questions!' Well, what was a father suppose to do?

He suspected Seaneen would be gone for a while, so he made sure the screen was set in front of the fire, and all was safe from wayward sparks. Closing her door behind him, he could see the lights were on in Sarah's bedroom. Perhaps once Seaneen had spent time with her, Sarah would be willing to let him know what was going on. For the moment he couldn't think of a thing he could do to help. Being a parent was not for the faint of heart.

The kitchen was clean and tidy when he came in through the side door. There was no indication they had served eight people for dinner a few hours ago. Dishes were put away, and all was ready for tomorrow's breakfast. Between Seaneen and Sarah, the country girls were learning and adapting to the daily routine like ducks to water.

"Evening, Mr. Duncan," James said, walking into the kitchen. "Any chance you might know where Seaneen might be? I promised her I would pop in this evening to say good night but it appears she has left her cottage. I do hope she is well."

"Nothing to worry about, James. She is spending time with my daughter, sharing secrets I would imagine."

"Well, good. I think I will retire then, it has been quite a big day for me. Thank you again for allowing me the opportunity to be part of Leigheas. I look forward to sharing more ideas with you and, of course, my deepest appreciation for your blessing of our engagement. I know it must seem rather sudden, but when you meet the right person, it just seems...well, right. And, between us, there was a fair amount of prayer involved."

"Good to know, James," Richard said with a smile, "I can see we will make much use of your wisdom around here. Good night, vicar."

The large clock in the reception room sounded half of the Westminster chime. Looking closer, Richard saw it was half-past eight, the appointed time he normally called Kaitlyn. They had quietly developed a habit of speaking on the telephone every two or three days. Retreating to his study he dialed the now familiar number and was a bit startled when she answered on the first ring, but took it as a good sign. Funny how insecure a grown man can be in the matters of affection.

"Good evening, you answered so quickly," he said not bothering to hide his pleasure.

"Yes," she said in a hushed voice. "Father fell asleep in his chair, and I pulled the telephone cord around the corner so as not to wake him."

"And I thought you were just anxious to talk to me," he teased.

"Always," she said with her lilting laugh.

"How are you? Has the store been busy?"

"I am fine, thank you, and yes, very busy. With Christmas a wee few weeks away, people are beginning their shopping. I wrap every gift with holiday paper and tie them up with a satin bow. Customers are so proud of their purchases when they leave. What is the news out in the country? Is Leigheas running to perfection?"

"You might want to make a cup of tea and get comfortable. It has been quite an odd few days."

"Cup of tea is made, biscuits are on the tray, I'm ready!"

One of the pleasures Richard had rediscovered was the simple joy of sharing news with someone. Kaitlyn was not only lovely and smart, but a very good listener. She rarely interrupted or offered an opinion unless asked and seemed to take a genuine interest in all he told her.

"Well, the most current turn of events has to do with Sarah and our newest guest. I don't think I mentioned that she began acting strangely shortly after he arrived."

"By strangely, what do you mean?"

"All of her work is done in the early morning hours and the rest of the time she keeps to her room under the guise of writing. I don't know, maybe she really is writing. It's just that this need for isolation and privacy only started after he arrived."

"Maybe she is suddenly inspired. Creativity often has a mind of its own."

"Perhaps, but tonight it took an even odder turn when I was visiting with Seaneen and I mentioned Sarah's behavior. As soon as I said the name of our new guest, she jumped up and ran out of her cottage and asked, or rather told me, not to ask any questions. What do you make of that?"

"That certainly is cause to think there is more going on than meets the eye. Has this new guest ever said anything about Sarah?"

"No, not a word. I have no idea what their connection could be."

"Sounds like a mystery that may take time to reveal. A positive note is Sarah is under your roof and Seaneen must know something about all this. You know she would never let any harm come to Sarah."

In all of their telephone conversations, Kaitlyn had seen the optimistic side of any situation and brought a comforting perspective. That was one of the many traits of this remarkable woman that attracted him.

"You're right as usual. Sometimes I forget that Sarah is an adult and her privacy should be allowed."

"Tell me what else is going on."

"Oh, where to start. Well, the other big news is that Vicar James Bradbury asked Seaneen to marry him tonight."

"That's quite exciting! And she said yes?"

"She did, but there's more to the story. He also inquired about staying on at Leigheas as sort of a 'vicar in residence.' Guests have naturally gravitated to him for spiritual matters and I think it would be a marvelous addition to our staff. As well as being available for guests, he has offered to do monthly sermons in the chapel. My mother would be so pleased. It is a marvelous idea."

"What a talented pair they will be. You have created such a wondrous place and it only seems to get better and better."

"It has been a blessing in many ways, not only for our guests, but for me as well. I was so lost after the shooting and planning Leigheas gave me purpose and direction."

"And a lovely home for you and Sarah."

"Absolutely, finally roots for us." Richard realized more and more how important it was for him to establish a real home for Sarah. He knew she would move away at some point, but hopefully Leigheas would always be here for her.

"How are your young ladies working out?"

"Surprisingly well. I don't know how we would've coped without them. The load is lighter now with most of our guests leaving before the holidays. Do you remember Ian?"

"I do. Isn't he the young man who was a bit overwhelmed by his promotion to head the family business?"

"Exactly right." Richard was astounded at how Kaitlyn remembered even the smallest details of a place she had never visited. "While he was here he spent quite a bit of time with our veterinarian Stephen, his son Henry, and with the farm animals. When he left, there was a very nice letter thanking me for his time here. He said he learned that confidence comes from within, and from being yourself, and not trying to please everyone around you. He mentioned how the relationship between Stephen and Henry was unconditional, and how the bond between the vet and the animals was built on mutual respect. Best of all, he wrote that he felt secure about going back to the family business and was most grateful."

"Oh, Richard. Isn't that everything you had hoped to accomplish?"

"It is, and more. Then, I heard from Edward, our guest who tried to control everything, that he had taken up bird watching with Marcus, our gardener. When he left this morning, he was quite enthused about nature and man's inability to control it. It was quite a revelation to him and he seemed to be oddly comforted by it."

"Have you ever heard the quote by Irishman Robert Lynd? 'In order to see birds, it is necessary to become part of the silence.' Perhaps Edward heard the silence for the first time while bird-watching. You may have produced a new world-class twitcher!" Again her delightful laugh made Richard smile.

"Twitcher? Is that a real term or are you making fun of me, the American?"

"You've not heard of twitchers? They are birdwatchers who are very enthusiastic about wild birds. I promise it is a real word, though a little on the slang side."

"So if I use that in a public setting, no one will fall down laughing?"

"It might depend on how you use it in a sentence."

"The English are very complicated people."

"I'm Scottish, not English. Best if you remember that, Laird of Leigheas," she said with an amused chuckle.

"Of course you are! Well now, Miss Scotland, are you still planning on visiting Leigheas day after tomorrow? I'm so hoping you are. Please include you father, if you like."

"That is so kind of you, I will ask him. Would around eleven be convenient?"

"That would be perfect," Richard answered.

"Then I will see you then."

"Good night, Kaitlyn. Sleep well."

The telephone line disconnected, but Richard held onto the handset with the somewhat silly look people have when they are smitten by another. It was as if holding the phone kept him connected to Kaitlyn. Reaching across his desk to place it back on the cradle, he saw Sarah standing in the doorway. He could feel his face reddening without having to look in the mirror. How long had she been there?

"Dad, are you busy? I think we need to talk."

## *Chapter Sixty-two*

# PETER:

## *A Story to Tell*

In the six days since Peter had been at Leigheas, he had fly fished with Richard Duncan three times, and had ridden miles across the entire estate with him numerous times, but never once had Sarah's name been mentioned. His best guess was that her father knew nothing about their relationship. After seeing Sarah that first night, Peter looked for her every day, but it was clear she was avoiding him with no interest in reconnecting. He racked his brain trying on theories of why she was so angry with him, but found no answer. Early in the morning of his seventh day at Leigheas an idea began to take shape. Their friendship began with the written word, so why not put his thoughts on paper and share his last few years with her? Perhaps it was time to bare his soul and re-live the painful collapse of his life. He came to Leigheas to face his demons and try to sort his future path. What better way than to write to his old friend? The Sarah he knew five years ago would understand.

By late morning, he had written over three full pages about what a dreadful, humiliating experience his trip to Italy had been–complete with sordid details. He wrote feverishly, afraid he might lose his nerve reliving it so honestly without holding back. It was excruciating and still so raw that at times that he felt physically ill. It clearly reminded him how far he had fallen. He wanted Sarah to know the whole story, but he also wanted her to know that he chose Leigheas not only to find peace with his past, but with the slimmest hope he would find her and renew their friendship. When he put a period on the last sentence, he realized how much he had been internalizing, and how good it felt to get it out. Feeling drained, yet happier than he had been in a long time, he was surprised to see a note had been slipped under his door. The small folded sheet had the Leigheas logo at the top and one hand written sentence, 'Please meet me in the kitchen at ten this morning.' He checked the clock and that was in five minutes. Quickly folding his three-page letter, he put it in an envelope and set it aside on the table. He grabbed his jacket and walked quickly to the main house. With every step, he tried to figure what this odd request was all about.

December arrived with cold temperatures and the blustery winds that were typical this time of year in the Borders. The kitchen felt warm and inviting after the short walk from his cottage. Richard Duncan was standing casually with his back leaning against the white marble countertop, holding a cup of tea.

"Good morning, Peter. I see you received my note. Thank you for coming..."

Before he finished his sentence, the door from the dining room opened and Sarah came rushing in. She caught sight of Peter, stopped in her tracks and he could see her jaw clinch. Glaring at her father, she spoke as though trying to control her temper.

"Dad, what is going on?"

Richard set his tea cup down on the counter, as if calculating exactly what he wanted to say.

"After we talked last night I realized the only way for you two to resolve this issue is to meet face to face. Sarah, you know that I am not in the habit of intervening."

Peter watched her give her father significant eye-rolling. Richard chose to ignore it.

"Peter, you never mentioned knowing my daughter in all the time we've spent together the past days, and Sarah, you have never, ever mentioned Peter in the five years you've known him until last night. It doesn't take a genius to see that there is something deeper going on here. I propose that you two take a walk over to the chapel where you can have some privacy and sort it out. Sarah, are you willing to listen to what Peter has to say?"

Without missing a beat, she answered firmly.

"No," and walked out the door she had just come through.

Neither man said a word. They both heard the front door slam shut. All the elation Peter felt by pouring out his soul in the letter to Sarah was ebbing away.

"Well, I guess that's that," Peter said with resignation. "I apologize for not telling you I knew Sarah when we first met. From the first moment she saw me, it was apparent that she was not pleased. The longer I was here, the more awkward telling you became."

"I promise you, Peter, I don't know very much about women, but I do know my daughter. She will be back."

As if on cue, Sarah came back in the kitchen and looked directly at Peter.

"I'll give you fifteen minutes."

Peter looked at Richard with admiration at his prediction of her return. Richard smiled and walked over to her jacket hanging on the hook near the rear door.

"I knew she forgot her coat."

They walked in silence toward the chapel. It was one of the few places Peter had not explored since his arrival. He had always been partial to this area of Scotland, hovering close to England's north border, however there was something very special about Leigheas.

"You must love it here," he ventured.

"Yes," was her one word response.

They continued walking. Peter looked at his watch.

"Just to clarify, did my fifteen minutes begin when we left the main house, or will it start when we arrive at the chapel? Because if it started at the house, I'm really going to have to talk fast to get it all in."

There was no answer, but he thought he might have seen a slight quiver in her lips. This gave him encouragement to continue.

"I mean, if you think about it, five years is……eighteen hundred and…twenty something days. So, you see, I need to know if I have the full fifteen minutes or if it's slipping away and I might only have, say, twelve minutes."

He cast a quick glance at her face, and noted the moment was gone and she seemed determined not to react at his attempt of humor. She walked on as though marching to war. They were approaching the stone chapel and stopped at the arched wooden door. Sarah took a deep breath and almost reluctantly pulled the heavy door open, allowing him to see the glorious simplicity of the interior for the first time. Neither one of them said a word. With his artistic eye, Peter took it all in–the stained glass windows with their divine subjects, the exquisitely hand carved cross at the front and the fine workmanship on the wooden pews. It was a captivating place. Sarah walked to the front pew on the right and sat down, leaving plenty of room for him. There was a reverence about the place, as though you could almost hear a heavenly choir softly singing. The spell was broken when Sarah spoke.

"Your fifteen minutes starts now."

Sitting down an arms length away from her, not too far, not too close, he realized this must be as difficult for her as it was for him. Would humor help?

"Do you think your lovely face could look just a little less miserable?" This was the best he could come up with as an opening line.

For some reason, she started to laugh unexpectedly but caught herself as if she remembered he was the enemy and went back to her stern face. He was perplexed and let a few moment pass before speaking again.

"Sarah, why are you so angry with me?" he asked gently.

"Because I don't want to like you again," she replied.

"Why? Even though five years have passed, I'm still the same Peter, your window friend. You have no idea how many times I wanted to contact you…"

"How dare you say that? You left and never looked back. Peter, five years ago I was young and obviously read too much into our friendship." Sarah stood up as if to emphasize her point. "I'm sorry, but I need to go. A friend from Edinburgh is arriving soon and I want to meet the car. Maybe we can continue this another time."

The wooden door closed behind her and left an echo in the small chapel.

"Didn't that go well?" he said out loud. "How could I be so stupid?"

It was obvious there was someone in Sarah's life who was coming to visit and her focus was on him. It would be natural that men would flock around her, trying to get her attention. Why would she wait for a struggling artist who hadn't been in contact for five years? Thinking they would take up where they left off was absurd. After his complete fall from grace in Italy and the struggle of the last year, why would any woman want to be with him? Yet…he felt there was still a small spark between them. After all, why was she so angry if she didn't have feelings? And, she did nearly laughed at his joke. Hadn't Richard Duncan said something about them 'resolving an issue?' What could that mean? Grasping at tender straws, it occurred to him that she probably had no idea how appalling his life had been. It was time to make a decision to either lay down on this wooden pew and hide in the chapel for the rest of his life or get up and face whatever lay ahead. He stood up and looked at the large, carved cross.

"I could use a wee bit of guidance, Lord."

By the time Peter left the chapel, he was on a mission. One stop at his cottage to pick up the letter he had written and then head to the main house and hand deliver it to Sarah. He entered through the front door, running into Meara.

"If you're looking for Mr. Duncan, he and Miss Sarah are in the kitchen with guests."

"Thank you, Meara. I wouldn't want to interrupt," Peter replied, knowing full well his intent was to interrupt and see who this man was that was after Sarah.

"I'm sure they wouldn't mind. They seem to be good friends."

He could overhear several voices speaking, one male for sure, and it wasn't Mr. Duncan. It sounded a little older than he expected, and very Scottish, but maybe Sarah liked mature men. His heart sank a little lower. 'Nothing ventured, nothing gained' he kept saying to himself over and over like a mantra. If it went really badly he would just pack up and leave Leigheas.

The talking and laughing stopped when Peter walked into the kitchen. The awkward moment passed as soon as Peter realized he knew the visiting guests.

"Peter! It's so good to see you. It's been far too long, what a lovely surprise," Kaitlyn said with obvious affection.

"Yes, lad, it's been far too long," echoed Thomas Turning, patting Peter on the back, then turning to Sarah and Richard. "Peter has been a customer since he was a wee boy. He could never get enough books about art and painting, and look at him now, quite an accomplished artist, I'd say."

"If I have had any success, Mr. Turning, credit must go to you for encouraging me all those years. You always had books set aside with my name on them when I would visit. It's lovely to see you both," Peter said with obvious relief that Mr. Turning could not possibly be a love interest of Sarah's.

Mr. Turning continued, "I'm sure I could find a few more books to set aside if you have time to pay a wee visit to the book shop. Let me think…it's been four or five years since you've been in."

"My father has a brilliant mind for remembering details," Kaitlyn said to Richard and Sarah, "especially about his favorite customers."

"I remember now. You bought a book by Jane Austen, I don't remember which one, there are so many, aren't there? And a Walter Scott book, and an odd, old book about motor cars by someone named Galloway Duncan, and….a lovely blank journal. I recall you said you were mailing them to someone very special."

Peter saw Sarah's eyes open wide as he looked directly at her.

"You are correct, Mr. Turning, I believe she quite liked them," Peter said.

Sarah answered, not breaking eye contact with Peter.

"Yes, she liked them very much."

# Chapter Sixty-three
# SARAH:
## *The Long Letter*

The rest of the day had been a blur for Sarah, remembering only snippets of conversations here and there. Kaitlyn and Thomas Turning were quite impressed with Leigheas and her father continued to be quite impressed with Kaitlyn. They toured the house and ventured out into the winter day to see some of the land. Peter accepted the invitation to join them for a leisurely lunch where the conversation was lively. Sarah chose to mainly observe the participants. The coincidence of the Turnings knowing Peter and both of them being at the same place at the same time seemed to be another divine appointment. The revelation that Peter truly had thought of her as special came as a surprise, but didn't erase what she had read in the article about him years ago, *'There is no one other than my cocker spaniel that I will miss.'* What a vexing puzzle this was. Listening to her father's advice, she had gone with Peter to the chapel, but once there realized she was terrified of getting involved with him again and left at the first opportunity. That probably wasn't fair as she sensed that he wanted to tell her things that would take longer than the fifteen minutes she allotted. Clearly, he had been through some trauma, or else he wouldn't have come to Leigheas. While she cared deeply about him and part of her wanted to comfort him, another part of her hoped he would disappear into the night forever. Okay, that might be a bit dramatic, she laughed to herself.

When he handed her an envelope with her name on it this morning, it was reminiscent of all their correspondence years ago. His familiar handwriting brought back the memory of how lonely those days had been. The words of her secret friend had often been a lifeline. She tucked the letter in her pocket like she used to do and saved it to read later alone in her room.

*Dear Sarah,*

*It's been a long time without you, my friend, and I have missed you more than you can imagine. By your actions, it's obvious I have done something dreadful. For the life of me I cannot fathom what act of folly I committed to make you dislike me so much. Please accept my sincere apology for anything and everything I might have done to distress you. You are the last person I would ever knowingly offend. Our friendship was one of the anchors I held on to when life spiraled out of control. I realize you have no way of knowing the journey I've been on these last years, as I have no knowledge where the years led you. If you will bear with me, I will start at the beginning and try to keep this concise.*

*Much of my early life was sheltered by my parents once I showed promise as an artist. When modest fame found me as a young man, so did a number of people who vied to get close to me to enhance their ego. Ultimately, most betrayed me and I became a wee bit cynical, and kept to myself in my studio. I welcomed my self-imposed isolation thinking that without the burden of friendships, I could focus solely on painting. My early fame faded and by the time you came along, I was still just as passionate about my work, but had become withdrawn and truthfully, pretty lonely. When we began corresponding I purposely avoided telling you about my artistic profession and for that I apologize. Since you were from America, I was pretty confident you would not know anything about me, but it had been a long time since anyone had liked me for me, not merely for the name at the bottom of a painting and I relished that. You were a breath of fresh air, so interesting and you made me laugh. I enjoyed hearing about your life and learning about you through your letters. Slowly you were becoming an important part of my daily structure and I looked forward to seeing you. On Christmas Eve, I was trying to make my way over to you when your father was shot. I cannot possibly imagine what you went through and can only tell you from my perspective, I was scared to death something had happened to you as well. Together with my parents, we tried to find out anything we could about you and your father, but a huge veil of secrecy went up after it occurred and no one was acknowledging the event ever took place. Thank God Mrs. McAughtrie knocked on our door and let me know you both were alive. Once you and I were able to exchange letters, and you were safe with Liam and his family, I was very relieved. Right after came the offer from Paulo Antoneli to apprentice with him and I became totally wrapped up in myself and moving to Italy. I must tell you though, the night before I was to leave, sleep eluded me. This whole Italian adventure suddenly didn't seem to be a very good idea, and when examining the reasons why, losing contact with you weighed heavily on me.*

*The first few months in Italy I spent learning Italian, watching the other apprentices and following Mr. Antoneli around. It was intoxicating to be the favorite pupil of a world famous artist. He would take me everywhere, introducing me to everyone as his protege. When I was finally allowed to paint under his direction, nearly half a year later, I felt my art ability was slipping. At his insistence I spent the next year and a half abandoning my technique and trying to emulate his style. His method of painting was completely foreign to me and I felt like I was starting over. All the while, he would praise my mediocre efforts as being brilliant. This did not settle well with the other apprentices who had been there far longer than I, and they stopped speaking to me. By the end of the second year I was questioning the wisdom of this experience. I began to see a different side of Mr. Antoneli–one that often drank too much, womanized and humiliated his students on a whim. There were always rumors about his darker side, but living it first hand was uncomfortable to say the least. Somehow another year passed and Mr. Antoneli began to travel more. However, when he did visit the studio he was less enamored with me. It was not unusual for him to savagely criticize my work in front of the others, then taunt me to argue back. After a while, one of the top apprentices, Raphael, became sympathetic to me. I was so desperate for friendship that I ignored all the signs that Raphael was involved in some dangerous schemes. All I saw was that he was charismatic and a bit exciting. He included me with his acquaintances outside the studio, all of whom were artists of some sort. They were fun, spontaneous and edgy, though they often drank heavily well into the morning hours. I had never known people like this, and they accepted me at face value. For a short time it helped me cope with the dreaded daylight hours with Mr. Antoneli, though I was hungover most days. Then things took a very bad turn. One evening I thought I saw Raphael trying to pass off one of his paintings as an Antoneli original to a tourist. Being unsure, I didn't say anything. A few nights later, I overheard him again telling another tourist the same thing. Not knowing what to do I walked toward Raphael and asked what he thought he was doing. Suddenly there were whistles blowing and police were all around us and we were hauled off to jail. Apparently, Mr. Antoneli was onto Raphael and his underground sales of Antoneli forgeries, and the transaction that night was a set up. Raphael and I were put in a large cell with other undesirable sorts. He was furious with me thinking I had something to do with him being caught. Everyone in the cell was Italian and I struggled to understand what was being said. The next thing I knew three men began beating on me and I honestly thought they were going to kill me. Guards broke it up and I was taken to the hospital to be stitched up. Mr. Antoneli showed up, even angrier than Raphael had been, thinking I had been part of the scheme. He shouted that he wanted me out of his studio and his life by the next evening. Twenty-four hours later I was wandering the streets of Florence with my suitcase and enough money for a bus ticket to Rome. For the next six months I washed dishes in an English tea room in the heart of Rome. They liked that I spoke English and knew I was badly in need of a job. As it turned out, Babington's Tea Room was a quite a famous place on the Piazza Sapgna and had been since the late 1800's. The owners were very generous, helping me find a cheap room to rent and offering all the food I could ever want. My time in Rome was mostly spent working, drinking all night and trying to remember every morning that I was living in one of the most artistic cities in the world. But it didn't matter by then. I was depressed, disgusted with myself and wallowing in my failures. My family had no idea where I was for months on end. Looking back, I think the trauma of all that happened in Florence left me damaged, physically, mentally and spiritually. I was now in my fifth year of being abroad, thoroughly miserable and declining badly. Early one morning I heard church bells ringing. I'm sure they rang every day, but for some reason that morning I listened with my whole being. I can't describe how it happened, but I found myself at the Anglican Church around the corner from my rented room. I sat alone on a wooden pew facing the tall alter and stared at the vertical stained glass windows for quite a while. When the bells stopped, their echo remained in the large church. For the first time in a very long time I could feel my pain lessen. The young vicar sat down next to me and waited until I was ready to talk. I won't go into all that happened, except to tell you that this kind man of God arranged my passage back to Scotland and my family. That was about five months ago. Since then I have struggled to find myself and where I belong. I fully realize that much of what happened was directly due to decisions I made. No excuses or blaming anyone else. Since being at Leigheas, I've realized it is time for me to get back to the basics, to forgive myself for the past, and grasp what lies ahead with both hands as a second chance. I guess what I'm trying to say is I am ready to come out of the shadows and face my future honourably.*

*Sarah, I've learned that our choices make all the difference and I am choosing to move forward as an open book, wherever God leads me. If you've read this far, I sincerely hope you will be willing to move forward with me as a friend, confident and whatever else might lie ahead. If this is all too much, and I understand it might be, then I want you to know you are one of the most extraordinary people I have ever known and I will always hold you close to my heart.*

*As always,*
*Peter*
*Your Window Friend*

She stared across the room, her mind spinning with so many

conflicting thoughts. There was much to digest in his letter. He certainly had found himself in a terribly compromising situation with Mr. Antoneli, but as he admitted, it was made worse by the choices he made. She was impressed with the honesty of his writing. He took responsibility and didn't claim to be a victim. He sounded as though he was coming out of a dark place, ready to live again with all the enthusiasm and eagerness he once had. Wouldn't it be something if the Peter she once knew could be back in her life? Yet, old hurts die hard. There was still the unexplained article when he left for Italy, making it very clear he had no regard for her.

Sarah had no idea how much time had passed until the grandfather clock chimed the eight o'clock hour. By now most people had retired to their rooms and all was quiet. The view from her window showed no moon or stars in the dark sky. She was pretty sure she could sneak over to Peter's cottage and slip a note under the door unnoticed. Hastily writing a short message and folding it up, she found her heart racing with guarded excitement. This felt like the old days.

Quietly making her way down the stairs, she could hear her father in his study laughing with Kaitlyn on the telephone. Whatever could they possibly have left to say? She and Mr. Turning only left Leigheas a few hours ago. No matter, she had her own errand to accomplish.

The kitchen was dark as she felt her way toward the back entrance. Throwing on her coat and Wellies, she softly closed the door behind her and stepped into the shadowy night. Suddenly, there was someone standing in front of her, only in silhouette. She fell backwards and stumbled on the bottom step, unceremoniously landing on her fanny.

"Sarah! It's me Seaneen. Let me help you. Are you hurt, lass?"

"No, no, I'm sure I'm fine" Sarah answered, caught between a jolt of surprise and the cold, wet puddle seeping into her pant legs.

"I'm terribly sorry I gave you such a fright. I never thought to run into to anyone this late. I was going to leave the list for the grocer on the kitchen table."

"Oh, Seaneen, it's certainly not your fault. I never thought I'd run into anyone either."

"What brings you out into a dark winter's night?"

Sarah was taken back to the day five years ago when she and Seaneen had delivered a letter to Peter in the midst of a snowstorm. The thought made her smile at what a good sport Seaneen was. Not much had changed.

"Would you like to walk with me to deliver a note to a certain guest?" Sarah asked.

Catching on immediately, Seaneen McAughtrie threaded Sarah's arm through hers.

"I can think of nothing I'd rather do," the older lady replied.

The two women walked across the damp meadow, passing several of the cottages lit only by dim porch lights. An owl hooted way up in one of the tall evergreen trees and startled them, which led to soft giggling. The note was successfully slid under Peter's door, without disturbing him.

"Let me walk with you back to your cottage," Sarah offered. "And I'll take the grocer's list back with me."

"I'd like that," Seaneen answered, then paused before continuing. "Shall I inquire about you and Peter, or just keep my nose on my face and not put it in your business?"

It was Sarah's turn to slide her arm through Seaneen's, as they walked along. She gave a bit of thought before answering.

"I'm not sure where this will go, but I know more now than I did before."

"You are a wise young woman, and I have full confidence you will do the right thing."

"Thank you, those are comforting words to hear. We will see. Now, what about you and your lovely gentleman? I'm genuinely very pleased for you, for both of you. I hope he knows he is marrying one of the best of the best."

"Ah, my sweet lass, I do love you as my own," Seaneen stopped near the front of her cottage. "What would you think about our wee wedding taking place on Hogmanay at the Leigheas chapel?"

"That sounds perfect! But you know that is only three weeks away?"

"Indeed, I do. The idea came from James. His closest friend, Vicar Giles Fisher, is available to perform the service that week, so we thought we would ask your father tomorrow."

"I'm sure it would be fine! This is so exciting!"

"Keep a secret?" the older woman asked.

"Of course," Sarah said.

"I'm going to ask your father to walk with me down the aisle."

"Oh, Seaneen…" was all Sarah could get out before tearing up and hugging her.

"And might you stand up with me?"

This brought another round of happy tears, and the agreement that the two ladies had much to talk about.

"Don't forget, lass, we need to start decorating the house for Christmas tomorrow."

"I won't forget. We can meet after lunch and make a plan."

Walking back to the main house, Sarah mused at how life was full of ups and downs. One must remember that when times are difficult, they never stay that way. Life certainly seems to have a way of righting itself.

## *Chapter Sixty-four*

# PETER:

### *Nothing Like a Wet Dog*

Peter woke up slowly from a hazy dream he instantly forgot. For a few moments he didn't know where he was, only that the room was pitch-black and chilly. The past few years he had awakened in a number of strange locations, so maybe it wasn't odd that he was confused.

He pulled the blanket up around his chin and listened to the rain pelting the windows.

Venturing one arm out of the covers, he turned on the bedside lamp, and found his drawing journal upended on the floor, with several pencils scattered nearby. He brought his cold arm back under the blanket and recalled that he was at Leigheas. He'd had a most astounding day yesterday. Unable to sleep last night, he had dug around his suitcase and found the journal he had thrown in at the last minute and began to sketch for the first time in a long while. Whether it was the relief of writing to Sarah or the surprise of seeing the always-supportive Kaitlyn and Thomas Turning, there had been a change in his thinking. Hope was a very powerful feeling that brought life to ideas. He was an artist and while he had lost sight of that, along with his confidence, it was now clear to him that it was time to stop sloshing in the past and begin creating to please himself. No longer did he need or desire anyone else's approval of his art. Scrambling out of bed and into warm clothes, he couldn't wait to resume his sketching. First, he needed to light the fire, then make a steaming cup of tea. Gathering up his journal and pencils off the floor, he laid them on kitchen table and was surprised to see yet another note pushed under his door.

"These people do communicate at the oddest times," he thought looking at the hands on his watch showing it was five o'clock in the morning.

Instantly he recognized Sarah's handwriting, and hesitated opening it. This could be really bad or really good. Was he ready to accept whichever way she went? A moment of vulnerability passed, replaced by faith that whatever it said, he would move forward with his life.

*Can you meet me at the chapel around seven in the morning?*
*S.*

Peter had no idea he had been holding his breath until a vast amount of air was exhaled. He would take that as a positive sign for the moment and not dwell on the possibility that she might still be done with him. There were two hours he could fill with drawing, tea, drawing some more and not thinking about Sarah Duncan. Ha! That was funny.

Rain continued to come down so heavily that seeing across the meadow was nearly impossible. Peter slid on his boots and a bright blue slicker that had kindly been left hanging on a hook near the door and grabbed an umbrella that was handy. Thankfully, the J.M. Barrie cottage was equipped with everything a person could need. He carefully tucked his drawing journal between his shirt and his wool coat, knowing it would stay dry with the slicker protecting it. Passing a mirror, he chuckled that all he needed was a red hat to resemble Paddington Bear. He was a bit early, but couldn't help it knowing he would see Sarah soon.

The heavy door of the chapel was hard to open with it's wet, slippery antique brass handle. Once inside, Peter felt the same awe he had the first time he visited…was that only yesterday? Today, the room was dimly lit to match the day outside, yet there was still an inviting feel about it. Sarah hadn't arrived which gave him time to get out of the wet slicker and walk around a bit. This hallowed place had a quiet peace giving thought that all was well in life. Or perhaps that was just Peter's wishful thinking.

"I have hope," he repeated like a mantra, "I have hope."

Then the door opened and Sarah rushed in pulling a soggy, rain drenched English cocker spaniel on a leash.

"I'm so sorry I'm late. The dog needed to go out and if I had taken the time to do that, then returned her to the house I would've been even later."

With that the dog shook her long hair, sending water drops across everything in near proximity, including both Peter and Sarah. Wagging her stubby tail, the sweet faced dog looked at the humans, waiting for attention.

Peter was the first to respond, "Thank you Maggie for a much needed shower. Was it that obvious I was in need?"

Her little tail wagged with even more enthusiasm and Sarah began to laugh.

"If I'm not mistaken, Seaneen left some towels in a closet in the back. It rains enough that guests often get a bit damp on their way here."

They sat on the chapel floor with the dog between them, both trying to dry Maggie's golden fur. Maggie was quite sure that grabbing the towel and running away with it was a new game. Before long Sarah and Peter were in fits of laughter chasing the dog through the pews trying to catch her. They finally settled down back on the floor with Maggie on Sarah's lap, happily panting after all the fun. Peter couldn't think of anywhere he would rather be.

"I'm glad you have a cocker spaniel. They are so eager to please and full of character," Peter said. "A little like me?"

The giggle that came out of Sarah was just what Peter had waited for. Dare he hope there could be a reconciliation? Sarah interrupted his thoughts.

"Peter, do you realize when you arrived at Leigheas and I opened the door, it was the first time I ever heard your voice?"

"I guess that's true. Was it what you expected?"

"It was very nice actually. After all, you could've sounded like a bull frog."

"A bull frog?" he answered incredulously.

Sarah puffed out her cheeks and made a loud, low pitched bellow, a bit like a foghorn.

"Yet another unknown talent of the lovely Sarah Duncan," he said laughing.

"That's what international schooling will teach you."

Peter mused for a moment, looking into her lovely blue eyes.

"Well, you could've sounded like a…peacock."

"A peacock? What on earth does a peacock sound like?"

"Are you telling me you've never heard a peacock's loud, incredibly annoying scream?"

"I had no idea they screamed. You thought I would sound like a screaming peacock?"

"Well, you could have. Aren't you glad you don't?"

"I am indeed."

"Seriously, did my voicc surprisc you?"

"Your voice is very pleasant, a bit deeper and more Scottish than I had imagined. It's quite agreeable," she answered.

Maggie grew tired of their conversation and had fallen asleep in Sarah's lap. The rain continued to pour outside, lending an intimate atmosphere to the two people sitting on the floor.

Sarah spoke first.

"Your letter tells quite a story."

"Believe it or not, I left out quite a bit," he answered a little self-consciously.

"I'm sorry it was so difficult. With such high expectations it must have all been very painful."

"I was far too young and naive to have been under the tutelage of Mr. Antoneli. He's undoubtedly brilliant, but with such genius seems to come a callus entitlement. One of the worst parts of this whole situation was when he told my parents I was an untalented, ungrateful wicked lad. That was their first clue that the famous artist was a might unhinged, but they didn't want to interfere as long as I chose to stay there. I might be many things, but as close as I have always been to my family they knew I had some bit of talent, always seemed grateful and they were pretty sure I wasn't wicked."

"How terrible for them to hear such awful things, no matter. They must have been very angry."

"They were for a long time, more so after I finally came home and they saw the change in me. My father wanted to take some action against him, but I just wanted to forget everything. It was really hard to come home a failure after a lifetime of support from my family. I knew I must be a laughing stock in Edinburgh with all the public attention I received before I left. Writing the letter to you yesterday was the first time I finally had the courage to face the demons and live through it again."

"I'm glad you shared it with me. I had no idea what you had been through."

Sarah gently stroked Maggie's soft fur and looked at Peter for what felt like an eternity. He knew intuitively to let her think out whatever it was she was about to say, so he kept quiet even though his heart was beating out of his body. Maggie opened one eye, looked up and snuggled further into Sarah's lap.

"Peter, there is something I need to know. I am a little embarrassed to bring it up and am struggling a bit with how to ask. I've carried this sadness for far too long, since you went to Italy…and I guess I just need to know."

"Sarah, you can ask me anything. I'm learning to be open and honest, no more hiding."

"During my months in Edinburgh You were very kind to me. Having moved so much in my life, you might think I would have become accustomed to being the new girl. When you add being naturally shy, and not having a normal family, I was feeling disconnected and lonely. No complaints, mind you. My father more than made up for no mother and I was very close to my grandmother before she passed away so there was no lack of love. But I always carried a sense of being different so I chose to live my life in books. Again, no complaints. Reading is where I've always gone to live in another world. My point, and I promise there is a point, is when you were attentive to me it meant so much and I'm afraid I developed quite a crush on you."

Peter opened his mouth to speak, but Sarah hushed him.

"You must let me finish, I may never have the courage to say any of this again." She took a deep breath and continued, "Your notes were entertaining and encouraging and lent an element of fun to my limited social life. When everything happened with my father, you were there and I held onto that. When you wrote to me about going to Italy, I must admit that while I was happy for you, selfishly I knew I would miss you very much. I was quite sure you would outgrow me by the time you returned, if you ever returned. Once my father and I left Shetland, we were in Edinburgh for a few days before we headed to London to sort our future. Seaneen McAughtrie joined us on the train, and left the newspaper article about you, along with some other magazines in my compartment."

Peter felt his breath leave as his body went completely still.

"You read the article? I never thought you would…"

"See it? It was a chance occurrence, I must say. Reading the first part I was confused by you being a famous artist and why you hadn't told me anything about that. I consoled myself that you must have had your reasons, and again, you had been so sympathetic to my problems, it was hard to be angry. Still, I was confused. It was only toward the end of the article that the bottom dropped out of my world."

In unison, they both said, "There is no one, other than my cocker spaniel, that I will miss."

"You know that line well," Sarah said.

Peter brushed his hair back with both hands, and looked at her with a rueful expression.

"Believe me, I never thought you would see that article."

"Apparently not," she said

"You have no idea how many times I've thought about it and what you might think if you ever saw it."

"Well, I realized that I had been a young, silly girl with an enormous imagination."

"Well, while much of that might be true," he said with a laugh, "and I'm not saying I agree with you, there's much more to the story. As I wrote in my letter, my trust in people was minimal when you came along. Knowing you had no idea who I was, meant that you liked me for me, and I really held onto that. It wasn't that I didn't want to share that part of my life with you, but our friendship was pure and simple. It wasn't complicated by outside influences."

There was a crack of lightening, followed by a loud thunder clap. A fresh torrent of rain began hitting the stained glass windows of the little chapel. The sleepy dog looked up at Sarah with her oversized brown eyes and long eyelashes, then put her head back down, secure to be in a warm lap.

"In an odd way, I can understand that," Sarah said. "In my case, I was afraid if we came back to Edinburgh, I would be known as the daughter of the man who was shot and I would lose my real identity. But that doesn't explain…"

Peter interrupted her.

"I'm getting to that. When the interview took place, I was in a really strange place mentally. Suddenly, I was a wee bit famous again and about to leave home on an adventure that had a thousand unknowns. I might have started believing my own press, 'the boy is a genius,' things like that, and for the first time I began to be cocky about who I was. Can you imagine such rubbish? When the writer was winding up the interview he asked about my personal life. Now, remember if you will at that time, you were exiled in Shetland, your father was at an unnamed rehabilitation centre and I still felt protective of you. I danced around answering the question, and the writer kept asking me for your name, insisting 'my public' wanted to know. There was absolutely no way I was going to divulge your name to the press. The only answer I could come up with was…."

And again in unison they both said, "There is no one, other than my cocker spaniel, that I will miss."

"Sarah, I have had a crush on you since you responded to my first note. I knew I was older than you were, but I was charmed by your intelligence, lack of guile and lovely sense of humor. My hope had always been that we would meet up in person and begin a genuine friendship. When I saw you in church at the Watchnight service all those years ago, I thought this was our chance. We both know how that ended. I am so deeply sorry that I caused you any pain by my well-meaning actions. Please accept my apologies, won't you?"

After what seemed like far too long, the smile he had longed to see nearly overwhelmed him. Not wanting to miss the moment, he couldn't stop his mouth from speaking.

"Right now I have very little to offer you, but I promise with all my heart that I won't let you down." Peter reached up on the pew next to him and handed her his sketch book. "I've begun drawing again, and feeling the passion I used to have. I can't wait to begin painting! I know it's asking a lot, but do you think you could wait for me–wait until I'm self-sufficient and could care for you properly?"

He watched as Sarah thumbed through each page, carefully examine each sketch, especially the one of her, before she answered him.

"I've loved you for nearly six years. I see no reason why I wouldn't wait a bit longer." Sarah gently laid the sketch book down next to her on the floor and held her hands out to Peter. The electricity was almost visible as they touched for the first time. Even Maggie the dog must have felt it. She stood up and shook her furry body all the way down to her stubby little tail, then walked away stretching her legs. She looked back at the humans as if to say, 'Time to go. I'm hungry.' Unfortunately, neither human noticed her as they shared their first kiss.

## *Chapter Sixty-five*

# RICHARD:

### *One Teaspoon for the Pot*

The ritual of making tea in the morning had become one of Richard's favorite traditions. Radiant warmth from the Aga stove kept the kitchen comfortable even on stormy mornings. He enjoyed his time alone in the morning, though he wouldn't have minded if Kaitlyn magically appeared. He reached up to the middle shelf for his Brown Betty teapot. The first decision of the day was which tea to choose. Lately, he had been partial to Earl Gray with it's flavor of bergamot orange, but Scottish breakfast tea was more full-bodied with a hint of malt and oaky-ness, like a good scotch whisky. But then Darjeeling tea from India had a brisk, fruity flavor he liked. After the dramatic weather this morning, he'd better go with the Scottish breakfast tea. A swirl of hot water in the old pot to warm it, then a teaspoon of tea leaves for each cup of hot water, plus one for the pot, just as his mother had taught him. In went the hot water, on went the teapot lid, then the anticipation of the fragrant aroma coming through the spout. Allowing time for tea to brew was always a lesson in patience.

As Richard took his first sip, Seaneen came in the side door, wearing a rain slicker and carrying a dripping wet umbrella.

"I thought you might be up, what with all that lightening and thunder. It's easing up a wee bit, but wasn't that a mighty storm?" she said hanging up her slicker and umbrella on the hooks by the door.

"It was indeed. I'm grateful it wasn't windy. The last thing we need are more downed branches and trees."

Seaneen busied herself in the kitchen while Richard drank his tea and looked out the window. There was a companionable silence between them, each lost in their own thoughts. The grandfather clock struck seven times. Out of nowhere Seaneen, turned to Richard.

"Richard? Would you give me away?" she asked with some urgency.

Without missing a beat he answered.

"I might sell you to passing gypsies, but give you away? No, you're worth at least a pound or two on the open market."

"Oh, you're full of it this morning, aren't you? You know perfectly well what I mean. When James and I get married, I was hoping you would walk with me down the aisle."

"I would be honored. I hope your planning on marrying at the chapel. It would mean a great deal to me."

Her face turned red and she looked flustered.

"Oh, Richard, I forgot to ask you if that would be all right. We've been thinking about it and we both love the chapel. How does the thirty-first of December sound? Yesterday James inquired if a friend of his would marry us and it seems that was the only day the gentleman had free. I'm so sorry I haven't mentioned it to you. I'm a bit ruffled with everything going on."

"New Year's Eve? Hogmanay? You do realize that is only three weeks away and Christmas is in between there."

"So Sarah reminded me last night. The wedding will be simple, and I've already sorted most of our Christmas preparations. There are a few details I wanted to speak to you and Sarah about..."

"Oh! I haven't told you, or Sarah for that matter, Liam called last night and he and the family would like to come for a visit on December twenty-ninth, although he thinks he may arrive ahead of the family for a meeting in London. With the guest cottages empty we can accommodate everyone. Is that all right with you?"

"My goodness, that is exciting news! They would be here for the wedding. My sister and her family will also be here for two nights, but they have booked rooms in Peebles. I don't know how this can all be any more perfect."

"Nonsense, they can stay here. We've plenty of room between the cottages and the bedrooms in the house."

"I wouldn't want to impose."

"Seaneen, we are family. Like it or not, you're stuck with us."

"I quite like it," she said hugging Richard. "And, by the way, Miss Turning would be most welcome at the wedding, if you'd like."

Before he could answer, the side door blew open and Maggie came running in, followed closely by Sarah and Peter, and a lot muddy tracks. A commotion ensued with rain slickers carelessly hung up, boots tossed toward the door and the wet dog being toweled off. A fair amount of laughter filled the warm kitchen. Maggie settled herself in front of the Aga, and the others made tea and settled in around the table.

"I'll pop out and share the all news with James," Seaneen said. "Be back in a jiffy, then we'd best start the planning."

It didn't take much for Richard to see that whatever the problem between Sarah and Peter, had been resolved in a most positive manner. They were holding hands while drinking tea and looking into each other's eyes. The sight might have made him roll his eyes, if he weren't wishing that Kaitlyn was here and they were doing much the same. He almost hated to interrupt their idyllic moment.

"Sarah, I haven't told you that Liam called late last evening wondering if the family could come for a visit between Christmas and New Years."

That caught her full attention and her enthusiasm bubbled over.

"Really? That's fabulous, wonderful news and what excellent timing. They will be here for Seaneen's wedding and Hogmanay. I'm so thrilled we will see them." She turned to Peter, "You remember Liam and his family kept me safe on Shetland, then turned out to be family. It was the best, oddest coincidence ever in the world."

"It certainly will be good to see them, but we've a lot to get done between now and then," Richard added to his daughters enthusiasm.

"We do, that's true, but nothing we can't handle."

Richard was beginning to see that nothing was going to dim the glow of his daughter's happiness. He was cautiously pleased, hoping she was right.

"I've got a notebook in the butler's pantry and we can begin a list," she said brightly. "I've learned you can accomplish anything with a list."

"Mr. Duncan, I will be here another week before I go to Elibank, which is only a few miles away, and I would be happy to help. It does sound like there's a lot to accomplish in a short time."

"You're a good sport, Peter. We will most likely take you up on your offer, thank you. Please call me Richard."

Sarah handed each man a sheet of paper and a pen.

"For your notes so you don't forget anything," she instructed.

"You know, I actually did run a consulate, Sunshine Girl, in case it slipped your mind," Richard reminded her with a laugh.

"Oh, Dad, that was ages ago. You're so much older now," she replied with a mischievous grin. "Although Kaitlyn doesn't seem to mind your advanced age."

She was met with her father's version of an evil eye, which only made her laugh. Seaneen returned with a stack of mail, setting it down in front of Richard.

"What did I miss? Oh my, Sarah has her famous notebook out."

"Apparently you can do anything with a notebook," Peter chimed in.

The next hour was spent discussing plans for the next few weeks. It was agreed Christmas Eve would be low key with just the family for dinner. Seaneen mentioned James had offered to lead a Watchnight service in the chapel. The big dinner would be on Christmas night with everyone, including James, Stephen and Henry, Kaitlyn and Thomas Turning and Peter's family if they were available. Seaneen said Meara and Brennan offered to help cook early Christmas day which would be a big help. The table could be set a day or two in advance. When talk turned to decorating the house and the chapel, the spirit of Christmas overflowed. Tasks were assigned, notes were taken, all in a happy, lighthearted atmosphere. Richard and Peter went to the attic to bring down boxes and boxes of decorations and made plans for a trip to the tree farm. Sarah and Seaneen headed to the butler's pantry to identify the things they would need to make the Christmas table perfect. It was a while before someone noticed breakfast had gotten lost in the shuffle, and the merry group gathered back at the kitchen table for a quick meal. Richard looked through the assortment of mail while enjoying his oatmeal, stopping suddenly when he saw the return address on one of the envelopes. The others at the table were busy in conversation and took no notice of him slipping the envelope into his jacket pocket or his face losing it's color. He took a breath before speaking to make sure his voice would sound normal.

"Sarah, when you've finished breakfast, would you meet me in my office? Take your time. There is just something I need to go over with you." Richard stood up and rinsed his bowl in the sink.

"I'll take care of that," Seaneen said, "you go on about your business."

"Thank you. And thank you, Peter for your help this morning."

It was taking all of his will power to keep his tone light and natural, though he was feeling quite the opposite. Once outside the kitchen, he felt his chest tighten in apprehension of what was to come.

# Chapter Sixty-six
# SARAH:
## *A Voice From the Past*

"This came in the post for you."

Her father's voice had an odd quality about it which made Sarah nervous. She stood in front of his desk as he held an envelope out toward her. If she didn't know better she would think his hand was shaking slightly. Something was off about all of this. Fear was battling curiosity and she couldn't seem to raise her hand to take the envelope.

"What is it?" she asked, hoping to prolong the inevitability of actually touching it.

"I suppose we won't know until you open it."

Her heart pounding, she took the envelope and read the return address. She involuntarily sat down hard on the leather chair, which thankfully was behind her.

"I am as shocked as you are," her father said. "This is the first communication from your mother since she left when you were a few months old. There are two names on the return address. I'm not sure what that means. Maybe you would prefer to read it in private."

"No. You open it," she said handing it back across the desk. "We should do this together."

Richard hesitated before taking it. He carefully slit the top of the envelope with a brass letter opener, and pulled out a sheet of thin, blue paper with Victoria's familiar handwriting. He handed it back to Sarah.

"Since it was addressed to you, I think you should read it first."

For the briefest moment Sarah thought she might throw up. Why did this have to come today? Just when she and Peter had reconnected and the morning had been so much fun. For the first time in a long while, all was good in her world. Whatever this was, it had all the earmarks of upending her happiness. She took a steeling breath and unfolded the paper. Out fell a small note card and newspaper clipping onto the floor. Before picking them up she read the letter silently, then looked at her anxious father, unable to say anything. Some moments passed before she began reading.

*Dear Sarah,*

*If you are reading this it means I have moved on to another life. Your father would like to think that I am in heaven, but I'm not sure I share his optimism.*

*It seems a bit too late, and honestly a little shallow, to apologize for not being in your life, but you must trust me that it was far better that I walked away. I simply did not want the responsibility of children. For whatever reason I was born without a maternal bone in my body. I hope you can understand that it had nothing to do with you. Your father is one of the kindest, most caring humans on this earth and I knew he would take good care of you. There is no doubt you are smart, beautiful and fascinating. My slight twinge of regret is not knowing you as an adult. We might have even been good friends. Alas, it was not to be.*

*For the last twenty years I have lived in Positano, a small village on the Amalfi Coast in Italy with my friend, Eduordo. I worked very hard at becoming an artist and was modestly successful, but more importantly I have been very happy. My hope for you is find your passion and follow it. Life will lead you on many strange journeys, but if you have passion it's like having a close friend who will keep you moving forward. My only words of wisdom to you.*

*The sale of my paintings allowed me to buy a small amount of land with a house and studio here. It has appreciated in value and is now worth more than I would've ever imagined. I have left half of it to you as my closest heir and half to Eduordo. If he chooses to continue living here, he will have the property assessed and will pay you half of the value. If not, he will sell and send you your half. He is a good man and very honest.*

*My beautiful daughter, please forgive me and know that I loved you the best way I knew how–from a distance. Live your life fully and don't miss a moment, it really is a grand adventure.*

*Your mother,*
*Victoria*

Laying the letter down on the desk, Sarah walked over to the large French doors that overlooked a vast meadow. The morning rain had left a mist in the air. The lump in her throat made it difficult to speak.

"Am I anything like her?" she asked without turning around.

"You are beautiful and smart like she is…or was. You have her big blue eyes and long, dark hair. But you are so much more than she could ever be. You have an open heart that loves and cares about people. Sadly, I'm afraid Victoria was very self-centered. It took me many years to come to terms with that."

The clock loudly ticked off the seconds in the silent room before Sarah spoke again.

"I don't know how to feel. I have a sense of losing something very important, but how do you lose something you never had?"

"Could it be you feel you've lost the opportunity of meeting her one day? You must have a thousand questions you would've wanted to ask her."

Sarah turned and faced her father.

"How do you feel?" she asked.

"I loved her very much. She was an extraordinary, independent woman who knew her own mind. Unfortunately, she hurt many people in her life. I feel very sad that she is gone, however I believe that she loved us as much as she was capable."

Reaching down to pick up the items that fell, Sarah saw that one was a note from Eduardo and the other was her mother's obituary.

"Eduardo says he would like to continue living in the house. He will have it appraised and send me half the amount soon. He added the name of an estate agent if we would like to arrange our own appraisal." Sarah looked at her father for a reaction.

"We would need someone who speaks Italian, but that is up to you," he answered.

"She said he is honest, so I don't see any reason to do anything further."

Sarah looked intently at the jagged cutout newspaper clipping of the obituary. It had a grainy photo of a woman who bore a scant resemblance to the only picture Sarah had of her mother, the one she kept in her Bible. The woman did appear to have large eyes and long, dark hair, but other than that nothing looked familiar. She scanned the sentences and all the positive adjectives describing Victoria Vivienne Duncan.

"It is very odd to learn about my mother's life in an obituary. It says her paintings 'reflected the unique charm of the coastal fishing village, as well as the natural beauty of the lemon and olive orchards.' Apparently, she had a small gallery in her studio which had a large following. 'Positano will be celebrating her life with the dedication of a large olive tree in the Piazetta across from the Church of Santa Maria Assunta where Victoria Duncan attended mass.' Was she always Catholic?"

"Not that I ever knew."

"Oh my," Sarah's eyes began get blurry. "It says, 'Victoria is survived by partner Eduardo DeLuca, former husband Richard Galloway Duncan…and daughter Sarah Anne Duncan.' There is a poem at the end:

'Please don't grieve for me<br>
For my life was as it was meant to be<br>
Near by the sea<br>
Unencumbered and free<br>
Please try to forgive me.'

Richard's arms opened wide and Sarah fell into them, sobbing on his chest as though the hurt would never end. Holding his daughter close, he was unable to wipe the tears running down his own face.

*"Dear Journal,*

*This was never intended to be a diary, but my need to write my feelings down is overwhelming.*

*It has been six days since the letter arrived and my emotions continue to swing much like a clock pendulum. Sometimes I am deeply sad, other times I forget she died, and in between I feel guilt, wonder, anger, curiosity, and remorse. I realize now that part of me wanted to meet her and know her. And that will never happen. Will this haunt me forever or will it find its place in the tapestry of my life?*

*Leigheas has been abuzz with activity preparing for Christmas, Seaneen's wedding and Liam's visit. With all the busyness no one seems to have noticed I have been preoccupied. Dad agreed not say anything to anyone because it was my news to share when and if, I was ready. Seeing his reaction to her death made me realize how much they cared for each other, if only for a moment in time. As children I think we are self-centered little beings who rarely think beyond ourselves. For the first time I got a real glimpse of my father as someone who had a full life before I was born. With my toe dipping into adult-hood, I am beginning to relate to my father more as a grown up and better understand him.*

*I have spent quite a lot of time the past few days pondering many things and praying for the right direction. If nothing else, my mother's death has encouraged me to examine what is important in life.*

With that thought in her mind, Sarah closed her journal.

## *Chapter Sixty-seven*

# PETER:

## *Finding a Christmas Tree*

The freezing temperatures were not unexpected given it was a week before Christmas. Time had flown as the items on the checklist had been completed and marked off. The only box not checked was finding a Christmas tree. Whether it was the persistent rainy weather that plagued the area or simply how close it was to the holiday, there was not a suitable tree to be found. Richard had been given the tree task, but reported he'd had one dead end after another in his search.

Peter was busy sketching in his cottage when Richard showed up at his door.

"I am a desperate man, Peter! There is not a single tree to be had in all of Great Britain. Do you have any ideas?"

"Come in, it's raw out there," Peter said ushering him inside. "I was afraid finding a tree could be a problem."

"There isn't a blasted tree within a hundred mile radius of Leigheas," Richard lamented, moving closer to the small fireplace as Peter handed him a hot cup of tea. "Having a tree is so important to Sarah, and I really hate to let her down."

"Well, I'm glad you asked…as I have a thought."

The relief on Richard's face was immediate. "You mean it? That would be an answer to prayer. I would be forever in your debt."

"Do you have a vehicle large enough to carry a tree? I know you were counting on having a tree delivered, but if we can convey it, I can pretty much guarantee a tree that Sarah will approve of."

"As it happens, I do!" Richard answered. "Would it be possible to go right away?"

"The sooner the better if it will make Sarah happy. She has seemed a wee bit withdrawn the past few days."

"She has a lot on her mind, but I agree with you. A Christmas tree is just what she needs. Do you know where the large, stone garage is out beyond the stables?"

"It's around to the left as I recall. Let me put on warmer clothes and I'll meet you there in ten minutes."

"I am very curious to know where this elusive tree is to be found. Where are we going?" Richard asked as he walked toward the door

"That part is a surprise," Peter answered mysteriously.

Even with a sweater, a coat, a hat, scarf, long socks, and Wellies, the walk to the stables chilled Peter. He had passed by the old garage several times on horseback while at Leigheas, but never had a reason to look inside. Plus, it was none of his business. As he approached the building, the big double doors swung open almost hitting him.

"Come on, jump in. I haven't driven this beauty in a while."

Peter stopped dead in his tracks and was thunderstruck.

"Bloody brilliant! That's a Tickford Land Rover! You own a Tickford Land Rover? How ever did you find it?"

"It came with the estate," Richard answered. "I'm guessing by your reaction, it's rather special?"

Being this close to a car Peter had only heard of for years was intoxicating.

"You don't know the history?" he asked, gently touching the tin plated spare wheel cover on the hood.

"Not a clue," Richard answered.

"Shortly after the war, Land Rover started selling cars designed after the American Jeep but ran into some problems. They teamed up with the Tickford people to make the car more luxurious?"

"This is luxurious?" Richard asked incredulously, looking at the rugged interior.

"Compared to the original Land Rover model it was," Peter continued, as he walked around the car. "Tickford was known for their work with Rolls Royce and Lagonda. This beauty has aluminum body panels, a one-piece laminated glass windscreen and lovely, padded leather seats."

"I had no idea she was a collector's item."

"Oh, she is. Look at the sliding side windows for ventilation. That was incredibly innovative for the time. Have you noticed the heater? That was revolutionary. There were only about 700 of these made and only a handful stayed in Great Britain."

"Well, I'm very impressed with your knowledge. Shall we take her out and find a Christmas tree?"

"Absolutely!" Peter answered with a huge grin.

"Now, where is it we are we going?" Richard asked again.

"It's not far. Turn left out of the driveway..."

Within fifteen minutes, the classic Tickford Land Rover was winding it's way down a long, tree-lined driveway.

"Welcome to Elibank. This is my grandparents home, though my parents are living here now as well."

"I had no idea this was so close to Leigheas. No wonder you know so much about this area."

"I've grown up on the estate, spending as much time here as I could. There are about two hundred fourteen acres, but most importantly like Leigheas, we have fishing rights on the Tweed. It has always been my favorite place to paint as well."

"It's really beautiful, but does our visit to Elibank have anything to do with a Christmas tree?"

"Well, it turns out I remembered we have a forest with Scots Pine trees."

The gravel crunched under the tires until Richard stopped the car in front of the large, white, harled and painted stone house. The pitched slate roof shared space with a number of chimneys and huge doors stood open under the enormous pedimented porch leading to the entry through carved double doors.

"My, this is magnificent," Richard said, looking through the car window at the house and the surrounding land.

"Most of the structures go back to the mid-nineteenth century, but here and there are parts dating to the seventeenth century. We even boast castle ruins on the property. There's quite a bit of history, including the Earl of Elibank, who was involved in a plan to kidnap

King Charles II in order to help Bonnie Prince Charlie take the throne. Needless to say, it ended badly. That was in 1752 and to my knowledge no one from Elibank has ever tried to over throw the monarchy since."

"Let's go in where it's a bit warmer."

"Weren't you the one just touting the Tickford heater?" Richard replied with a laugh.

Peter wrapped his scarf closer around his neck and watched his breath form a misty cloud as it condensed in the chill. Richard followed him through the carved doors to the bright entry hall.

"Hello? Hello?" Peter called as they walked down the hall.

"Peter, is that you?" A male voice answered from a room further along the way.

"It is and I've brought a friend. Are you busy?"

A tall, lanky gentleman with a close cropped beard and a friendly smile came into the hallway and beckoned them into the warm drawing room.

"No, no. Come in. It is bloody cold out there today, warm yourselves by the fire."

"Father, this is Richard Duncan, Richard this is my father Stuart Michael-McGregor."

"Very nice to meet you," Richard said, shaking Mr. Michael-McGregor's hand.

"Believe me, Mr. Duncan, the privilege is mine. I've heard quite a bit about you."

"We are here on a mission, Father. Do you think Grandfather would mind if we cut down a Scots pine from the forest?

"I'm sure he wouldn't mind in the least. If you remember you and your Grandfather planted many of those trees when you were a wee boy."

"By the way, where is Grandfather?"

"He and your Grandmother are in London for Christmas with your great aunt Prudence. Your mother is on the telephone with your sister and it looks as though she won't be home for Christmas either."

Without hesitation, Richard spoke up. "We were planning on inviting you and your family to Leigheas for Christmas dinner if it didn't conflict with your plans."

"How kind of you. Allow me to speak with my wife and I will let you know, though I can see no reason why we couldn't. Now, do you need some help with that tree?"

"We brought an axe. Will that suffice?"

"Let me put on my heavy jacket and we can get a saw as well from the outbuilding."

"Oh, Father, before you go out the front door, there is something I need to tell you," Peter said with mock seriousness

Stuart looked quizzically at his son.

"What is it, Peter?"

"Outside that door, in our driveway…is a Tickford Land Rover!"

"No!" Stuart said in astonishment. "Then why are we in here? Let's go!"

The only person more intrigued with the old Land Rover than Peter was his father.

He looked at every part of car, inside and out, asking questions that Richard was helpless to answer.

"If only your grandfather was here. This is fantastic. It's the first one I have ever seen in person. What a cracker!" Stuart exclaimed.

"I'm going to have a word with mum while you ogle. Don't leave without me."

Peter disappeared into the house, but hearing his mother still on the phone stood in between the two doors to stay warm. It became obvious by their conversation that neither Richard Duncan nor his father knew he was there, not that he was trying to eavesdrop.

"Mr. Duncan, first of all, let me tell you how much we appreciate all you have done for Peter in the weeks he has spent with you. It was heartbreaking to see my only son so disconsolate about every part of his life. That dreadful man drug Peter through hell and back, then walked away with no shame or remorse. There was a time when we considered legal action, if nothing else, to prevent him from doing it to another young artist. Ultimately, at Peter's request, we let it go." Stuart paused for a moment and looked across the wide expanse of pastureland. "His mother and I were at a loss how to help when he came home. Truthfully, I think we both felt a little guilty for not stepping in earlier."

"I can understand your frustration and helplessness. Being a parent has never been for the faint of heart. I must tell you, though, after spending a fair amount of time with Peter, he really seems to have faced his problems and come out the victor. He's enthused about painting again, and appears to have quite an attachment to my daughter, who by the way is equally attached to him."

"Yes, Sarah has been important to him for a very long time. We first learned about her when you were…when you had your accident. He was frantic to find out if she had been hurt and where she was. At the time, no one knew if you were dead or alive, if you don't mind me saying so."

"It's hard to believe that was six years ago on Christmas Eve."

"You know what they say, time flies? Once Peter found out from your housekeeper that you were alive and Sarah was safe, he began eating and sleeping regularly. Until then he had been looking a wee bit ragged."

"Interesting! Seaneen told him. I had no idea about any of this."

"The fact that Peter was able to help your CIA and FBI locate the man who hurt you, was a miracle."

"What? I have no idea what you're talking about. You're saying Peter knew where Conrad Ratchford was hiding? This doesn't make any sense, I'm very confused."

At this point, Peter decided he had better step out and finish the story, knowing his father might embellish it a tad, and he was feeling a little uneasy eavesdropping.

"Actually, Richard, my father is correct. It's a bit of a twisted tale, try to stay with me," Peter said. "Jonquil, is the daughter of our neighbor in Edinburgh who went to the same school Sarah attended and heard about your…accident. By the oddest coincidence, several weeks later, Jonquil happened to overhear her mother speaking on the telephone to Mr. Ratchford, who, as it happens, is her mother's brother, so he's Jonquil's uncle. The conversation centered around Mr. Ratchford doing something dreadful in Edinburgh, possibly killing someone, and wanting Jonquil's parents to rescue him from

Iceland before some foreigners got to him."

"But how did you get involved?" Richard asked, looking puzzled.

Peter's father jumped in, "Jonquil was afraid her parents were going to help Mr. Ratchford escape again. She had met Peter and knew about his friendship with Sarah, and was desperate to protect her parents."

Father and son were interrupting each other in an effort to get the story out. Richard looked from one to the other, slightly bewildered, as it all unfolded.

"When she came to me and related all that was said and I asked enough questions to assure the details were accurate, I knew I had to do something."

"Then Peter came to us and we all agreed that he must alert the American Consulate."

"They came to the house, interrogated me, found the information valid…and the rest is history," Peter finished the story with finality.

"Does Sarah know any of this?" Richard asked.

"No," Peter answered a little embarrassed. "I was just at the right place at the right time."

"You pretty much changed the course of our lives, Peter. I must admit to being a little stunned by everything you've told me, but it certainly reinforces my belief that you are quite an exceptional young man."

"Thank you."

Feeling a little awkward by all the emotion, and in typical British fashion, Stuart Michael-McGregor cleared his throat."

"Don't we have a tree to cut down?"

Richard tossed the keys to the Tickford Land Rover to the elder Michael-McGregor.

"Would you care to drive?" he asked.

## Chapter Sixty-eight

# SARAH:

*Today is the Day*

The colossal Christmas tree became even more perfect when Sarah learned it had actually been planted by Peter and his grandfather. Last night they wrangled the Scots Pine into a stand and placed it in the largest reception room, jokingly referred to as The Elephant Room due to it's enormous size. As it was getting late, it was decided they would all meet the following evening for dinner and tree trimming.

Sarah woke up the next morning with one thought in her mind and said it out loud as though telling the world:

"Today is the day!"

Last week had been a blur as she tried very hard to stay in the moment, but her heart and attention were elsewhere. This feeling of falling down a rabbit hole must end and it must end today. With a firm resolution and a prayer for guidance, she began to make a plan.

For starters, she would sneak out for a quick trip to Edinburgh. Everyone was otherwise occupied today, so the house was unusually quiet. Without detection, she walked down the long drive and caught the bus. It took far longer than going by car, but she wanted to accomplish her goal and return home before anyone missed her.

The ride to the big city was uneventful with very few people on the bus. Before long she walked into Cavanagh's Antique Shoppe on Cockburn Street and just as she hoped, Maeve and Robbie had everything she was looking for. Her gifts were wrapped in traditional paper with satin ribbons and in less than two hours Sarah was back on the bus headed home. The long drive gave her time to gather her thoughts and write notes in her journal. She titled the page 'Today is the Day.'

It was a short distance from the bus drop-off to the gate at Leigheas, then the long walk down the driveway. By the time she reached the house, she was chilled to the bone and ready for a hot cup of tea. Seaneen and the girls were busy in the kitchen making preparations for dinner.

"Lass, where have you been in this weather? Have you heard there is snow predicted tonight? Kaitlyn arrived a wee bit ago and told us."

"My goodness," Sarah said, hoping to avoid any explanation of where she had been. "It is freezing out there so I'm not surprised. Where is Kaitlyn?

"She'll be down soon. Just taking a moment to freshen up."

"Is my father in?"

"He is in his office with Liam, who arrived earlier than we thought. Aye, it's good to see the lad. It's been far too long."

"I'm so glad he's here, tonight especially." Sarah said. "I'll run upstairs and change, then be down to help you."

"Take your time, lass, we've about got it ready. And where was it you said you were?"

"Just a few errands," Sarah answered vaguely. "and It looks like I made it home just in time. Everything smells delicious. Brennan, could you put the kettle on? I'd love a quick cup of tea."

Hiding her bag of treasures from Cavanagh's under her coat, she walked quickly toward the stairs.

"My favorite cousin, Sarah!" Liam called after her, as he left Richards's office.

In her excitement at seeing him, the parcels she was holding fell with a clatter on the marble floor. Torn between hugging Liam and retrieving her gifts, she gave a quick one-armed greeting and quickly bent over and tried to gather them up.

"I really am over-the-moon pleased to see you, but I must run upstairs." She turned about halfway up and looked at the bewildered Liam. "Really, I am absolutely thrilled you are here, tonight especially."

"And what's so special about..." he asked, but she was long gone.

For the first time in Sarah's memory, dinner was set in The Elephant Room. Looking around she wondered why they didn't use it more often. The walls were covered in a pale yellow silk, with towering windows and French doors looking out on the garden and trees beyond. Her father had installed special lighting outside so that it was fairy-tale magical at night. On the far wall was an enormous fireplace and mantle with comfortable seating scattered around the big room. An oval, antique burled-wood dining table had been placed in the center of the room, with the freshly cut tree dominating the far corner. The fragrance of fresh pine carried throughout, bringing a sense of anticipation.

"It's really a special room, isn't it?" Richard asked, walking in alone. "We should use this room more often."

"I was just thinking that, but maybe we could give it a nicer name."

"Or we could just fill it with elephant memorabilia." he laughed. "I'm afraid it will always be known as The Elephant Room. If I'm not mistaken, wasn't that your idea after identifying it as the largest room in the house?"

"Not one of my better ideas."

Her father reached over and put his arm around his nearly grown daughter.

"How are you? I've left you alone to sort this out, but I worry about you. Is there anything you want to talk about?"

Reaching up, she gave her father a kiss on the cheek.

"I love you, Dad."

"I love you too, Sunshine."

She looked eye to eye with him like she used to when she was trying to get her way.

"Today is the day," she said with conviction.

At that moment the door swung open with Seaneen, James, Peter, Kaitlyn and Liam laden with dishes of food. There was the happy noise of friends bantering, enjoying each other's company as the steaming platters were set on the table.

Dinner lived up to the aroma that preceded it and was heartily enjoyed. As the last of the apple cake with thick cream on top was gone, Richard stood up.

"I don't believe that tree will trim itself. Shall we get to it?"

Sarah rose from her chair and looked around the table, then took a deep breath.

"Actually, not yet, if you don't mind. Could you sit for just a few minutes more?"

Her father dutifully sat down as she picked up the bag of gifts she had hidden nearby. She walked around the table, leaving a small wrapped package in front of each person, then returned to her chair. All eyes were on her.

"Recently I received news that my mother died. As most of you know, she chose to go her own way and live completely unconnected to her family. I'm not judging her for this, after all, how could I as we never met, but I do know that is not the way I want to live my life. Her death hasn't been easy to accept and has uncovered a deep pain I didn't know I carried. At the same time it has caused me to examine my personal choices and decide how I want to go about navigating my own way. Each of you here have, in some way, shaped who I am. You have loved me, taught me, inspired me, and shown me the importance of always being there for one another. After days of confusion and truthfully feeling a bit lost, I woke up this morning with clarity towards my future. Today is the day I begin my journey with intentionality and with your prayers and support. I have decided to quit my job in London and become a writer. There are hundreds of book ideas floating in my mind and my passion is to put words on paper and make an ever so slight difference in the world. My dream right now is to create a series of children's books with each story making the point that everyone has gifts to share and our differences are what make the world a fascinating place." She paused to take a breath before continuing. "In front of you is a small gift chosen to acknowledge and thank you individually, and with each comes with a special request."

She looked to her immediate left and began with her father.

"Dad, you've loved me unconditionally and whole-heartedly, sacrificed for me and given me the most amazing life a girl could ever imagine. Bringing up a girl, especially through the teenage years, could not have been easy, but you never let me down. You raised me through the eyes of love and with a firm hand."

Richard methodically unwrapped his package and found an antique silver star ornament inside.

"You will always be my guiding star." She paused to compose herself. "If it is all right with you, may I move home and work from Leigheas? It has always been an inspirational place for me to write."

"Absolutely," was all he could get out, choking back his emotion.

Sarah quickly went on before she lost her nerve.

"James, you're the newest to my family and I have watched you bring such peace and joy to everyone you've come into contact with, especially Seaneen." Sarah saw her friend smile and blush. "And while we haven't had the chance to spend much time together, I hope to remedy that very soon." She gave a nod and James opened his gift of a lovely antique silver cross. "If you are comfortable with the idea, would you consider holding a small service in the chapel in memory of my mother? I've been thinking that it might help bring some closure for me."

"I would be honored," the vicar answered solemnly.

Turning to Liam, Sarah continued, "Liam, from the first time we met you've been watching over me. Of course, at the time I didn't have a clue, I just thought you were annoying. But in the face of danger you protected me without a moment's thought for yourself. You took me into your family's home to keep me safe, then had the good sense to be my cousin."

Liam took her compliments by turning red and shaking his head. He opened his gift to find an antique round ornament with engraved words 'Celtic Warriors Shield' in the center.

"I will always think of you as the warrior who saved my life in so many ways. My request of you is this: when we were in Shetland, you held my fragile existence together by sharing your comforting wisdom through stories, or sometimes just in conversation. May I draw on those lessons for my books?"

"My Sarah girl, of course you can, if you think they are worthy. Though to my memory, you were the brave one who soldiered through so well for one so young. Finding you as my cousin has been the highlight. Oh, of course, that includes you too, Uncle Richard."

Sarah turned to her right.

"Kaitlyn, by now you must be wondering how you ended up with this crazy lot of people. I have included you because your kind words spoken to a stranger on a train has made all the difference. When I asked your views on my decisions, your wise counsel was to 'follow my passion.' So, if this doesn't work out, it's your fault," Sarah added with a laugh. "Seriously, it was exactly the words I needed at that time. They stuck with me, obviously."

Untying the ribbon, Kaitlyn unwrapped her gift of a small, square antique tin tile ornament with an enameled red heart in the middle. On the backside were the words 'Follow your Heart.'

"Thank you, Sarah, for including me. I do believe we were a wee bit kindred souls from the moment I sat down with you. I knew you were searching for something and I only shared what I knew to be true. And besides, meeting you has changed my life as much as it has yours." Richard reached for Kaitlyn's hand.

"My favor of you, Kaitlyn is to guide me as I write, honestly and gently pointing out errors, changes or kindly telling me it's garbage. Between you and your father, you are the most well-read people I've ever met and I trust your judgement."

"I can easily tell you on behalf of both my father and myself we would be thrilled to be part of your new career. You are a writer, Sarah Duncan, and that is very exciting."

There was a long pause as Sarah looked to her dear friend Seaneen McAughtrie.

"And how do I properly thank you, Seaneen? You have been there from my first day in Edinburgh offering your comfort, wisdom, quiet, loving presence and hot tea and scones. You became not only my friend, but my confidant and partner in crime. Like Liam, you were silently protecting me, though I never knew it. You went far out on a limb to connect me with Peter when I was in Shetland and I know you could've gotten into big trouble for that. Then you came back into my life when Dad created Leigheas and continued to be there for my university days and beyond–always my champion."

After wiping away a stray tear, Seaneen opened her package. She lifted up an ornament consisting of pair of ornately carved antique silver angel wings about three inches long, attached with a red ribbon.

"You are my angel on earth." Sarah reached her hand out to Seaneen. "My request of you is to let me help in the running of Leigheas. With your new marriage, I suspect you two will want to travel and spend time together. Now don't get me wrong, I'm not letting you off the hook, Leigheas will always need your guiding hand. We found when you were recuperating from your accident that we could exist, but it wasn't pretty."

"Aye, my sweet lass, you stole my heart the first time we met. You were so shy, and always escaping to your room to read a book." Giving Sarah a wink, she continued "And we did have some lovely adventures we will keep between us. I will look forward to spending time with you as you learn the running of this fine house. Mind you, I may not give you all my secrets, I still want to be needed."

All eyes turned to Peter, the last to open his gift, as he locked eyes with Sarah. She opened her mouth several times to speak, but nothing came out. Finally, with a look heavenward she found her voice.

"Peter, your kindness to a young girl who was so lost, changed my life forever. You became more important than I think you will ever know. Your first wave grew to become a treasured communication that brought a dimension to my life I had never known. Friendship with someone around my own age was a new experience for me and you proved to be everything I could've asked for. The years separated us and we have each traveled bumpy roads, but through the grace of God, we have reconnected at what I'm sure is exactly the right time."

They held their gaze as though no one else was in the room. She broke the moment.

"You can open your gift now."

Peter smiled self consciously and tore off the ribbon and paper. He held up a bronze circular claddagh ornament, with two hands holding a heart, with a crown on top.

"I do realize it is Irish and not Scottish, but the meaning of friendship, loyalty and love seemed to perfectly fit our relationship." Sarah could tell he was quite taken with it by the way he kept running his fingers over the carving. "And my request of you, Peter Michael-McGregor is to illustrate my books. I will be at Leigheas and you will be at Elibank and I can't think of anyone I'd rather share my dream with. Oh, please say yes."

Without hesitation, Peter rose from his chair and took three steps to Sarah. Holding her face in his hands, he whispered, "Yes!" before kissing her in front of God and everyone at the table.

It was late in the evening when the tree was fully trimmed. The last bit of business was each person finding a spot for their special ornament Sarah had given them. The tired tree decorators sat around The Elephant Room, warmed by the fire and admiring their handiwork. Richard and Kaitlyn had slipped out for a moment and returned with a large bottle of champagne and seven glasses.

"This has been quite a night and I believe it calls for a toast before we end it," he said popping the cork and pouring out the bubbling wine.

As they held up their glasses, Sarah spoke from her heart.

"Richard Duncan, Seaneen McAughtrie, Liam Morrison, James Bradbury, Kaitlyn Turning and Peter Michael-McGregor… you are without a doubt the things I love best about Scotland."

THE END

# Acknowledgements

Four years ago when I began writing ***Window Friends*** it was a bit of a secret. It stayed that way until fairly recently when I finally put my big girl panties on and let a few people in. I was not prepared for the support, kindness and assistance that came my way. Without the following people ***Window Friends*** would still be just a dream, handwritten in dozens of spiral notebooks. There are no words to adequately thank those who contributed. However, now that I call myself a writer, I will try.

To Greg Dow, my incredibly supportive husband. As the only one who knew about the book from its inception during a walk on a side street in Edinburgh, Scotland, you kept my confidence and allowed me the time and space to fulfill my need to write this story. I might add this included several trips to Scotland, which I think you were really okay with. Your belief in my ability never wavered and you were always there to listen, critique and cheer me on. ***Window Friends*** wouldn't exist without you. Love you.

To my brother, Chris Darley, who listened long-distance to hours of me prattling on about characters, plot lines and story details. Your generous gift of time and caring are more appreciated than you will ever know. Everyone should have a brother like you–unconditionally supportive in every way. Thank you.

To my two Sarahs, each of you played an integral part in birthing ***Window Friends***.

My lovely Sarah Rauchas in Edinburgh (or Johannesburg, South Africa depending on the year), as the second person I told about the story, you encouraged me and gave me confidence I sorely needed. The pleasure of several visits to your absurdly charming Victorian cottage created the perfect backdrop to weave my tale. Thank you.

My dear Sarah (Sally) Hogenauer, you were the first person to actually read the entire first draft when I emailed it to you while I was in a covid-induced fever. Thankfully, you liked it and didn't have to join the witness protection program because you couldn't face me. Your valuable knowledge, input and continued availability for every question is a testament to real friendship. Thank you.

To close friends Skip and Shannon Novakovich, your gracious willingness to spend time and offer expert advice on the pen and ink drawings made all the difference. Shannon, I am so grateful to you for reading the book, for your input and your very funny side notes. You are both a blessing. Thank you.

To Natilee McGill, while always adorable, when did you grow up into such a smart person? Without you there would be no beautiful website or social media presence. Seeking your advice on so many things is a delight. Thank you.

To Susan Brenning, while you live in Norway, your impact on the book coming to fruition is enormous. You stepped in with comprehensive advice when I was feeling discouraged about what step to take next. It will be a lovely day when we finally meet in person. Thank you.

To Scott Armstrong, my long-time friend, compatriot and gifted photographer, your enthusiasm and talent brought forth portrait photos I didn't hate. In fact, I actually liked them! Thank you.

To my friends and family who encouraged me every step of the way, daughters Alex Sanford and Christen Bagwell; sons Ben Dow and Charlie Dow; niece Mica Darley-Emerson; and BFF Rozanne Tucker, a heartfelt thank you.

To Hope*Writers, a community dedicated to helping writers make progress while learning to balance the art of writing with the business of publishing. Your amazing staff and online concept have led to making dreams come true for so many. Special thank you to Sara Ward.

To Chrissy Wolfe, finding you through Hope*Writers has been an enormous blessing. Thank you.

And I want to thank God most of all for everything.

Printed in Great Britain
by Amazon